Jeanne pried herself out of the mud and started walking. A few paces brought the hilltop into view. Something – someone – lay there. She moved faster. Someone else had fallen victim to whomever or whatever had left her drenched and defenseless in a cemetery. Together, they would make sense of things.

Before she reached it, she discerned that the supine figure was male. His legs were spread, and his arms extended from his sides, like someone making a snow angel. He seemed to be transfixed by the pouring clouds above him. "Hello?" Jeanne said.

A few more steps brought her to the hilltop. Her eyes registered the stillness of the man's chest before she saw his face. His mouth hung open, a dark O. Red splotched his nose and cheeks, residue of blood that the rain had not yet washed away. The nose itself looked flattened, sliced open on both sides. The eye sockets were empty.

She knelt beside him and placed her hand on his neck. The flesh was cold. "SOMEBODY!" she yelled. Her joints ached, and her bruised hip throbbed. She had slept on the side of a muddy hill, and now she was cold, wet, aching, hungry, and standing next to a murdered man. The word "ritual" came into her mind. Someone had taken his eyes and destroyed his nose. A perverse impulse forced her to look into the O of his mouth. It was voided, tongueless. He had been murdered and ritually mutilated. She wondered about the order of events.

A sense of danger straightened her spine. No one could have left this man here without noticing her on the hill. More than likely, what had happened to her was connected to what had happened to him. She didn't recognize the man, but somehow, they were linked.

Burning the Middle Ground

by L. Andrew Cooper

Book I of *The Last World War*

a BlackWyrm book
Louisville, Kentucky

BURNING THE MIDDLE GROUND

A BlackWyrm Book
BlackWyrm Publishing
10307 Chimney Ridge Ct, Louisville, KY 40299

Printed in the United States of America.

ISBN: 978-1-61318-138-6
LCCN: 2012952227

Cover Design by Dave Mattingly
Edited by Jodi Black

First edition: November 2012

"'Now I want you to tell me just one thing more. Why do you hate the south?'

'I dont hate it,' Quentin said, quickly, at once, immediately; 'I dont hate it,' he said. *I dont hate it* he thought, panting in the cold air, the iron New England dark: *I dont. I dont! I dont hate it! I dont hate it!*

— William Faulkner, *Absalom, Absalom!*

Prologue: False Start

Ronald had the facts. Brian McCullough was seventeen when it happened, a senior in high school. His sister Fran was ten. The father, Matt McCullough, worked as a veterinarian despite being a real MD. The mother, Linda McCullough, had advanced degrees in psychology and taught special education at the middle school. Everyone knew that the family didn't go to church, and everyone knew that Matt was having an affair. When the term "open marriage" broke into the town's vernacular that summer, the God-fearing people of Kenning, Georgia were scandalized. Fran heard someone describe her family as "godless," and she asked a teacher what the word meant. The teacher said "godless" meant people who were going to Hell. Afraid, Fran joined First Church of Kenning. There, she heard the Reverend Michael Cox's sermon on the sanctity of marriage, which beseeched the righteous to redress the unholy.

Ronald, a web journalist, would describe what occurred the following Tuesday with care. He would be humorless and exact, embellishing only for effect. He imagined Brian walking home from school. The boy noticed that the front door of his family's large two-story house was open. Fran must have forgotten to shut it all the way. But why were his parents' cars in the driveway? They weren't supposed to be home for another hour at least. Brian walked faster. Without knowing why, he broke into a jog.

Stan Johnson lived next to the McCulloughs. Stan kept a handgun in a locked metal box on a shelf in his garage because his wife had a strict rule against letting guns in the house. Every boy in the neighborhood knew that the lock on the metal box was rusted and that the Johnsons hardly ever bolted the garage window. More than once, "Wanna go look at a gun" had been a dare at a boys' sleepover party.

Brian couldn't have been thinking about Stan's gun when he entered the house. Ronald imagined the boy having little on his mind when he called "Hello?" and closed the door behind him. "You know you guys left the front door open?"

Nobody answered. His voice shook the house's quiet stillness, bouncing off walls, finding no response. The place seemed empty, but the cars in the driveway suggested otherwise. His parents must have come home early for some reason, and the only reason he could think of was Fran, maybe trouble at school. Maybe a teacher had called their parents in for a conference. Mom and Dad had gone for the conference and then taken Fran home, and then maybe they had gone out for ice cream. The convenience store that sold cones and scoops was two miles away, but the day was pleasant enough, so maybe they had decided to walk. Maybe they had expected to meet up with Brian on the way over. He hadn't seen them, but he had taken his new shortcut, and they couldn't have expected that. He had nothing to worry about.

There was a faint smudge on the bottom stair. The foyer had a dark hardwood floor, but they had covered the stairs and the second floor with off-white carpet about a year ago. Dad had joked that since both of his kids were finally out of their Kool-Aid phases, they could risk the investment.

The smudge wasn't quite a footprint, but it might have been left by a shoe. It was brown, but it wasn't the right color for Diet Coke. Fran had started raiding Mom's soda supply over a month ago. After a few evenings of jittery babbling at the dinner table, Mom and Dad had taken Brian's suggestion about limiting Fran's consumption of what he called "nasty acid – with bubbles." Fran had forgiven him for the resulting one-can-per-day restriction.

Brian called up the stairs: "Hello?"

Sound traveled well in the house; if they were home, someone would have responded. The cars in the driveway, the open door, the smudge on the stairs: by themselves, they didn't mean anything was wrong, so they didn't justify his nervousness. Figuring he was just hungry, Brian decided against searching for his family upstairs and in favor of seeing if any of the ham from Sunday's dinner remained in the refrigerator.

To the left of the main stairs the foyer turned into a short hall that led past the dining room and ended at the kitchen. The hallway floor was the same dark wood as the foyer, but the kitchen had blue faux-marble tile, and there he noticed more smudges. They weren't the size of a whole shoe, but they were too regular to be anything other than tracks. They might have come from a heel, something sullied by a dip in a brown puddle that the rest of the shoe had missed. Brian couldn't divine a direction from the tracks.

They either started or ended at the open doorway for the stairs down to the unfinished basement.

"Hey – are you guys down there?"

Light from the kitchen stopped halfway down the stairs, and Brian was on the brink of darkness before he realized he might want a flashlight. Deciding that blind groping would suffice for finding the light switch at the landing, he continued downward, unready for the object near the bottom that tripped him. He broke the fall with hands and knees and tumbled onto his side, hugging a leg whose kneecap howled agony.

"Goddamn it, OW!" The sound was strange in the confined dark space; he felt embarrassed, as if he had been caught talking to himself. He waited for the pain to subside and struggled to his feet. Brushing dust from his jeans, he chided himself for the stupidity of coming down without a flashlight, of coming down at all, of being so worried, of thinking—

When the hand swiping dust found something sticky, his head turned toward the half-lit stairway. Eyes adjusting, he could distinguish the outline of the object that had tripped him. A shoe. It was a man's shoe, too small to be his, so it had to be his father's. He limped closer and saw it was more than a shoe.

Dad's left foot rested on the third stair from the bottom, and the leg extended from it diagonally. Brian must have fallen over him. "Dad? Sorry, I didn't see you there, I—"

The right leg splayed out away from the stairs, as if Dad had been trying some kind of weird stretch. Brian felt it in his stomach before his brain signaled the alarm. He lurched forward, found the light switch, and flipped it.

Dad's eyes were open, and he was lying on his back in a brownish red pool. "Dad!" Brian collapsed to his knees on the concrete at his father's side, not sensing the new jolt from his damaged kneecap. He shook his father once and stopped. Dad must have fallen down the stairs, and moving a man with a broken neck could kill him. Brian pulled his arms away. "Dad, can you talk?"

No answer. Brian's shaking hands hovered above his father's chest, wanting to touch, wanting to intervene, but afraid. The space between his hands and the chest remained constant – Dad wasn't breathing. He allowed two fingers to make contact with the neck, hunting for the jugular. He didn't find a pulse, so he tried the other side, wishing that the CPR training in health class had been this year instead of freshman year, because he was stupid and he couldn't remember how, because he kept searching and failing and trying again.

When he accepted that there was no pulse, he realized he was kneeling in his father's blood. So much blood couldn't have come from a fall. Brian's convulsing hands tipped Dad's head back until his mouth fell open. Brian couldn't remember how many breaths – one, two, three, and then he scooted so he could plant his palms squarely in the center of the man's chest and push, one, two, three, four, five, and then breaths, one, two, and then compressions, one, two, three, four, five, six, and then breaths, and then compressions, and then Brian realized that his father's lips were lukewarm and that tears were running down his own cheeks.

"Please, no." The sound filled the basement and made him aware of his surroundings, aware that there could be something else wrong, that maybe— "Mom!"

In the room's most distant corner, she lay face down on the concrete, at the center of her own brownish-red pool. Barely standing, Brian lurched through the distance between his parents and flipped his mother onto her back. Her nose was crooked, broken, perhaps, when she fell forward, clutching her breast where the bullet had entered. He had seen too many similar configurations of flesh on TV not to know that he was looking at a bullet wound, that his mother had been killed by a gunshot.

Did Dad run?

She had been shot in the chest, but he had been shot in the back, on the stairs, going up. Whoever had done this had been downstairs when they found him, and the intruder had shot Mom in the chest, and Dad had turned to run for help or for—

"FRAN!"

Brian bolted for the stairs. He stumbled when he stepped on his father's leg but kept going, taking three stairs at a time and screaming his sister's name. The tracks led him through the kitchen, into the foyer, onto the next stairway. "Franny are you up here! It's me Brian are you okay? Franny answer me please!"

He came to his own bedroom first and looked in but felt stupid for looking in because she wouldn't be there, she'd be in her own room, which was next, where he looked in and saw her sitting on the edge of her twin-sized bed and he jumped at her, threw his arms around her, squeezed her, and lifted her from the bed, saying "Franny Franny oh God Franny we'll get help I'll get you out of here oh God thank God you're okay!"

The girl was warm in his arms but unmoving. She was breathing, but her shoulders and neck were limp. "Fran are you okay what did they do to you oh God Mom!"

Fran wriggled, so he put her down. He knelt beside her, feeling the pain in his knee but not caring, and started to check her for injuries. Her hands were in her lap. One held a gun.

The sight knocked him backward, away from his ten-year-old sister, onto the off-white carpet. Her shoes had only smudged the stairs, but his had left deep tracks all around. His were bloodier than hers because she had stepped over their parents before the pools had become wide and deep.

"Fran?" He heard the horror in his voice as his mind put together enough details not only to imagine but to believe, for a moment, what she had done. He got back on his knees and said, "Fran, what happened?"

The question rippled the girl's posture. Her shoulders straightened, and her neck lifted her head. Her eyes met his, and he saw in them something he had never seen on TV or anywhere. He saw his sister's expression, and his jaw fell open. With an arm that looked too frail to lift it, Fran raised the gun to her right eye and fired.

Stan Johnson pulled into his garage at his usual time and saw that the window was open. He looked for the metal box and found it empty. He called the police, who discovered a group of bike-riding boys who had seen Fran McCullough walking around the Johnsons' house. A uniformed officer named Winston Beecher knocked on the McCulloughs' front door. No one answered, so he went in. The bloody footprints prompted him to call for backup, but he didn't wait before rushing up the stairs. He found the boy in his sister's bedroom, presumably in the same position as when the little girl had splattered her head on the bedspread and walls.

Brian McCullough did not speak for a year.

Schism

1

The lobby of the Sleep E-Z Motel had two small round tables with three chairs each. A narrow, rectangular table with only three legs leaned against the wall, supporting two coffee makers and an open box from Dunkin' Donuts. Taped to one of the two coffee makers, a piece of paper boasted in kid-print lettering, "Sorry – NO DECAF!" All of the donuts had bluish frosting and polychromatic sprinkles. As Ronald poured brown liquid into a Styrofoam cup, he studied the donuts. He didn't notice the overflow until the heat hit his knuckles.

"Fucking-A Christ fuck!" he said. He lifted the cup to his lips and sipped, leaving a clean circle with a brown corona on the table. Once he had drained the cup's content to a safe level, he grabbed three napkins. He slapped one of them on the spill, wrapped another around his cup, and used the third to grip a donut. Choosing a chair that faced the lobby's glass front door, he sat and began the business of sprinkle removal.

Half a donut and two cups of coffee later, the front door's bell jingled and made way for a beige-uniformed man. The officer was more than six feet tall. Thinning brown hair framed a boyish face. Muscular arms filled his sleeves, and a small, protruding gut made his gun belt look uncomfortable. Ronald put him at about thirty, old enough to be fit and fat at the same time, young enough to be unaccustomed to an unruly body. The age estimate made the officer the elder at the meeting, but Ronald expected to manage the situation.

He stood. Using the napkin from his coffee to rub any stickiness from his right hand, Ronald said, "You must be Deputy Beecher. I'm Ronald Glassner." Hand clean, he offered to shake.

Deputy Beecher tucked his hat under his left arm and grasped Ronald's hand with crushing force. "Sorry I'm late," he said. "I went to the wrong motel."

"You mean there's another one around here?"

Beecher nodded. "We've got two nearby on account of being close to the interstate. They do good enough business I suppose."

"This town is full of surprises," Ronald said. A tilt of his head indicated the table. "There are donuts. They have... sprinkles. Help yourself."

Beecher slapped his stomach. "It's not all true what they say about cops and donuts." A forced chuckle followed the observation.

"I wasn't thinking about that," Ronald said. "I'm just sorry I can't be a better host. Maybe I could buy us a real breakfast somewhere?"

"Nah, already ate. Mind if I sit?"

Ronald gestured at the chair farthest from his. "Please, be my guest."

"Much obliged." Beecher took the far chair, and his hat took the near. "It's been quite a morning already." He seemed to expect agreement, so Ronald nodded. "I went over to Vincent's Pizzeria to look into a problem they've been having with their trash. People keep putting in bags that don't belong."

Ronald imagined a bare foot sticking out of a trash bag stuffed deep inside a dumpster. "Any idea who did it?"

"Vincent swears it's the barber shop next door."

"Were the bags full of hair?" Ronald imagined a collage of suburban dyes.

Beecher gazed at Ronald's coffee cup. "Nah, nothing like that."

"May I get you a cup of coffee, Deputy Beecher?"

"Please, call me Winston! And no thank you. I've already had three this morning. I'm trying to cut down. Makes me nervous." He sighed. "So how do you like Kenning so far?"

"It seems... quaint."

Winston shook his head. "Did you know that 'quaint' means 'cunt' in Middle English?"

Surprised, Ronald laughed. "No, I did not know that." He locked eyes with Winston while he took the final sips from his cup. "If you don't mind my asking, how does a cop from a small Georgia town know that?"

Winston gave his posture a playful stretch. "Chaucer cracks me up," he said.

Further conversation revealed that Winston had taken quite a few classes at the community college in Tifton before pursuing a career in law enforcement. "I read that you got some kind of award after the Tragedy," Ronald said.

Winston nodded. "I didn't do much of anything to earn it, though. I mean, I broke protocol when I rushed into that house... and then, when I saw the boy, I didn't apprehend him like I should have."

Ronald reached for the tape recorder in his jacket pocket. "Do you mind if I record this?"

"Better that you don't misquote me," Winston said. "This is going on your website, right?"

"Actually, I'm doing a book. Once the *American Sane* site took off, publishers started calling, so there'll be interest."

"And you really got famous by keeping a diary on the web?"

With a thin grin, Ronald said, "Yeah, a blog, and now it's expanded quite a bit, more of a 'zine. I've got three freelance contributors doing regular work for me, NYU students, and I have to wade through a ton of unsolicited submissions at the site's contact address. The advertising revenue was enough to quit my day job."

"Uh-huh," Winston said. "Good for you."

"I see." Ronald cleared his throat. "Well then, I really appreciate you taking the time to talk to me. I know it must be hard to dredge up painful memories from so long ago."

"Not that long."

"You were saying about how they gave you an award?"

Winston explained that the award didn't come until later, after they had closed the investigation. On that Tuesday, he had entered the McCullough household with probable cause and discovered a blood-covered seventeen-year-old boy in a room with his dead sister. The gun was in the sister's hand, but anybody else's first thought would have been that the boy had killed everyone, Menendez brothers-style but white and Southern. That was everyone else's first thought, but not Winston's.

Winston said that Brian McCullough looked "like a puppy impaled on a pike." The boy's eyes were wide and innocent but glassy and dead. A lock of dark blond hair hung down to his nose, the only streak of color on an ashen face. His mouth hung open. Winston heard wheezing as the boy sucked breath. Otherwise, the room was silent.

The officer positioned himself between Brian and the gun. "Are you injured?" he said. There was blood on the boy's jeans and shirt, but it didn't seem to be spreading, and the patterns didn't look like they had come from the boy's body. "You're Brian McCullough, right?"

Brian blinked at the sound of his name.

After repeating the name and the question about injury several more times, Winston said, "We have to clear the scene." He wondered if "the scene" sounded heartless. He wondered if the boy actually heard and comprehended what he was saying. "I'm going to lead you out of here."

The boy said nothing, so Winston set a hand on his arm. At first Winston imagined that he would have to carry the boy over his shoulder, but Brian's legs started to assist as Winston lifted. Winston considered holding the boy's hand but figured leading him by the wrist would be better. They walked down the stairs slowly. Winston tried to avoid smearing the bloody footprints; he reckoned he had already spoiled enough evidence.

Winston had Brian sit in the back of the patrol car and left the door open, hoping to establish trust. He got on the radio, requested an ambulance, and found out the sheriff would be there shortly. When Sheriff Hadderly arrived, Winston told him that it looked like a suicide and that someone should track down the parents.

The way he thought about the parents was, as he would say to many interested parties, the damnedest thing – he never even thought about searching the house. He had an idea of where Matt and Linda McCullough worked, so he was thinking about yellow pages and school directories, not basements and bloodbaths. The sheriff was on the scene for less than five minutes before he ran out of the house, gun drawn.

"You watch him! You watch him!" Sheriff Hadderly shouted.

Winston wasn't even sure who he was supposed to watch until the sheriff shoved his hands into the back of the patrol car, yanked Brian from the seat, slammed him against the sidewall, clamped cuffs on him, and Mirandized.

While the sheriff berated him for not following the tracks from the foyer to the other two corpses, Winston thought about where Brian's mind must be. He didn't suspect the boy the way Hadderly did. His soul knew the boy was a victim, not a perpetrator. While everyone else was thinking about Brian being tried as an adult and getting the death penalty, Winston was thinking about how sad it was that the person in town with the best training to deal with Brian's trauma was probably his dead mother.

"I stuck up for him," Winston said. "I called the public defenders to make sure they'd be on their way, and I visited him in the holding cell, talking to him even though he didn't talk back.

When the ballistics and gunpowder tests came back saying there was no way the boy had done it, everyone started worrying about lawsuits and such because of the way they had all treated him. But then everybody remembered me being there for him and decided I had represented the better part of Kenning and the county police. So Sheriff Hadderly made up this certificate for me, and I got my picture mounted on a plaque in the main office. It's still there, if that's the kind of thing you want to look at for your book."

"I might do that, thank you," Ronald said. "What happened to Brian then?"

"Well, I suppose he spent a few weeks in a state facility on account of him not talking. While he was there he started writing things down. By that time all the legal questions were answered, but I guess they had him write about it for therapy."

Ronald tried to control the gleam in his eye. "Do you know – do those writings – still exist?"

"You'd have to ask Brian about that," Winston said.

"And how... would I do that?" Asking regular people to relive the town's most painful memory was hard enough. How would he ask a young man to recount the murders of his entire family?

"Call him up," Winston said. "He's in the book. Still at the same house, so it shouldn't be too hard."

Ronald wondered how hard it was to remove bloodstains from a concrete basement floor. "The same house where it happened?"

"The very one. His parents left him with life insurance money, but not enough for a seventeen-year-old kid to set up on his own, even though the courts gave him the right to act as an adult. The house... well, he couldn't exactly sell it because everyone knew about it. And he needed a place to stay. So he stayed."

Ronald reexamined Winston's thinning hair, boyish face, and broad shoulders. Winston returned half a smile. "Would you mind showing me the McCulloughs' house?" Ronald said.

2

That night, Ronald posted to *American Sane*:

I've felt vaguely menaced ever since I crossed the border into what I still think of as the Red States, but when I got into Deputy Beecher's car, I knew I was lost behind enemy lines. Once we pulled out of the cigarette-encrusted parking lot of the hovel they call a motel, the burly cop asked if I "was going to make this whole thing about gun control." How could *I* be responsible for making "this whole thing" about gun control? How could a story about a little girl blowing away her parents not *already* be about gun control? I've read headlines saying the McCullough Tragedy was the South's Columbine. As if what happened near Paducah, Kentucky in 1997 wasn't enough (Google it, Sane Ignorants). Such comparisons don't do any good. People love their guns, and they don't care how many children die as long as they get to keep loving their guns. When the cop pointed out that he was a card-carrying member of the NRA, I wasn't the least bit surprised.

We stayed pretty quiet for the rest of the drive over to Brian McCullough's house. I have to admit, when I first caught sight of McCullough, the first word in my head was *iconic*. Here was a guy who had survived something so nasty that it might be too controversial to put in a horror movie. I expected him to be a skinny, sad, blubbering idiot, the kind of guy who plays chess in coffee shops and threatens to tell you his story if you get too close. Instead, behold! A picture ripe for the cover of a magazine. Brian was standing in his front yard *chopping wood*. Who the fuck chops their own wood? Sweat gleaming on a perfect, shirtless body, he raised an axe over his head to bring it down, *thwoop*, splitting a log with more confidence than I have when I slice a cheesecake. Deputy Beecher told me that Brian is a handyman and a pretty good amateur carpenter. Christ on crutches, a fucking *carpenter*!

Stay tuned, Sane Readers. Soon, I'll have my first full-fledged conversation with Mr. All-American, the Tragedy Survivor.

3

Brian sat smiling at his computer.

"Jeez, Brian, I'm really sorry I ever brought that jerk over here," Winston said.

Brian shrugged. "He said I have a perfect body. That's pretty nice."

Winston patted Brian on the back and leaned up against his desk. "Is 'burly' an insult?"

"No," Brian said. "Well, maybe." Insult or not, "burly" described Winston well, and he did keep his NRA card in his wallet. Winston had shown it to him when they had gone on their first hunting trip. Brian didn't care for the website's tone, but Ronald wasn't entirely wrong. Years ago, people had tried to get Brian involved in some sort of anti-gun campaign. Brian had declined, but that didn't mean he was happy about where Mr. Johnson kept his gun.

"You wouldn't mind, would you, if this Ronald Glassner was... you know... funny for you?" Winston cleared his throat and fidgeted with the stapler that sat on the corner of Brian's desk.

"You think he's gay?"

Winston looked around the room. "Yeah, I do. I mean, that's okay with me and everything, but what he said about you—"

"I can handle a scrawny reporter," Brian said. "Like I said, it's kind of flattering."

"I'd think so. Most folks wouldn't."

Brian rolled his eyes and faced the computer screen. The logo for *American Sane*, a demonic-looking clown with a U.S. flag on its forehead, bopped in the upper left corner. The title on the page was "Kenning, Georgia: Day One."

"So," Winston said, "are you still willing to talk to him again?"

"Probably. If he comes over." Ronald would write about him no matter what he did, so Brian preferred to speak for himself.

"You better bet he'll come over here," Winston laughed.

"I'm not sure," Brian said. Yesterday, Ronald had seemed uneasy.

The doorbell rang. Brian pushed his chair away from the desk and looked up at Winston. "That's timing," Winston said. "I'd bet you fifty dollars it's him."

They walked to the front door together. Brian saw Ronald through the peephole. The reporter's head was too big for his shoulders, and his reddish-brown hair seemed to be molded by what the woman who cut Brian's hair called "product." The short, skinny man wore a brown jacket and a maroon tie despite the soaring early-April temperatures.

Brian opened the door wide enough for Ronald to see Winston.

"Hi there." Ronald shifted his feet on the welcome mat. "I didn't expect to see both of you here."

"I just came by to show Brian something on his computer," Winston said. "It was pretty hilarious."

Ronald became paler. "Computer?"

"Yeah," Winston said, "it's a funny little invention that some of us around here like to use from time to time." Brian smiled at Winston's smirk. "What's even funnier is that we were just talking about you. Like they say, speak of the devil."

Ronald looked toward his feet. Contradicting his tie and slacks, the reporter wore tennis shoes. Ronald looked back up. "May I come in?"

Taking a step back, Brian said, "Sure. I've got Coke in the fridge."

"No thanks," Ronald said. Stepping inside, he seemed to study the dark wood floor. "I had Starbuck's a little while ago. I was very happy to see a Starbuck's here."

"We've got indoor plumbing, too," Winston said.

Ronald looked up and turned toward Winston. Brian took another step back. "Look, I obviously upset you. Was it something I said on my website? Did I get something wrong?"

"Wrong?" Winston thought for a moment. "I don't know about that. I guess I sort of thought your whole website was a little bit...." He thought again, and his face lit up: "Quaint."

Brian stifled a laugh. Ronald tilted his head back so he could look Winston in the eye, and he grinned. "I totally deserved that." He offered a handshake. "Friends?"

Winston growled while he shook Ronald's hand. "I'd best be going. I got another complaint about trash showing up in weird places. Damnedest thing."

Brian was about to close the door behind Winston when Ronald said, "Wait, stop. Do you mind if we go outside?"

"Sure," Brian said. "After you." They reached the front step, and Brian waved at Winston as the squad car left the driveway.

Ronald stepped out into the front yard. "You still mow lawns?" he asked.

"Huh," Brian shrugged. He had expected Ronald's first question to be about That Day. "Yeah, but I call it landscaping. I do gardens, lawns. I put in that bird bath in that yard on the corner. You see it?"

"Gorgeous," Ronald said, squinting.

"How'd you know I mow lawns?"

"Somebody mentioned it in one of the articles. I've read everything ever written about you."

Brian thought about mentioning the box of old report cards that his mother had kept in the basement but decided not to. The basement would come up soon enough. "What brings you by, Ronald? I've got a fence to do today."

"I'd like to schedule our first real interview." Ronald paused. "I could have done that over the phone, but I wanted to check on something."

"What?"

Ronald cocked his head to one side, a signal for Brian to look in that direction without seeming to. Brian glanced. He saw yards, houses, and parked cars. "What am I looking at?" Brian asked.

"You see that blue sedan with dark windows?"

Brian shielded his eyes from the sun and looked again. "Looks like Jake Warren's car. He lives down at that intersection."

"Does he always park so far from home?"

"Guess not. Why?"

"Show me the back of your house," Ronald said, and they walked. When they had cleared the high wooden fence, closing the street from view, he said, "That car was there yesterday, too. And last night I saw it parked near the motel where I'm staying."

"Huh."

"What does Jake Warren do?"

"He's an accountant, I think," Brian said. "And he's a deacon at First Church."

"That's *the* First Church, right? The one—"

"Yeah, that one." The one where Michael Cox gave the sermon some people said had inspired Fran to do what she did.

"Okay," Ronald said. "Tell me something else. Is there a little girl who lives next door?" He gestured toward the Johnsons' house.

"No. Three boys. Why?"

Ronald shook his head, and his demeanor seemed to melt. For a moment, he didn't seem like a hotshot writer on a mission; he seemed like a worried young man. "It's just that I saw... thought I saw... well, I'm sure it isn't important." The former persona returned. "So, Mr. McCullough, are you free tomorrow afternoon for a long chat? I want to hear it all, from your point of view. I've got to get it right. Otherwise, I'll spend the rest of my life apologizing to people like Deputy Beecher."

4

The reporter couldn't have picked a worse time to reopen the wounds of the McCullough Tragedy. This Sunday, Jeanne Harper would inaugurate New Church of Kenning with her first sermon, and even though the Tragedy was indirectly responsible for her decision to start preaching, she wanted her church to focus on Kenning's future, not its painful past.

Jeanne had attended the Princeton Seminary, but before the Tragedy, she was always happy to stay out of church business. The town's churches – Baptist, Episcopal, Methodist, Nazarene, and Presbyterian – all seemed more or less the same. At the end of the day, she only cared about her salvation through Jesus Christ and her fellowship with other believers, and that meant that any reasonable, Protestant church would do. Christ's love was about bringing mankind together, not pulverizing humanity into squabbling fragments. She attended First Church simply because it was the largest.

The murders made national news five years ago, and everyone searched for reasons. On the day the headlines appeared, Jeanne had a conversation in the checkout at SmartShop Grocery that forecasted the impending controversy. "Isn't it terrible?" Barbara Fehn asked. "How could somebody so young...?"

"There's just no way to understand it," Jeanne said.

"It almost rattles your faith, doesn't it? I mean, just two days after that sermon and everything. Poor Reverend Cox, bless his heart, must be terribly shaken up."

"What do you mean?"

"Well," Barbara said, "I assume *you* were in church on Sunday."

Jeanne nodded.

"Well then, I assume you heard what everyone is calling *the* sermon."

Jeanne had to think for a moment before she recalled that Reverend Cox had had one of his more political days. "It wasn't his best."

Barbara huffed. "I should think not. Did you know the whole thing was aimed at the McCullough girl?"

Jeanne knew that Fran McCullough had attended – the girl's mother drove her to church but didn't go in – but Jeanne didn't see a connection between a ten-year-old girl and a sermon about the sanctity of marriage. "No," she said.

"Apparently your pastor made statements about dealing harshly with sinners, and that girl took him a little too seriously."

The boy at the checkout told Jeanne the total for her groceries. As he ran her credit card, she turned to Barbara. "So people are saying Fran McCullough killed her parents because of what Reverend Cox said?"

Barbara seemed to have trouble lifting the two gallons of milk from her cart to the conveyer. "It stands to reason there's a connection. That's what people are saying."

In the days that followed, Jeanne waited for the Reverend's response as accusations grew from gossip into official concern. The Reverend didn't attend the town meeting where people assembled to light candles, share grief, and discuss what, if anything, the town needed to do. The early service at First Church wasn't usually the most popular, but on the first Sunday after the Tragedy, people stuffed themselves into the pews and aisles long before the scheduled start time. Reverend Cox did not appear. Instead, Deacon Warren selected mournful hymns and invited people to talk about the heartache they all felt. The early service merged with the late service; most of the town came to speak, cry, sing, and pray.

Two weeks later, a new pastor moved down from Macon to fill in for Reverend Cox "indefinitely." Jeanne kept attending First Church, but she also started to invite friends to her house for casual Bible studies. The people in her small group reported that they saw Mrs. Cox from time to time, but the preacher's wife offered little information, describing her husband as "unavailable" or, occasionally, "convalescing."

The government had no interest in holding Michael Cox responsible, but townspeople demanded that the Reverend speak out about his "role in the killings." Through the course of a month, the outcry rose to its zenith and diminished. A few people speculated that Michael Cox no longer lived in Kenning. Most simply accepted that the McCullough Tragedy had broken him, that he had chosen to remove himself from the town's leadership instead of making his accusers go to the trouble.

Michael Cox waited three years to set the record straight. Without saying anything to the congregation at large, the church leaders posted a sign by the main driveway: "Sunday Reverend Cox Wrestling with Deliverance." No one had forgotten the circumstances surrounding the Reverend's disappearance. Everyone had an opinion about his return.

"Those people are just opening up old wounds and filling them with salt!" Barbara Fehn said.

While she understood their perspective, Jeanne did not agree with those who said Michael Cox had misled, betrayed, and abandoned the people of Kenning. He had let the town down, but as a Christian, Jeanne believed in forgiveness, so she'd wait to hear what the Reverend had to say. He was a charming, intelligent, and spiritual man. His repentance would be a model.

As the title "Wrestling with Deliverance" suggested, the sermon focused on Jacob's night-long battle with the angel. "The night of my struggle has been long and dark," Reverend Cox said, casting himself as Jacob. He continued, "I have received the angel's blessing, and I know that I must once again stand up for God's people! I must repeat His words, His laws, and His teachings, and I must understand their consequences, because no matter what else they may seem to be, they are the Lord working to advance His divine will!" The Reverend's gift from the metaphorical angel was not absolution for the pain his words had caused. It was confirmation of his righteousness. He declared that he had done nothing wrong, and he suggested that the crimes of the parents had spawned the crimes of the daughter. The Reverend implied that the McCulloughs had gotten what they deserved, and Jeanne was furious.

She wasn't alone. When Jeanne spoke her mind, she had a ready audience. She had no intention of leading a movement, but she soon found herself a rallying point for almost half the congregation. There were meetings, debates, and prayer groups. Reverend Cox, once again at the helm of First Church, expressed understanding and regret for all the bad feelings. The hand he extended to the disgruntled took away many of Jeanne's de facto followers, but it did not satisfy her. Despite his talk of unity, Michael Cox never admitted to or apologized for the suggestion that Matt and Linda McCullough had deserved to die, and thus he allowed the suggestion – correlated to the idea that Fran had been an agent of God – to take root in the congregation that accepted him.

Jeanne stopped attending First Church and issued a general invitation for people to join the Bible studies she led in the spacious home she had inherited from her father, who had been mayor. At first, the majority of Kenning's faithful eyed these meetings with suspicion, but as the Bible studies grew from a handful of friends into groups of twenty, thirty, and forty, most of the town began to respect them. The meetings gave rise to the idea of a new church, and less than two years later, the non-denominational New Church of Kenning broke ground.

5

Seventeen-year-old Melanie Grayson had attended Jeanne's Bible studies since the beginning, and Jeanne had come to rely on her. Other than the people Jeanne paid to help her, Melanie was the only person whose interest in New Church seemed comparable to Jeanne's. When the news came, Jeanne had to fight for self-control.

"*This* Sunday? They're going to start it *this* Sunday, of all Sundays?" Jeanne smoothed out an imaginary wrinkle in her skirt. She should have known that somehow, Michael Cox and the rest of them would find a way to sabotage her efforts. They weren't spiteful, exactly, but they were competitive, and Jeanne could easily imagine Reverend Cox and his men sitting around a table to discuss how they might "handle the New Church problem."

Jeanne and Melanie sat in the main office behind the sanctuary of New Church. "I'm sorry, Ms. Harper," the girl said, "but my dad said the youth group would be helping out with the revival this weekend, and since my kid sister is a part of it, I have to go."

"Don't blame yourself, Mel. You've done more than any one person should do to help me out, and I can't thank you enough." Jeanne sighed. "I can do without you this Sunday, I guess, but I'm sorry you won't be there to hear my first... sermon? Is it fair to call it a sermon? I never felt like I was preaching during our Bible studies."

"I'd love to hear it," Melanie said.

Jeanne stood up and paced. The office furniture had come from her own home, making this room the only one in the building that looked at all ready for the weekend. More pews were supposed to arrive tomorrow. "So they've decided to do a revival. I guess I should have expected it since it's Easter, but since they didn't do one last year, or the year before, I can't think it's a coincidence, can I?"

"It's not. They did this on purpose."

"I suppose I'll have to go talk to them." Jeanne fetched her purse and took out her car keys.

"I'll go with you."

"Walk me to the car," Jeanne said, "and help me think of what to say. But I have to do this by myself."

As they made their way through the sanctuary's scant disordered pews and half-opened boxes of hymnals, Jeanne wondered again if she had made all the right decisions for the building. New Church included none of the dark reds and ostentatious gold that usually colored altars and pulpits. The vaulted ceiling seemed classic, but other design features shouted modernity. The carpet was light blue, and the trim and pillars were blond walnut. Jeanne hoped she would eventually be able to replace the huge front window with stained glass, but for now, it was transparent, letting more pure sunshine into the sanctuary than she had ever seen in a church before.

The front doors were heavy. That, at least, seemed traditional enough. She pulled on the handle with both arms, stood behind the door, and gestured for Melanie to exit first.

Melanie said thank you, stepped through the doorway, and screamed.

Jeanne's first thought was that Melanie's heel had gotten caught on a loose brick, sending her tumbling down the steps. A burst of adrenaline flung the door wide, and Jeanne rushed out.

Melanie stood on the second stair, uninjured. A hand covered her mouth. Jeanne looked at the uncovered portion of Mel's face and saw a mixture of fear, disgust, and sadness. Tears welled in the girl's eyes. Jeanne asked, "What is it?"

In response, Melanie pointed to the bottom step. Two cats, one a solid blue-grey and the other a yellowish tabby, lay there with gashed sides, torn faces, and blood-matted fur. Melanie asked, "Who would do such a thing?"

"They must have fought," Jeanne said. "Killed each other."

6

Not long after sunset, Ronald went exploring. He needed to know the town well – inside, outside, daytime, nighttime – to give his book authenticity. The postings about his travels on *American Sane* were frivolous, not intended to do much other than satisfy the lefty minions whose interest in his "sharp wit" lured the advertisers who paid his bills. The book about the McCullough Tragedy would be different. He had something serious to express. He would transform from a wit into a *voice*.

The Sleep E-Z Motel occupied a revealing position at the edge of town. If he walked in one direction, he'd end up in real live cotton fields, where the souls of murdered slaves probably still sang spirituals. If he walked the same distance in the other direction, he'd end up in the center of town, on the street with the Starbuck's, McDonald's, and Wal-Mart, or on the parallel lane with three of the town's five – soon to be six – churches. Taking either direction, he'd end up in the middle of a shameful symbol of everything wrong with American history and culture. The cotton wouldn't be particularly interesting at night; the town center might be. By the time he reached the street corner with the Starbuck's, which was closed, he regretted his decision.

The quiet streets highlighted the one thing that Kenning had that New York lacked: a feeling of total safety. If he wore drag or a Yankees T-shirt, he would risk getting clobbered by an anonymous baseball bat, but otherwise, he might stroll along any of the streets for hours without worrying about muggings, drive-bys, or any of the other urban delights he had gotten bored with writing about. A narrow alley connected Main Street – it was actually called Main Street! – to a lesser thoroughfare, and he didn't hesitate to walk down it.

When he emerged on the other side of the alley, he saw the sign for Vincent's Pizzeria. He must have passed the dumpster that Winston mentioned. He returned to the alley and looked, wondering what strange plot had turned trash bags into a matter for police action. Ronald lifted the dumpster's lid and unleashed an odor that brought his stomach to his throat. The scent was a greasy blend of pepperoni and death, and as the lid slammed back down, Ronald considered indefinitely foregoing all specimens of cheesy pie.

"Arf! Arf! Arf!"

A short-haired Chihuahua scampered into the alley from the direction of the pizzeria's main entrance, attracted, perhaps, by the carrion stench. "Grrrrrrrrrrrr."

"Greetings, puppy." Ronald didn't dislike dogs. Dogs disliked him. He feigned a lunge in the dog's direction and stomped on the pavement, hoping to frighten the thing off. It held its ground, deepening its tiny engine-noise of hate. "Persistent bugger," Ronald said. "Shouldn't you be trapped in Reese Witherspoon's handbag?"

As if offended, the dog charged at him. Ronald took an involuntary step backward before he realized that being charged by a Chihuahua was an occasion for mirth, not flight. Ronald's unmoving posture did not deter the beast, which, leaping, slammed into his shin with bruising force and tumbled to the ground. "That hurt you more than me," Ronald said. He bent down to make sure the prone dog hadn't sustained too much injury. His hand paused mid-reach – was he really about to touch a dog that had just given itself a concussion to spite him? Before the hand could withdraw, the dog snapped to its feet and launched open jaws at Ronald's fingers.

The fingers escaped, but Ronald didn't have time to process another move before the Chihuahua resumed the offensive, targeting the bruised shin with its teeth. It scurried over a tennis shoe, slipped its head beneath the cuff of his slacks, and bit. The leg responded with a reflexive kick, dislodged the dog's teeth from torn skin, and sent it upward in an arc, flying two, five, ten yards before crashing onto the lane beyond the alley. There, it did not move.

Ronald imagined the recrimination that would follow the assault's discovery, townsfolk seeing him and shouting "Dog killer!" He had never intentionally injured another creature in his life. Despite the animal's obvious malice, he would have to follow it to where it had landed. He would have to determine his level of guilt.

When he stepped forward, pain shot up from his bitten shin. The dog had done damage. He limped on, stopping just shy of the alley's exit, and saw what waited. A gigantic, grayish-white mastiff stood by the steps of the pizzeria, staring in his direction. When Ronald and the mastiff made eye contact, growling began, and the nearby streetlight was bright enough for Ronald to detect tensing muscles, a poise to strike.

"Nice doggy, good doggy. I'm sorry I hurt your friend." He took a backward step, moving slowly. "Go get help!"

"Woof! Woof! Woof!"

Ronald didn't mean the suggestion about "help," but the universe responded. A few yards behind the mastiff, a large Doberman approached. Ronald took another step back, and the Doberman picked up speed. "Oh, *fuck*," Ronald said, and he, the Doberman, and the mastiff started running.

Ronald heard the dogs closing his small lead as he crossed through the alley. He made a quick turn back onto Main Street, gaining ground. Main Street looked deserted, but Ronald screamed for help anyway. Running, he glanced over a shoulder. New panic flared when he realized that a third dog, a mid-sized terrier, had joined the chase. His pursuers had officially become a pack of wild dogs.

Ronald turned another corner, darted through another alley, and ran down another street, passing a post office, a bank, and a vacant lot. The dogs lost ground when he made the quick turns, but they were still after him, and the straight path down the road was allowing them to gain. Another alley, two more quick cuts, and he was back on Main Street, trying to remember the form he had mastered on the high school track team and yelling "Aaaaaaaah" in the hope that Winston or some other kind, intervening soul might appear.

Down by the McDonald's, he spied another human. She wore pink sweatpants, a white T-shirt, an orange fanny pack, and a pink sweatband that constricted her head's fluttering flock of bleach-blonde curls. The woman was jogging toward him, but at only a little over five feet tall, she wouldn't be much help against his pursuers. Drawing near, he shouted, "Run!"

She fixed her eyes on him, uncomprehending, and stood still on the sidewalk as Ronald bolted by. "Ruuuuuun!" he shouted again.

He couldn't help slowing enough to glance back at her. She looked from him to his wake, where the three dogs were running and turning their attention to her. She rotated toward Ronald, opened her mouth to shout, and toppled to the pavement as the dogs rammed against her back.

Ronald stopped, breathless, indecisive. The woman was going to be mauled. He could join her, adding to the dogs' supper of human flesh, or he could keep running until he found someone else, summoned aid that would undoubtedly come too late.

He took off his jacket, wrapped it around his right arm, sprinted back to the dog-covered woman, and attacked. His first kick removed the terrier from the pile. It yelped and tumbled back, but the kick wasn't as effective as the one that had sent the Chihuahua flying. The terrier regrouped and charged at Ronald. He whacked it with his coat-covered arm, kicked it onto its side, and stomped on its neck.

"Get them off get them off get them off!"

The woman was crying, howling, as the mastiff and the Doberman tore into her. Ronald dove at the mastiff and lost his footing, adding more weight to the pile on top of the woman. Struggling to lock the mastiff's head in the crook of his left arm, he saw the woman's blood-smeared face, one eye closed, the other wide in terror. Human screams and hungry growls surrounded him as he managed to wrench a dog away from the woman's shoulder. Ronald rolled on his back, taking the mastiff with him, but his arm wasn't strong enough to immobilize the beast. It squirmed until they lay chest to chest, the dog on top. It started clawing.

Trying to keep his left arm's grip tight enough to prevent the mastiff's reddened teeth from reaching his neck, he turned his head toward the woman in time to see the Doberman abandon the meal it was making of her ear. It jumped toward him. Ronald forced his jacket-armored right arm into the Doberman's gaping mouth, but as he did, his hold on the mastiff weakened. He felt teeth pierce his shoulder and neck before he blacked out.

7

Melanie was sitting in her AP Biology class Wednesday morning when Principal Bledsoe's voice sounded over the intercom: "Would any teachers who have a free period please come to the front office as soon as possible?" She dismissed the call, concentrating on her obsession. She hadn't eaten meat since yesterday, when she'd found the dead cats on the doorstep of New Church. Her reaction might seem silly to some people. Animals die. They kill each other. Death and killing are natural. They studied such things in class. Melanie didn't care. Nature was gross, and she didn't have to eat it.

Ms. Fuggle turned back to her model of a Skinner box and lectured for several minutes before Mrs. Kemp, an English teacher, entered the classroom without knocking. The two teachers excused themselves and disappeared into the hall. Melanie strained to listen. Some of the teachers' words – "hospital," "attack," and "plague" – prompted her to break school rules. She fetched the cell phone from her purse's secret compartment and pressed the number one.

"Hey Mel," Brian answered. "What's up?"

"Listen, I only have a minute. Is something happening?"

"Huh?"

"Something weird's happening. I think it's connected to those cats I told you about."

She heard Brian's breath catch in his throat. "Did you hear about the dogs?"

"What dogs?"

Brian told Melanie about the attack. "Do you think I should send something to the hospital? I mean, for the reporter guy?"

"His name is Ronald," Melanie said. "And you might send something. There's a flower shop in the hospital."

"I'm not sending flowers."

"Fine, send a balloon. You need to make him like you if he's going to write about you. But that's all beside the point." Melanie huffed frustration. "Have you heard anything else?"

"If you mean other than—"

"Melanie Grayson!" The voice was Kemp's.

"Gotta go." Melanie shoved her phone into her pocket. She braced for a teacher's tirade about the rudeness of today's teens.

"Thank you, Melanie. Class, I'll be filling in for Ms. Fuggle for a little while. She had some business."

Melanie looked from Kemp to the Skinner box and made a connection. If something were going wrong with local animals, Ms. Fuggle would be a reasonable person to call.

"You see, class," Kemp began, "it seems like some people have been hurt by, well, wild animals, and I'm covering your class until the buses get here. School will let out early."

A boy in the back of the class shouted "All right!" A few others started clapping. Melanie pondered the stupidity of letting children out of school when dangerous animals were outside hurting people. When the buses arrived, Bledsoe exhorted everyone to be very, very careful and to stay indoors.

The students hurried out, but Melanie lingered, waiting for a moment alone with Kemp. "I'm sorry to bother you, ma'am, but can you tell me where Ms. Fuggle went?"

Kemp pondered. "Well, Dr. Early, the veterinarian—"

Her suspicion confirmed, Melanie drove toward the vet's office and parked two blocks away. A loose mob stood at Early's front door. Some of them carried cages that jumped in their arms; others wore bandages. As she navigated through the crowd, pushing toward the door, she gathered information. Mary White said all the science teachers had joined Sheriff Hadderly and Dr. Early inside, doing tests on animals, food, and water. Selma Evans said the CDC was sending a woman doctor named Kelly Pratt down from Atlanta to make the tests "official." Kyle Amory said that as many as seven people had been hospitalized. Several of the forlorn and bandaged crowd members confessed to hurting or killing their pets in self-defense.

Melanie was opening the vet's glass front door when the crowd's anxious chatter softened to a murmur. The glass reflected turning heads and bodies. Melanie heard a booming baritone: "Funny, isn't it, these times we're living in?"

She turned in the voice's direction. Michael Cox's average-height, neatly-coiffed head was barely visible from her position. The voice was his, and something, something at the root of her feeling about the cats, made her abandon the door and move toward him.

Someone said, "What do you mean, Reverend?"

"I'm reminded," Cox responded, "of the book of Ezekiel in the Old Testament. The prophet foretells God's justice for the wayward people in Jerusalem. God did not take too kindly to the sinners' abominations, and he showed no pity."

Melanie thought about the word "abomination" and what some religious leaders had said in the aftermath of Hurricane Katrina. While thousands of people were still sick, homeless, and suffering, preachers like Cox had called the hurricane God's justice. She moved closer to the voice.

"The Lord said, 'I will send upon you famine and evil beasts, and they shall bereave thee.'" Melanie could see the preacher clearly now. His hair was almost as black as hers, and he had intelligent eyes, a warm smile, and broad shoulders. He continued, "I call what's happening here at this doctor's office funny because people forget who's really in control. It's *God* who shapes the will of the animals. When we deny Him, they turn against us."

Someone in the crowd shouted "Amen," and Melanie had to object: "So there's no point in trying to do something about all these people getting hurt? We should just wait for God to sort things out? Whatever happened to the idea that God helps those who help themselves?"

"Melanie Grayson," Cox said. He stepped from his immediate circle and stood in front of her. "I'm glad we'll be seeing you at the revival this Sunday. If you came to church more often, you might know that that particular adage is not in the Bible. God helps the helpless; when we surrender, He delivers us."

Melanie would not retreat. "So you're telling us to sit and wait? To do nothing?" She knew he wouldn't answer. He might provide some nugget of canned wisdom to maintain his station in the crowd, but he wouldn't provide direct instructions.

"Yes," Cox said. "I am telling you to do nothing and wait. Go home, people! See to your families, and trust God. He will provide an answer."

At his command, the crowd dispersed. Melanie stood dumbfounded, routed by a clear statement of faith undergirded by plain logic. She had to agree: standing in front of the veterinarian's office did no good, and she would only slow down the tests if she went inside and insisted on information. Like the majority, she went home.

8

On *American Sane*:

A gay man running for his life down the dark streets of a Southern town is not, I would think, a particularly uncommon phenomenon, but the pack of errant pets that pursued me might have turned some heads, had there been heads to turn. But no, Sane Readers, I was all alone last night, going for a walk, taking in the scenery of the unscenic town called Kenning, Georgia. I was pondering how safe the streets seemed when some of the town's lesser denizens decided to make a meal of me. I fended off the first dog's attack with ease, but when three of its friends – one of which certainly weighed more than I do – decided to join the fray, I ran for my life. Luckily and unluckily, I happened upon a female jogger, who became the monsters' new target when I sped past her. Earning the title "hero" inscribed on the card that came with the get-well balloon I'm looking at as I type, I returned to offer aid.

I didn't arrive in time to save the woman's ear, which I'm told will be surgically reconstructed, but I probably saved her life, offering my body as fodder instead of hers. One of the dogs ripped a chunk from my shoulder, missing a major artery by, as the doctor said, "that much." I passed out and awoke in a hospital bed.

I have often wondered why people in little towns like Kenning feel more threatened by terrorists and criminals than New Yorkers do, and I have often condemned them for rushing to arms when they are clearly secure. According to such logic, Barbara Fehn was stupid to carry a tazer when she went for a nighttime jog on Kenning's safe streets, but had she not kept 50,000 volts in her fanny pack, we might both have bled to death on Main Street U.S.A. The woman I saved has returned the favor. *Merci*, bellicose Red States, *et pardonnez-moi*.

9

When he answered the door, Ronald wore nothing but pajama bottoms and had his left arm in a sling. Brian noted the stitched lacerations on Ronald's torso and held up the six-pack of bottled water. "Here," he said. "I got the last one they had at SmartShop."

"Come in," Ronald said. "To be honest, I thought you Southern boys always showed up with beer. Could I be mistaken in this stereotype as well? Are you not a fan of the brewsky?"

Brian stepped inside and set the water on the table by the window. He surveyed the room. Twisted sheets and blankets topped a queen-sized bed, and several packages of gauze occupied the surface of a dresser. A holstered gun sat on top of the television next to the remote. "Is Winston here?"

Ronald looked toward the bathroom and then back at Brian. "Yes, he is." His voice got louder: "Yes, Brian, Winston is in the bathroom washing up!" Squinting, he continued, "The deputy was kind enough to drive me home and help me change the dressing on this shoulder. I guess they train cops for stuff like that."

Brian nodded.

"So hey, good to see you, Brian," Ronald said. "Why don't you sit? Sorry I don't have anything to offer you. Actually, thanks to you, I do. Would you like a cup of water?" Before Brian could reply, Ronald walked back toward the bathroom and knocked on the door. "Deputy, would you mind handing me a cup for our guest?"

Brian heard a toilet flush, and the bathroom door opened. Winston came out. One hand held a wrapped plastic cup, and the other fidgeted with his shirt collar. "Hey, Brian, good to see you."

Brian nodded.

"So, um, Ronald and me were just talking," Winston said, "about how strange all this stuff in town is. All these animals going crazy. It's the damnedest thing."

Brian sat at the table. "That's why I brought the water. Everybody's saying something must have gotten into the town's water supply."

Winston retrieved his gun belt from the television. "Is there anything in the news about it? I mean, is it happening in other places?"

"Just here, far as I know," Brian said.

Winston looked from Brian to Ronald and cleared his throat. "Well, I should get going. There's a lot of work to do. If you two will excuse me." He set the cup on the table and exited.

"It seems like one or the other of us is always driving him off, doesn't it?" Ronald took the other seat at the table. "You'll excuse me for not getting dressed. Putting on a shirt is unpleasant."

Brian nodded. "Did the hospital give you something for it?"

"A shirt?"

"The pain."

"Ah, yes," Ronald said. "They're quite lovely, actually, these little pills. Would you like one?"

"No thanks."

Ronald looked around the room, tapping the table with his right hand. "So," he said.

"So," Brian said.

"So, uh, what brings you here, Brian?"

"We were supposed to talk today. Interview."

Ronald stood up and doubled over, falling back into his chair. "Oh, *fuck*," he said. "Remind me that there is a slow, gentle art to standing up."

"Can I get you something?"

"No. In fact, I was standing for no reason at all. I slept most of the day. Now I have a lot of nervous energy."

"Nervous?"

Ronald sighed. "Being attacked by wild dogs can do that to you. Make you nervous." Silence followed, and Brian watched Ronald scan the room. His eyes settled on the balloon floating over his suitcase. "Ah-ha! I bet you can help me with a little mystery. Who's Melanie Grayson?"

"Huh? Why?"

"I got this balloon with this card signed 'From Brian McCullough and Melanie Grayson.' I'd show it to you," Ronald sighed, "but that would involve standing again."

"It's, um, Mel wanted to send something."

"And Mel is…?"

Brian blushed. "Kind of my girlfriend."

"Is it serious?" Ronald asked.

"What?"

"The *relationship*," Ronald said. "Have the two of you been together long?"

Squirming in the chair, Brian said, "It's complicated."

"Oh *really*," Ronald said. "Tell me. I love complication."

"This can't be part of the interview."

"Oh?"

"Promise me I won't read about this on your website tomorrow."

Ronald straightened in his chair, winced, and said, "You have my word."

"Okay," Brian said. "You see, her parents don't know about us. And she's sort of still in high school."

"Oh, *scandal!*"

10

An hour after Brian left, Ronald heard Winston's comforting voice announce that the crisis was over. He and his officer brethren drove through Kenning with megaphones, spreading the news. Tests said the water was safe. The town's pets, their blood work normal, were returning to their calm, loving selves.

The next morning, Ronald met Winston in front of Kenning's garbage dump. "Thanks for coming," Winston said. Beads of sweat stood out on his high forehead, and dark dampness blotted his uniform. "It's just the damnedest thing. Sheriff Hadderly told me to go home, that it was no big deal, but I think it is a big deal, and I don't know what to do."

Closing the door of the rented Jeep stirred the air. Ronald slapped one hand over his mouth and another on his stomach, trying not to gag. Pain from his stretched wounds combined with stench to ebb consciousness.

"Smells bad, doesn't it?"

"Oh God *fuck* does it smell bad!" Ronald said, steadying himself. "I didn't expect a garbage dump to smell like roses, but this is *beyond*."

Winston nodded. "Uh-huh." He looked back over his shoulder at a mound of trash, and despite the heat, he shivered. "There's something wrong here."

The large officer was being timid with information, and instead of feeling annoyed, Ronald felt worried. He didn't know how to interact now that he and Winston were suddenly close. Ronald didn't dislike relationships. Relationships disliked him. "So there's something you need to show me that you couldn't tell me about on the phone," he said. "And it sounds like you're doing something against your boss's orders. You are a man of mysteries. Care to explain?"

"Here." Winston gave Ronald a handkerchief. "I keep these in my glove compartment."

"Thanks, really, but—" Ronald sniffed demonstratively and felt immediate regret—"my sinuses are mercilessly clear."

Winston shook his head. "Use it to cover your nose and mouth. For a smart guy, you're pretty slow sometimes." Winston smiled, and Ronald smiled back. "Look, just follow me, okay?" Ronald did as instructed, and the two men walked toward the piles of compressed garbage. Winston moved fast, almost forcing Ronald to jog alongside. "Dave Holcomb runs this place and called us this morning," he said. "He was rambling about how people need to show respect and that they shouldn't go leaving things where they don't belong. Did you know that it's not even legal to bury your pets in your back yard?"

Ronald realized what he was about to see just as Winston pointed. "I thought it must have been my fault," Winston said, "because I didn't say anything when I found the bag of bones out by Vincent's Pizzeria. You know, I sort of thought somebody had just cleaned up their attic and hadn't wanted the rotting rats in their own trashcans. Sure, it wasn't the right thing to do, but was it really worth tracking somebody down over? The bones were mixed in with other stuff, you know, normal household trash stuff. I thought the rotting cat in the other bag was just a coincidence, and then the thing with the dogs and you, and I sort of forgot."

Ronald didn't understand how one could forget garbage bags full of corpses showing up where they didn't belong, but he decided to let that point go. In front of him, three trash bags sat nestled amidst objects less easy to identify. Torn plastic revealed their contents: ears, tails, fur.

"I'm guessing that whoever was hiding their trash in other people's dumpsters finally decided just to bring it here. Then an animal must have caught a whiff and come over to check it out. You see there," he pointed out some stripped parts a few yards away from the bags, "some wild thing had itself a nice supper."

Ronald thought about the Doberman eating Barbara Fehn's ear. "This whole mess started Tuesday," Ronald said, "and today is Thursday. A lot of people must have killed some animals in self defense before it stopped. I took out one or two myself." Ronald didn't mean to sound proud, but he did. "How awful," he appended. "Maybe these bags are just some kind of cleanup effort we didn't hear about?"

Winston walked deeper into the valleys of trash. Ronald followed. "That's what I thought at first," Winston said. "Or kind of hoped. Until I noticed that there." He pointed to another bag. It had also been torn open, but the tears looked more precise. "I saw that bag and thought, why would another bag not look crushed like the rest of the stuff here? And I decided to look in."

Unable to resist, Ronald brought his hanky-covered face closer to the bag's opening. The things inside looked different from those in the other bag. Flesh was grey, far more advanced in decomposition. "My God, this must have been happening for a long time."

"Uh-huh. The way I figure it, somebody has been saving them up, and after what happened over the last couple of days, they figured nobody would pay much attention to some bags of dead animals."

The wind blew again, but Ronald was prepared. He braced himself against odor's onslaught and said, "What did Sheriff Hadderly say about this? Surely, if you and I can tell at a glance that these animals are more than two days dead—"

"I know, I know, and I showed him, and I told him, and he just repeated that it had all come from what happened the other day and that I shouldn't worry about it. He said 'drop it.' I don't have much better to do. Why would he want me to drop it?"

"You think Hadderly knows something."

Winston nodded. "He was acting funny this morning. Kind of glazed over, and he was tugging at the fingers of those gloves he always wears like he was nervous about something."

Ronald looked at his shoes. "You realize that what you're saying might upgrade this whole situation from a freak occurrence to a conspiracy?"

"Uh-huh."

"I hate to use a cliché," Ronald said, "but I have no choice. What the *fuck* is going on?"

11

"Join us at First Church this Easter Sunday for a Revival of
Tradition, Fellowship, and Spirit! New members are welcome —
don't miss it!"

Beneath those words, which appeared in big, bright, blue and
yellow letters, a calendar listed events throughout Easter Week.
Beneath the calendar, in smaller print, a note read, "The events of
the last few days have shown that our town has never needed the
healing light of Jesus Christ more than we do now. Let's bring the
town together in an act of unity to celebrate and praise Him for
our deliverance!"

The fliers were all over town: in mailboxes, on telephone poles,
under windshield wipers. First Church had launched an all-out
campaign, and Jeanne couldn't help feeling that she was the leader
of the opposition party. She might have been wrong, but as she
read the small print, she felt accused of trying to tear the town
apart by opening New Church on Easter. The dead cats on the
church doorstep had deflated her resolve to confront First Church
leaders on Tuesday, but nothing would stop her today.

The walk to First Church took less than fifteen minutes. With
each step, Jeanne's anger grew. Of course Melanie was right — of
course they had planned the revival to reduce attendance at New
Church. First Church already had a large sanctuary, and they were
setting up tents to extend their capacity to the thousands. Jeanne
had forty or fifty people who would definitely be in the pews this
Sunday, but for her church to survive, she would need a much larger
congregation. First Church's advertising campaign was a
preemptive strike, an attempt to squash the opposition before it
could organize. And now, Thursday, late afternoon, Jeanne didn't
have time to plan a proper response. Strategically, First Church had
made a good move, one she should have anticipated. But since when
were churches about strategy, move and countermove?

She maneuvered through the familiar hallways behind the
sanctuary to Reverend Cox's office. A black plaque with gold

lettering announced "The Rev. Michael Cox" on the closed door. Jeanne raised a fist in the air, hesitated, and knocked.

No answer.

She knocked again, hard enough for the solid wood to hurt her knuckles. When no answer came, she tried a third time, creating duller thuds with the clenched side of her hand. The knocking was pointless. The Reverend was probably out posting fliers or spreading the word about how being First is so much better than being New.

A click preceded a loud clack, and with a creak, the door opened. The face that greeted her did not match the name on the door. Jake Warren's tall, narrow body filled the gap in the doorway. His cheeks puffed out with chewing, which caused his grey thin-rimmed glasses to bounce on his nose. Jeanne hardly knew him. Deacon Warren had lived in Kenning for seven years, and during that time he had won the town's respect by lending his financial services to the church. His thick silver hair and the lines around his eyes put him at sixty-something, a decade ahead of both Jeanne and Michael Cox.

"Deacon Warren," Jeanne said. "I'm surprised to see you. I was looking for Reverend Cox."

He nodded and chewed for a moment before gulping down whatever he was eating. The movement of his neck seemed exaggerated as he swallowed, the Adam's apple swelling and sinking as dinner descended. "Excuse me, Ms. Harper," he said. "I was just having an early supper. Mike brought me some leftovers from a salmon Sara, that's Mrs. Cox, made. There's plenty left. Care to join me?" He pulled the door wide and gestured toward the neat meal laid out on the Reverend's desk.

Jeanne peered in; she had never seen this room before. Dark wood furniture kept the place from being bright, but a big brown sofa, soft leather high-backed chairs, overstuffed bookcases, and a colorful model of happy, cartoonish animals proceeding two by two into a tiny ark made the place seem friendly. Behind the large desk, in the room's rear corners, were two closed doors. One of them might have been a closet. "Do you always eat in Reverend Cox's office?"

"Mike likes to use this room to counsel members of the congregation and to conduct church business," the deacon said, "but when he's really hard at work, he prefers to stay home." He walked around to the far side of the desk, gestured for Jeanne to take a chair across from him, and sat. "I use the desk sometimes when I've got church-related paperwork. And I sure have some now! Even with the church's exemption, there's tons to do. I think it's rude to have taxes due at Easter, don't you?"

Forgetting the anger that had brought her here, Jeanne smiled and took a seat. The meal in front of her looked less like leftovers and more like a feast: fish, a basket of bread, a dish of Southern-style green beans, and a carafe of something that looked like wine.

"May I pour you a glass?" the deacon asked. "It's not real wine, just grape juice. And it's not what we use for Communion, if that's what you're thinking. Heh heh heh."

The scent was powerful: Jeanne had forgotten lunch. "Actually, yes, if it's no trouble. The beans look delicious."

"Say no more." He stood and went to the door in the back right corner. He returned with a paper plate, a plastic cup, and a plastic fork. "This is all I can offer, I'm afraid. Is that okay?"

Jeanne nodded, and Jake Warren served. She sampled the beans, commented on how good they were, sipped the juice, and remembered why she had come. "So Reverend Cox is at home now, is that right?"

"I couldn't tell you," he said. "All I know is that he's not here. Is there something I can help you with?"

The man's broad grin revealed his top teeth, square incisors and long canines. Jeanne tried to keep her own smile from faltering and straightened her back. "You know, you probably can help me. Deacon Warren, I—"

"Please, call me Jake." He speared his fork into the salmon's large Tupperware container.

"Jake," she said. "Fine. Look, I'm afraid I've got a bone to pick with you."

"Oh?" He washed down fish with grape juice.

"Yes." Jeanne stirred her beans with her fork. "And I expect you might be able to guess what it is." She hoped she sounded stern.

"Please excuse me for eating," he took a bite, "but I didn't have lunch." Chew, swallow, drink. "You're upset about something, that's clear. I hope the plans for your church are going well?"

"They're going fine, they – that's precisely the point! You know all about my plans and you're doing everything in your power to upset them!"

Jake took a long drink from his cup, set it on the table, and said, "Whoa, now, what's this? What have I done?"

"I don't mean you specifically. What I'm talking about," she unzipped her purse and took out the flier, "is this." She slapped it on the desk. "What's the meaning of all this advertising – what are you trying to prove?"

He looked over the flier and smiled. "I think that's part of what the Young Evangelists are doing. The kids are very excited about the revival. People talk about how bad the kids are today. I think they're wrong. What do you think?"

"I think some of the kids are – what are we talking about! Look, it's obvious to me and to everyone I've talked to that First Church is putting on this big show as a kind of, I don't know, power play, an attempt to muscle out New Church. As you must know, we're holding our first services this Sunday."

"I see." He took another bite of fish and held up the lid of its container. "Would you like any?" Jeanne shook her head no, and he closed up the salmon. "Look, Ms. Harper – may I call you Jeanne?"

"I don't care what you call me."

"Fine then, Jeanne. Well Jeanne, I can't claim not to know about your big opening. I really do wish you the best. But you can't expect us not to go ahead with our Easter plans. You know this is one of the two biggest holidays for every church in town, and despite all the bunnies and chocolate eggs, I feel that Easter is the one day of the year that most people devote wholly to the celebration of the Lord. I know you feel like you've got a calling and a mission, but so do we. And we want to touch the souls of as many people as we can this Easter – the whole town, if possible."

"I – oh!" All of Jeanne's anger returned, but it rendered her impotent. Jake Warren made complete sense, but something about his words seemed sinister. The dark wood, the gleaming grin, the happy animals on their way to the ark: they seemed like etchings on a plastic film that she could peel away to reveal a ghastly truth. Her attention turned to the door in the back left corner, and she felt a wave of nausea. There was no reason for her to think these things or to feel this way. She told herself that Jake was right, that she should withdraw, and the nausea became stronger. She pushed the plate of green beans away. She imagined vomiting all over the desk, and her heart rate jumped.

"Jeanne, you don't look well." Having finished his own, he took a bite of Jeanne's beans. Chewing, he said, "Perhaps you'd like to lie down?" He gestured toward the brown sofa.

"No, thank you." She tried to will the nausea away, and her heart beat faster. "I'm fine." She took a deep breath. "And I will *not* lie down!"

"Okay," the deacon said. "Let's cut to the chase, then. What do you hope to accomplish by being here? What in the world do you want me to do?"

"I... nothing." Jeanne tried to take another deep breath, but it felt shallow, cut off. Her chest was tight, and her heart pounded. "Yes, something! Admit it! Admit that all of this – all of your plans, your fliers – are part of some kind of competition you imagine we're in!"

He walked around the desk, toward her. His path took him by the door in the left corner. As he passed it, Jeanne's eyes stuck on the door's knob: big, brass, shiny, reflective. Her heartbeat pulsed in her ears. "You're the one," the deacon said, "who seems to be imagining some kind of competition." He sat in the chair next to her, so close that their knees were almost touching. She felt a kind of static electricity between them, an aura that made her flesh creep. "You're the one who came here in anger today. Wrath is a sin, you know. You're the one," he leaned close, "who wants to divide our congregation over the McCullough Tragedy, still, now, after so many years. How Christian is that?"

The man's closeness made her heart pound harder. She tried to slow her breathing and failed. "It—" breath "—sounds—" breath "—like—" breath, pause. She closed her eyes and stopped breathing, trying to find steadiness, trying to calm the muscle that threatened to explode from her chest. She found no calm, but she found strength: "By calling me un-Christian, you prove I'm right."

Jake Warren stood up and walked around to the rear of Jeanne's high-backed chair. She sensed him through the chair's wood and leather, hovering over her, dwarfing her, collapsing her. Thump thump thump thump thump thump thump. His voice floated downward, muffled by the thick rhythm in her ears, "You may be right," he said, "but what does that mean? Can you tell me that?"

Her vision blurred, and her fingers tingled. For the first time, she thought *heart attack*, and the fear triggered adrenaline that gave her heart rate another boost, three beats a second, maybe more. She felt cold sweat above her eyebrows. The tingling crept up to her wrists.

"You realize," the man said, "that we do not question your church's right to exist." He set a hand on Jeanne's shoulder, causing a shock to rush to her center and rebound to her extremities. Her mouth opened wide to draw air, but none came. She tried to form words and failed. The deacon continued, "But you must also realize that in every conflict, there are sides, winners and losers, just and unjust. You understand?"

The hand did not move from her shoulder. The voice in her mind screamed for help, for air, for release from Deacon Warren's cool grip, but her mouth did nothing, and her heart fluttered. Pain filled her chest, her stomach, the bottom of her throat. Her vision became blurrier, and her arms felt numb. She thought she heard the deacon say, "We couldn't go forward without you," and she lost consciousness.

12

In the dream, Ronald heard his own voice calling "Mommy! Mommy!" The sound traveled over the concrete floor, up the wooden steps, through the kitchen, down the hall, and into the foyer, where the front door had just opened. Mommy had gotten home first; she would hear him calling and rush down the stairs. She did, and he hid the gun behind his back, saying "Mommy, come and see!" Mommy looked angry. Why had he left school early? Why had he called her, saying there was an emergency? She approached, half-scolding, half-concerned. He bowed his head, bashful, and waited until she was close enough. When she was an arm's length away, he raised the gun and pointed upward, firing into her chest. He dodged her body as it fell forward. He stepped over her, moved a few feet away, and waited for Daddy to come home. He arrived in minutes, and calling out brought him down the stairs. Daddy saw Mommy lying down and looked at Ronald, questioning. He must have detected something on Ronald's face because he started to retreat before he saw the gun. Daddy turned to ascend, and Ronald fired a second time.

Ronald awoke with a start, sat up quickly, and clutched his healing skin, which hurt from sudden movement. He raised his good arm and pressed his hand to his ear, hoping to push away the gunshot's illusory ringing. Injured and awake in an uncomfortable motel bed on a Thursday night, Ronald sensed something suspiciously like clarity telling him to get up, pack his suitcase, and leave. He was supposed to be chronicling Kenning's past. He was not supposed to be investigating a conspiracy involving dead animals, the town sheriff, and God knew what else. He was not supposed to be having dreams that put him in the shoes of a little girl committing parricide.

The lamp in the motel parking lot was as dim as ever, but his room seemed brighter than usual. Ronald pondered the strange illumination until the fog of sleep cleared, and then he detected the cause: the light was on in the bathroom. He didn't remember leaving it on. As he inched toward the bed's edge, planning investigation, he murmured, "You're paranoid." The sound seemed naked in the half-lit room, exposed, fragile, and lonely. He shuffled toward the bathroom, bracing himself for the attack of the intruder who had turned on the light. "Really paranoid."

The bathroom was small, so Ronald, standing in the doorway, narrowed the hiding places to two: between the door and the wall to his left, or behind the opaque white shower curtain to his right. He wrapped his fingers around the cold door handle and stepped backward into the main room. Before the door could click shut, he gave it a hard shove and watched it swing toward the wall with crushing force. The door slammed into the wall, but he heard no startled cry, no gasp of pain.

He stepped through the doorway and turned toward the door. He pulled it back and peered behind: nothing. "Fucking *nuts*," he said, and the sound reverberated from porcelain.

One hiding place remained. The bathtub was behind him. He would turn, grab the curtain, and throw it open, pain from his injuries be damned. The window in the wall beside the tub had perma-fogged panes. The opening was too small for a grown person. Whoever was waiting in the tub – and no one was, of course – was trapped there.

Ronald felt a soft touch on his bare back and screamed. He spun on his heels, right fist arcing, and punched with all his strength. The fist slammed into cold, yielding vinyl. The shower curtain was too flimsy to absorb any of the force, so his spin continued, wrapping his arm in white and bringing the curtain rod down with a crash. Ronald's frantic left hand searched for something to steady him, found the door, and pushed it closed, making the attempt to regain his footing the final twist that sent him sprawling on the bathroom tiles.

The shock blurred his vision. As it cleared, he looked down at his shoulder, where the effort to keep from falling had caused him to burst a stitch. A thin trickle of blood made its way down his left arm. "Fuck me, I'm an idiot," he said. He must have left the window open to let out steam after his last careful shower. He had knocked himself down trying to attack the wind that had pushed the shower curtain into his back. "Idiot, idiot, idiot," he said, and, grasping the toilet for support, he got to his feet. He turned to examine the bathtub.

The tub was empty, and the window was closed.

Apparently, the shower curtain had decided to reach out and touch someone. Ronald tried to laugh, but the joke felt hollow. Whatever the curtain's intentions had been, it was inanimate now, in a heap on the floor, half-attached to the fallen rod.

Tap tap tap.

The sound came from the main room, from the window that faced the lamp-lit parking lot. Ronald sighed, repeated "Idiot," and walked toward the noise.

The tapping continued, confirming itself as a phenomenon more substantial than the suspicions that had drawn him into the bathroom. As he passed the bed, he switched on a lamp, and when he got to the table, he switched on another lamp. Making sure of his footing, he reached toward the drape cord and pulled.

The uncovered window revealed his Jeep, a white van, two other cars in the lot, and a dark blue sedan across the street.

Tap tap tap.

The sound came from the door. Well-trained by urban living, he had secured both the bolt and the chain before going to bed. Nothing would get in, but he could look through the peephole to discover who was trying. He stepped closer and looked.

At first, he saw nothing. His eye rolled up, nothing, to the left, nothing, to the right, nothing, down — a head of dark hair. On either side, a shoulder clad in the puffy sleeves of a child's fancy dress. The face, barely visible, was long, pale, and familiar. Fran McCullough's. Her grey-blue eyes were gone, but her head tilted back, directing the empty sockets toward the peephole.

Ronald stumbled back and said "God *damn* it!" He lurched forward, threw off the chain, flipped the bolt, and yanked the door open.

Nothing.

"That's great, Ronald, really great. You *really* need to go home." But he wouldn't, couldn't. He had to understand; he had to *know*.

13

Jeanne woke up drowning. She felt water in her nose and mouth and realized she had just tried to inhale it. Her lungs rebelled in spasms, convulsing her whole body, forcing her torso to rise. The open slits of her eyes detected grey light through a wet film. She was not underwater, so all she had to do was get control of her lungs and breathe. Balled hands joined together and slammed into her diaphragm. The spasms became a cough, and she was vomiting liquid, spewing muddy water and mucus from her nose.

Water dripped from her eyes. The world took shape. She was lying in mud. Her face had been in a puddle that was rising every second with the fast-falling rain. Her clothes, the skirt and blouse she had put on this morning, Thursday morning, were drenched and sticking to her cold, shriveled, goose-pimpled skin. The ground beneath her was on an incline, the side of a hill. Getting handholds in the mud, she pushed herself up to a sitting position. Not far away, she saw headstones. Lightning flashed. She was sitting in a cemetery during a thunderstorm.

A nearby tree, half-covered with new leaves, looked familiar. The irregular rows of headstones, some old, some new, summoned presence of mind. This was Hart's Cemetery, the largest burial ground in the town proper, the one connected with First Church. Jeanne's most recent memory flashed. She'd been sitting in Reverend Cox's office, talking to Jake Warren. A strange sensation had overwhelmed her, and she'd fainted. She'd woken up here. How had she gotten here?

"Hello?" she called. "Is there anybody here?" Thunder answered.

Her right hip hurt. She was bruised but otherwise uninjured. She spotted her purse nearby; she hadn't been robbed. Her silver watch was on her left wrist, as always. She looked at it: a quarter past nine. The glow behind the dense clouds was morning. Friday. She had lost more than sixteen hours.

Jeanne pried herself out of the mud and started walking. A few paces brought the hilltop into view. Something – someone – lay there. She moved faster. Someone else had fallen victim to whomever or whatever had left her drenched and defenseless in a cemetery. Together, they would make sense of things.

Before she reached it, she discerned that the supine figure was male. His legs were spread, and his arms extended from his sides, like someone making a snow angel. He seemed to be transfixed by the pouring clouds above him. "Hello?" Jeanne said.

A few more steps brought her to the hilltop. Her eyes registered the stillness of the man's chest before she saw his face. His mouth hung open, a dark O. Red splotched his nose and cheeks, residue of blood that the rain had not yet washed away. The nose itself looked flattened, sliced open on both sides. The eye sockets were empty.

She knelt beside him and placed her hand on his neck. The flesh was cold. "SOMEBODY!" she yelled. Her joints ached, and her bruised hip throbbed. She had slept on the side of a muddy hill, and now she was cold, wet, aching, hungry, and standing next to a murdered man. The word "ritual" came into her mind. Someone had taken his eyes and destroyed his nose. A perverse impulse forced her to look into the O of his mouth. It was voided, tongueless. He had been murdered and ritually mutilated. She wondered about the order of events.

A sense of danger straightened her spine. No one could have left this man here without noticing her on the hill. More than likely, what had happened to her was connected to what had happened to him. She didn't recognize the man, but somehow, they were linked.

Jake Warren.

At the very least, Jake Warren would know what had happened to her after her fainting spell, but as she looked at the mutilated corpse, she realized that Jake Warren's knowledge probably meant complicity. But that made no sense. She was angry at First Church, and she had never cared much for the unctuous deacon. But murder?

Her head turned left and right. The sensation of not being alone, of being watched, tensed her muscles, made her plot directions for escape. She needed a phone, and she remembered Melanie arguing that a "woman like her simply had to have a cell phone." She didn't. She started walking. Main Street wasn't far.

She walked toward a police car parked in front of the Starbuck's. The car was empty, so she stumbled toward the coffee shop. A bell rang as she pushed the front door open. The smells of fresh coffee and rich pastries turned her stomach. A young man behind the counter topped a steaming white cup with whipped cream. A woman near the cash register watched him, waiting for her treat. Two men sat at a table by the large window overlooking the patrol car. Their conversation halted, and one of them stood. "You look like you got caught in it," Winston Beecher said.

She shuffled toward him. "Please," she said. The noise was soft, and her lips quivered. "Please, I... I need help."

Deputy Beecher rushed to her side, and the other man, who had one arm in a sling, stood. "Ms. Harper, what's the matter? You look... uh, troubled."

The man who had been sitting with the policeman joined them. "I, I need to talk to you," Jeanne stammered. She imagined eavesdroppers panicking. "Maybe not here."

"My car is parked right there," Deputy Beecher said, pointing. "Tell me where I can take you."

The man with the deputy extended his unfettered hand. "I'm Ronald Glassner. I don't believe we've met."

The policeman blushed. "Forgive my manners! Ms. Harper, this is Ronald. Ronald, this is Ms. Harper."

Jeanne took the offered hand, and Ronald said, "I've read about you and New Church. I'm very happy to meet you. Your first name is Gene, right?"

She forced a smile and said, "Pleased to meet you. And it's Jeanne, like from a bottle. The spelling confuses people." She struggled to persist in pleasantry. "I've also heard about you. You're writing about Brian McCullough, aren't you?"

"As a matter of fact," he said, "I am, and it's—"

"Wait," Jeanne said, her head falling forward. "Wait, I'm sorry to be rude. This is important. Deputy Beecher—"

"Call me Winston, please!"

"Winston, please, I'll follow you to your car."

Winston led. Jeanne stayed close behind him, and Ronald stayed close behind her. She decided not to object, and when they cleared the coffee shop's exit, all three ran through the rain to the car and piled into the front. Jeanne ended up in the passenger seat, Ronald behind the wheel, and Winston in the middle. "So," Winston said. Jeanne looked at him and felt warmth and goodness.

The tightness stiffening her aching body began to fade. She wanted to speak, but she couldn't, not yet. "So," Winston said again. He cleared his throat. "Um, Ronald and me were just talking about how quiet it is in this town when it rains. It's Friday morning, but you'd think it was Sunday."

Friday morning. She took a deep breath.

"Ms. Harper, should I take you to a doctor?" Before she could answer, Winston continued, "Look out, Ronald. Switch places." What followed might have made her laugh under different circumstances. The large policeman tried to lift himself over while his small friend climbed under. Winston couldn't keep clear of the seat, so he collapsed on Ronald, who gasped under the weight and kicked, knocking over the CB radio. Jeanne set the radio right while the two men finished their exchange. When Ronald settled into the space next to her, he fixed the lapels of his sport coat and waved. "Now then," Winston said, shoving his key into the ignition. "We'll head to the hospital and get you checked out."

"No," Jeanne said. "Wait. Go... go to Hart's Cemetery."

Winston cranked the engine. "Hart's Cemetery? What for?"

"A body," Jeanne said. "A dead body."

"Logical," Ronald inserted.

"Ten-four." Winston backed out of the parking lot. "Maybe you'll explain on the way?"

The circuitous drive around to the cemetery's entrance took longer than Jeanne's direct walk had, and in those minutes, Jeanne described how she had been at First Church yesterday, blacked out, and woken in the cemetery this morning. She described the dead man. When she mentioned the empty eye sockets, Ronald fidgeted. Winston got on the radio and requested that Sheriff Hadderly meet him "at the scene." Driving, Winston turned to Ronald and said, "I didn't want to call him, but I had to. I learned that lesson five years ago." Ronald nodded, and Jeanne didn't understand.

In less than half an hour, the rain stopped, and the three of them stood around the body with Sheriff Hadderly. "That's Dave Holcomb," the sheriff said. Ronald and Winston looked at each other, acknowledging something that Jeanne couldn't follow. "He's a drunk," the sheriff said, tugging at the fingers of his gloved left hand, "and I'd be willing to bet that he did this to himself."

"The eyes?" Jeanne said. "How could a man do that to himself?"

"Birds, probably," the sheriff said. "It's grisly, but it happens."

"Ms. Harper," Winston said, "let me take you home. You can get into some fresh clothes and then come to the station and give us your statement."

"Yes," the sheriff said, "get these people out of here, Deputy. They've got no business being here, and you should know better."

14

The windshield wiper on the driver's side kept sticking to the glass, making a sound that compounded the obnoxiousness of Stefanie's prattling. "And you know what else?" Stef said.

Melanie kept her eyes on the road. If her twelve-year-old sister kept insisting on distracting her, they would crash. The drive home was taking forever. Rain had started trickling again while she was waiting for Stef in the middle school parking lot, and now it was torrential, adding to the tiny lakes that made Melanie slow down to avoid hydroplaning. "No, what else," Melanie barked.

"Rebecca says her family's going to come to the revival this Sunday, too, even though they usually go to a whole different church. That's, like, five different people I know who are coming to our church instead of their own this Sunday!"

"Yay," Melanie said.

"And really, Mel, I know Dad is making you go but I still think that you helping out is just such the right thing for you to do. I mean, really! It's totally the place to be this Sunday. I mean, I know you're friends with that what's-her-name Harper lady who is putting together that weird New Church that everybody keeps talking about like it's some kind of cult or something, but I swear you won't regret being a part of this thing! Everybody, I mean *everybody*, is going to be there, and we're going to sing songs and the Young Evangelists are really going to be an important part of everything. Oh my gosh, did I even tell you? Bobby and some of his friends at the high school are in a band! It's a Christian Rock thing, and they're going to play in the tent on Monday, and it's going to be so awesome! You know Bobby, right?"

Melanie knew Bobby Sutton. He had dropped his Algebra book in front of her so he could bend down and look up her skirt. "Christian Rock *is* awesome," she said. She couldn't help the sarcasm. Stef's sudden interest in all things holy seemed misguided and pathetic, but then again, what pre-teen's interests weren't misguided and pathetic? She looked at her sister. "So what's the name of Bobby's band?"

"Oh my gosh, you'll never believe it, they're called Faith Healer, which is, like, so cool, because it's like they heal by faith *and* heal people's faith all in one! Oh my gosh, there's Bobby now!"

Melanie's head turned back toward the road, and her foot slammed the brakes. A group of kids, ranging in age from Stefanie's to her own, was crossing the street. She stopped only a few feet from them. They seemed to be coming from a white van parked on the side of the road. Melanie put both hands on her car horn and pressed.

"That's so rude! Stop it!" Stef said. Melanie stopped, still stunned by the near-accident. "Can I go with them?"

"What? No!" The kids in the street took slow, deliberate steps through the rain. Melanie counted eight. Bobby and another boy walked in front, and two rows of three walked behind. The formation seemed to march.

"Oh, come on! It's the Young Evangelists! Mom and Dad won't mind. They're probably on their way to church, and I'll be going there *anyway* tonight. It'll save you from having to drive me!"

"Simmer down!" Melanie sounded like their mother. "You'll get soaking wet in three seconds. You're staying in this car." For emphasis, Melanie pressed the button for the electric locks.

Bobby and the other group leader were almost to the other side of the street when all eight of them stopped. Bobby turned, made eye contact with Melanie, and pointed at her. Melanie remembered *Invasion of the Body Snatchers* and expected the boy to drop his jaw and sound a weird, alien alarm. Melanie put her hand on her sister's shoulder and said, "You'd better listen to me and *stay right there.*"

"But why? You're not being fair!" Stefanie whined.

Channeling Mom again, Melanie said, "Because I said so." She was too busy monitoring the group in front of her car to observe her sister's reaction. The cluster behind Bobby didn't turn in unison to stare at Melanie – which was a relief – but one by one, they did turn to face her car. Bobby took a step toward them, and Melanie put her hand on the gear shift. "What are they doing?"

"They see me! They want me to come with them!"

Stefanie's words roused a chill. When the other kids started to move, her grip on the gear shift tightened. "Don't you *dare* open that door," Melanie said.

"But!" Bobby tapped on the passenger-side window.

"But *nothing*," Melanie said.

Stefanie huffed. "Mel, you're being a total bitch!"

The abrupt shift in her sister's vocabulary almost made Melanie smile, but the tapping at her window cut the good feelings short. A girl she didn't recognize stood beside her car, beckoning. "What the hell do they want?" Melanie whispered.

"I told you! They want me to go with them! Come on, *please?*"

Tap tap tap tap tap tap tap tap tap tap tap.

Melanie looked around. With the same deliberate pace, two kids walked toward the back of her car. The group of eight was forming a circle, surrounding them. "No way," Melanie said.

"Please!"

The hand on the gear shift yanked it into reverse, and Melanie's foot mashed the accelerator. Tires squealed on wet road. The kids surrounding them jumped back, looking, for a moment, startled and animate. Looking, for a moment, human.

Melanie berated herself for her overactive imagination as she made a three-point turn. They would have to find another way to go.

15

After the trouble on Tuesday and Wednesday, the Hobermans wanted a doghouse big enough to help manage their three black Labradors. It needed collapsible internal walls so the dogs could be either all together or separated. It needed locking doors, strong enough to act as a cage but pleasant enough to be a luxury accommodation. Brian drew a line on a board with a tape measure and picked up his handsaw. Now that the rain had stopped, he was anxious to finish.

The whining of brakes in his driveway seized his attention. He yanked the saw free, set it aside, and leaned the board against his portable worktable. Dragging his forearm across his damp brow, he turned and saw Melanie get out of her car. The muscles in his neck and shoulders loosened, and the ache in the worn skin of his palms subsided.

Mel didn't come straight for him. She turned toward the passenger door, and Brian noticed that someone was waiting inside. The door opened, and Stefanie stepped out. "What are we doing here? You said we were going home. Since you wouldn't let me go with them I've got to go home and clean up and get back there and there might not be enough time for everything especially if you have to stop and make smoochies with your stupid boyfriend."

"Sssh!" said Mel. "As far as anyone else is concerned, he's *not* my boyfriend, got it?" Mel didn't seem to notice that anyone nearby could have heard her. She didn't even acknowledge that Brian was standing there, ten yards away, sweaty and waiting. "I swear I don't know why I trust you and drive you around everywhere all the time."

Stef folded her arms across her chest – where Brian discerned evidence of a starter bra – and stomped her left foot. "Fine then, go talk to whoever he is and make it quick. I'll stay *right here*."

"Fine." Mel turned toward Brian and waved. "Hi," she said, letting the pitch of the vowel fall with her posture.

"Hey there." Brian looked down at his sawdust-freckled skin. "I was just... working."

She approached. Closer, her eyes revealed more than the weariness in her voice. Floating in worry, they weren't far from fear. "I'm sorry to bother you, but I just—" she stopped to swallow tears. "We were on our way home, and I came here because I didn't know what else to do."

He closed the distance between them, figuring she wouldn't mind too much if he smelled bad. "It's okay," he said. "Glad you're here."

"I—" She faked a laugh. "It's stupid."

"Tell me."

Mel sighed. "I was driving Stef home from school. It was raining. There were these kids from First Church... crossing the street. They just looked *wrong*. And it was like they were after us."

Brian put a finger under her chin. "I'm a mess," he said, "but I'd hug you if you'd let me."

They embraced, and Brian held on until he felt her back relax into his arms.

"Will you two please HURRY UP!" Stef yelled.

Mel pulled back and wiped moisture from her eyes, smearing makeup. "We're both a mess," she said. "I wish we could just get in the car and go, you know? Until all of this is over."

Brian shrugged. He understood what was happening in Melanie's head. Ever since the animals had gone crazy, she'd been saying that *something* was coming. Something bad. "Maybe we could," he said.

Mel looked back at Stef, who was pacing. "No we couldn't. Not now. I can't leave her alone with... them. You didn't see them."

Brian nodded.

Stef came toward them. "If you're just going to stand here while I wait for you then I might as well just tell Mom and Dad where we've been and what you're doing."

Mel turned, put hands on hips, and posed Big Sister. "Was that a threat?"

"Uh! You're such a dork! You know I have to go!" Stef's words said she was defeated. She stormed away.

"I can't stay," Mel said. "I have to take her home. Sooner or later, if we make her mad at us, she *will* tell."

"And?" Brian said.

She gave him a teasing Melanie-smile. "You're in a strange mood, aren't you?"

"You'll be eighteen in a couple of months," he said.

"AHHHHHHHHHHHHHHHHHHHHHH!"

Brian jumped, causing the downward arc of the saw to clip his jeans instead of his flesh. Stumbling back, he saw Stef. She wielded the handsaw like an ax. Seeing she had missed him, Stef spun toward Mel and raised her weapon for another strike.

Yelling, "Mel look out!" he dove toward her, pushed her away from Stef's swing, and knocked her to the ground. "Stefanie what are you doing?"

The girl's chest heaved, raking air into her lungs. Her rounded shoulders, flexed arms, and solid stance banished girlishness in favor of berserker rage, but her face was placid, still, with lips parted to release the quieter but unceasing sound, "Ahhhhhhhhhhhhhhhhhhh."

From the ground Mel yelled "Don't hurt her!"

Ready for self-defense, Brian faced off with her, trying to decide whether talk would work. "Stefanie, listen to me," he said.

She stepped left, so he stepped right, and they started circling. Melanie scrambled away, watching in horror. Stefanie's movements told Brian she was sizing him up, awaiting her moment, but her eyes showed no calculation. They were as empty as the mechanistic hum of her voice. "Ahhhhhhhhhhhhhhhhh."

"Stefanie," Brian repeated. He couldn't have explained the thought behind the next words: "Stef, is that you?"

"Ahhhhhhhhhhhhhhhhhhhhh."

Circling, Brian tried to get closer. The saw was sharp. He didn't think she could use it well enough to overpower him, but she could do real damage. He had to get it out of her hands. "Stefanie."

She swung at him, and he leapt aside. Thinking the attempt would leave her unbalanced, he rushed in, trying to knock her down without crushing her. She dodged him as easily as he had dodged her.

They resumed their circle. From the corner of his eye, Brian saw Melanie get up. Her expression seemed dazed, and her hands clamped on her backside, where the force of falling had probably left pain. He had an idea, but he didn't know how to tell Mel what to do without Stef knowing—

Saw teeth bit into his right side. He saw it coming too late to sidestep but early enough to pull away, turning a potential gash into a thin bloody line. His left hand reached to cover the wound while the right went out, a block. Keeping in step with the girl, he heard his own question, *Stef, is that you?*, and answered it: this was not the girl he knew, not the kid who had been threatening to tell on her big sister.

Melanie came closer, watching, charting a circle that encompassed theirs. He hadn't told her what to do, but she was doing it anyway, positioning herself behind her sister while Brian held the girl's attention. The droning "Ah" went on, and it almost sounded like a plea. One moment, it told Brian to stay still, to let her attack, and the next, it begged for help.

The plea became a scream when Melanie's hands locked on her sister's upper arms. Mel tried to yank her sister's arms back but caused them to flail, whipping the saw blade in all directions. Risking another slash, Brian charged. He brought his right forearm down on Stefanie's with enough power to break her grip on the saw and perhaps her arm with it. The saw fell to the dirt, and as Stef recoiled, pain shattering her placid expression, Mel crossed the girl's arms behind her back and immobilized them.

Stef's heavy breathing erupted into sobs. Confusion, fear, and pain melted her eyes. The "Ah" became words: "Let me let me let me let me let me." Her body went limp, and Melanie caught her as she fell.

"Let me," Brian said. Taking Stef into his arms, he saw that she was still conscious. Her voice faded, but her lips went on forming the same words.

Let me let me let me let me let me let me let me.

16

On *American Sane*:
What qualifies as "normal" in a town like Kenning, Georgia?

Two days have passed since my last post, during which I thrilled you with a tale of my daring escape from deranged dogs. It turns out that my attackers were but a specimen of a much larger apeshit happening. Every animal in town seems to have gone temporarily insane, turning on their owners and otherwise being very, very naughty. Something so violent and outré has to have a *cause*, Sane Readers, and I would expect the town to turn itself inside out in search of said cause. Teams of scientists should descend upon us, wearing hazmat suits and scouring the countryside for a meteor fragment emitting electromagnetic crazy beams designed to corrupt our four-legged friends. Helicopters should fly overhead, dissecting woods and alleys to uncover the secret camps of evil terrorist dog whisperers. The town's business should be concentrated, constant, chaotic, and anything other than *as usual*. Chatter about the event should fill every populated corner of town, but what are people talking about instead? Which church they'll attend on Easter Sunday. *En masse*, the people of Kenning seem to have dismissed the phenomenon as "just one of those things."

If horrors such as these pass so quickly into the realm of normalcy in small Southern towns, I can begin to understand how even commoner horrors – and yes, I think of racism, homophobia, warmongering, et cetera – thrive here unmolested. I came to Kenning in search of understanding, so perhaps I'm just getting what I asked for. I will try to pass along more anthropological wisdom as it becomes available. If you don't hear from me for awhile, I'd appreciate it very much if you would worry.

17

Winston looked over Ronald's shoulder, toward the motel bed on which Ronald's laptop computer hummed. "You're working," he said. "I'll come back later."

The officer's voice dripped with a childish disappointment that Ronald found pleasing. "Actually, I was just finishing up. After you dropped me off, I decided to get in touch with reality again. If I don't send word on a regular basis, my readers are likely to gather a posse and come searching for me." Instead of inviting Winston in, Ronald stepped out beside him. "THAT'S RIGHT," he shouted at the town. "PEOPLE WILL COME LOOKING FOR ME IF ANYTHING HAPPENS!"

"Who are you talking to?" Winston asked.

Ronald went inside and gestured for him to follow. "Oh, anyone who'll listen, especially the type of anyone who might be missing their sensory organs."

Winston closed the door and locked it. He sat at the table near the window. "You're getting around pretty good," he said. "And you've still got that shirt on."

Claiming a corner of the bed instead of another chair at the table, Ronald nodded. "I'm still taking those delightful little pills, and even though I had a setback last night, I believe I am recovering."

"Setback?" Winston abandoned his chair and moved toward a spot on the bed nearer Ronald. "What happened?"

The bed sagged in response to Winston's weight, almost causing Ronald to teeter onto the large officer's legs. Ronald scooted away and turned. "Oh, nothing. I burst a stitch. It didn't bleed. Much."

"You want me to have a look?"

Ronald stood and took the chair that Winston had abandoned. "The offer is kind, but no thank you. After this morning, I expect you'd have more on your mind than checking my wounds."

"This morning, right. What was it you wanted to talk about? Before Ms. Harper came in and that whole mess started?"

Squinting, Ronald said, "It's nothing."

"I'm a cop." Winston gestured to his uniform, stiff hat to shiny shoes. "I know bullshit when I smell it."

"Yes, and your nose must have been mightily offended when the sheriff arrived at the cemetery. Have you ever heard of a bird eating a dead man's eyes and tongue?"

"No, I haven't," Winston said. "But before we get to that, I need to know what you wanted to talk about."

Ronald hadn't gotten back to sleep after the dream about Fran and its eyeless-visitor sequel. He'd sat by the window, waiting for sunrise. "You're relentless."

"I suppose," Winston said. "Now tell me what's the matter."

"It's nothing," Ronald said, "except that I'm going insane. And hallucinating! What fun!"

"Does it have something to do with your pills?"

He hadn't thought of that. "Maybe. But I doubt it. The warning label on the bottle mentions nothing about dead girls knocking on your door in the middle of the night."

"Huh?"

Ronald took a deep breath. "Last night I dreamt I was Fran McCullough and then I woke up and she was knocking on my door."

Silence. Winston seemed like he was about to speak. More silence.

"Okay, so is this the part where you ask me to take a ride in the back of your car?" Ronald stared at Winston until he returned eye contact. When he did, Ronald broke off, letting his eyes trail to Winston's forehead, the sprigs of hair beneath his hat, and the color on his rounded cheeks. They both smiled.

"So it was a dream," Winston said.

"Dream, hallucination, sure," Ronald said. "That's what I thought. Or that's what I mostly thought, but here's the thing: it happened before. The first time I went to Brian's house, I saw a girl over by his neighbor's place. I didn't think it was Fran McCullough – not then – but I thought there was something peculiar about her, even though I didn't know what it was. And there was a dark blue sedan parked on the street."

Winston looked like he had something to say, but Ronald held up a hand to stop him. "I asked Brian about the car later. He told me it belonged to Jake Warren."

"From First Church," Winston said. "The man Ms. Harper went to see."

"You're with me. Good. Last night, when I saw Fran again, the car was parked right over there." Ronald pointed at a vacancy beyond his window. "I've been seeing a lot of that car lately."

"So you think Jake Warren has something to do with these things you've been seeing," Winston said.

"Your powers of ratiocination rival Sherlock Holmes's," Ronald said. "Sorry," he added. "That was rude."

"You're a jerk," Winston said. "It's part of your charm."

Ronald's eyes fell to the floor. The implications of what Ronald was about to say would require Winston to jeopardize his job, maybe more. He would be upset if something bad happened to Winston, for whom he now had proprietary feeling. "Okay, so here it is. I'll lay it all out. There's one more detail that I think is important, and it's something you'll just have to believe."

"Okay, shoot," Winston said.

A crack about the NRA's influence on Winston's diction rose to his lips, but Ronald squashed it before it could escape. "You see, in this hallucination of mine, there was something very odd about Fran McCullough's appearance."

"Uh-huh?"

"You see, she didn't have any eyes. Just empty sockets, like—"

"Like Dave Holcomb," Winston finished.

"Yes."

"And Dave Holcomb was the one who found the bags full of animals at the dump."

Ronald hadn't remembered that, but he said "Yes" anyway.

"So what you're saying is that the things you're seeing, what happened to Jeanne Harper, what happened to Dave Holcomb, what happened to the animals... it's all connected. And it's got something to do with Fran McCullough, which means it's got something to do with Brian. And Jake Warren's involved in it all somehow. That's what you're saying, right?"

"Not exactly," Ronald said, "but it'll do."

Winston stood up and adjusted his belt, making his gun do a side-to-side dance. "Come on," he said. "Get your shoes on."

"Where are we going?"

Winston fetched Ronald's tennis shoes from the other side of the room. "Telling the sheriff about any of this wouldn't do any good, so we've got to do things on our own. We've got to talk to Jeanne Harper again. When I drove her home, I had a feeling like she wasn't telling me something."

"Okay." Ronald accepted the shoes and stepped into them. "Let's go."

"Wait a sec, I'm not done ratiocinating yet. We've got to talk to Jeanne Harper, and even though it's going to suck to tell him what you told me, we've got to talk to Brian. I say we go to Brian first, get a sense of whether seeing that blue car by his house means what you think it means. Then we go talk to Jeanne. And after we do that, if we're still thinking the way we're thinking, we'll have ourselves a little talk with Jake Warren." Winston smoothed out the front of his uniform. "Now where did I put my hat?"

Ronald grinned. "You're wearing it."

18

The thunder and lightning had ceased, and now the only sounds were oscillations of downpour and quiet. Jeanne lay in bed. Her body hummed with exhaustion. When her eyelids sank, giving in to comfort, she pulled them open, refocusing on the sounds of weather and pushing herself to think. Winston Beecher and his friend Ronald had seemed more interested in her take on the morning's events than the sheriff. When Winston dropped her off in front of her house, he told her that she could call him on his private cell phone if she needed anything. He said, "For official police business, of course, you call 911 or the station number, but if you just want somebody who's got a, you know, open mind, you call me up on this number." He handed her a scrap of paper with the number on it. "You hang on to that."

The scrap of paper sat on the nightstand next to the cordless telephone. If she used it, her involvement in this – and she was sure there was a "this" – would deepen. Maybe it would be okay if she learned nothing more about the dead body, okay if she avoided the implications of that word, "ritual," which her mind had attached to the dead body's mutilations. Maybe there was a logical explanation for what had happened to her. Maybe she had left Jake Warren's office, taken a walk in the cemetery, tripped on something, and hit her head. Of course, she didn't have any bruises on her head, and she never took walks in cemeteries, but somehow, things might come together and make some sort of non-sinister sense, and then she would....

Jeanne fell asleep.

She woke up gasping, arms flailing, desperate for the air that her dream of drowning had denied her. Sitting up, she found herself in her own bed, safe and away from the mud and water she had woken to this morning. She planted a hand in the center of her chest and monitored her heart rate's decline. Closing her eyes, she forbade tears.

Her eyes reopened. Bright green numbers on her alarm clock broke through darkness with the numbers 8:19. Her ears searched for sounds of rain and found a quiet disturbed only by the faint rumble of an engine. To be audible, the car had to be close, either in front of her house or in her driveway, a visitor. Twilight glowed around her bedroom window. She reached over and switched on the lamp by the phone. Hoping she'd have time to change before she heard the doorbell, she rolled out of bed, crossed to the window, and peeked through the blinds. She saw a blue sedan by the curb near her mailbox. Dark windows kept her from seeing the vehicle's occupants.

She left the window for the closet and turned on the bedroom's overhead light. Slacks and a plain, comfortable shirt would have to suffice for whatever visitor was coming. The sound of a car door slamming encouraged her to hurry through buttons and head for the stairs.

She turned on the hall light as she left her bedroom, and even though she could see well enough without it, she turned on the light in the stairwell, too. Halfway down the steps, she paused. Two tall, narrow windows, covered with translucent white drapes, flanked her front door. One of the draped rectangles framed a shadowy shape. Someone was standing by the door. She waited, expecting the bell to ring. It didn't.

Her bare foot hovered over the next step. The shadow-shape in the window didn't move. It was large enough to be a person, but it was indistinct. Whoever had been in the car had had plenty of time to reach the door. Why didn't the bell ring?

Jeanne thought of the phone on her nightstand, the scrap of paper with Winston's number. For all she knew, Winston could be the person at the door, the person who would, at any moment, ring the bell. Or maybe the shadow-shape in the window wasn't a person at all, just some trick of light, and maybe the person parked in front of her house was going to a neighbor's, so of course the doorbell wouldn't ring, and maybe...

Maybe she should just go down the stairs, turn on the porch light, and see for herself. The hovering foot met carpet, and she descended another step and another, watching the shadow-shape and bracing herself with each movement for the jarring sound of the doorbell.

At the bottom of the steps, she stood directly across from the window-framed shadow-shape. It was still indistinct, distorted by the white drape. If she pushed the drape to one side, she might reveal nothing, or she could reveal a narrow man, someone tall enough to make the shape, someone facing her through the window instead of standing at the door.

Annoyed with herself, she crossed the foyer and flipped two more light switches. Bright bulbs filled the foyer and the front porch with yellow light. Verifying that she had, in fact, fastened the bolt on the door, she reached for the drape and pushed.

No one.

The porch light helped her see that the dark blue sedan was still on the street. She recognized it: she had noticed it in the parking lot of First Church last time she was there. She didn't know for sure, but it was reasonable to think the car was Jake Warren's. Jake Warren wouldn't have parked in front of her house to go visit one of her neighbors. He was here for her.

Calling 911 to say that she suspected the car parked near her house might belong to someone who might have a desire to hurt her would be ridiculous, but she was nevertheless certain of danger, and she did have someone to call. She stepped toward the stairs.

The lights went out. No glow lit the top of the stairs: the lamp in the bedroom was out, too. She froze in place and took a deep breath. The door behind her was a way out – a way toward the blue sedan, toward whatever figure had made the shadow-shape in her window. For now, the door was locked, and Jake Warren or whoever had been standing at the door was probably still outside.

The stairs were another option. If the power had gone out, even the bedroom clock would be dark, and she'd have no way to read the scrap of paper with Winston's number. If she moved carefully, she could find her way to the kitchen, to the flashlight she kept in the drawer by the sink. She started moving, feeling along the wall. After a few steps, she turned back. Her long, pointed umbrella, the one with the duck-shaped handle, was in a stand by the door, easy to find in the dark. She could carry it like a sword, ready for defense.

With one hand gripping the umbrella and another moving along the wall, she made her way to the kitchen, found the edge of the counter, and used it to guide her toward the sink. When her fingers touched cold metal, they moved down and felt for the drawer handle. A floorboard creaked behind her.

She spun, umbrella out, swinging. Her weapon connected with something, and she heard a crash. The vase she kept on the kitchen's center island fell to the floor. She heard the glass shatter but couldn't see where it was. She pulled the umbrella closer to her body, ready to swing again. "If you come any closer," she said to the darkness, "I *will* hurt you."

No response. She waited to hear the creaking of another floorboard, any sign of movement other than her own. Nothing came. She was standing barefoot in the darkness on a kitchen floor now covered with shattered glass. She may or may not have been alone.

She bowed her head, said a silent prayer, and reached behind her, toward the drawer handle. Pulling it open by degrees, she listened for movement in front of her. She held the umbrella ready. The drawer squeaked, and she stopped herself from swinging at the darkness again.

Sensing that the drawer should be wide enough, she let her hand dip in and feel for the cylindrical plastic flashlight. She found it, wrapped her fingers around it, and held her thumb on the switch. She paused, collecting herself. In a single movement, she withdrew the flashlight, turned it on, aimed it in front of her, and jabbed out with the umbrella, hoping to take her blinded opponent by surprise.

The space before her was unoccupied. Fallen flowers lay on the floor, untrodden amidst sparkling particles of glass. She allowed herself to blink. Maybe she was being silly. Maybe the car wasn't Jake Warren's, and maybe this was a normal blackout, and maybe...

Something knocked her back against the edge of the sink, and in her surprise, both hands opened, dropping the flashlight and umbrella. The flashlight landed with a crack and went out. Before she could steady her footing, another blow hit from the side and knocked her down. Disoriented in the dark, she didn't know where she had fallen. She didn't feel glass beneath her, but depending on where she was, any move might have pierced skin.

She had no reason not to scream: "HELP ME!!!"

"And why would I do that?" Jake Warren's voice answered.

"Deacon Warren." She didn't know how he had gotten in, but that didn't matter.

"Yes," he said. "Good guess. Perhaps you're wondering what I'm doing here?"

Jeanne sat up. She would stand, and if glass particles stabbed her feet, she would not scream. "Yes," she said. "I would like to know." On her feet, she began to get her bearings. She had fallen away from the glass. She needed to hear his voice again to know his location.

"I'm wondering something, too," he said. She still couldn't tell where he was. She began to sweep her feet out around her, searching for the tools she had dropped. Finding the umbrella, she leaned forward and took it. "Every time I see you," he said, "I always wonder the same thing."

Jeanne kept searching for the flashlight with her feet as her hands prepared to use the umbrella as a bludgeon. "Can you see me now?"

"Yes," he said. "I can. Is this what you're looking for?"

A strange sound, something coming toward her, made her jump back in the darkness. It was a rolling sound. The flashlight made contact with her toes.

"Try it," the deacon said.

Before leaning over to pick it up, Jeanne struck out with the umbrella. It passed through empty air. "Okay," Jeanne said. She retrieved the flashlight and tried the switch. Nothing.

"Give it a little shake."

She did, and the light came on. She made a sweep of the room in front of her and turned to search behind her. Nothing.

"Don't you want to know what I'm wondering?" he asked.

"Sure." She stepped forward. "I'd love to know."

"Watch your step," he said. "I'd hate for you to get blood on the stairs."

Why did he say stairs? Exits and other phones were closer. How did he know she was thinking of going upstairs?

"I always wonder," he said, "how a woman like you ended up alone. I mean, here you are, fairly wealthy, fairly attractive, well-educated, well-respected... except it's hard to respect an unmarried woman, isn't it? I mean, a widow, maybe, but a woman your age who has *never* been married?"

Jeanne kept the flashlight moving, checking corners, checking behind her, for any sign of the source of the voice that seemed to come from everywhere. "Are you proposing?"

Jake Warren laughed. "Not exactly."

She was out of the kitchen now, almost to the stairs. The flashlight kept moving, revealing untenanted corners and places behind furniture that she'd have to approach to search. She stayed on course, not yet sure if she would choose the front door or the stairs.

"Why are you here?" she asked.

"You know why I'm here," he said. "Or don't you remember?" The voice was teasing. It knew she didn't know. As she moved, the voice seemed to move with her. Could she be imagining it? Could this be some mental aftershock of the day's events?

She reached the foyer. "I'm sorry. I had a busy day. Did we have an appointment?" She stepped toward the front door.

"Don't do that," he said.

Knowing he meant to keep her from the door, she leapt at it, flipping the bolt and turning the knob without dropping light or weapon. The door opened wide, and for a second, she saw the porch and the shadow-shape standing there, as inchoate as it had looked through the drape. The doorknob slipped from her fingers, and the door slammed shut. Something grabbed her, enveloped her from behind, lifted her from the ground, and threw her. She landed on the stairs, hard. Winded and dazed, she listened to the sound of the flashlight that had slipped from her hand and was rolling down steps. It reached the bottom and went out.

Strange, static-filled air pricked at her skin. The sensation focused on the back of her neck. Warmth like human breath blew across her cheek. She got to her hands and knees, abandoned the umbrella, and crawled, up, up the stairs, around the corner, toward her bedroom. She jumped on all fours through the doorway and, on the other side, kicked the door shut behind her. She got to her feet and secured the weak lock.

"I'm calling the police!" she yelled. She didn't need to be able to see Winston's scrap of paper. She had more than enough reason to dial 911.

The phone rang. Jeanne screamed. "Leave me alone!"

The phone rang again. Was it him? The idea was irrational, but nothing happening was rational, and she knew if she answered the phone, she would hear that voice again, his voice, and she would crumble, would lose her mind completely—

It rang again. If she lifted the receiver and heard Jake Warren's voice, she could hang up, dial, get help. She had to be reasonable. With the phone's ring as a guide through the dark, she found the receiver and brought it to her ear. "Hello?" she whispered.

"Hi, Ms. Harper, this is Winston Beecher—"

"Oh please Winston please please you have to help me!"

She heard movement on the other end. "Slow down, Ms. Harper. What's going on?

"Winston, please, he's here!"

She heard muffled shouting on the other end. When Winston spoke again, he sounded like he was running. "We're on our way, Ms. Harper. Tell me – who's there?"

"Jake Warren!"

"Jake Warren is attacking you?"

"Yes!" She hadn't seen him. She hadn't felt a hand on her. "I mean – maybe. I don't know!"

The running sounds stopped. "Ms. Harper, I—"

No one was banging on her locked bedroom door. No one was threatening her, not now. "I, I didn't see him," she said. "I heard him! I heard his voice!"

"Ms. Harper, tell me what's happening."

"I don't know! I saw his car... and the lights went out... and there was his voice... and something pushed me, picked me up, threw me—"

"Stop for a second. Jake Warren's car is there? What kind of car is it?"

The question was absurd. "It's blue! I don't know! I'm not even sure—" Feeling around the bed, she found her way to the window. By the light of a distant streetlamp, she could see well enough to know that the car was still there. "It's blue," she said again, "with four doors, and the windows are dark. I don't know the make on it – maybe a Lincoln, a big one."

"That's good, Ms. Harper." She heard him put down the phone and say something to someone else. "Ms. Harper, I believe you're in trouble, and we're coming, but there's something – I think – Ms. Harper, what you're describing sounds like Jake Warren's car, but I have to tell you – I'm leaving Brian McCullough's house right now, and, and – Jake Warren's car has been parked near here for at least a couple of hours."

Jeanne dropped the phone. The car was gone.

19

"You're awake," Melanie said.

Stef's eyes closed again, and Melanie watched a shudder pass through her sister's body. "How are you?" Melanie asked.

The girl's eyelids squeezed together, furrowing her brow. "My arm hurts."

"Sorry about that," Brian said. "You'll have a big bruise. I don't think it's broken." He looked remorseful as he spoke, guilt-ridden for disarming the girl who had sliced open his side. Melanie had helped to secure the bandage after his shower. Brian kept a hand near the shirt-hidden spot.

Stef sat up, moving the arm to demonstrate that it was whole. "I'll be okay. But it hurts."

"I have Tylenol," Brian offered. "I'll go get it."

Alone with her sister now, Melanie decided to assess the damage. "What do you remember?"

Stef looked around her. Melanie could see that her sister was taking in Brian's bachelor-style living room, the big TV on a too-tiny table and the PlayStation controllers on the floor. Tears trickled down the girl's cheeks. "I remember."

Melanie sat beside her and wrapped an arm around her shoulders. "Do you... do you know why you... did what you did?"

Stef shook her head and looked up at Melanie, pleading. "No. It was just like, you guys were being so slow, and I needed to go, go to the church, and so I was walking, and then I saw myself... picking it up, and I saw myself swinging it, and, and...." She broke down. "I'm sorry I'm sorry I'm sorry!"

"Shhh," Melanie said. "It's okay. Nobody's mad at you."

"But they are!" she shouted, pulling away. "I have to go! That's all I remember, this feeling, I have to go, have to. But I don't want to now! Let me... let me stay here!"

Melanie said, "You don't have to go." But they couldn't stay here. Melanie had already ignored her cell phone's chirps twice, sure that it was her parents looking for them. Dad would be angry.

"Here you go," Brian said, entering the room with high volume and fresh cheer. "Two Tylenols and one Coke." He handed the pills and soda to Stef. "Should fix you up for now." He positioned himself to sit on the couch with them, and then he moved, taking the rocking chair opposite. "Anything else I can get you?"

Stef shook her head and swallowed the pills.

"Did Winston and Ronald say when they'd be back?" Brian asked.

"I don't think so," Melanie answered. "They were going to Ms. Harper's place to pick her up. It shouldn't take more than half an hour."

Brian left the rocking chair for the window that overlooked the front yard. Pulling back the curtain showed them both that the dark blue sedan, Jake Warren's car, was still parked on the lamp-lit street.

Returning to his chair, Brian said, "I'm so sorry."

Melanie and her sister both looked at him. "What are you sorry for?" Melanie asked.

Brian looked at Stefanie. "I'm sorry you got hurt. I don't want anybody to get hurt."

Melanie wanted to go to him, to kneel by his chair, take his hand, and tell him everything would be okay.

"You know I love you, right?" he said to Melanie.

"Of course I do." Melanie didn't move from the sofa.

"I don't want anyone to hurt you," he said. "Either of you. I need you to trust me. I'll stop them. I promise."

Brian was difficult to fathom. Everything about him – every move, every tone, every decision, every breath – seemed laden with what had happened to him. What the town and the papers called the McCullough Tragedy was his. She and Brian had been together for months now, but sometimes Melanie couldn't help thinking of the Brian she knew *about* instead of the Brian she knew. The Brian she knew, taciturn but stable, needy but strong, must have radiated from the Brian she knew about, the one who had witnessed the destruction of his whole life, the one who had spent time in a mental institution, scribbling directions and desires but few insights into the irreparable damage, the thick sheen of scars just beneath his skin.

20

As Winston's car turned into Brian's driveway, Ronald suggested that they all go into the house for a rest. Jeanne sat with her arms crossed over her stomach and her fingers tucked behind her elbows; Ronald shouldn't have been able to see that her fingers were shaking, but he could. They parked, and Jeanne jumped out, rushing toward the sedan parked in the street. Approaching behind her, Winston asked, "Is that the one?"

"I can't be sure. But it looked like this." She made a circuit, examining doors, windows, tires. "*Exactly* like this."

"I'd swear it was here the whole time," Winston said. "I kept an eye on it after I heard about what happened with Brian and Stefanie Grayson. With everything else, Jake Warren's car seemed like too much of a coincidence, and I'll be damned if he managed to drive away and come back without me see—"

"What happened with Brian and Stef?" Jeanne asked. "Are they all right?"

Ronald cleared his throat. "You know, Winston, it might be better if all of this waited for another t—"

"They're fine. The girl was inside asleep when we left. Damnedest thing, but according to Brian, she kind of flipped out and attacked him."

Jeanne's arms dropped to her sides, making her shaking hands plain for all. "Attacked?"

"With a handsaw," Winston said. "Cut him pretty good, too. He said it was like she was... somebody else."

"So Brian called you," Jeanne said.

A noise from the front of the house made Ronald turn. Brian came out first, followed by Melanie and her mildly psychotic sister. Ronald turned back to the group around Jake Warren's car and signaled a hush, which they ignored.

"We got here by coincidence," Winston said. "We were already coming to talk to Brian about Jake Warren and even about Brian's sister Fra—"

Ronald kicked Winston's shin, making him hop.

"Hey guys." Brian joined the car-enfolding arc formed by Ronald, Winston, and Jeanne. He gestured behind him. "Mel and Stef have to go. Their parents have been calling."

Jeanne broke away from the arc and headed for the girls. Ronald watched them. Melanie seemed about to speak, and Stefanie seemed apprehensive, as if she would step away. Jeanne opened her arms to them, and the girls fell in. A minute passed, and by the erratic shaking of shoulders, Ronald knew that all three in the huddle were crying.

"We have to do something," Brian said.

"Agreed," said Winston.

"We all need sleep," Ronald said. "There's nothing we can do right now."

Silence followed. Brian and Winston seemed deep in thought. Ronald turned toward the women, who were breaking their embrace and saying goodbyes. No one said anything until Melanie's car pulled away and Jeanne rejoined them. "Now then," Jeanne said, "about this car."

"What about it?" Winston said.

"Has anybody tried the doors?"

Without answering, Winston pulled the handle on the driver's door. Locked. Jeanne checked the adjacent door, and Brian walked to the far side to try the remaining two. Shaking, pensive heads acknowledged that all doors were locked.

"I'll break a window," Brian said.

"Why not?" Winston said.

Winston circled toward Brian, and Jeanne followed. Ronald jogged to catch up. "*Why not?*" he asked. "Winston, you're a cop. You can't just go breaking into people's cars."

Jeanne started knocking on the glass. "Jake Warren, if you're in there, get out now."

"What the fuck? Why the hell would he be in there?" The locals seemed unfazed by Ronald's questions. "Am I the only one holding on to a shred of sanity here?"

"Break it," Jeanne said. Brian walked away.

Ronald snapped his fingers in front of Winston, who was gazing into the car's black windows. "*Hello?* Earth to Deputy Beecher?"

Winston grabbed Ronald's snapping fingers, tightly and then gently. "Ron."

The truncation of his name grated on his nerves. *"Winnie,"* Ronald said. "It's illegal."

The burly cop rolled his eyes. "Okay, fine. Think about it. You heard what I told Jeanne about Sheriff Hadderly. He's not himself anymore, and even if he were, there's nothing the law can do because we've got nothing to go on. So what do we do? You made a connection between this car and seeing a dead girl with no eyes on your doorstep. Ms. Harper made a connection between this car and being attacked by something like – can I call it anything else? – an invisible force. 'Sanity' and this car don't go too good together, do they?"

Ronald was willing to grant the point. He was preparing a different objection when Brian returned, holding a heavy stone in one hand. "Stand back," Brian said. Accepting defeat, Ronald took the first backward step, and the others followed. The sound of shattering glass was surprisingly soft.

After the electric locks clicked, Brian and Jeanne opened the nearest doors, and Winston walked around for the others, letting streetlight and moonlight wash over the seats. The interior was shiny, pristine leather. A briefcase lay on the passenger seat, and on the backseat lay an umbrella and a stack of books. One of the books was a Bible. The light was too dim to read titles, but Ronald thought he could make out the word "Accounting" on one of the other spines. Another spine was without label, red and worn.

Brian leaned in and reached for the briefcase. "Wait," Jeanne said. "I've been thinking about what Jake Warren said to me."

The three men stood around her, listening.

"He said he wondered why I never got married. I guess everybody in this town wonders. A single woman is a suspicious thing, a feminist, a witch, or worse." Ronald had a fairly good idea of what "worse" might be. "I was engaged once," Jeanne said. "I knew Charlie in college."

She took a deep breath. "He died. Car accident. I guess the people who knew about it figured I was too heart-broken to start dating again, and years later, when I came back with my degree from the Seminary, I let them think that I had chosen to be a kind of nun, married to God. It was an absurd idea, but I saw no reason to fight it."

Ronald agreed. Being a nun was absurd.

"My feelings about religion are different from a lot of people's," Jeanne said. "I'm not literal. I see the truth behind scripture, and the goodness behind dogma. Faith helped me to understand why I don't need a husband. What people seem to forget is that Jesus Christ taught that loving humanity, loving yourself, and loving God are all the same thing. That kind of love is more than enough."

Ronald usually tuned out sermonizing. But Jeanne's way of speaking, her sincerity, the depth of her eyes, kept him rapt.

"That love is all I need from religion. At least, that's what I thought." Jeanne's back straightened, and Ronald noticed that her hands no longer shook. "I only believed in Hell as the state of being distant from God. I thought that angels and demons were psychomachia, figures representing our internal struggles to be worthy of Christ's divinity."

Ronald knew what was coming, and he wanted her to stop.

"I was wrong." Jeanne looked into the eyes of each of her rapt listeners in turn. "Ronald, you've seen things, impossible things. Brian, you said that Stefanie wasn't herself, that it was like somebody else was in control, right? Like she was possessed?" Brian nodded. "And Winston, you described the sheriff the same way. And like you said, I was attacked by an *invisible force*."

Jeanne waited until she was sure that her audience had reached the solution of her equation. "Jake Warren asked me about why I never married because he wanted me to know, to realize how wrong I had been. Religion is about more than comfort. Evil is real."

"Now wait a minute," Winston said, "Ms. Harper, you've had an extraordinary day, but—"

Silencing him, Jeanne extended her arm and pointed a finger into the backseat of Jake Warren's car. Ronald's eyes followed Jeanne's direction. She didn't point at the books. She was pointing at the umbrella, which was long and had a handle shaped like a duck. "That umbrella is mine. I had it with me when the demon attacked. And if you're right about this car not moving, that's impossible, right?"

The men stood stunned. Winston was the first to speak: "I don't know about demons, Ms. Harper, but I do know that something's wrong here." He looked around at Brian and Ronald. Ronald knew Winston was searching for support as he tried to drag them all back to reality, but Ronald was too tired, and too far swayed, to assist. "I know something else, too. If Jake Warren and Ms. Harper both handled that umbrella, there'll be fingerprints. Even though I don't trust the sheriff in all this, now I do think that's it's time I acted like a cop. I'm going to call this in. And don't worry, Ronald. I'm not the one who broke the window, so there shouldn't be too much trouble."

Ronald nodded as Winston stepped away to use his cell phone. While Winston told the phone about Jeanne's home invasion, Jake Warren's car, and the rest of the details that had a basis in reality, Ronald, Brian, and Jeanne stayed where they stood, staring at the funny duck-shaped umbrella. Ronald was startled when Winston returned. His face looked pale. "Well," he said, "There's... news."

They waited.

"The folks down at the station are already very interested in Jake Warren. Sheriff Hadderly had a couple of boys looking into Ms. Harper's story. It would seem that... they found him a few hours ago. His wrists and ankles were gashed, like a suicide, but there wasn't any blood. He's been dead at least since this morning."

21

"Get some sleep?"

Ronald nodded as he slammed the Jeep's door behind him. "I can't say I fancied waking up to return to this lovely place," he gestured outward, "but I did sleep."

Brian followed Ronald's gesture. From a distance, the colors in the heaps blurred into brown, making the heaps themselves look like rolling hills instead of garbage. From the opening in the tall fence that marked the dump's entrance, the swarms of newborn insects looked like heat-distortions in the air. At any range, once detected, the smell was unmistakable: rank waste and putrid death.

Brian said, "You and Winston didn't come back here after they found Dave Holcomb. As far as you know, nobody's been back?"

Ronald looked much better, wearing a yellow dress shirt that brightened his reddish hair. His usual jacket had stayed home. "I talked to Winston this morning, and he said that as far as he knows, Sheriff Hadderly is still telling people to stay clear of this place." Ronald sniffed. "In any other circumstance, I would heed the sheriff's wisdom."

The two men stood a few feet apart, in range for a handshake. Brian's hand moved up and down by his side, waiting to reciprocate an offer. Ronald's head cocked to the right, and an eyebrow rose. He looked away, toward the rising sun, then back. "So, um, yeah, Winston said he's sorry he couldn't be here, but with yesterday's two dead people, he had no choice but to head to the station first thing." Ronald smiled.

Brian smiled. He tried to still the hand by his side.

"So," Ronald said.

Brian nodded.

"So." Ronald repeated the sunward glance. "So."

Brian cleared his throat.

"This would be easier if I were here to interview you, wouldn't it?"

Brian nodded.

"I suppose that my cross-country search for American quirks to exploit on my website is a type of investigative journalism, but I never pictured myself going to such lengths to find a story." Ronald looked out at the piles of trash. "And this place is...."

"Long," Brian finished.

Ronald set a hand on Brian's shoulder, and Brian didn't flinch. "Yes, my friend, you are right. This place is *long*. Shall we journey inward?"

"You remember where you found the bags?" Their mission was simple. If Jeanne was right, Dave Holcomb's death had not been natural, and the trash manager's connection to the dead animals seemed a likely enough motive. Mel and Stef were at home, grounded. Jeanne had business at New Church. Winston had work as a real cop. That left Ronald and Brian to do the sleuthing.

Ronald walked, and Brian followed. "There were markers," Ronald said. He pointed to a stripped carcass in their path. "Winston referred to that lovely heap as some animal's 'nice supper.' I found the description rustic, though not exactly bucolic."

Brian didn't know the word "bucolic." He noticed a torn trash bag with a large swarm. "Is that one of them?"

Pinching his nose shut, Ronald crossed to the bag. After a quick glimpse, he returned. "Yes. The one with the older bits," he pointed, "must be over there."

They strolled further. Brian didn't know the size of the dump, but as the piles rose around them, it seemed huge. Some of the heaps were on a kind of grid, and some were more random. The valleys among the stacks linked into a maze. Without all the broken glass, sharp metal, and dead things, it might have made an excellent playground.

"Here we are," Ronald said. "We have relocated the bags of dead animal parts. Yay. Now what?"

Brian shrugged. "Don't know. Look around, I guess." His eyes started picking through the area around the bag. There were sticks of broken furniture, scraps of plastic, yard waste, and car waste. "What are we looking for?"

"Human remains, maybe. Winston said we ought to check this place out again. Last time we were here, we discovered evidence of a cover-up. Now, we're looking for evidence of what's being covered up."

A loud crash made both men's heads jerk upward. To their right, junk tumbled from the top of a trash heap. Brian searched for signs of what had caused the miniature avalanche. It might have been a bird. "A lot could hide in here."

Ronald stepped closer and looked where Brian was looking. "Très ominous. Do you see something up there?"

"No." Brian heard the sound of something else tumbling, this time a few yards from the first avalanche, but he couldn't see what fell.

"Okay then." Ronald walked further into the dump. "Like I was saying, we need to keep our eyes open. We need to think about *causes*. If we bar Jeanne's demon theory for the moment, maybe we're looking for, I don't know, syringes. Strange bottles. Something left over from whatever the Bad Guys used to make the animals go insane."

Ronald moved faster as he spoke, and Brian doubled his pace to keep up. "Eyes," Brian offered. "And a tongue. They were missing from Dave Holcomb's body."

"Right you are." Ronald stopped. "But I don't think we'd be lucky enough to find those lying around in here, do you?" Ronald scanned the surrounding piles.

A faint, high-pitched scratch, like a nail skipping across a sheet of metal, sounded behind them. They looked back. The dump's entrance was no longer in sight.

"I can't ask," Ronald said.

"Ask what?"

"I can't ask," Ronald repeated, "because if I do ask, I'll increase the probability of your answer being yes."

"Chances are none if you don't ask," Brian said. "So I guess you're right."

"Such cleverness." Ronald looked at the tops of mounds to their left and right. He gazed ahead. "Based on the way the piles look, I think the older part of the dump is ahead of us."

"Ask what?"

Overhead, a bird screeched. "That was a buzzard, wasn't it," Ronald said. "Do you have buzzards in the South? I imagine them out West, you know, circling bulls' skulls nestled prettily in the sand."

"Actually," Brian said, "people sometimes call Georgia 'The Buzzard State.'"

"Oh really? There's that cleverness again." Behind them, Brian heard more metallic scratches. Ronald started walking again, toward the older part of the dump.

Brian kept up. "We won't find anything if you keep moving this fast."

Ronald stopped. He looked over his right shoulder, then his injured left. "I know."

"What were you going to ask me?"

From the top of a pile to their left, Brian heard three distinct sounds, crunch, crunch, crunch, like someone stepping on aluminum cans. Looking in the sounds' direction, Ronald said, "I was going to ask," he took a deep breath, "if you feel like we're being watched."

"Now that you mention it," Brian said.

"See! I shouldn't have asked."

Not realizing his intention until he did it, Brian stepped closer to Ronald, who did the same. The two men turned, back to back. They surveyed the hilltops. "Demons don't need to stalk people, do they?" Ronald asked.

"Don't know. They might do it for fun."

Ronald stepped away, and the two faced each other again. "You're wicked. Really, who'd follow us out here and bother... climbing up those dangerous piles just to... watch us?" During each pause, Ronald's eyes seemed to pick through a different crack in the heaps. "I mean, I felt like that blue car was following me, but Jake Warren couldn't be stalking us. He's dead."

"That didn't stop him from stalking Ms. Harper last night."

"Touché," Ronald said. "What's that up ahead?"

Brian followed the direction of Ronald's finger, which would guide them further into the maze of rubble. "It looks like a tool shed."

"It's undoubtedly where Dave Holcomb used to sit and write his diary, you know, the one where he recorded all his horrifying discoveries, the one we'll be reading when the demon decides to strike."

"Diary?" Brian asked. Ronald had a way of talking about things as if he'd already lived through them.

"You don't read much fiction, do you?" Ronald seemed to study him.

"No. I'm more into, you know, *Popular Mechanics*."

Crunch. Crunch. Silence.

They returned their attention to the sloppy wooden structure, which was too large to be a tool shed. The door had an unfastened padlock on it. They hesitated. Brian fought the urge to look behind him. Ever since Ronald had mentioned it, he had felt sure they were being watched. "Do you think we're trespassing if we go in?" Brian asked.

"Of course. We're trespassing already." Ronald took a deep breath and winced, his shoulders folding inward. "All right then," he said with a hand on the door, "after me."

Ronald led them into the shack, and Brian shut the door behind them. The inside looked better than the outside. The shack contained two chairs, in good shape but probably still salvaged from the heaps, and a desk against a windowless wall. The desk's surface was clear. On the wall by the desk hung a calendar. On it, a woman with large, bare breasts waved at them.

Ronald pointed at the calendar. "A thing of beauty in a land of ugliness."

Ronald was able to crack jokes about anything. "Should we look in the drawers?" Brian asked.

"Why not," Ronald said. They searched the desk and found no diary: nothing but schedules for the dump's fleet of trucks, a cardboard box, taped shut, and a stack of paperbacks. Ronald held up one of the books, entitled *Passion's Kiss*. On the cover, a long-haired, shirtless man was kissing the neck of a woman in a white see-through gown. "You see? Beauty."

"What do you think is in the box?" Brian asked.

Outside, there was a loud clang, metal falling on hard ground.

"It's too small to be a severed head," Ronald said, "which is a relief." He took a large set of keys from his pocket. From the jangling wad, he picked out a Swiss Army knife. Cutting the tape, he said, "I guess it could be a baby's head. Are you ready?"

"Ready," Brian said. A new sensation, a spark of fun, passed between them.

They opened the box. "Oh look," Ronald said. "Treasure."

Brian saw rings: class rings, wedding rings, and the kind with cheap stones that show up in bins at shopping malls. He saw two digital watches and a plastic pearl necklace.

Ronald held up a class ring that looked just like Melanie's. "If this were still on a finger, we'd have something."

"YOU BOYS HAVING A GOOD TIME IN THERE?"

The voice was familiar, but Brian couldn't place it. Ronald dropped the ring back into the box. "This can't be good," Ronald said. "Do you know who that is?"

The shack had one window, but it was on the side of the structure opposite the door. The voice was coming from the blind entryway. Brian stepped up to the door, prepared to pull it open, and answered Ronald's question: "No."

"I have a guess. Open it." Brian did, and Ronald stepped out. While his eyes readjusted to the sunlight, he heard Ronald say, "Good morning, Sheriff!"

Shielding his eyes with a saluting hand, Brian joined Ronald and searched for Sheriff Hadderly. He didn't see him.

"Look up," Ronald said.

Halfway up a mound of trash, Sheriff Hadderly clung to a protrusion. His arms and legs bent back, making his chest the closest thing to them. The sheriff was in his uniform, without the cowboy hat and dark sunglasses. The sun hung over the sheriff's position; shadows covered his face. Something about him looked wrong.

"We were just leaving," Ronald called up. "What are you doing up there?"

In answer, Sheriff Hadderly hopped down. The distance to the ground was more than four yards, but his landing was smooth. Brian's gaze caught on the sheriff's bare feet. The arches were so high that each step left a strange, talon-like mark in the dirt. Coming closer to them, the sheriff said, "Keeping an eye on you boys. I'd say you being here is suspicious, wouldn't you?"

Ronald took a step back. Brian noticed the sheriff's hands. The usual black gloves were missing. The nails were long, as thick as fingers, and pointed. The sheriff's arms hung at his sides, swinging as he moved. Brian joined Ronald, noticing that they had less than two yards to go before their backs would be against the shack's wall.

"We didn't mean to cause trouble." Ronald's eyes moved back and forth between the sheriff's face and hands. "We'll be on our way."

"Not quite," the sheriff said. He stopped, facing them. Bent elbows kept the misshapen hands at belt-level, a gunslinger at high noon.

"This is bad," Ronald whispered.

Brian nodded.

"Looks like you forgot your boots, there, Sheriff." Ronald pointed at the sheriff's pointy feet.

"Wear them when I have to." Hadderly looked down. "They're not too comfortable these days." The top of his head showed salt-and-pepper hair. No horns. "I remembered my gun, though." The sheriff smiled, showing teeth.

"When I say three," Ronald whispered, "start running."

Brian nodded. He waited for Ronald to count.

"THREE!" Ronald screamed.

Surprise at the missing numbers cost Brian a second, and Ronald was off, running ahead of him. Brian caught up and passed him, but as he pulled in front, he realized he didn't know which way to go. He had to slow, to let the injured man who had led them here lead them out.

They turned right, left, went forward, turned again. Ronald wasn't leading them out; he was leading them away, further into the maze. Brian wouldn't argue.

Ronald stopped. Brian kept going but looked over his shoulder and saw the sweaty back of Ronald's yellow shirt. Brian turned and rejoined him when he realized what Ronald had already figured out: the sheriff was not on their trail.

"Okay," Ronald said, catching his breath, "maybe I overreacted."

Crunch, crunch, crunch, clang! The two men's chins rose heavenward and dropped back down as jaws gaped. Sheriff Hadderly was following, but he had taken the high road, leaping from trash pile to trash pile, clinging to garbage like a squirrel on bark, spanning impossible distances with each thrust of his legs.

"Oh *fuck*," Ronald said.

They turned around and started running again. Brian hesitated but couldn't help taking the lead, using his longer legs and better form to get ahead, get away from the pounding noises of Sheriff Hadderly landing and launching, matching their distance on land with distance through sky. Brian sensed Ronald behind him, losing ground a little at a time, and he thought that, before he turned another corner, he would stop, wait—

A shadow passed over them, and they both stopped. Brian stepped backward until Ronald was at his side again. They both stared at the sheriff, who had landed on the ground in front of them, cutting them off.

"Now boys, where do you think you're going?"

Brian's eyes searched trash piles for something he could use as a weapon. He wouldn't find anything that could match a bullet, but if he—

Ronald grabbed his forearm, yanked it, and started running back the way they had come. Brian stayed still, facing off with the sheriff. If Hadderly wanted to shoot them, to end the chase, he could.

"Brian McCullough, shouldn't you be running after your little friend right now?"

He didn't need more encouragement. He turned and ran, catching sight of Ronald just as he turned a new corner. Keeping his eyes fixed on Ronald, closing the distance again, he concentrated on the noises, the clanging, the banging, the quick scratches of fingernails on metal, the tumbling of trash as each of the sheriff's leaps caused another avalanche, and he realized they could run and run but never outrun, but they would keep going, keep running until the sheriff decided to stop them.

Another turned corner revealed the opening in the dump's tall fence. Ronald was dashing through it. Brian saw the keys in Ronald's free hand as he slowed to find the right one for the Jeep's ignition. Almost caught up, Brian felt another shadow passing overhead.

Hadderly landed atop the fence, perching, separating Brian from Ronald. Ronald opened the Jeep's door and waited, watching.

"Go ahead, leave him!" the sheriff called. "I'd rather have this one."

Brian's arms and legs tensed, bracing to find out what the sheriff could mean by *have*. Hadderly's eyes fixed on him. The sheriff leaned back on his haunches, preparing another leap. "GO!" Brian shouted, looking away from Hadderly, toward Ronald.

"Yes!" the sheriff cried. His eyes locked with Brian's, not breaking away as he called to Ronald again, "Leave him! You're not part of this!"

Without taking his eyes from the sheriff, Brian searched his periphery for anything he could use as a weapon. He heard the Jeep's engine crank and start and noticed a splintered plank of wood in the nearest pile of trash. He broke for it, hearing the squeal of the Jeep's tires as he sprinted back toward the maze.

He didn't look back, didn't wait for another shadow to soar over him, didn't turn to see what made the loud crash. Brian got to the board, pulled it from the pile, and turned to fight.

The Jeep was wrapped in links of steel, and a human lump lay on the ground in front of it. The driver's side door opened, pushing through the fence that Ronald had brought down. Ronald got out, shook his head, and looked at the human lump.

The sheriff wasn't moving. Brian stepped forward, gripping the splintered board. Ronald had rammed the fence, and the sheriff had fallen. Brian couldn't see Hadderly's head.

Ronald paused a few feet from the sheriff. "He's not moving," he said.

Brian stopped at a similar distance. "No, he's not."

Ronald took a step closer. "He must have been jumping right when I hit the fence. I must have knocked him off balance."

Brian nodded.

"I think he fell on his head."

Brian stepped up to the sheriff's crumpled form, ready to pummel it with the board. Nudging the body with his foot, he unraveled it, revealing the head. The head looked fine. The angle of the neck did not.

"I think he's dead." Ronald sighed relief. His eyes widened. "Oh God – please tell me he's not dead!" Ronald dropped to his knees by the body, feeling for a pulse in the contorted neck. "Oh god*damn* it," he said.

"What?"

Ronald stood up. "What do you mean, what? We just killed the sheriff, that's what."

Brian nodded.

22

"Why did you take his shoes off?" Winston was being obtuse.

"We didn't," Ronald said.

Winston bent over and poked one of Sheriff Hadderly's toes. "What happened to his feet?"

Ronald looked at Brian, who shrugged. "I don't know," Ronald said. "It's the damnedest thing."

"That it is." Winston walked away from the body. "You know, me and Glen weren't best friends or anything, but I hate to see him like this. He was a decent man."

"What got him," Brian said, "got him before today."

Winston turned. "Huh?"

Ronald stepped between his companions, pressing his left shoulder against Brian and setting his right hand on Winston's back. He hoped to be a conduit of reason. "What Brian means to say is that the Sheriff Hadderly who chased us through the dump was *not* a decent man. I dare say he might not have been a man." He pointed at the corpse's arched feet and clawed fingers for emphasis. "Did we mention that he could fly?"

"You said he could jump really far," Winston said. "That's not the same thing."

Brian sat down by the body. He seemed to address the corpse as he spoke: "I remember the way he was with me, shoving me, yelling at me. Screaming about what a monster I was. Showing me pictures of... from the basement. That Day."

Separating Ronald's hand from his back and returning it to Ronald's side, Winston said to Brian, "He and the others just had the wrong idea. I know he was sorry later. He said as much to me."

"Not to me," Brian said.

"Okay, I'm sorry to break up the spontaneous wake that's developing here, but when I called you, Winston, I said we had an E-mer-gen-cy. You get that, right? This is big, big trouble." Ronald paced between Brian and Winston. One of them had to snap out of his funk and share Ronald's perfectly reasonable panic.

"What do you want us to do?" Winston asked.

Ronald threw up his good arm. "I don't know, let's sing a song!" He huffed, preparing a tirade. His glassy-eyed companions looked at him. They didn't seem exasperated or even the slightest bit impressed. "Okay. I get it. You guys are reacting to this in a much calmer fashion than I am. Good. Maybe you're thinking more clearly, then, and can answer a little question that may seem of mild importance: what are we going to do with the body?"

"Do?" Brian asked.

"I wish I'd brought a camera," Winston said. "I'd swear Sheriff Hadderly's feet didn't used to be like that. We should have some pictures of them."

"Yes, and we can put them on the front page of the Kenning Gazette, right under the headline that says "YANKEE HOMO SLAYS SHERIFF." Overhead, a bird screeched. "Thank you!" Ronald shouted toward the bird. "At least somebody here is thinking practically. 'Leave the body here,' says Mr. Buzzard, 'and we'll have ourselves a nice supper!'"

"Ronald," Winston said, "shut the fuck up."

Ronald couldn't recall Winston using the word "fuck," and the syllable surprised him. He decided to heed the order and stand still.

"Thank you," Winston said. "Now Brian, you saw everything, right, and you can say it was an accident."

"It wasn't," Brian said.

"Well it might as well have been!" Ronald said. "Who'd expect a man to be sitting on top of a fence like that anyway? Am I right?"

So they had reduced the charge from murder to vehicular manslaughter. Ronald was not satisfied, but he chose to stay silent.

Brian stood. "Who'd run into a fence like that by accident? It's not hard to see."

Come on, people, think *self-defense.*

"I guess since there are two of you, you might say that Hadderly attacked you, and it was self-defense," Winston said.

Thank you.

"That's tough," Brian said. "We were trespassing."

Yes, and the dead man was a cop. People aren't supposed to defend themselves against cops. Maybe Brian was too young, but had Winston slept through the Rodney King episode of American history?

"Yeah, and I guess saying you killed a cop in self-defense won't get much sympathy."

"So what are we supposed to tell people?" Brian asked.

Somebody needed to remember that, before he died, Sheriff Hadderly had not been himself. He may, in fact, have been "possessed" by "demons." The words were Jeanne's, not Ronald's, but they deserved consideration. If they were, in fact, the enemies of an evil conspiracy that had already infiltrated the police force, to whom should they broadcast their responsibility for the recent murder of a chief minion?

"Maybe we can't tell them anything," Winston said. "Maybe Ronald's right. Maybe we've got to do something with the body."

Thank you!

"What?" Brian asked.

Ronald bit his tongue. His two companions meditated. Biting his tongue became painful. Brian and Winston thought some more.

"Jesus Christ, people, we're standing in the middle of a fucking garbage dump, for God's sake!!!"

23

Mom, Dad, Stef, and Mel stood behind their assigned chairs at the dinner table, not joining hands until Dad said the words "Let us pray." Hands linked and heads bowed. Dad spoke first. There seemed to be a direct correlation between the length of Dad's nightly prayers and the depth of Melanie's hunger. Tonight, on the eve of Easter, with pork loin waiting on the table to break Melanie's day-long fast, Dad would pray a sermon.

"And forgive us, Lord, when we stray from our duty to You. Stefanie is pure in body and spirit, and her heart longs to serve Your will. Forgive her for allowing false influences to lead her astray." Dad only used words like "astray" in prayer. "Spare her from temptation, and help me to defend her purity."

Melanie swallowed, hoping to dislodge the lump in her throat. She knew that by "false influences," Dad meant her. Last night they had returned from Brian's to a three-hour screaming match. She and Stef had announced their intention to skip the rest of the weekend's activities at First Church, and Dad had said that their decision was as "inconceivable" as it was "unsupportable." He confiscated Melanie's cell phone and car keys, explaining that they could go to church or go nowhere. In the middle of the night, she had sneaked a call on the land line to tell Brian she wouldn't be able to join him for Saturday morning's excursion to the dump.

The prayer continued: "And as for my other daughter, please, Lord, help us. Help us to forgive her trespasses." Trespasses? "Help her to see the inevitable end of the path she walks. Help her to repent, and cleanse her from the stench of sin." Stench of sin? That was new. She felt her father's eyes on her, but she kept her head bowed and eyes closed. "We thank you for this food, oh Lord, and for all your blessings."

Mom's turn came next. She listed the things for which she was thankful. Stefanie's list followed, then Melanie's. Melanie emphasized her thankfulness for Jeanne Harper.

They sat and began the meal. Melanie watched Dad saw the meat with his oversized steak knife. He took a bite and spoke while chewing: "You want to go hear that Harper woman preach instead of keeping your promise to First Church."

Melanie looked at Mom. She needed to know if Dad had relented and was about to give her permission or if he was luring her into a trap. Mom's focus stayed on her plate. "Jeanne Harper is a good woman, Dad. Her faith is a good influence on me, and I think it would be a good influence on Stef, too."

The clank of her father's knife dropping on his plate startled her. "So I suppose you think she's more godly than Reverend Cox?"

Melanie had to be careful. "Not more godly. Godly in a different way. I know you and I disagree about Michael Cox, Dad." She cleared her throat. "I don't question his goodness. I just think Jeanne's – Ms. Harper's – faith speaks to me in a different way. She's the sort of woman I'd like to be."

Dad dragged the end of his knife along the plate as he lifted its handle. He hewed another chunk of meat with a single stroke, stabbed it with his fork, and brought it to his mouth. Chewing, he said, "So you want to be like her, and I suppose you want your sister to be like you, is that it?"

Mom set down her fork and looked at the gravy boat at the center of the table. Last night, she had expressed anger, backing up her husband's rants without question. Tonight's withdrawal was ominous.

Stef grabbed the salt and shook it over her corn and potatoes. Mel didn't expect her sister to join the dinner's verbal melee. "I guess," Mel said, "I want Stef to be happy."

"Like you?" her father asked.

Melanie had no answer.

"Like you," her father repeated. "You want your sister to be a whore. Like you."

Melanie dropped her fork and pushed back her chair, absorbing the shock. Her mother grabbed the gravy boat and poured, flooding her potatoes. Stefanie blinked in surprise, looking from her father to her sister and back again.

Standing, Melanie said, "I am not a who—"

"Sit down," her father barked. He sawed at the pork.

The lump in her throat felt like a grapefruit, and she knew that swallowing would do no good. With the slight volume she could muster, she said, "I will *not* sit down. Not until you apologize for calling me that awful word."

"Sit down, whore," he said.

"I won't."

"You will!" He stood. His chair slid out behind him and tipped over, crashing on the floor. He pointed at her with the steak knife as he spoke: "You will sit down or I will *sit you down*."

"Nathaniel," Mom said, "put down the knife."

Dad looked at his hand and seemed surprised by what he saw. He set the knife down on his napkin. Staring at his elder daughter, he said, "Sit down."

"Dad," Stefanie said.

Melanie took a deep breath. "No, Stefanie. Stay out of it." She took a step toward her father. "This is between me and him."

He reached back and moved the chair, stepping toward her. "I don't know if there's anything left between you and me."

Closing the space between them, she looked him in the eye as she spoke, straining against tears. "I don't know what you're talking about. Are you really that mad about this weekend?"

"My daughter lies with every breath," he said. "Since you won't sit down, maybe you'll tell me what you want. Is it that cell phone of yours? Do you want to call that McCullough boy again from your own phone, so you can go over there and flash him those bold eyes and spread your legs—"

"SHUT UP!" she cried.

He slapped her. The blow was fast and hard, stinging. She felt her cheek already swelling as her hand rose up to cradle it. Tears trickled around her fingertips. "I can't believe you," she said, turning around to make a stormy exit.

Pain ripped through her scalp as her father caught her hair and yanked her toward him. Releasing the hair, he shoved her shoulder, spinning her around to face him. "You will listen to me, God damn you!" he shouted.

"I HATE YOU!" she screamed.

His open hand swung at her again. She saw it coming and turned, trying to dodge. The hand met her ear and the side of her head, skewing her balance, pushing her toward the floor. She landed with a thud.

"Nathaniel!" her mother said.

"Quiet, Tatum," he answered. "It's time someone slapped some sense into this girl. Otherwise she's lost to us."

Getting to her hands and knees, Melanie started to crawl away. Her vision was blurry, and her head was pounding.

"You won't go anywhere," Dad said, "other than your room. And you won't come out until I let you out."

Using the side of a chair to help her to her feet, Melanie nodded. During the next two hours, she didn't move from the center of her quilted double bed, where she lay clutching a pillow and thinking. For the second time in two days, a strong man had pushed her to the ground. Brian had meant to help her. Dad had not. Her bruises didn't register the difference.

A knock roused her. Moving was difficult, but she opened her door, hoping her sister had brought food.

Her mother stood circumspect. "Shhh."

"What?" Mel whispered.

Mom held up Melanie's cell phone.

"Why?" Melanie asked.

Tatum Grayson shook her head. "Because I said so," her mother answered.

24

Brian followed orders while Winston directed the burial, explaining what the "folks from forensics" would do when they found the sheriff's body. The body's discovery was inevitable: their job was to delay its detection and remove all signs that could link it to them. When he handled the sheriff's bare feet, the familiar sensation of lifeless flesh infected Brian's fingers.

Later, Winston said that he and Ronald had to "discuss" Ronald's immediate departure from town. "When he says 'discuss,'" Ronald corrected, "he means 'argue about.' It won't be pretty, Brian, and you'll be better off on your own." The two of them left Brian at home, alone.

Brian sat in the rocking chair in his living room. The doghouse was still in his front yard, where circling tracks advertised yesterday's brief combat with Melanie's sister. The telephone saved him from more distant memories of a little girl gone mad. "Hello?"

"Brian," the voice said. He almost didn't recognize her.

"Mel, what's wrong?"

"I need you to come. Come now. Come get me. Take me away from here."

As he parked his truck, Brian felt the touch of dead flesh lingering on his hand. He balled his fist, counted to three, and stepped out of the car.

Melanie's house was a block away. She had assured him that her parents were in bed, but he didn't want his truck detected by an idle glance through a bedroom window. Brian didn't know what Mr. Grayson had done. He didn't have to. Melanie's plea was more than enough reason for him to load the ladder into the truck and break the speed limit. With the ladder balanced on his right shoulder, Brian walked toward the Graysons'.

According to Melanie's directions, her room was the only one with a second-floor window on the left side of the house. Facing the house from the street, Brian wondered which "left" she meant. His current left seemed likely, but if she had been looking toward the street during their conversation, envisioning Brian's approach, Brian might end up knocking on the parents' window instead of the plotting teen's.

Hinges squeaked as Brian locked the adjustable ladder into the "A" position. He waited for the house to respond to the sound. It didn't. He climbed, stopping three rungs from the top. Melanie had said she wouldn't be able to come through if he couldn't be there to give her a hand. She was scared of heights. Brian wasn't fond of them, either.

The window loomed dark above him. He could see the curtains were open, but he could discern nothing through the black panes. Once he reached the top, he would see better – and whoever was inside might see him. Melanie had said that she couldn't risk a light, so she'd be waiting in darkness for him to tap. Of course, she might have been waiting in darkness on the opposite side of the house. There was only one way to know.

Brian took a deep breath and ascended. Nearer the window, he could make out the dim shapes of furniture, including a double bed, mussed but untenanted. He scanned the room for a Melanie-shape and saw none. Reaching out, he clenched his knuckles for a soft rap.

Wood popped, and the window slid open. The startling sound made Brian jerk back, and the ladder teetered. Melanie appeared in the window frame as Brian wobbled toward it. Sensing that if he grabbed her, they both might fall, he directed his arms toward the windowsill and clenched it, pulling himself halfway into the bedroom before his feet confirmed that the ladder stood steady.

"Shit!" Melanie whispered.

"Hi," Brian coughed. Stomping on the ladder to test its sturdiness, he pulled his torso back outside.

"Shh! Could that thing be any louder?" Keeping her voice hushed, Melanie gestured to the ladder.

"Sorry," Brian whispered. "You ready?"

Melanie smiled, and Brian made out tear-tracks near the corners of her lips. She had pulled her long hair into a ponytail. She had on jeans, a t-shirt, and a backpack. She was ready. "Some rescue," she said.

"You think?" He grinned, extended his hand, and hesitated. The residue of death clung to his fingers, and he didn't want Melanie to touch it. She reached out for him, and without thinking, he pulled away.

The sound started as a growl, but it grew into a guttural yell. Brian imagined a boar ramming his heels as the force punctuating the yells jarred the ladder again, again, again. Brian's arms flailed, and Melanie seemed to drift through the window as she screamed, "Daddy no!" Brian's eyes sank and saw Mr. Grayson, one leg on the ground and the other extended, kicking the ladder, knocking it away, leaving Brian with nothing under his feet but air. A microsecond of falling, a hand clasped his, and his body swung and smacked the vinyl siding. He heard Melanie grunt and felt himself rise. Dazed, he looked down and saw Mr. Grayson pushing the ladder further away to gain access to Brian's dangling legs.

"Reach up with your other hand! I can't hold you!"

Brian's arm reacted before his brain could process. His left hand gripped the windowsill as his right slipped from Melanie's fingers. Holding all his weight with one wrenched arm, Brian scurried against the wall until his right hand could grasp the sill. He started pulling himself up and saw Melanie on the floor beneath the window, her legs still braced against the wall from supporting his weight.

Brian was about to greet her again when his pants tightened against his calf and started pulling him downward. "Mel!" was all he had time to shout before his body slipped through the window and his death-coated fingers missed their last grab at the sill. He fell, taking Mr. Grayson, who was pulling on his leg, down with him.

Melanie's father slowed Brian's descent as they collapsed. Brian's back hit grass-covered ground, and his legs smacked against the other man's chest. His mouth opened to draw breath, and for an instant, his legs didn't respond. Brian struggled for air as every muscle clenched, waiting for his brain to assess injury.

"Get off me!" Brian felt Mr. Grayson toss his legs aside and saw the large man's form rising. He had to get up, to prepare for the next attack, but he was dazed, winded, unable to move. Mr. Grayson grabbed Brian's shirt and pulled, helping him to his feet before slamming him against the house. Brian heard "Son of a bitch!" and felt a fist pound his face.

Suspended in Mr. Grayson's grasp, Brian watched the man's free hand pull back for another blow. The fist came at him and stopped before contact, restrained. Melanie was on her father's back, grappling with him, yanking him away. The grip on his shirt released, and Brian sank to his knees, realizing that Mel had somehow made it down the stairs, through the front door, and to the house's side in a dazed instant.

Brian's shoulder smashed against earth. Blinking and wavering, he watched his girlfriend and her father struggle. He saw Mel push off from her father's back and stumble away, almost felled by the momentum. Mr. Grayson turned on her and swung a fist, missing. An alarm sounded in Brian's head, forcing him up, away from the ground. Legs intact, chest inflating, mouth spitting out the blood that gushed from his nose, Brian took three long strides, grabbed Mr. Grayson's shoulder, spun him, and punched him in the jaw.

Brian dodged Mr. Grayson's slow riposte and punched again, connecting with forehead and knocking the older man to the dirt. Melanie appeared at Brian's side, yanking his left arm. He didn't feel the pain in his already-swelling face or his bruised backside, but he did feel a bolt from Melanie's yank: it was the same arm that had held his weight while he was dangling from the window. "He could've killed you!" Mel shouted, more at her father than at him.

Mr. Grayson was sitting up. He looked like he could stand. "Whore," he spat.

Brian looked at Melanie, whose body convulsed with something like a laugh. "Asshole," she said. "Brian, we're going."

"Wait a second," Brian said. The words sounded funny, distorted by his puffy, blood-smeared lips. He walked past Mr. Grayson, who watched unmoving, and picked up the ladder. He couldn't quite lift it over his right shoulder, so he dragged it, scraping it along concrete as they traversed the block back to his truck. Windows started glowing in each house they passed, lighting their way as they limped by.

25

"Something is wrong in Kenning."

Jeanne listened as her words resounded through the sanctuary. They floated over the empty pews, and they ripped through the full ones. Barbara Fehn sat near the front, holding her husband's hand. Bandages still covered much of her head. Jeanne hadn't expected to see Barbara or half of the other people here. First Church might have had thousands in their sanctuary and in the adjoining tent, where speakers and screens made Michael Cox larger than life, but Jeanne had done well, garnering a hundred, maybe more.

Ted Early sat near the back. He wasn't an avid churchgoer. He was here because, like so many others, he knew that Jeanne spoke the truth when she repeated, "Something is wrong in Kenning." She looked at Dr. Early, and she looked at Kyle Amory, who sat two pews closer with his wife and two daughters. They knew. "We all know," she said, not looking at her notes. "We know, but we don't know how to talk about it."

The heavy double doors opposite the pulpit opened, flooding the sanctuary with light that forced Jeanne's eyes to slits. The blue carpet, the blonde wood, the hundred faces wide-eyed and waiting blurred into sun. They began their slow refocus as the doors folded shut, and Jeanne saw two more people joining the pews. Elation filled her lungs as Brian and Melanie, bruised and hobbling, found seats and opened a Bible.

"We all know that something is wrong in this town, but we don't know how to talk about it. We've been together this morning, and we've sung songs, and some of you shouted 'Hallelujah!,' and others of you didn't know if shouting hallelujah is something we do in this here *New* Church." The last line came out with a twang. Jeanne smiled, and the congregation smiled with her. "It's Easter Sunday, and you know what I say?"

A pause.

"I say hallelujah!" The words landed on the congregation like a stomp of her feet. The jolt lingered in the air, straightening the spines of her listeners. "I say hallelujah because something is wrong in this town, and it's Easter Sunday, and Christ is risen, and we're here together. Hallelujah!" The cadence in her voice was strong, unfamiliar, but hers. The sermon continued, weaving themes of resurrection and the town's salvation together with commentary on the hypocrisy of so-called Christian leaders, and she did not hesitate to mention Michael Cox by name.

Jeanne paused when the church's heavy double doors reopened. Blinded, she continued the verse from memory: "'But one of the soldiers with a spear pierced His side, and—'"

The doors closed, and Jake Warren stood opposite her in a pressed grey suit, his silver hair flawless, his hands clasped at his waist, his lips curled, smiling around teeth so white she could see them from the pulpit. "Uh," Jeanne said.

No heads turned toward the aisle as Jake Warren walked down it. Faces in the pews filled with anticipation, expecting her to finish the verse. They either ignored the dead man passing between them, or they didn't see him.

Jeanne looked down at the Bible, and her shadow made the pages easier to read. As she searched the page for her place, Jake Warren moved through the second pew from the front, took a seat, removed his glasses, and fixed his eyes on her. She backtracked: "'But when they came to Jesus, and saw that he was dead already—'"

The doors opened again, and no one turned toward the fresh flood of light. Adjusting more quickly now, Jeanne's eyes saw the same tall form emerge through the sun, the same silver hair, the same curling smile, the same thin-rimmed glasses. Jake Warren stood at the sanctuary's entrance. He also sat in a pew.

Blinking, Jeanne looked from one Jake Warren to the other. Traversing the distance between the two, her eyes landed on a third, sitting next to Kyle Amory's youngest daughter. The Deacon's white teeth sparkled in sunlight that narrowed with the closing doors.

Lowering her head again, Jeanne read, "'For these things were done, that the scripture should be fulfilled.'" She cleared her throat and faced the congregation. Jake Warren sat in the second pew; he sat near the Amory girl; he stood in front of the closed double doors. Scanning, her eyes discovered a fourth, sitting next to Melanie. "Mel—," Jeanne began, and she saw Melanie's expression, puzzled, recognizing her name misplaced amidst scripture. Jeanne breathed. "'That the scripture should be fulfilled,'" she said. Head down, blinking at the pages in her shadow, Jeanne told her congregation, "You see, Jesus' life and death mark the fulfillment of God's promise, and His word, which He passes to us through the writings."

She delivered her thoughts, her hopes, about the power of the scripture. As she spoke, Jake Warren was everywhere, in the second pew, the fourth, the seventh, the twelfth, in the center aisle, in the side aisle, behind her, with the small choir she'd assembled, grinning at her, grinning at the altar, mocking her, mocking the cross, a testament: she would fail.

Nobody else saw him. Jake Warren was here, dead, impossible, filling the pews, filling the aisles, positioning himself, his selves, among them, blinding them to his presence, watching them, watching her, grinning, powerful. Friday he had died, bloodless and mutilated, and she hadn't expected to face him today, Easter, in her church, surrounded by friends who saw nothing, who couldn't help her, who'd think her mad if she so much as uttered a word about the man, the men, the demons, the forms who were standing now, rising from the pews, walking down the aisles. A dozen Jake Warrens approached her. They converged on the pulpit, surrounding her. Her hands shook as fingers fumbled for her next marker in the scripture. The circle of Jake Warrens tightened, formed a wall. She looked, tried to see Dr. Early, tried to see Melanie, and all she saw was him, white teeth, silver hair, clasped hands.

Head bowed, she read the final verses from the Book of John, and she told the congregation that the words meant that Christ died in part so that they could read about his death, so that they could find his words and his example and understand the teachings for themselves. They didn't need preachers, they only needed—

The Jake Warrens were close enough for their breath to tickle her cheeks. There were too many of them for one circle, so they radiated out from her, concentric, around the pulpit, around the altar, grey-suited arcs distorting her voice with terror, making the sound of the Word quiver on her tongue.

"A-a-a-and turn to the Book of Matthew, verse, I mean chapter twenty-eight, the final verses...." She forced her vocal cords to squeeze out sounds that could leap over the wall of men, demons, breathing on her, grinning at her, reaching out with wrinkled hands. She finished the verses from Matthew, explained that though Christ commands his disciples to teach, he still says *all* power is His, and under her breath she said to the Jake Warrens, HIS, not YOURS, you damned thing, you abomination, you—

"The Book of Luke gives us another question, 'Why seek ye the living among the dead?' Why? WHY?"

The last question was almost a scream: she hurled it like a hammer, and its force pulverized her audience. They didn't see the arcs of men around her, the hands, reaching. They didn't feel the cold depression of Jake Warren's finger on her cheek, pushing against her jaw, filling her with horror and nausea and the need, almost irrepressible, to be silent. *Almost.*

Jeanne closed her eyes. She could still sense them standing around her, could still feel them, cold, touching her, but that was their limit. They couldn't throw her, couldn't bind her, couldn't stop her, not here. "God's will is for us to know His sacrifice and to know the scriptures for ourselves! God's will is to join our will with His!" She continued, shouting, keeping her eyes closed but raising her fists in the air, daring the Jake Warrens to touch her, to demonstrate their reality so she could show her congregation what they really faced, what was really wrong with Kenning.

A sound like thunder shook the sanctuary. Jeanne heard surprise and confusion murmur through the pews, and she opened her eyes. The heavy doors opposite her stood open, wide, blinding the congregation that turned to look with amazement. Wind couldn't open those doors without the strength of a tornado. The air was still, and the Jake Warrens were gone.

26

Neither of them had spoken for half an hour. Ronald lay on the bed, staring at the ceiling of his cheap motel room, thinking about how much his life had changed in only a week. He looked at the scabs on his torso and the bandage on his shoulder. He would leave Kenning today, and whenever he felt like writing, he would probably thrill the Sane Readers with an allegorical map of his body from the waist up. He wouldn't tell them about Winston, lying silent beside him, staring at the same ceiling. Ronald was used to leaving people behind, and he wasn't used to missing them. The present mixture of dread and longing felt alien.

A knock made them both sit up. Ronald was on top of the covers in boxer shorts, so he volunteered to answer the door. Grabbing the sling from the nightstand, he inserted his left arm. He glanced over his shoulder as he shuffled away from the bed.

Brian and Melanie stood in the doorway. The sling that held Brian's left arm was white instead of blue, but otherwise, it was identical. "We match," Ronald said.

"I guess so."

"What happened?"

"Got hurt."

"Fighting evil?"

Brian shrugged and winced.

"Sure," Melanie said. "Fighting evil."

Ronald looked at the bruises on Brian's face. "Is Winston here?" Brian said.

Glancing back into the room, Ronald spied Winston pulling his pants on. "No point in denying it, I suppose." He gestured for the couple to enter.

"Relax," Mel said, crossing the threshold. "It's about time Beecher found himself a nice man." She waved at Winston, who was buttoning his shirt.

Brian's lumpy face contorted. "You knew?"

"Duh," she said.

Winston appeared at Ronald's side, fully dressed, as Brian closed the door. Being the only mostly naked person in the room was suddenly awkward. "Hey there, Brian-and-Mel," Winston said. His smile was fake.

Melanie waved, and Brian nodded. The four of them stood, quiet corners of a square. Ronald spotted yesterday's clothes in a heap on the floor and thought about putting them on. Disrupting the square seemed drastic.

Winston cleared his throat. "Hey, so you guys were looking for me?"

"Actually," Mel said, "we wanted to see you both. We thought this was the best place to check."

Ronald and Winston looked at each other. How had they become a public couple in less than seven days?

"We came," Brian said, "to say goodbye."

Ronald broke away from their rigid configuration. "That's it – I'm getting dressed!" He dashed for his pants.

Winston, stifling a laugh, snorted, and the sound was obnoxious enough to be contagious. As Ronald dressed, Brian snorted, and Melanie snorted. Winston's turn came, and he broke into a full guffaw, which Brian-and-Mel echoed.

Calming, Brian said through a bright smile, "So, uh, I guess the argument went well for you two, huh?"

Ronald decided on a Polo shirt instead of yesterday's button-up Perry Ellis, which was still smudged from the trash-heap burial. "What, you guys don't fuck after a fight?"

Winston snorted, but Melanie blushed. Brian's smile faded.

"Oops," Ronald said. "Sorry."

"So," Winston said. "You came to say goodbye because Ronald's leaving, or...?"

"We're going, too," Mel said. "Brian and I – there's no reason to stay anymore."

"What happened?" Winston asked.

"My father *happened*," Mel said.

Winston nodded. Fully dressed, Ronald imagined Winston left alone in Kenning and said, "So you guys are just skipping town? Where will you go? Melanie, what about your sister? And what about Jeanne?" The significance of the date occurred to him. "Oh, shit! Did either of you go to her service this morning?"

"We both did," Brian said.

"You, Brian?" Winston asked.

Brian shrugged and winced. "Mel wanted to."

Melanie crossed to the table by the window and claimed a chair. This was the first time that Ronald had seen her in a dress: it was a simple, Easter-appropriate blue thing that reached to her hose-covered calves. The dress's pleats and folds flattened her chest, straightened her curves, and made her long, curling-ironed hair seem like a child's attempt to look grown up. As the girl's face fell into her hands, it struck him that Melanie was, technically, a child. "How rude of me," he said. "Why don't you both sit down."

Brian sat and reached out for her, placing his hand on the table at a holdable distance. "What's wrong, Mel?" She lowered her hands but didn't accept Brian's gesture. Ronald sat on the edge of the bed, watching them. Winston sat beside him.

"It's Stef," Mel said. "I'm still not sure that leaving her is the right thing. I'm still not sure that—"

Outside, faint chimes drifted on the air. The sounds of bells grew, becoming chords, becoming a familiar tune. The noise stopped Melanie's lament. It froze them all, and Ronald asked, "What *is* that?"

"It sounds like a hymn," Melanie said.

"'Christ the Lord is Risen Today,'" Winston said. "First Church plays it every year at the end of the late Easter service."

Brian said, "Impossible."

"They do," Winston insisted.

"Impossible," Ronald agreed. "The church is more than a mile away. It'd have to be deafening for the people in town."

Along with the bells came voices: "Ah, ah-ah-ah-ah, le-eh loo-oo, yah!"

"He's right," Mel said. "We couldn't hear the words from here, no way. How?"

The voices became louder: "All creation joins to say, ah, ah-ah-ah-ah, le-eh loo-oo, yah!"

Rising, Winston said, "Wait a minute." He crossed to the clock radio on the nightstand and turned it on. Static. He rolled the knob until they could hear more distinct sounds, and then: "Raise your joys and triumphs high, ah, ah-ah-ah-ah, le-eh loo-oo, yah!" The radio echoed the sounds passing through the window.

"Outside," Brian said, "it sounds like bells, live bells, not recorded."

"Ah, ah-ah-ah-ah-ah, le-eh loo-oo, YAH!"

Winston turned the knob until the static became another station. They heard the same bells, the same voices, "loo-oo, YAH!" Outside, the ringing bells sounded as if they might have been across the street rather than a mile away. Winston turned to another radio station, and another, finding the same sounds, on AM, on FM, everywhere.

Ronald started pacing. "How could a church do that? How could a church in a small town commandeer the airwaves? How—"

"Brian," Melanie said, standing. "We'll come back for Stef. You're right – we wouldn't be able to take her with us now anyway. We have to go. Now."

"I still need to go back to the house," Brian said, "and get some things. All you've got is that dress and the other stuff in your backpack. We have to—"

The noise got louder: "Where, O death, is now your sting?"

Melanie took the hand that Brian had offered across the table. "Get up," she said. "We have to go. I don't feel right."

Ronald heard her words and felt the effect at the same time. The music vibrated in his bones, filled his chest, and made his skin tighten, and even though he hadn't even known the name of the song two minutes ago, the lyrics came to him, urging him to sing.

"DYING ONCE, HE ALL DOTH SAVE! AH, AH-AH-AH-AH, LE-EH LOO-OO, YAH!"

"Winston," Ronald said, half-shouting. "I think she's right. Let's go. You and me. Let's get in the Jeep and drive."

Melanie was at the door, dragging Brian behind her. Brian's lips were forming silent syllables, "Alleluia." She opened the door, and the song was even louder, gaining volume, gaining harmonies, gaining voices, men, women, children, blending into one.

The four went together. Brian's truck was two spaces over from the rented Jeep. "We'll follow you," Winston said. "Just go." When his words ceased, Winston started humming the tune that enveloped them. Ronald tossed him the keys and walked around to the passenger door. He wanted to say something, but he was afraid that, if he opened his mouth, the song would come.

"SOAR WE NOW WHERE CHRIST HATH LED! AH, AH-AH-AH-AH, LE-EH LOO-OO, YAH!" Amidst reverberations, "soar" sounded like "sour."

Ronald buckled himself in, and Winston held the key close to the ignition. Ronald wanted to ask, *What are you waiting for*, but when he opened his mouth, he only heard:

"FOLLOWING OUR EXALTED HEAD," with "Following" like "Falling."

The hand that held the keys shook, as if Winston's arm pushed at a barrier in front of the ignition. Looking across the parking lot, Ronald saw Brian's truck still where it had been. He strained to hear the rumble of an engine, but all he heard were voices and bells. With eyes closed, he opened his mouth and forced out sound: "Winston... come... on... let's... GO!"

"MADE LIKE HIM, LIKE HIM WE RISE!" with "Made" like "Mad" and "AH, AH-AH-AH-AH, LE-EH LOO-OO, YAH!!"

Ronald reached over and wrapped his right hand around Winston's, pushing it toward the ignition. The resistance wasn't between the key and its slot: it was in Winston's arm, and in Ronald's own.

The bells slowed, building to the final line as sopranos soared on a descant: "OURS THE CROSS, THE GRAVE, THE SKIES!!!" Every word sounded as it should.

"AH,   AH-AH-AH-AH-AH,   LE-EH,   LOO-OOOOOOOO, YAAAAAAAAAAAH!"

All sound stopped. There were no echoes, no static streaming from the open motel room door. There were no birds, no cars. The sound of his own breathing was thunder in Ronald's ears.

Wrestling with his vocal cords, Ronald managed, "Try again."

Together, their hands guided the key into the ignition. Hand in hand, they turned the key, waiting for the cranking engine to shatter the silence outside.

Nothing. "Try again."

Nothing. "Please."

Nothing.

Ronald released Winston's hand, unbuckled the seatbelt, and got out of the Jeep. Dazed, he walked toward Brian's truck. Winston stayed close behind. Brian emerged from the driver's side, Melanie from the passenger's. "Yours too?" Brian called as they approached.

Ronald nodded. "I think if we tried any other car in this lot," he said.

"It wouldn't work," Melanie finished.

"And if we tried any other car in Kenning," Winston said.

"It wouldn't work," Brian finished.

Melanie looked at each of them as they gathered by the truck. "Where can we go? What can we do?"

The men nodded. "I can't leave," Winston said. "Not now. I have to go back in... to town... to make sure... everyone's okay."

Ronald stepped closer to Winston. "I'll stay with you, I'll go with you back to town, and we'll check things out, if you promise to leave with me tonight, on foot if we have to."

Wrapping his uninjured arm around Melanie's shoulders, Brian guided her closer to the other men. They all stood close enough for an embrace. "We'll stay together," Brian said. "We'll check things out, go back to my place, get supplies, and then leave. Together."

27

Alone, Brian walked through Kenning's center, down empty street after empty street. On Sunday, most of the shops would have been closed anyway, but the windows in the big chain stores should have been bright, hawking marshmallow bunnies and other confections. The doors of Wal-Mart and Starbuck's didn't budge. No kids ran through the field by Town Hall, where the annual Easter Egg Hunt should have been. The churches, even First Church, stood quiet. Only New Church's doors were open. Brian climbed the stairs and stepped into the sanctuary. Mere hours ago, a hundred people had filled the pews, and Jeanne had delivered her fitful, inspirational sermon. Afterward, people had waited in line to thank and congratulate her, as if by closing her eyes, shaking her fists, and shouting scriptures, she had offered the entire town salvation. Now, the deserted pulpit looked small.

"Ms. Harper?" Brian called. "Jeanne?"

His voice echoed through the sanctuary and brought no reply. He turned around in the doorway, noticing the doors: they hung wide, but Brian could see no hooks, no stoppers, no mechanisms of any kind that could keep them in place. The doors pressed against the walls as if the force that had blown them open still lingered.

Jeanne wasn't in her office. The halls beyond the sanctuary were as empty as Kenning's streets. Outside again, Brian saw the sun dipping beneath the horizon. He headed home.

When he reached his street, the remaining sunlight allowed him to see Ronald's backside protruding from the doghouse in his yard. As Brian approached, more of the man's body vanished within the structure.

"Careful," Brian said. "That house doubles as a cage."

Ronald's body bounced when Brian spoke. Brian heard the collision of Ronald's head with the doghouse's low roof. "Ow!"

"Need help?"

Ronald crawled backward until he could stand. He brushed off his knees and said, "No, thanks, I'm fine." He rubbed the back of his head. "Where's Melanie?"

Brian looked at the ground. "She... after we saw how deserted everything was, she said she had to go home and check on Stef. She made me promise not to follow her. Said I wouldn't be welcome, you know, since I punched her dad in the face."

"You punched Melanie's father in the face?"

"Twice," Brian said.

Ronald shook his head and grinned. "How manly."

"Where's Winston?"

Ronald took a deep breath. "Well, after he made the brilliant suggestion that our foursome split up so we could cover more ground – to which, you might recall, I objected strenuously – he realized that he should go check at the police station, and that I couldn't go with him. *Because.*"

"Because?"

Ronald nodded. "Right. So he told me to wait back here, he'd only be a minute, which was, of course," he looked at his watch, "almost two hours ago, which I suppose isn't long since he's on foot and the police station is God knows where, but I can't say I'm altogether pleased. By the way, I thought you people in small towns didn't lock your front doors."

"Sorry." Brian unlocked the door and gestured for Ronald to enter. Brian followed him to the living room, where he sat on the edge of the couch and slapped his free hand on his knee.

"So," he said.

Brian moved the rocking chair across from his guest and sat. "So."

"So we can't leave because Melanie and Winston will come looking for us here, and if we stay, we'll go crazy wondering if whatever ate the rest of the town—"

"Ate?"

"Figure of speech." Ronald cleared his throat. "I hope."

Brian considered laughing but decided that Ronald wasn't trying to be funny. "We could leave a note on the door. Mel has a key – I gave it to her last night."

Ronald stood. "It's nice when romantic gestures intersect with practicality. Let's go."

Brian led Ronald through his shortcut to Melanie's house. Along the way, streetlights greeted the dusk, emphasizing the lack of children in the yards and cars in the streets. When they arrived, Brian concealed himself behind a tree. If someone other than Mel or Stef came to the door, Ronald was supposed to say he had interviewed Mel at New Church earlier this week but wanted to make sure he had all the facts straight. Ronald had called the excuse "lame but workable."

A minute passed between Ronald's initial knock and his jab at the doorbell. Brian let his eyes wander from the front porch to the windows. A few of the houses on the street had lights on, but all of the Graysons' windows were dark. Brian considered going through the neighborhood from door to door, knocking on each until someone, anyone, came to answer.

Ronald rang the bell again, and then he stepped past the low-cut holly tree to the left of the door and leaned toward a window. The curve of his body suggested that he was pressing his face against the glass, straining to see forms in the darkness. After a moment, he turned toward Brian, raised his right hand in a gesture of defeat, and joined him by the tree.

The walk to the police station was longer. As Ronald grumbled about the stupidity of putting the police so far from the center of town, the last remnants of sunlight faded, leaving them with moon and stars to guide them through yards and irregular patches of trees. When they reached the small, one-story building with three police cars and a white van parked in front, Ronald said, "I never imagined that a police station for an entire county could be... so... *cute*."

Brian couldn't think of the place where he had spent the longest hours of his life as "cute." "The holding cells are in that building over there," he pointed. "The county jail is a few miles off."

The station's glass front door provided a full view of the lobby, which was empty. The door was locked. "Does crime not occur on Sunday nights?" Ronald's voice seemed strained. Knocking on the glass, he shouted, "Hey, Winston!"

No reply would come, but Brian waited for Ronald to exhaust hope.

Stepping away from the door, Ronald shoved his right hand into his pocket and pulled out his cell phone. "You know, there's no harm in trying again." He pressed a button. "No service." An emphatic finger poked the phone repeatedly. "Naturally. I don't imagine there's a pay phone anywhere?"

"Not that I know of."

"Not that it would work anyway. The phone at your house wasn't working this afternoon, and something tells me that the local telephone repairperson is just as missing as everyone else." Ronald took a deep breath. "WINSTON!" His head jerked from side to side, spreading the sound. "WINSTON! JEANNE! MELANIE! ANYBODY!!!"

"Shh!" Brian thought he had heard something before, but now he was certain: on the wind, voices. "Listen!"

"What?"

"Shh!" Singing voices.

"Oh fuck," Ronald said. "This again."

Brian lowered his voice. "I think it's coming from that direction." He pointed and started walking.

"Oh, right, let's walk *toward* the crazy religious people with magic powers."

Brian stopped, grabbed Ronald's uninjured shoulder, and said, "You want to find Winston?"

Ronald nodded.

"Then *calm down.*"

The words worked their way through Ronald's face. Brian could see the struggle: Ronald felt talked down to, and he was right to be angry, but Brian was also right, and being angry would do no good. Ronald lifted Brian's hand from his shoulder, squeezed it, dropped it, and said, "Okay." He walked toward the singing.

Brian followed. The sound led them away from the station and through a grove of pines. When the trees opened out onto one of Kenning's few four-lane roads, Ronald reached back toward Brian and stopped him. "Over there," he whispered.

About fifty yards away, three people stood on the asphalt at even distances from one another. Each person held a candle and sang, "Jesus be Jesus in me." The singing was softer than the earlier hymn, effortless, as if the natural result of exhalation. Ronald looked beyond the street. "How far does it go?"

Brian didn't understand what Ronald meant until he gazed out further and saw flickering. An arc comprised of more singers and more candles spread from both sides of the street, disappearing into trees. "Let's find out."

"If we cross," Ronald whispered, "they'll see us."

Brian looked at the three unrecognizable figures in the road. Their erect posture suggested attention, devotion, paralysis. "I wouldn't mind seeing them move," Brian said. "Even if it's to chase us."

Ronald gazed at the human arc. "Where does this road lead?"

"North," Brian said. "Out of town."

"Of course." Ronald sighed. "Let's cross."

Their movement triggered no response from the singers, who continued the slow melody, "No longer me, but Thee." Brian and Ronald moved through the patch of trees and into the unused field, where more people stood. Some of them had candles, and some of them didn't. All sang. With eyes on the singers instead of the way ahead, Brian and Ronald kept walking, keeping their distance from the arc as they passed into a residential neighborhood. At the edges of yards and cul-de-sacs, the singing wall continued, "Resurrection power, fill me this hour, Jesus be Jesus in me."

Another neighborhood, more trees. "It's a circle, isn't it," Ronald said. "They surrounded the whole town."

Brian nodded. To surround the town, they would need thousands. More than could fit in First Church and its tent. They would need almost everyone who lived in Kenning.

"Someone must have seen us by now," Ronald whispered. "What happens if we walk toward them?"

Brian started for the nearest singer. As he closed the distance, he lost track of Ronald. A face in the moonlight became distinct. It was Marty Fisher, who worked at the Southern Trust bank. Brian knew the singers and, somehow, the song. He had been walking around in a growing haze of fear, but what was he afraid of? He knew them, knew *this*, and it was right. His heart had been pounding, but now, as it calmed, he felt warm. His skin tingled, and his shoulders became light. The pain in his arm, the throbbing in his face – everything dissipated, making his steps easy as they brought him closer to Mr. Fisher. He felt glad for the words as they passed through his lips: "No longer me, but Thee!"

The weight careening into his back didn't bother him, but when he found himself face down on the ground, another man climbing off of him and grabbing his legs, he felt anger and started to kick.

"Come... on! Stop it Brian! Ow!" The plaintive tone became harmonious, "Resurrection power, fill me this – NO!"

Ronald dragged him across the ground in quick jerks, struggling against kicks. Brian sang as dirt smeared against his bruised face. Swelling with the rhythm, he yanked his leg free from Ronald's weaker grip, rolled over, and got to his feet. Ronald's left arm was out of the sling, and he was circling, coming around to stand between Brian and the singers. "Jesus!" Ronald spat, and before Brian knew what was happening, Ronald's hands slammed into his chest, pushing him back. "Be!" Another push, "Jesus!" another, "in!" another, "me!" Ronald's shoulder smacked against Brian's hip, and he stumbled as Ronald drove him back, back, away from the singers, until Brian's heel hit a loose rock, and they both fell.

"Holy Christ fuck OWWWW!" Ronald yelled, rolling away.

Brian blinked, shook his head, and felt the urge to sing leave him as he gasped for air. "Ow!" he echoed.

"Are you," Ronald said, huffing, lying on his back, gripping his left shoulder with his right hand, "you?"

"Huh?"

"You walked away and were just... gone... singing... and I went after you, and I ...was... Christ! Fuck! Ow!" Ronald's grumbling trailed off as he fought for breath. After a calm moment, his tone changed: "We can't leave, can we?"

Brian didn't answer, but he didn't have to. The closer he had gotten to the singers, the closer he had been to joining them. If Brian and Ronald tried to leave, they would increase the force that sealed off the town.

"Fuck," Ronald repeated. "I never thought I could tackle a guy your size. I think I ripped open my stitches again, and my—" He interrupted himself with a loud sniff. "What's that smell?"

Brian closed his mouth to let the air enter through his nose. "It smells like... cooking."

"What's up there?" Ronald pointed ahead, parallel to the singers in the direction they had been taking.

"That's part of the Bledsoe family land," Brian said. "They own a lot of acres around here. Jim Bledsoe is the principal at the high school. Sometimes he lets the kids use his land for events, you know, after a big game or something."

"Events. Like bonfires?"

Brian sniffed again. The air didn't smell like marshmallows and hot dogs. "Maybe."

Brian and Ronald walked together, passing through more trees. They saw the glow before they reached the clearing. The human arc continued through and beyond the field, and a smaller circle surrounded the blazing fire. The people in the smaller circle weren't singing. They watched the flames.

"What are they doing?" Ronald's voice was loud enough to reach Brian through the crackling of the bonfire, and it was loud enough to stir the fire's audience. A man disengaged from the circle. Brian ducked halfway behind a tree and crouched. Ronald huddled with him, and together they watched the broad-shouldered form step toward their position in the trees.

Michael Cox called out, "Hello?" The baritone tore through the night, eclipsing the gentle singing and sending shivers down Brian's spine. He looked into Ronald's eyes, saw controlled terror, and hoped his own composure would hold.

"What watchers are with us in the woods?" the Reverend called. "Who has come to join our celebration?" Behind him, the flames leaped, bringing his shadow closer. The dancing orange made the preacher half-silhouette, half-man. He blended with the shifting darkness, reaching out.

Brian told himself not to move, not to breathe. The singing had come from him before, unbidden, uncontrolled, and his legs had betrayed him, carrying him closer to their power. Now a step, a slip, any muscle that yielded to the Reverend's call might have the same effect, hooking him, dragging him, delivering them both. He concentrated on stillness, focused on stifling the tremors that wanted to radiate from his heart to his hands. Ronald's body echoed Brian's thought as it trembled against him. Brian prepared to grab him, hold him, muffle him, save him.

"Feel it! Feel the power of the voices joined together! Feel the force of the faith of your brothers and your... sister! Yes! We will *all* submit to the power of the Lord, to His Divine Might, to His Supreme Will!"

Brian wanted to go, to join them. He needed to know the release he had only tasted when his voice had erupted in song. Fighting, he concentrated on holding himself and Ronald in place. Something helped him – the smell, sweet but horrible. Its nausea rooted him.

Michael Cox stepped away, walking around the circle devoted to the flame. When he moved, the Reverend left an opening in the circle, allowing a direct line of sight to the fire itself. Brian heard Ronald gasp, and he saw why.

Protruding from the fire: a blackening hand.

The Prayer Room

1

Mike surveyed the sorry state of his office. Extra music stands from the choir, a stack of chairs for the monthly dinners in the fellowship hall, and half-empty bags of pretzels from Wednesday's meeting of the Young Evangelists all competed for territory in the cramped space. Yesterday, he had had to move a stack of books from one of the high-backed leather chairs to the floor so that Cathy Sutton, a woman from his congregation, could sit while they chatted about the upcoming bake sale. Remodeling the sanctuary to add more pews had left First Church of Kenning with no room for storage. The Reverend Michael Cox's office had turned into an all-purpose closet.

He walked to the window. The afternoon sky was grey. Staying in the cramped office seemed better than going home. Sara waited for him. She was making a casserole, something with cheese and potatoes.

A tiny pyramid of brownish powder sat on the corner of the windowsill. With his hand on the sill for support, Mike leaned in for a closer look. He added his other hand and started to kneel. As he recognized sawdust, he heard a pop and felt the sill give way. He fell backward, smacking his head on his desk and pulling a chunk of wood with him.

Dazed, he looked at the giant splinter in his hands. Tiny bodies clung to it. He sat up and confirmed his suspicion: where the wood had crumbled, insects raced. Most of the scurrying forms were antlike but whitish-yellow. The way they writhed in the wood reminded Mike of maggots, but he knew what they were. "Great," he said. Termites were feasting on the church. He set the separated chunk of wood on what remained of the sill and got to his feet. "Wonderful," he said. "Perfect."

The voice came from behind him: "What's perfect?"

Trying not to look startled, Mike turned. A tall, thin man stood in his doorway. The silver hair beneath the rim of the man's white Panama hat suggested age, but a warm smile gave the eyes behind thin-rimmed glasses youthful energy. He carried a shopping bag. It looked heavy. "I didn't mean to sneak up on you," the man said. He leaned forward, as if he wanted to enter but would never intrude.

Mike wiped his hands on his pants, maneuvered around his desk, and stepped over two stacks of books. "Not at all." He approached the stranger. "It's good to have a visitor on such a gloomy day." The man did not move. "Would you like to come in?"

The man removed his hat with his free hand and walked in. "Thank you," he said. "I was hoping to have a word with you."

"Sounds serious," Mike smiled. "You look familiar. Have we met? I'm Michael Cox." He extended a hand.

The man put his hat back on and reciprocated with a firm, quick handshake. "Jake," he said. "Warren. I'm new here, but you might have seen me at the service this morning. I like to sit close so I can hear the choir better." His accent was wrong – whatever city he was from, it wasn't nearby.

"Won't you sit down?" Mike set an example, crossing back toward his desk chair as he said, "People who know about acoustics will tell you that the singing actually sounds better from the back of the sanctuary. But me," Mike sat, "I'm like you. One of the reasons I started preaching was so I could be near all those beautiful voices." He chuckled and was pleased to see the man grin while he took the offered chair. "I'm glad you decided to join us. How'd you like the service, Mr. Warren?"

"Oh, please, it's Jake." Jake settled into the chair, set his bag on the floor, and laid his hat on his lap. "And the truth is, I spent the whole morning thinking I finally found the right church for me. I've moved around a lot in the last few years, and even in other towns like this one, it seems like all the churches are trying too hard to be modern, to make sure they appeal to everybody." As Jake talked, his speech took on a rhythm similar to Mike's. "Don't get me wrong, I saw plenty of young people who felt the spirit in your congregation. What I mean is that, well, it's a relief to find a more traditional gathering." Jake cleared his throat. "I don't mean to carry on. You seemed busy when I walked in, frustrated. Did I interrupt something?"

Mike swiveled toward the damaged windowsill and pointed. "That," he said. "I was feeling frustrated over *that*."

Jake stood, setting his hat on the edge of Mike's desk. "What, the rain?"

"No," Mike said, still pointing. "Look closer."

Picking up the shopping bag but leaving the hat on the desk, Jake circled toward Mike. Before Mike thought to warn him, he saw Jake's smile melt into surprise as a stack of books caught the man's feet. The bag flew from his hand, spilling on the floor, but Mike leapt from his chair in time to grab Jake's shoulders and save him from similar sprawl.

Jake's hands clasped Mike's arms as he regained his posture, and for a moment, they might have been dancing. A chill rushed through Mike's spine and made the skin on his neck feel rigid. He released his visitor, who stepped back and said, "Thank you. How clumsy! I made a mess of your office."

On the floor, Mike saw new books blending with the old. Several hardbound volumes that Mike didn't recognize mingled with the toppled pile of theology texts. By the far wall, a small, faded red book with worn corners lay in a shadow.

Mike brushed his hands on his pants. "Please, as if this place wasn't already a mess."

"I see what you're talking about."

"Excuse me?"

"Oh, heh-heh." Jake blushed. "I didn't mean that your office is a mess. You should see mine at home. What I mean is, I see what you mean about *that*." He pointed at the windowsill. "You've got quite an infestation."

"Darn it, I thought as much." Mike sighed and sat back in his chair, letting his head droop. Looking up, he saw that Jake had shifted his position but stayed close, leaning on a corner of the desk less than three feet away. "I honestly don't know what we're going to do about it."

Jake sank back until he was almost sitting on the desk. "What you do is call an exterminator, pronto. Let this go, and the floor could fall out from under you."

Mike imagined plummeting into the basement through fragments of half-eaten wood. The church kept the basement closed off – it was no good for storage because it flooded at least twice a year. "I know you're right," Mike said, "but we might have to close the church if the termites have got as far as I think."

Jake was sitting on the desk now. "You might have to close for a couple of days, but the exterminators work pretty fast nowadays."

Mike shook his head. "That's not what I mean. Anyway, I don't want to trouble you with church business. What was it you wanted to have a word about?"

"It's no trouble. What did you mean?"

Sharing his thoughts with the stranger couldn't make things any worse. "The fact is, if we've got major damage – what I mean is – if we've got to get the builders back here – we just did some remodeling – and, well, the point is, we can hardly afford the exterminators, much less whatever rebuilding we'd have to do."

"How bad off are the church's finances?"

The question seemed pointed, even impertinent, but Jake's grin, which had returned along with his balance, encouraged Mike to trust him. "You want to know the truth? I don't even know! The man who used to do our books, Bart Granger, God rest him, died of a heart attack about a month ago, and we haven't been able to get things straight since."

Jake slid off the desk. "This is kind of a rhetorical question, but do you believe in Divine Providence?"

"Of course." Mike preferred to think of the termites as the devil's work rather than God's, but he was willing to entertain counterintuitive notions.

Jake leaned to the floor and grabbed a book, *Basic Accounting for Churches*. "I don't know why I brought this with me, except to prove I know what I'm talking about—"

"What *are* we talking about?"

"I'd like to join your congregation, and I thought that, if you needed me, I could offer you my services, free of charge. I'm a freelance accountant and financial advisor."

Thirty minutes later, Mike and Jake shook hands a second time. This handshake lasted longer, and as they parted, Mike thought that the man's arrival had indeed been providential. Jake was going to straighten out their books. Jake had said that with a little time and good management, he'd bet – if he were a betting man – that the church would not only be solvent enough to repair the damage but also ready to fix the water problems in the basement and the storage problems, too. He knew an architect who would probably volunteer some work. In just a few months, they could remodel the office and give it direct access to a newly finished storage space below.

Gathering papers from his desk, Mike got ready to follow Jake into the gloom that stood between him and home. A glance at the window surprised him: the writhing activity in the broken sill had almost ceased. Only a thin line of termites remained, leading from the window to the floor. Their path pointed to a book that Jake must have left behind. The faded red volume with worn corners was the center of a swarm.

Mike followed the trail, wincing as the bottoms of his shoes crunched against whitish bodies. The squirming piles parted before him as he reached for the tome. Its spine and cover provided no information, so he turned to the first page and read the title: *The Alchemy of Will*, by Dr. Allen Fincher.

2

The book sat on the double swing in Mike and Sara's garden. The faded red volume seemed innocuous in its surroundings: purple, pink, and orange azaleas marked a trail through the yard, and the last blooms of the dogwoods framed the property with wavering white. Not far from the swing, Sara's patch of roses was ready to triumph over Mike's meager lilies once the warmth of May took hold. Fluffy clouds specked the bright blue sky. The setting seemed wrong for a conversation about blasphemy.

"Hey there, Reverend." Mr. Warren's voice came from the side of the house. "I appreciate the invitation. I had no idea this side of town had such lovely houses."

Mike looked at his home, manicured hedges and fresh white paint. His favorite feature, the porch, began by the back door and continued around one side. His second-favorite feature, the second-floor balcony, was attached to his bedroom. The other rooms on the second floor, unoccupied bedrooms, gathered dust. His third-favorite feature, the attic they had converted into a private study, was where Mike spent most of his time, planning sermons and dealing with church business. "We're blessed to have such a nice place in such a nice town."

Each man stood by one end of the swing. "I've been thinking," Mr. Warren said, "about other things we might do to raise money for the church. Bake sales are fine, but an attendance drive would work better."

"I appreciate the thought, Mr. Warren, but I'm afraid I've reconsidered our... partnership." Mike wanted to be stern, not condescending. People looked up to him so often that he couldn't break the habit of looking down.

"Oh really?" Jake Warren glanced at the swing. "I see you found my book." He sat by the book, and as the seat swung back with his weight, he opened it. The rim of his white Panama hat merged with the red cover, hiding his expression. "Looks like you might have read some of it." He closed the book and set it in his lap, leaving space by his side for Mike.

"Mr. Warren, I—"

"You stopped calling me Jake. Didn't like what you read very much, did you?"

"It's blasphemous!" Mike didn't mean to shout, but as the adjective exploded from his lips, his arms flew into the air, doubling his volume.

Jake Warren set his hat on top of the book. He looked up at Mike. "Come now, I agree that Dr. Fincher wasn't a traditional Christian, but does that make what he has to say blasphemous? Allen was an anthropologist, so he writes from a more... global... perspective. Don't tell me you're the type of preacher who refuses to read about others' beliefs."

"Allen? Do you know this man?"

He laughed. "No, Mike. Allen Fincher died almost a century ago, in Massachusetts. He was a Harvard professor. I just happen to have studied his work."

"That's my point!" Mike's arms flew out again, and he realized he hadn't yet made his point. "What I'm saying – what I mean to say – is that I don't see how a man of the sort you claim to be could study such garbage." He took a deep breath. "And it's not garbage because it's different from what I believe. It's garbage because it attacks the foundation of my belief! You know this book compares the Crucifixion to pagan forms of human sacrifice, as if God had to sacrifice His son to work some kind of hocus-pocus?"

"Sit down, please," Jake Warren said, "and maybe we can stop shouting." He gestured toward the empty space on the swing. Mike took a seat as far from the other man as possible. "Look, I know that Dr. Fincher can be hard to take. You have to understand the times he was living in. Even half a century after Darwin's drivel, no scholar, no matter how tactful, could challenge the mainstream way of seeing things without being ostracized. So Dr. Fincher decided not to be tactful at all."

Mike shook his head. "Mr. Warren, are you trying to tell me that there's a tactful way to say that the redemption of mankind was like black magic?"

"Yes. Believe it or not, I am." He looked down at the hat-covered book. "That's the point of *Alchemy of Will* – there's a way of understanding the powers of all religion, all mysticism, as manifestations of the one true God Almighty. Allen Fincher was pious in his own way. Martin Luther was accused of blasphemy, too."

Mike decided to laugh. "Jake, you can't compare this guy to the father of the Reformation."

Putting on his hat, Jake picked up the book. "I don't know. We'll just have to see." He stood, forcing Mike to swing backward. "Look, Reverend, you obviously think my reading habits make me unworthy to serve your church. While I think it's a good church, and I think I could help it survive, I won't stay where I'm not wanted." He sighed and glanced at the house. "I appreciate the invitation, but you'll have to tell Mrs. Cox that I'll take a raincheck on that cup of tea. Good day." He started down the azalea-lined path toward the gate.

Mike grabbed an armrest and pushed himself out of the swing. He thought of calling for Jake to wait, but he hesitated, and the man was gone.

3

"Will you pray with me tonight?"

Sara sat on the far side of the bed. When Mike spoke, she set her nail file on her nightstand. "I haven't gotten down there with you for weeks. What makes tonight any different?" The king-sized bed sagged in the middle; they had once slept close to one another. Now they occupied distinct sides, and recently, Sara had not come close to his.

Mike's arms pressed against the edge of the mattress. His knees, covered by thin pajamas, burrowed into carpet. "I just need you by my side today."

"What's so special about today? It's Tuesday." She leaned against a bank of pillows. "Nothing unusual happened today." She thought. "Unless this is about that man you invited over to not have tea with you." She smirked. "You know, it might be a sin to invite someone over for tea without intending to serve him tea. It's basically a lie. Who knew that tea had the power to ruin men's souls?"

"I would have given him tea if he'd wanted it." Mike's knees were starting to ache, and he wished he hadn't asked her anything at all. "But Sara—"

"Look, Mike, if this is another sermon about the long suffering of my Biblical namesake, I tell you, I've had it. I'm not going to pray to a God that did this to me. I'll keep up appearances – go to church, bake cookies, do all the other preacher's wife things – but when we're alone in our bedroom, I'm not going to pretend that everything hasn't changed."

Mike rose from his knees and sat on the bed with his back to his wife. "Nothing's changed." They had tried and failed to get pregnant for years. Sara insisted on trying all the pills and injections, even when they made her sick. A month ago, she had started losing sleep and complaining about feeling hot. When she said she had missed two periods, Mike rushed her to the doctor. The doctor pronounced "premature menopause," and Sara kept saying, "but I'm thirty-eight," over and over. The doctor said she might keep trying, but when she got home that afternoon, she buried her latest prescription in the garbage. "Nothing's changed," Mike repeated. "I love you, and God loves you."

"I love you, too, Mike, but we'll both get through this better if you just *stop*."

"Stop? What is that you want me to stop? Praying?"

She grabbed a pillow from behind her, hugged it against her chest, and lay flat. "No, pray all you want. Pray all day, pray all night, pray until the church makes enough money for you to get us that new car, and pray until this great big house is so full of praying that you don't notice how empty it is. Just stop asking me to join you."

Mike wanted to explain her error, but he knew better. She had allowed herself to drift further and further, tethered to him by the thinnest of ropes, and then she had cut the connection. Now no words would prompt her to fill the vacancy by his side. He returned to his knees.

4

They met by the gate. The first words out of Mike's mouth were, "Does it work?"

"Hello, Reverend," Jake said. "I'm happy you invited me back. You know, I'd love a tour of your garden. Are you the gardener, or do we owe all this beauty to your wife?"

Opening the gate, Mike repeated, "*Does it work?*"

Jake took a few steps on the azalea-lined path and stopped. "Does *what* work?"

"This... book, this alchemy. Does it work?"

With a hand on Mike's back, Jake said, "Walk with me." They walked. "If by 'does it work,' you mean, is he right, then yes, it works. But are you ready for that answer? Why am I suddenly welcome in your company again?"

"Those words," Mike said, trying not to think about the hand on his back, "they're like... spells. How can that not be witchcraft? How can that not be... evil?"

"We stopped burning people at the stake a long time ago," Jake said. "'Witchcraft' turned out to be a number of different religions, and while people of those faiths need us to witness to them, they're not evil. And they're not entirely wrong. That's why the conversion of Europe happened so quickly – we still have much in common with our pagan ancestors."

"But the spells," Mike said.

"Spells! All Dr. Fincher did was write down the religious ceremonies he observed around the world. To us, they look like spells, but to other cultures, the Lord's Prayer and the Apostles' Creed might look like spells, too. That's where Dr. Fincher gets one of those comparisons you thought were blasphemy. Spells, prayers, they're all the same thing: attempts by man to use his will to reach a higher will, the Will of God. Because no matter who you pray to, there's really only one God who hears prayers, right?"

"I suppose." The reasoning was heretical, but Mike could follow it.

"And the words you pray don't matter. Ultimately it's about a connection with God. Am I right?"

Mike looked at his inquisitor in silence. They reached the swing and faced it without sitting. Jake said, "Remember what the Apostle Paul says in the first Epistle to the Thessalonians: 'Pray without ceasing.' I believe that if you say a prayer enough times, the power of prayer becomes part of your breath. How did the saints accomplish miracles?"

"Through faith," Mike said.

"Yes. Faith turns their wills into conduits of the Divine. What do you know about St. Anthony of Padua?"

"Look, Jake, I studied these things, but I'm not a Catholic, and I—"

"One of St. Anthony's miracles was to appear in two places at once. It's called bilocation. Several other saints were known to manifest it. I—"

"Listen, Jake, I called you over here to say I'm sorry, and though I should be more accepting of how you see things, I don't think—"

"Turn around," Jake said. Mike stayed still. Jake took a deep breath and ordered: "Turn around *now*."

Mike turned. What he saw might have knocked him over, but the hand on his back kept him steady. In front of him, he saw the azalea-lined trail they had just walked. Blossoms of purple, pink, and orange stood out as if from behind a screen, and the screen itself was a different image: his office, dark wood and crowded shelves, stacks of books and music holders, bags of pretzels, high-backed chairs, a splinter of wood. He and Jake were standing between his office window and his desk, and they were standing in his back yard, in front of the double swing on the trail of flowers. He reached toward the lion-shaped bookend on the corner of his desk, and for a moment, his hand felt cold metal.

"This can't be happening," Mike said.

Jake's hand slid from Mike's back to his arm without breaking contact. Jake stepped forward, dragging his hand along Mike's shirtsleeve until their fingers clasped. Another step forward, and Jake was passing through the desk, slowly pulling Mike behind. Jake led them through a chair, and they reached one of the azalea bushes. He stretched down, picked a blossom, and set it in Mike's free hand. "You feel it, don't you?"

Mike felt soft petals. "This is... the devil's work."

Jake shook his head. "Not the devil, Mike. This power belongs only to God and to those who serve Him. God shows us miracles to inspire faith. Now watch." He walked back through the chair, leading Mike by the hand. Standing so his body and the desk stayed separate, Jake leaned over and grabbed a silver pen from Mike's desktop. He loosened his grip on Mike's hand but did not release it. In the space he created, he set the pen. "Hold this," he said, and he pulled away.

They stood on the azalea-lined trail. Around them, the air was open, and the day was bright. There were no traces of office furniture. In his hand, Mike saw his silver pen. "How?" he said.

Jake grinned, showing teeth. "It's like uttering a prayer until it becomes part of your breath. You need time," he said, "and practice."

5

Mike's suggestion that he and Sara reschedule their dinner with Alice Granger had met with guilt-tripping disdain. Wasn't he obliged to look after the widow of a man who had served First Church so well? On his way downstairs to answer the door, Mike almost tripped over Sarge, Sara's cat, a grizzled calico with long whiskers and one eye. Mike usually had little to do with him, but tonight, he wished he could follow the veteran's example, hiding upstairs and waiting for leftovers.

He opened the door and saw Alice leaning toward the bell, ready to poke the button a fourth time. "Hi!" she said. The tight brown curls on her head made her hair look like a wig, but otherwise, she looked pretty, with subdued makeup and a conservative dress. "I was beginning to think nobody was home!"

"Sorry we made you wait," Mike said. "Won't you come in?"

In response, Alice held up a bottle. "Sara said the veal is in a white wine sauce, so I thought maybe a pinot grigio. The charming man at the shop recommended it, so I hope it's good!" She waited for Mike to accept the offering.

"I appreciate the thought, but Sara and I don't drink—"

"Speak for yourself!" Sara tapped him on the shoulder and gestured for him to step aside. "I'm sure it's lovely, Alice. I'll open it and let it breathe." Mike didn't think white wines needed to breathe, but he would not correct the error. Sara took the wine and pulled Alice through the doorway. "Why don't you and Mike sit at the dining room table? I need to finish mashing the potatoes, and then I'll serve."

Mike and Sara usually ate in the kitchen, but tonight Sara had set places at the long dining room table, two at one end and a third at the distant other. Mike took the solitary position. Alice hesitated before taking the chair on the side instead of the place opposite Mike. Glancing at the table's floral centerpiece and the candelabra on the sideboard, she said, "You and Sara have such nice things!"

Mike unfolded his napkin in his lap and mumbled, "Thank you. Sara gets all the credit."

From the kitchen, he heard a cork pop. Clinking glasses signaled Sara's entrance. In one hand she held a bowl of salad, and in the other she balanced three stems. She set the bowl by the centerpiece, a glass by her own place, a glass by Alice, and a glass by Mike. "No thank you," Mike said.

"Don't be rude," Sara said.

"It's not rude to set an example," Mike said. He looked at Alice. "I preach abstinence, and I try to practice it. I didn't imagine you and B—" he cleared his throat, "I didn't think you'd be a drinker, being so involved in the church."

Alice looked down at her empty plate. "Jesus drank wine."

"That's right," Sara said. She moved the bowl toward Mike and tilted the tongs toward him. "'Drink wine with a merry heart.' It's Ecclesiastes, I think." She exited.

Sara didn't usually quote Bible verses, especially not lately, but she was right. Mike served himself salad, looked around, stood, and carried the bowl to Alice. "Thanks," Alice said. Her voice sounded pinched.

As Mike rearranged the napkin in his lap, Sara returned with the platter of veal piccata in one hand and the bowl of mashed potatoes in the other. "'Wine is a mocker,'" Mike said. "'And whosoever is deceived thereby is not wise.'" He looked at Alice. "That's Proverbs, chapter twenty, verse one."

Sara exited, returning in a moment with a bowl of green beans and the bottle of wine. "I'll see your Proverb," she set down the beans, "and raise you a Psalm. Psalm 104 praises the Lord," she poured for Alice, "for making the wine," she poured for herself, "'that maketh glad the heart of man,'" she poured for Mike. Standing at her own place, she raised her glass and said, "Praise the Lord!" She gulped half and sat.

Had she studied for this encounter? "The body is the temple of the Holy Spirit." Mike pushed his glass away. "That's Corinthians." He couldn't remember *which* Corinthians. "I don't believe in polluting God's temple."

Sara served veal, potatoes, and beans for Alice and herself. She kept the dishes at their end of the table. "I'd offer you some of this food," she said, "but the sauce for the veal has wine in it. It also has butter. I mashed a whole stick of butter in with the potatoes, and the beans not only have butter, but some really fatty bacon, too. And if you're really concerned about polluting your temple, you might push away that plate of salad, because the dressing is simply full of high-calorie oil. And there's egg in the mix, too! You know you need to watch your cholesterol." She speared some of the fat, limp, delicious-looking beans with her fork and raised them to her mouth.

"Shall I ask the blessing?" Mike glared. The beans didn't pass between Sara's lips; her fork clattered on her plate. While Mike prayed with his eyes closed, he felt his wife's fixed gaze prickle his face. When he finished, he carried his plate to the women's side of the table and served himself.

"I'm so sorry I caused all this trouble," Alice said. "I didn't think a bottle of wine would... oh, I just didn't think."

That night, after Mike got under the covers and turned out the light, Sara said, "I think Alice had a miserable time."

"She did."

Sara sighed. "I went too far. I'm sorry."

Mike looked at his wife's face, visible in moonlight. "What were you trying to prove?"

"Can't you just accept my apology?"

The moonlight made her face look softer, younger. He leaned forward and kissed her cheek, enjoying how the delicate skin felt against his lips.

When he pulled away, her fingers brushed against her face, as if exploring the sensation he had left. She shook her head, dismissing it. "Are you seeing that friend of yours again tomorrow, what's his name, Jake?"

"Yes," Mike said.

"We should have him over for dinner sometime. Or maybe him and Alice together. No wine, I promise." She kissed him on the mouth, a peck, and said goodnight.

6

Jake pushed the metal lion-shaped bookend from the corner of Mike's desk, clearing a space to sit. He took off his glasses and set them aside. Mike kept his back to him, watching reflected lips move in a windowpane. "Tell me, Reverend, do you think Christ condones war?"

"I'm really not up for more catechizing."

"Okay. What are you up for?" The panama hat came off, finding a place on the desk next to the lion.

Mike turned and saw that what he had thought was a smudge on the window was really a reddish-black streak across Jake's forehead. "It's not Ash Wednesday, and you're not Catholic," Mike said. "What's that?"

Jake's head sank to his chest, directing a light chuckle at his lap. "You don't want to answer my question," Jake said, "but you expect me to answer yours."

"Fine then." Mike left the window and took a seat in one of the high-backed chairs that faced his desk. Jake swiveled on the desk's edge to follow him. His right hand rested on the metal lion, almost petting it. "I've read Aquinas," Mike said, "and I agree with the standard argument for just war."

"And you remember what Paul writes in the book of Romans, about how the minister of God does not bear the sword in vain?"

This morning, Sara had left the batter in the waffle iron until it turned black. Mike found her kneeling in front of the trash can, scraping out the charred breakfast and weeping. When he offered to help, she cried harder. Small things had baffling impact, but Mike was tolerant. "Yes." He took a deep breath and let his eyes drift from Jake to papers on his desk. "I remember."

"Then tell me," Jake said, *"who the fuck do you think you are?"*

The question took a moment to seem real. "Excuse me?"

Jake slid off the desk and started walking toward him. "I said, who the FUCK do you think you are, Reverend? Sitting there thinking about something you're afraid to say while I talk about something you're afraid to do?"

Mike's back became rigid. "Jake, I—"

"You *what*, exactly? You don't appreciate my *harsh language*?" Jake's voice was menacing. "Get off it, will you? Just a second ago, your shoulders were slumped so low that you looked like a faggot trying to suck his own dick. Be a man!"

Legs tense, Mike felt his feet pressing against the carpet. If he stood, his face would be inches from Jake's. He grasped the arms of the chair. "We're in a church! We're in *my* church!"

"*Your* church? Do you really think this is *your* church? A man who, a few weeks ago, would have been content to let the building get eaten by insects while he just sat there, watching? A man whose congregation is crying out for leadership, for strength, for direction, while he just sits there, watching?"

Mike's vision was sharp, and his breath was quick. The leather-covered arms of the chair strained against his clenching fingers.

"*Your* church," Jake continued. "Really? How long do you think the congregation will put up with you? They *know*, Michael! Sure, Sara comes to the services, and she volunteers for Cathy Sutton's little bake sales and Amanda Kitchener's ridiculous craft fairs, but she's not keeping it *secret*, Reverend. The way she looks at you, the way she looks at the whole church—"

Mike's hands ached to form fists. "Watch it, Jake."

"Or what?" Jake laughed. "Come on, when I first met you, I thought you were a man of God, a man of vision, but now I have to wonder, are you really a man at all?"

"Watch it." Why was Jake doing this? And why was he letting Jake get to him?

Jake stepped between the chair and the window, engulfing Mike in shadow. His voice became softer: "A so-called man, a so-called minister, who tries to convince his congregation to follow God's ways but can barely follow them himself, who can't even get his *wife* to do a good job *pretending* to believe the bullshit he—"

"Enough!" Mike rocketed from the chair, and his hands, palms flat, collided with Jake's chest. Jake stumbled backward, stopping against the desk. "I don't know what you're trying to prove, but I won't listen to this." He inhaled and waited for the breath to calm his racing pulse.

Jake laughed. "Everything you do is a joke, Michael. Everything you claim to believe is a lie. You're afraid, that's all. You're afraid to ask me for what you really want. You fucking *coward*. You don't believe in God. You believe in fear, and you hope there's a heaven where you can go because you're afraid of death, and you pretend there's a God who created you in His image because you're afraid of your own reflection, and you lie about Jesus saving souls because you know that, if you had a soul, it would be hollow and simpering, just like you."

"Shut up, Jake."

"That's all religion is, right? Fear of death mixed with fear of your own pathetic nature. You want to believe that Jesus rose from the dead because otherwise, nailing people to crosses and burning them at stakes would just be more evidence of the brutal, animal law that *really* governs men's natures. Especially yours. Come on! You're too smart to buy into the millennia of bullshit, aren't you? The wars fought in God's name were just excuses to steal and conquer. It's all nothing to you, as long as you've got your pretty house in your pretty garden and that fancy new car you've been saving for. It's all nothing! It's lies, excuses—"

"Shut up!" Mike's hands formed fists.

Jake pushed away from the desk, bringing his face too close and echoing with mocking glee, "Shut up? Is that what you say to Sara? All of this sounds a little too familiar, doesn't it? It's what she thinks now, right? And deep down, you know she's smarter than you. You know she's right. You want to think of yourself as Abraham, God's chosen, and you want to think you can't have children because God is testing you, but really, you know He's not, because really, you're just an impotent fuck—"

Pushing Jake's chest with the left fist gave the right arm room to swing. The punch connected with Jake's face, smashing his nose in a spray of blood. Jake spat and laughed as he teetered and collapsed onto the desk. "Is that all you can do? I've seen it, Mike! I've seen that fear in you, the way you look at women, any woman, Cathy Sutton, Alice Granger—"

Mike grabbed Jake's baby blue shirt, lifted him from the desktop, and slammed a fist into his face until buttons popped and the shirt slipped from his fingers. Jake's body fell back, smacking his head against the metal lion as he crumpled onto the desktop. Jake was silent and still. His eyes were closed, and his chest neither rose nor fell. Mike saw blood on the papers behind Jake's head. Was he dead?

A rhythmic sound began, slow and deep at first but rising in pitch as it got louder, becoming rapid, like a giggle. Jake's blood-covered eyelids popped open, and parting, grinning lips showed reddened teeth. "Coward! Weakling!" The voice was pure glee, and Mike saw the metal lion, spotted red, and imagined Jake reaching for it, grabbing it, swinging it. The idea seized him, moved him, brought his hand to the lion and lifted it, gripped it, pulled it up, and brought it down. The metal crashed against the strange smear on Jake's forehead, which cracked, on his bent nose, which flattened, on his reddened teeth, which shattered. The lion slipped from Mike's hand. It thumped on the floor behind him.

In front of him, his office window looked out on the bright day. The town was quiet. No one was near. As always, Jake had closed the solid door behind him when he'd entered. No one had seen or heard the Reverend Michael Cox commit murder.

Mike turned around, away from the window and the bloody body on his desk, and stepped toward the door. As he realized what he'd done, he realized it was right, the just execution of a blasphemer. Extending from a blood-spattered shirt cuff, his hand grasped the door handle.

"Honestly, Mike, if you hadn't done it then, I don't know what else I would have said. My creativity has limits." The voice, distorted as lips worked over missing teeth, spun Mike around. Jake stood in front of the desk, the bright window behind him. He reached back and picked up his stained hat. "Ruined. I guess we all make sacrifices." He snickered, but the mirth faded, and his face became serious. "Now I know, Mike. Now I know you have what it takes to be a warrior for God. We won't do what you've been too afraid to ask for. We won't make Sara fertile. But we can do so much more."

Mike stood dumbfounded, and as new teeth pushed shattered fragments from the gaps in Jake's mouth, Jake said, "You have to promise never to kill me again, though." He laughed. "I came prepared today, but usually I'd find having my face mashed in far less pleasant."

7

The one-story building that served as the county sheriff's office had its glass front door propped open. As he walked through the parking lot, Mike could see the lobby's orange faux-leather sofas and the counter where Sheriff Andy Perkins stood tapping a pen against his chin. Andy was in his mid-sixties, well-liked, and very good at his job. That he was five-four and weighed about 140 hampered no one's confidence in his ability to enforce the law. Andy ran unopposed almost every time the sheriff's office appeared on the county ballot. When someone ran against him, that someone lost.

Jake's apparition appeared by a parked police car. He wore a green polo shirt and khaki slacks; a plaid golfer's cap had replaced the white panama. If Sara looked in their back yard, she would see the same man, in the same outfit, sitting on their swing, admiring the early-summer blossoms. Jake had said that Mike should perform the morning's errands by himself, but a part of Jake would tag along to offer advice. Since the incident with the metal lion, Mike had studied *The Alchemy of Will* dutifully. He didn't need a babysitter. "So," Jake said, "are you ready to see the man who plays Barney to this town's Andy?"

With minimum volume, Mike answered, "That joke is what kids today call 'lame.'"

"Kids these days wouldn't even get the reference," Jake said. "Shall we continue?"

Mike nodded and crossed through the doorway. Andy looked up from the papers on the counter and set down the pen. "Well how do you do, Reverend." He looked left and right and said, "What can we do for you today? No trouble at the church, I hope."

"Oh, it's nothing like that," Mike said. "I just stopped by to have a word with a member of my congregation. Is Glen Hadderly around?"

"Glen!!" Andy shouted. "Last I saw him, he was playing solitaire on the new computer. It's a slow day."

"A slow day is a good day, right?" Mike smiled.

"That's right," Andy said. "Glen!"

The man who emerged from the back was not Barney Fife-ish. His average height made him tower over the Sheriff, and his dark hair, flecked with early grey, looked too well-coiffed to admit goofiness. Deputy Hadderly moved with casual confidence, and the pleasure he showed at seeing Reverend Cox was merely polite. "Hey there, Reverend. What can I do for you? No trouble at the church, I hope."

"No," Mike said, "no trouble. But I'm hoping you can help me with something. Can we have a word in private?"

Creases appeared and disappeared on Andy's forehead before the sheriff picked up his pen and returned his interest to the papers on the counter. "Yeah," said Hadderly, "I guess so. Sheriff, do you mind if we use the interrogation room?"

"The interrogation room," Jake said. "That's Glen's baby. Ever since he became a deputy, he's been after the sheriff to make the station more 'professional,' which means more like the police stations on TV. The new room even has a one-way mirror."

"Sure," Andy said to Hadderly. "Go right ahead."

"I'll keep an eye on the other side of the mirror," Jake said, "and warn you if the good sheriff decides to play spy."

Glen and Mike settled on opposite sides of the interrogation room's round table. "What's up, Reverend?" Glen said. "It's kind of strange meeting in private."

Mike looked up at the mirror and wondered whether Jake had to maintain an apparition while watching from the other side of the glass. "I know it is, Glen, but I'm wondering if you can do a favor for me, and it's not the kind of thing we can really talk about in public."

Glen laughed, and Mike frowned. "I'm sorry, Reverend, but it's funny. You know, you being a preacher, and me being a cop, and you asking me to keep some sort of secret."

Mike nodded. "Well, what I have to say is unusual." He searched his memory for the details that Jake had provided. "You used to work at the power plant with Nate Grayson, right?"

"That's right." Glen's expression turned severe.

"I hit a nerve. Bad memories?"

Glen tilted his chair back and propped his booted feet on the table. "You could say that. It's just you mentioning Nate Grayson. Me and him don't really get along."

"Oh? Why's that?"

"Because." Glen crossed his feet. "Look, I know the Bible probably says something about not holding grudges."

Passages sprung to mind, but they seemed contrary to the day's purpose. "Forgiveness is hard," Mike said.

"The thing is, Nate got the promotion I deserved just because he has a college degree. So yeah, I guess you can say that place has bad memories."

"So you quit the plant and decided to become a cop." Mike knew Jake's information would be accurate. Jake had proven his mastery of *The Alchemy*. Mike had no reason to doubt.

"That's right," Glen said.

"And are the... opportunities... any better here?"

Glen looked at the mirror and shrugged. "Same shit different day, if you'll pardon my French."

"I understand." Mike pulled out the high school yearbook he had taken from the public library. "What if I told you there's going to be a robbery today. What if I can show you exactly who's going to do it. What if I could help you recover the stolen property and look like a hero, as long as you promise not to look too hard for the actual thieves?"

"What, is this something that somebody confessed to you, and you have to keep it secret or something?"

"Something like that."

8

Alice stood at the hulking do-it-yourself photo printer, pressing buttons between glances at prints. Mike snapped his fingers in front of her eyes, which did not blink. "She really can't see or hear us, can she? It's like we're not even here."

Jake moved toward him. "We are here, in a way. And if you keep concentrating on getting her attention, you eventually will."

Careful to avoid touching her, Mike retracted his hand and walked toward the center of the store. The photo printer was perpendicular to the main checkout. The pharmacy counter was on the other side of the front entrance, visible from the registers but separated by an expanse of white-tiled floor. The tiles reflected the ceiling's fluorescent lights. As he moved, Mike's presence did not disturb the glare.

Mike clapped his hands, making a sound that should have startled the whole store. Brett Martin, the pharmacist, did not look up from his book. Mike recognized the teenage girl at the register but couldn't recall her name. The clapping sound did not disrupt her ennui. In the aisle of cold and flu remedies, Matt McCullough, the veterinarian who had pronounced Sara's half-blind cat "fit as a fiddle," stared at the label on a bottle of cough syrup, undisturbed. Ness Green, the store's only other customer, hovered near the feminine hygiene products, looking back and forth from a list in his hand to an array of tampons. Ness looked puzzled and afraid, unaware of anything beyond the daunting task before him.

"Don't you feel like we should warn them?" Mike asked. "Couldn't something go wrong?"

"Something could," Jake said, "but these kids, Randy and Ashley, aren't violent. They're not too bright, either. Today's supposed to be their big move. All they need is enough money to make it to Los Angeles, where Randy will sell the drugs they've stolen to valium-addicted Beverly Hills housewives and Ashley will become a famous actress. Kind of asinine, isn't it?"

"Kids' dreams are naïve. That's what makes them kids' dreams." Mike sighed. "They're just misguided."

"Uh-huh," Jake said. "Don't tell me you're losing your resolve. Maybe I misspoke when I called them 'kids.' They're both nineteen. And they're lost." He joined Mike by the front entrance. "I heard your little *dreamers* debating whether they should put pantyhose over their heads or wear sunglasses. They chose the sunglasses. That's why Glen can claim to recognize them from the security tape." Jake's expression turned from bemused to serious. "I also heard Randy bragging about how he'd 'pop a guy' if anybody got in their way. It was just to impress the girl, but anyone who can talk so callously about murder is beyond 'misguided.'"

"Promise me, Jake. Promise me that, if something goes wrong, if innocent people are going to get hurt, we'll do something."

"Innocent people?" Jake said. "Sure. I'll tell you if I see any."

A bell jingled as both of the front doors opened, making room for the sunglasses-wearing teens to enter side by side. Randy's zipped leather jacket concealed his beltline, where he had probably tucked the revolver. The heavy red sack on Ashley's shoulder looked more like a suitcase than a purse; she would probably use it to tote their plunder.

Jake stepped aside as they approached, but Mike was too slow. Randy walked through him, causing a sensation like a fly swatter smacking against Mike's innards. The store vanished, and Mike was back in his attic office, sitting on the floor cross-legged, still in the meditative pose that he and Jake had assumed for the hours leading up to their transportation.

"Damn it, no!" Mike shouted. He stood up, kicked over the ashes of the "offering" he and Jake had made in order to "focus Mike's will," and leaned over toward Jake's placid face. "Wake up! Come back! Bring me back with you! Jake! Jake! JAKE!!!"

The placid face stretched in a smile. "No need to shout. I can hear you." Jake stood up from the attic floor. The wideness of his eyes told Mike that he was still seeing the store, experiencing the scene that Mike was denied.

"How come you're there and I'm here? How come you can do all this and I—"

"Shhh," Jake said. "You don't want to break my concentration, do you? Calm down. Remember, if you can't manage it, all you have to do is take my hand."

Mike shoved out his hand as if for a handshake. "Fine! Take me back."

"Shhh," Jake said. "Not until you calm down. Remember, you have to focus on being there and not being seen. We can't afford—"

"I'm focused!" Mike shouted. He took a deep breath, not needing Jake's sneer to tell him how absurd he sounded. "What's happening?"

"Well, I'm having trouble following them and you at the same time," Jake said, "but Matt McCullough is standing at the photograph machine, talking to Alice, and Ness Green is still building up the courage to buy tampons. Randy and Ashley are at the pharmacy counter. Randy's using a low voice, but I can tell he's already asking Brett to open the safe, and in a moment—"

"I'm calm," Mike said, nodding at his waiting hand. "Please. Take me back."

"Don't let go." Jake took his hand. "You won't be able to manage on your own again until you've really taken the time to focus."

They were back in the store, mere feet from where Randy stood at the pharmacy counter, unzipping his jacket to show Brett his gun. "Look, dude, just open up the narcotics safe and fill this bag." He cocked his head toward the red sack on Ashley's shoulder. "Nobody has to get hurt. Fill up the bag, and give me whatever you've got in the register." When Randy talked, his lips curled up and revealed shiny metal braces.

Panic lurked behind Brett's stern expression. "Young man, just what do you think you're doing? We've got cameras, and the police—"

The gun came out of the jeans, and Randy leveled the barrel at Brett's nose. "Cops? Did you call the fucking cops?"

Mike imagined little Andy Perkins storming the store, a blazing gun in each hand. It wouldn't happen, but Randy didn't know that. "Jake, I—"

"Shhh," Jake said, squeezing his hand.

"No!" Brett said. "I didn't signal anybody. But it's a matter of time before someone walks by and sees you, and somebody'll recognize you, and then it'll be over. Don't ruin your life over this."

Randy pulled back the hammer on the revolver, and his finger tensed against the trigger. "Man, I will *end* your life if you don't start filling up this bag." Ashley turned her head toward him. Mike didn't need to see her eyes to know that she was questioning whether Randy might really be up to a killing.

Brett went over to the safe, opened it, and started to fill the bag. On the other side of the store, the checkout girl still looked bored, and McCullough kept chatting with Alice.

"Hurry up, man. Don't waste space with the worthless shit, either. You know what I'm after. Give it to me, or I will *end* you." Ashley's jaw dropped in disbelief while Jake's hand covered his mouth, masking a titter. Mike wondered which piece of Hollywood garbage had given Randy the "end you" line.

Brett stopped filling the bag and came up to the counter. "Son, I don't know what you want. I don't know about the... street value... of these things. They're medicines that people need. Think about it, son. You don't want to do this."

The gun shook in Randy's hand as it pointed at the pharmacist; the finger on the trigger remained tense. With a slightly different vocabulary, Randy said what Mike was thinking: "I'M NOT YOUR FUCKING SON, SO SHUT THE FUCK UP AND DO WHAT I FUCKING TELL YOU!!!"

The yelling snapped everyone in the store to attention. McCullough, Alice, and the checkout girl turned toward the pharmacy counter and gaped at what they saw. McCullough, not mindful of his volume, said, "Alice, call the police!"

Randy whipped around with the gun, and as startled Ashley reached for his arm, he fired. The checkout girl screamed. The bullet obliterated a display of disposable cameras, and McCullough grabbed Alice, shielding her.

Mike lurched toward them, rushing to join in Alice's defense. Jake's firm grip halted him. As Mike's hand squirmed for release, Jake's expression reminded him that there was nothing he could do. He took a deep breath, feeling his chest – part of the body he'd left in the attic – swell around his racing heart.

Brett held up the red sack, trying to recapture the robbers' attention. "Hey, it's okay, nobody's calling the police. I've got what you want here, narcotics, amphetamines, steroids...."

Randy wasn't listening. "All of you! Get your asses over here!" The gun pointed at McCullough, Alice, and the checkout girl. "MOVE IT!!"

Putting up their hands, palms flat and empty, the three hostages made their way to the nearer side of the store. "Get on your knees! Put your hands behind your head!"

Ashley said to Randy, "Hey, um, *Billy*, we don't need to get these people involved. This guy here is going to give us what we want." She turned to Brett and nodded. "Right?"

Raising his hands in surrender, Brett said "Right." He did not resume bag-filling.

Randy stepped toward the hostages, who were on their knees. He pressed the gun against Alice's forehead.

"Steady, Mike," Jake said.

"If anybody tries anything, I will put a fucking bullet between this bitch's eyes. Got it?" Alice's face quivered, and her chest convulsed with sobs. Randy turned around, his back to the kneeling hostages, and aimed at Brett. "Get back to work!" Brett put more packages into the red sack.

"We've got a problem," Jake said.

Mike looked at Alice, still on her knees and shaking in terror. "I know."

"No," Jake said, "you don't. Look." With his free hand, he pointed to Ness Green, who had abandoned tampons and begun sneaking toward them. As long as Randy and Ashley kept their backs turned, they wouldn't see him, but they wouldn't keep their backs turned for long.

"Lord help us," Mike said. Perhaps a prayer could activate *the will* and stop Ness Green. Mike searched for words, but nothing came. "Jake, do something."

"There's nothing I can do, not in time," Jake said.

"We can't just watch!"

"Our only other option is *not* to watch."

As Ness crept closer, Brett set the sack on the counter. "I got everything you might want from the safe. We're almost done." His voice was shaking. He was going to try something brave. "There's more, more that I can give you, but before I do that, I want you to let one of the women go."

McCullough looked at Alice, and Alice looked at the checkout girl. Randy and Ashley kept their backs to them, focusing on the pharmacist. Mike and Jake divided their attention between the gunman and Ness, who stepped closer, closer, quiet, but not silent. McCullough noticed him. Alice noticed him.

"YOU DON'T TELL ME WHAT TO DO!!" Randy screamed. He pulled back the hammer and prepared for a second shot. "Open the register! Give me the cash!"

With fumbling fingers, Brett typed in a code, and the register drawer popped open. He scooped out wads of cash and threw them in the cloth sack. Focused on his task, he didn't see Ness emerging from the aisle, crouching, stepping, his shoes making tiny clicks as they collided against the shiny white tiles. The three hostages, hands behind their heads, watched Ness. Mike could feel his hand sweating in Jake's grip. Back in the attic, moisture seeped between their palms.

"It's not much," Brett said. "Just the starter for the day plus a little from—"

"Just give me what you've got."

"Okay." Brett's gaze broke away from the cash drawer, the sack, and the gun. It drifted over Randy's shoulder and connected with Ness. His voice tried to keep Randy's attention, repeating, "Okay," but his eyes stayed fixed on Ness.

Ashley noticed first. She turned and yelled "Stop!"

The sound spun Randy around, and his tense finger squeezed the trigger. For a moment, Mike thought he could actually see the bullet as it flew from the barrel, cut through the air, and slammed into Ness Green's chest. Ness collapsed, bumping into Ashley as his fall closed the distance between them. A puddle of blood spread quickly on the white tiles, bright under the ceiling's panels of fluorescent light.

Ashley and the checkout girl screamed. McCullough abandoned his prostrate pose and dove at the injured man, turning him over and covering the wound with his hands.

Randy pointed the gun erratically, at Alice, at McCullough, at Ness, at Brett. "Nobody else move! NOBODY!" He bent toward McCullough, who was keeping pressure on Ness's wound. "Is he dead?"

"Not yet," McCullough said. 'We need an ambulance."

Randy reached behind him and grabbed Ashley. "Get the bag!"

Shaking as badly as the two women who were still on their knees, Ashley snatched the sack from the counter. Randy led her to the doors, yanking her arm whenever she fell out of step. Seconds later, Mike heard their tires squeal as they sped down the street.

"The bullet missed the heart, but I need some help with the bleeding!" McCullough yelled. Brett abandoned the counter and took the veterinarian's place as wound-holder. McCullough ordered the checkout girl to call the police as he checked Ness's eyes.

The teenage girl dialed, and Alice snapped to awareness. Her hands slipped from behind her head. Her body tipped forward, and she started crawling toward McCullough, saying "Help me, help me."

"We're leaving," Jake said. "We have work to do."

9

The supplies were already in the trunk of Jake's Lincoln, so they just had to drive to the preordained spot on the four-lane road that led out of town. Jake kept tabs on Randy and Ashley while he drove, assuring Mike that the criminals wouldn't elude them. Mike didn't argue. Jake seemed comfortable driving in one place while spying in another, but his comfort wasn't contagious.

Jake pulled the car onto the road's shoulder and into the grass beyond. Rolling slowly, he maneuvered into a grove of pines and parked when the woods surrounded them. "We can leave the car here until we're done. Nobody will see," Jake said.

The sun hung low on the horizon. Light was orange and fading but still bright. Mike longed for the cover of darkness, and he wondered what his longing signified. "How can we get them to stop?" Mike asked. "A roadblock?"

"Get out of the car and I'll show you."

Mike kept his eyes on the road as he climbed out of the passenger seat and made his way to the Lincoln's front. No one drove by.

"Do you remember what Dr. Fincher writes about the will and perception?" Jake asked.

"We don't have time for catechism." Mike rubbed his hands together to stem a shiver. The evening was warm, but he felt cold.

"Illusion," Jake said, "is a gift of the will. Self-delusion, the delusion of others, beauty and horror – it all comes from the mind's eye. We see things as we imagine them more often than as they are. The greatest power is making others see the world as you want them to. I'm paraphrasing Allen's more eloquent prose—"

"Please, just tell me what we're doing!"

"Give me your hand," Jake said. Mike complied. Jake produced a long pocket knife from the rear of his slacks and opened it. The blade sparkled in the orange sunset. Mike glanced at the road, saw no cars, and fixed his attention on his hand, palm out and waiting. "Ready?" Jake asked.

Mike took a deep breath and held it, letting the word "Why" hiss through his teeth.

"Because," Jake said, "even I need help to access the greater gifts." He placed the top of the long blade where Mike's wrist met his hand, pushed, and started to drag. As skin parted in a widening line of red, Mike clenched his jaw and froze the air in his lungs. The knife continued until it slit the web between two fingers. By then, blood was pooling. Mike winced as Jake raised the knife toward his mouth. Expecting Jake's tongue to extend and, vampire-like, lap at the fluid, Mike felt relieved when the flat of the blade only pressed against Jake's lips. Jake's face scrunched, spreading the fluid like lipstick, and in a low hush, he started to chant. His eyes stared into nothing as his hand reached for Mike's. Lifting the bleeding palm toward his face, Jake kept chanting, and he did not flinch as he pressed the bleeding wound into his eyes.

Mike fought the urge to yank his throbbing hand away from Jake's face. Eyelashes tickled the wound, and the words on Jake's bloody lips blended from recognizable English into one of the foreign tongues from the pages of the *Alchemy*, one of the languages that Jake described as "dead but nonetheless lively." The soft, lilting phrases almost kept Mike from hearing the sound of an approaching engine.

"Jake," Mike looked over his shoulder, "someone's coming. Whatever you're going to do, do it now."

Jake pushed the hand away, revealing his face, raccoon-like with blood. Behind red bubbles, his eyes were open. His painted lips kept chanting, and the noise of the engine drew nearer. Mike positioned himself behind a tree and watched as the white van came down the slope that ended at the grove where Jake had parked. "Jake," he said. "Now, Jake." Mike looked over his shoulder at the reddened face.

Chanting stopped, and Jake blinked. Without a word, he grinned.

Mike returned his attention to the road. Where four smooth, well-painted lanes had been, a line of rubble marked the edge of a chasm, a crater of collapsed asphalt at least ten yards across. The white van's tires screeched, and as the van smashed into it, Mike read the sign that said "Danger!"

Mike heard the opening of the van's door before a torrent of curses announced Randy's frustration with the roadblock. Randy circled around the front of the vehicle, kicking the felled signpost as he walked. The passenger door opened, and Ashley jumped out, screaming, "Just go around it for God's sake!"

Jake tapped Mike on the shoulder and said, "Get the dart guns out of the trunk." Mike needed a moment to comprehend before he complied. He fetched the guns, and they took the shots at close range.

Mike lifted Ashley into the van by himself, but he needed Jake's help with Randy. He was slamming the van's rear doors when a brief siren blast forced new sweat to sprout on his cold skin. The sunlight was almost gone, and the flashes of red and blue from the top of the squad car cast mad shadows in all directions.

"Howdy, Reverend!" Mike turned and saw Glen Hadderly, his thumbs hooked into his gun belt, swaggering in Mike's direction. "You look like shit, if you'll pardon my French."

"Pardon," Mike echoed. "Yes, of course." He knew how he must look. His short-sleeved, button-up white shirt was untucked and soaked to the point of translucence. Most of the moisture was sweat, but some of it was blood from his sliced hand.

"You been working?" The deputy's expression was suspicious, not as conciliating as it had been in response to the implied promise of promotion. "You look tired."

"Oh," Mike said.

Hadderly noticed the pit in the road. "What the hell happened?!?"

"Um," Mike said. "Meteor?"

Jake abandoned his spot at the edge of the illusory chasm and walked along the van's side. Mike gawked at the dart gun dangling in Jake's left hand. "Good evening, Deputy," Jake said. "Hot night, isn't it?"

"Hold it," Hadderly barked. "Is that a weapon?"

"What, this?" Jake held up the gun. "It's just for tranquilizers. Perfectly harmless, unless you're afraid of a good sleep."

"All the same, I'd as soon you drop it." The deputy stepped forward, shifting stern eyes from Mike to Jake and moving one hand closer to his gun. "And what the hell is all over your *face*, Mr., um..."

"Warren, but you can call me Jake. I work with Mike at First Church. And it's nothing for you to worry about. Just some red stuff I was using."

The deputy looked incredulous. "What are you two up to? *Reverend?*" Mike pressed his back against the van's doors. "What happened to the road?" He paused and squinted at Mike. "What are you hiding in that van? What's really going on here?"

Jake tucked the dart gun into the rear of his pants and moved into shoulder-patting range. "Come now, Deputy Hadderly, if we wanted to hide something from you, would we have told you where to find us?" He gave the rhetorical question a moment to settle. "You *are* a little early, though." He patted.

The deputy shook off the reassuring gesture. "I had to get out here quick. The faces on that security tape were so plain I had to ID them right away, or else somebody else would. Not long after, Gus Tannen called and said his van was missing, probably taken by his niece Ashley. Andy decided to give the state troopers a call, and there'll be road blocks all over the place in no time. And they'll be looking for this van." To punctuate his point, Hadderly drew his gun and tapped it against one of the van's rear windows. Mike was sidling away, praying for the deputy's confusion to make him unobservant, when Hadderly did a double-take at the window and shouted "HOLY SHIT!" Hadderly leapt backward and pointed the gun at Mike and Jake. "You two stand together! And don't move!"

Ignoring both halves of the contradictory command, Jake moved further from Mike, toward the deputy. "We made you a promise, and we're here to keep it, Glen," Jake said. "What are you so upset about?" He halted his approach when the gun was only inches from his cheek.

"Those... those kids! Those are them, right? The robbers! Are they... dead?"

Jake reached up and gently slipped the gun from Glen's fingers. He tucked it into the rear of his pants, and Mike wondered whether the weapon-tucking gesture, done twice in two minutes, were practiced. "I'll give that back when you've calmed down."

Glen's arms fell to his sides. "What are you? Some kind of vigilante Bible squad?"

With a shout of delight, Jake clapped his hands and gestured toward Mike. "We are! Isn't that right, Reverend?"

Mike nodded. He couldn't get over having said "Meteor."

"To answer your question," Jake said, "they're not dead. There's nothing wrong with them, unless, like I said, you've got a problem with a good sleep."

"You shot them with the tranquilizer gun," the deputy interpreted.

Jake put his finger on his nose. "You got it." He patted Glen on the shoulder. The man did not resist. "I'm awfully glad you came early. Otherwise we wouldn't know your comrades are looking for this van. My car is parked right over there," Jake pointed at the grove of pines. "We've got to move these two delinquents again. I can pull the car closer, but we're pretty pooped, so I hope you won't mind helping. One should fit in the trunk; the other gets the backseat."

In Glen's face, Mike could see Jake's calm, rational language battling the deputy's better instincts. "But what did you tranq them for? What are you going to do with them?"

"It's not exactly a vigilante thing," Jake said. "It's more of a *reform* thing. We're going to re-form these criminals, and we're going to reform this entire town. You've seen it yourself, the direction we're going — the direction the entire country is going! Don't you think it's time for a change? For the return of real values? For a rebirth?"

The words might have come from one of Mike's sermons.

"You wait here," Jake said. "I'll go get my car." He walked toward the trees.

Mike nodded at Glen. Glen gazed at Mike, the battle ongoing in his face, and then looked back up the road. "Wait! Wait just a damned minute!"

Jake stopped, and Mike pressed his back harder against the van.

"What the hell happened to the goddamned road? Did you say a *meteor* hit?"

"No," Mike said. "I said 'meet here.' Because the, uh, sinkhole marked the place where we were supposed to meet."

"Uh-huh," the deputy said. "Don't ever take up a career in politics, Reverend."

Mike nodded.

Returning, Jake called out, "Do you have your flashlight with you, Glen?"

Glen turned from Mike to Jake. "It's back in the car."

"Go get it. Then meet me by that hole."

"I should arrest you guys," Glen mumbled. He went back to his car. Mike said nothing. Jake was handling the situation, and anything Mike did would make it worse. Glen retrieved the flashlight, and Jake led him to the edge of the sinkhole. Mike followed at a distance.

"Shine your light down there," Jake said. Glen directed the beam into the illusion. "Looks deep, doesn't it?"

Glen picked up a piece of rubble and dropped it in the hole. Five long seconds later, they heard it hit bottom. "That's no ordinary sinkhole," the deputy said.

"Right," Jake said. "Now pay attention." With no buildup or warning, Jake stepped over the pile of rubble and walked across the chasm, appearing to take step after step onto empty air. He stopped in the middle, turned, and waved. "What do you think now, Glen?"

Mike couldn't see the deputy's face, but he could imagine his expression.

"Take a step, Glen. I promise you won't fall."

The officer seemed uncertain, but his leg extended, testing the empty space. Mike didn't know if he would float, fall, or simply disrupt the illusion.

The leg retracted. "You're crazy!"

"I'm standing on thin air," Jake said. "Give crazy a try!" Glen's head shook back and forth, a vigorous refusal. "I tell you what," Jake coaxed. "Mike, take his hand. If he starts to fall, pull him back, okay?"

Mike took the deputy's hand. Perplexed, hesitating, Glen looked from the chasm to Mike, from Mike to Jake. Glen's head shook again, another refusal. Mike nodded and forced a smile. Glen took a deep breath, closed his eyes, and squeezed Mike's fingers so hard that Mike ground his teeth. The deputy took his first step onto nothingness. After the fourth step, Mike released him, and he walked on his own to meet Jake in the center.

Jake reached behind him and produced Glen's gun. Inserting it into Glen's holster, Jake said, "We need you, Glen. We're more than vigilantes. This thing, this sinkhole, it isn't real, and it'll be gone as soon as we are. But we're real, and so are you. Are you ready? Are you ready to make something of yourself? Of this town?"

Glen lifted and dropped his legs, stomping. He jumped. "It's like there's nothing there – I don't feel anything under me – but I'm not falling."

"Will you help us?" Jake offered a handshake, and Glen accepted.

Half an hour later, Deputy Hadderly reported that he had found the van abandoned on the side of the road. All of the stolen drugs and money were inside, but the perpetrators had fled. Nevertheless, Glen's heroism was assured.

An hour later, Mike and Jake hauled Randy and Ashley into the basement of First Church. Stumbling in darkness, they entered through the plastic sheets that had replaced the outer wall of Mike's office. The plans called for a stairway, but now a ladder provided the only access from Mike's office down to the newly partitioned space that would become the Prayer Room.

Mike guided the limp bodies through the hole to where Jake waited to catch them. By the time they had Randy and Ashley laid out on the makeshift altar of wooden crates, Mike wanted nothing more than to go home, get in bed, and think about how nice Sara's backrubs had been in the early days of their marriage.

"Tell me, Jake, what was in those darts? They haven't moved. I'd think they were dead if they weren't breathing."

"They're not dead. They can't be dead for this."

This. Until this moment, Mike had been able to avoid thinking about *this.* He could get lost in the abstractions of just war and the greater glory of God and how, by adopting Jake's mission, he was advancing Christ's Church no matter how abhorrent his acts would be to Christ Himself. Abstraction was easy. The cutting would be hard.

"Undress them," Jake said. "I'll get the tools from the car."

Mike started with Randy. He lifted the boy's torso and guided his arms from the leather jacket. Randy's hands and back scraped against the wooden crates as Mike jerked the T-shirt around bony shoulders. Yanking off the jeans proved tougher than the T-shirt, but Mike managed. He stopped at the underwear. That could stay unless Jake said otherwise.

The girl proved easier to undress because her clothes weren't as tight. Mike felt less like a pervert but more sinister as he exposed Ashley's braless breasts and skinny thighs. He wished the stirring in his pants would stop.

Jake appeared on the ladder, carefully moving from rung to rung while he balanced a suitcase handle in his fingers. Keeping his eyes from the girl, Mike said, "What took you so long?"

"You didn't notice? Ashley's shoes came off when we were dragging her across the grass. I couldn't leave them there, so I had to carry them back to the car." Jake looked exasperated but firm. In his companion, Mike detected none of the hesitation, none of the heaviness, that he felt filling his own chest and swallowing his own skin.

"Silky panties and tighty whities," Jake said. "You got shy at the last minute, didn't you? You men of the cloth, all alike." Jake flashed his toothy grin and set the suitcase on a clear corner of a crate. He flipped the latches and revealed ropes, rags, scalpels, and saws.

"You can't back out now, Mike. We've come too far. Think of how I cut open your hand. And that metal lion you smashed into my face – it didn't feel *good*, believe me. The greatest acts of will require the greatest sacrifices. This is God's law: He followed and affirmed it when He sacrificed His only son. Are you with me? Will you stand among the ministers of God, taking up the sword as He commands?"

Blood drained from Mike's face. The cold that had haunted his skin all day turned to intractable ice. He nodded.

"Good. Then take this scalpel and cut off their undies. Remember to start saying the words before you start sawing. The left arms go in the north wall, the right in the south. The legs go in the east wall, and the heads in the west. They should, of course, face the East. We'll leave the torsos in these crates for now, until we get the real altar built. Don't worry about the smell: they'll be as incorruptible as saints."

10

First Church's renovation continued. Weeks passed as sheet rock partitioned the basement and bricks formed the office's new outer wall. Jake's workers were quiet and steady. Mike wanted to hurry them, but knowing what they were sealing into the walls downstairs, he left them alone. When late-August humidity was at its most miserable, the workers declared their job done. Absorbing his remade office's thick silence, Mike stared at the mahogany paneling that had replaced his window. To his right was the door to his new storage closet. To his left was the door that led down.

A loud knock preceded the squeaking of hinges. "Reverend?" a familiar voice called.

Mike turned and saw Cathy Sutton. She wasn't alone: her six-foot-three teenage son Chad was in tow, wearing the scowl he broadcasted whenever she forced him to attend church. "I'm sorry to barge in, but – oh my goodness! Doesn't this place look *grand*!"

Mike savored a three-second pause before he switched on his warmth. "What do you think? It's not too much, I hope."

"Oh, I don't think so," she said. "All that dark wood looks classy. I guess you'll miss the sunshine, though." The woman beamed at him, and Chad rolled his eyes.

"I do, but the architect said the window had to go. I guess it makes the room more private." Mike shrugged. "That's not all bad."

She blushed. "I didn't mean to say I didn't like it. I love it! It's dignified, like a preacher's place should be."

"Thank you, Mrs. Sutton." He usually called her Cathy. "What brings you here today?"

Leaving the door wide open behind her, she crossed toward the desk, taking one high-backed chair for herself and gesturing for her son to sit in the other. "Well, I'm sorry to bother you with it, but we have a little problem that we hope you can help us with."

"Oh?" Mike looked at Chad, who, despite his enormous shoulders, was trying to disappear into the leather padding around him.

"*Yes*," said Mrs. Sutton. "Oh, I'm ashamed to admit it, but it seems Mr. Chad here thinks he's better than everybody else, so much better that he doesn't have to go to school, not even on the first day!"

"I don't think I'm better," Chad grumbled.

Mrs. Sutton gave her son a reproachful look and said, "Reverend, I was hoping you could tell my son how Jesus feels about truants."

Mike imagined Jesus weighing in on high school attendance policies. "God commands us all to show self-control and be the best people we can, and that means going to school, Chad."

"Jesus didn't have to go to Kenning High," Chad rebutted. "Did they even have high schools back then?"

"Shush!" said Mrs. Sutton.

"Actually, that's a pretty smart question," Mike said. "Mrs. Sutton, I'd be happy to have a talk with your son, man to man. Actually, your timing is great, because there's something I could use his help with, too. What do you say, Chad, do you mind spending an hour or two with a stiff-necked preacher?"

Chad half-laughed, glared at his mother, and said, "Sure."

Cathy Sutton left her son in Mike's care. Looking at the door to the left of the now-windowless wall, Mike said, "Do you pray, Chad?"

"Sure," the boy said.

Mike chuckled. His back stayed to his audience. "I guess it's like when a dentist asks if you floss. If a preacher asks if you pray, you kind of have to say yes, don't you?"

"Sure."

"Sure," Mike repeated. He opened the door and faced the boy. "I doubt you even know how to pray, Chad. Come downstairs with me. I want to show you something I've been working on. It's a new room, a place where your conscience can have a one-on-one with the Almighty. A place where people learn to pray."

11

Two swings, two slides, and monkey bars formed the centerpiece of Kenning's only park. "Strange, isn't it," Mike said, "two childless grown men sitting on a park bench on a Saturday morning?" Jake remained quiet. Beneath the plaid golfer's hat, his eyes were fixed on the playset. Two girls were dangling from the monkey bars, and another girl sat on a swing, with a blond-headed, pimply-faced boy pushing from behind. "Care to tell me what we're doing here?"

"There's Chad," Jake said, "right on time." He pointed at the lumbering form who had parked his car on the far side of a baseball diamond. Chad walked toward them, with another boy, his younger brother, close behind. "No, Chad, not to us. To the swings." The boys' direction changed.

"What's Bobby doing here?" Mike asked.

"Who?"

"The other boy with Chad. His brother."

"I'm guessing Cathy Sutton made him tag along," Jake said. "It won't matter."

"Matter to what?"

"To our test," Jake said. "The Prayer Room is new to me, too, you know. I read about it in one of Allen's unpublished papers, about a chief who governed his tribe from a hut made from human bones. We're not exactly following the script. We must proceed with caution."

Mike felt sweaty and tired and irritated. "You could let me in on more of your plan, you know."

"What makes you think I have a plan?" Jake said. "I'm an opportunist. There – now you and your brother want the swings."

Mike watched Chad approach the blond boy, who was about six inches shorter and half as wide. "Hey," Chad said. "Me and my brother want the swings."

Mike barely heard Bobby say, "We do?"

"You two take turns with that one," the blond boy said. His posture straightened. He seemed to recognize the interlopers. "My sister and me aren't finished yet."

"Come on, Chad," Bobby said. "Let's go throw the football or something."

"You need both swings," Jake said. "Take them."

The girl on the swing arced back toward the blond boy, who gave her a slight push without turning away from his challenger, who said, "You two stop, or I'll make you stop."

"Buzz off," the blond boy said. He turned toward the girl in the swing, who had to be his younger sister, and gave her a push. The two girls on the bars ceased monkeying. They stood ten feet from the swings, watching the scene as it developed. Two women, perhaps mothers, watched from a distant bench.

Chad shoved the blond boy, who stumbled away from the swings but didn't fall. Regaining his balance, the boy shouted, "BACK OFF! The swings don't belong to you!" He fumed but maintained control.

Chad shoved again, adding the weight of his shoulders, and forced the boy to the ground. The swinging girl looked behind her and yelped at her fallen brother. In response, Chad's arm grabbed one of the swing's chains and shook it, causing the seat to sway wildly and the girl to fly out. Cradling her knee, she sobbed.

Backing away, Bobby searched around, noting the women on the distant bench and Mike and Jake on the near. The distant women's heads swiveled to and from the mounting violence, debating intervention. Mike's legs tensed, ready to spring up, but he didn't move. Jake's relaxed form watched.

The blond boy hopped up from the grass and sprinted toward his sister, shouting "Franny!" at the top of his lungs. Chad motioned for his brother to take one of the swings while the boy examined his sister for injuries. Finding a skinned knee but nothing life-threatening, the boy circled toward his sister's attacker and charged. His weight wasn't enough for a tackle. Chad grabbed the boy's shirt and punched him in the face. The boy fell again, and Chad returned his attention to the swing.

The sister stood up, favoring her knee, and called to her brother. Chad shouted for her to get away from the swing. Bobby put a hand on Chad's shoulder, asking if they could go. The women from the bench stood up and took a tentative step. Jake stood, engrossed. "Wait," he said.

Chad's head turned toward Jake, away from the fallen boy, who rose quickly from the grass, wiped tears away from the eye that would later be black, and charged again. His shoulder connected with Chad's arm, catching him off guard and spinning him. The blond boy's feet twisted in the dirt as he directed one fist at Chad's jaw and another at Chad's stomach. Chad faltered, doubling over, and the blond boy unleashed a torrent of quick punches at the larger boy's gut. Behind his brother, Bobby made jerky movements, first toward Chad and then toward the blond boy. The women from the bench approached, but seeing that the underdog was about to best the bully, they froze. The blond boy nailed Chad's jaw a second time, spun around, and landed a kick in the center of Chad's chest. Chad collapsed.

Mike stood beside Jake, who applauded, shouting "Bravo!"

"What?" Mike said. "Why?"

"Our little soldier found an adversary." Jake's voice was gleeful. "He's one to keep."

"Chad?"

"No," Jake said. "The other one."

12

The weight of Sarge's cage pressed valleys into Mike's legs. If the woman at the counter didn't call their name in the next five minutes, he was going to set the thing on the floor and walk out. "Would you please remind me why we're here?"

Sara patted the top of the Pet Carrier and pressed her nose against the door's metal grate. "We're here because Sarge isn't feeling well." She spoke in her cat voice, soft, high-pitched, and coddling.

"No," Mike said, "that's why *you're* here. Why am I here?"

Sara's glare drilled deep. "Because you're a loving and supportive husband."

Inside the cage, Sarge shifted positions. Mike wondered if the cat's ceaseless shifting would leave bruises. He looked at his watch. The receptionist had three more minutes. "How do you *know* the cat isn't feeling well?" The half-blind creature always looked plaintive. More than once, Sara had referred to Sarge's "struggles with depression."

"You haven't noticed the vomit all over the floor?"

Piles of pinkish, half-digested cat food speckled with clumps of fur were common enough on their carpets. "You'll recall that I switched to hard-bottomed slippers for that very reason," Mike said, "two years ago. What's so special about the current vomit?"

"It's *yellow*! That can't be normal."

"So now you're an expert on cat puke."

"No," Sara said. "That's why we're here. I may not be an expert on cat puke, but Dr. McCullough is."

"I see," Mike said. "So, as a loving and supportive husband, I must share in the gathering of puke wisdom. I recall the exhortation to patience in the first letter to the Thessalonians."

"I'm sure you do." Her eyes kept their hold on Mike's, fathoming. "It won't be long now. Pretty soon, you'll be able to run and play with your little friend Jake."

In the months of Mike's training, Sara had never spoken an unkind word about Jake Warren. "What is that supposed to mean?"

"It means," Sara said, "that these days you seem far more interested in running all over town with that... man... than you are in spending any time with your wife."

"Maybe you should try to be more pleasant company," Mike said.

"Maybe you should make me a member of your secret club," she volleyed.

Mike was preparing a rejoinder when the receptionist called, "Sarge Cox?" When he'd given Sara his last name, he hadn't expected her to pass it on so blithely to anything with four legs and fluffy fur.

"Right here." Sara stood.

"You and Sarge can go on back." The receptionist smiled. "Dr. McCullough is waiting in room two."

Dr. McCullough was an enigma. He had graduated from a first-rate medical school and then studied to be a veterinarian. Whatever had caused McCullough to become less useful to society had not removed all skill: with vestigial knowledge of human anatomy, the pet doctor had kept Ness Green's bullet wound from being fatal.

"Reverend Cox, Mrs. Cox, how do you do? Please shut the door behind you in case the little one decides to bolt." McCullough patted the paper-covered examination table. "Set the cage right here and tell me about the trouble." The pet doctor was close to Mike in height, but his frame was smaller, and his hair was lighter. It was the same shade of blond as his son Brian's.

Mike claimed a nearby chair, and Sara described the thrills of finding the contents of Sarge's stomach deposited on the stairs, the bedspread, the hall rug, and even the kitchen counter. Nodding as if each detail were an essential piece of a masterwork puzzle, McCullough contorted his eyebrows and lips into expressions of concern.

The yellow in Sarge's vomit might simply be bile, but the vet wanted to perform tests. As Sara gave McCullough *carte blanche*, Mike felt familiar creeping along the back of his neck. Since summer had turned to autumn, Jake had been following him, invisibly observing Mike's deployments of Fincher's methods. The tightening of neck skin and the stiffening of hairs signaled Jake's spying presence, and now, the sensations reminded him that he had business with McCullough beyond vomit-talk.

"Why don't you leave Sarge with me for a little while? I'll run the tests, and you and the Reverend can go out. We should be ready in a couple of hours, and I promise to take good care of him in the meantime."

"Joy," Sara said. "An afternoon on the town with my loving husband."

"Mr. McCullough," Mike stood, "it occurs to me that I've never seen you on a Sunday. Do you mind if I ask which church you attend?"

"Yes, Mike, he minds," Sara said.

McCullough cleared his throat. "Actually, Linda and I aren't really churchgoers."

"Don't you have two young children?" Mike asked.

"Well, Brian is hardly young anymore." The pet doctor smiled. "Linda and I are already bracing ourselves for his college exodus."

"Exodus," Mike repeated. "Good word. Do you read the Bible with your kids?"

McCullough's face lost some of its brightness. "Look, Reverend, I have the greatest respect for men of your profession, but I don't think it's appropriate—"

"If the Lord is missing from your children's education, are they really educated, do you think?"

"Mike, please," Sara said.

"Frankly," McCullough said, his eyes on the Pet Carrier, "I think your Lord is a little too present in my children's education. I believe that the Constitution's guarantee of freedom of religion also means freedom from religion, which means that religious teaching needs to happen outside of our public schools. Like I said, I have the greatest respect for the service you provide to members of our community, but I don't appreciate your not-so-subtle hints about the way I choose to raise my kids."

"There's no need to lecture me," Mike said. "I just asked you a simple question. Maybe you should wonder why you feel so defensive."

"Please excuse my husband," Sara said. "His work requires a measure of... *zeal*."

Mike laughed. "And by 'zeal' I think my wife might mean obnoxiousness." He grinned and extended a hand for shaking. "I apologize if I offended you."

McCullough walked around the table and reciprocated the gesture. "And I apologize for my strong reaction."

Without releasing the vet's hand, Mike said, "No hard feelings, I hope." His mind searched for the words he had studied, and he remembered Jake's instructions for maximizing the efficacy of silent prayer.

McCullough relaxed his fingers but didn't pull away from Mike's grip. "No hard feelings. No need to worry – Sarge will still get my best care." McCullough's reassuring laugh strained as the handshake became more uncomfortable.

"Thank you, doctor." Sara's eyes switched from the shaking hands to Mike's face, commanding her husband to cease.

The handshake continued as words circled through Mike's brain, blending from a foreign dialect into English that found voice: "Thoughts, offering, body, conduit, *let me, let me.*"

"Excuse me?" asked the pet doctor, tugging at his trapped hand.

"Let me, let me."

"Mike, we should go," Sara said.

"Let me, let me," Mike said. "Go?"

Sara took the men's clasped hands and pulled them apart. "Yes," she said. "Go."

Wiggling his hand in the air, McCullough led the way, opening the door and stepping through. "Oh!" he shouted. "Sorry! I didn't expect anyone to be standing there."

McCullough stepped back toward Mike and Sara, revealing the victim of the doorway crash. Alice Granger straightened her blouse, touched the tight curls on her head, and said, "I'm sorry I surprised you! It's just that Cindy told me you were back here, and I thought I'd—"

"I thought I asked you not to come by here anymore," McCullough said, half-hushed.

"I, uh," Alice said, and then, "Oh! Sara! Reverend Cox! I didn't see you there! I'm so sorry I interrupted! I just had a question for the doctor. I didn't realize he wasn't alone."

"I didn't know you had any pets," Sara said. Her expression was as quizzical as Mike felt. Despite the tension between them, husband and wife united in curiosity.

"I'm... thinking of getting a dog," Alice stammered.

"I see," Sara said.

Mike saw too.

13

Mike and Jake saw many things.

They saw the Sleep E-Z motel, where Matt McCullough arranged clandestine meetings with Alice Granger. On the Thursday after the Sarge-puke consultation, Mike sat in his attic and watched McCullough tell his receptionist, Cindy, to "cover for a little while." The look on Cindy's face said she knew what he meant. If his wife Linda called, Matt would be with a patient. He wouldn't be on one of the Sleep E-Z's superannuated mattresses, playing with Alice's tight curls and perky breasts.

McCullough parked his car on the side of the E-Z's lot furthest from the street. As he crossed toward room six, he looked over each of his shoulders once, twice, again. A tap at six's door summoned Alice, who wore a half-unbuttoned blouse and jeans that Mike found shockingly tight.

Alice flashed a lascivious smile when McCullough stepped through the doorway, but McCullough's face stayed firm, serious. He asked why she had felt it necessary to come to his office the other day. She told him she'd needed to talk, and she insisted a trail of phone calls could be just as bad as office visits.

"Really? You still think so, even though that preacher and his wife took less than two seconds to figure us out?"

"They *did?*" Her face reddened.

"They did."

McCullough sat on the bed and rubbed his face. "What are we going to do? We can't keep this up. Linda will find out. The whole *town* will find out. There aren't any secrets in Kenning."

Mike thought of the Prayer Room and laughed. His projection sat on the edge of the bed next to McCullough. The mattress did not sag or squeak in response.

"And what if Linda knew? What if the town knew? After what we went through together, could anyone blame us?" Mike knew the look on Alice's face. She needed validation, something to keep her from falling further into the abyss that had opened at Bart's death.

"Are we even talking about the same town? Of course they'd blame us." McCullough was right, but he was wrong for saying it. His words exploited the still-grieving widow's vulnerability.

Alice started crying. McCullough gave her his shoulder. Sitting on the bed, they embraced. Mike stood, walked around them, and repositioned himself next to the woman. His hand rose from his side and moved toward Alice's slender back, the soft veiled skin where shoulders sloped into spine. His fingers hovered, and they snapped back when the blouse started to peel away. McCullough guided the garment down her arms and let it constrict her, pushing her shoulder blades together and her breasts out, toward him. As McCullough leaned in and kissed the front of Alice's bra, Mike traced the rear strap with a pinky in the air, not making contact until a sudden move forced the plastic clasp against his fingertip.

The sensation rippled through his arm and made the attic waver into visibility around him. He kept his concentration, maintained his place, and heard Alice say, "What was that?"

"Shhh." McCullough kissed her on the mouth. Mike reestablished himself in the motel room, the attic forgotten. Alice shifted her arms so the blouse could slide off, and as he removed her bra, McCullough angled her toward the mattress. Mike scooted away from contact as the couple spread out, McCullough pressing himself on top of Alice, rubbing her arms with grasping hands. He released her and pulled off his own shirt before pressing down again, skin to skin, rubbing the blond hair of his chest across Alice's hard nipples.

Alice's hands reached for McCullough's backside and shoved fingers beneath the rim of his pants. She squeezed him, and his back arched up, leaving Mike a clear view of the greedy, ecstatic expression on Alice's face. Mike stood when her hands made a similar thrust on the opposite side, grabbing and pressing until McCullough gasped, pulled away, and flopped onto his back. Alice stood up next to Mike, almost stepping through him. She unbuttoned her tight jeans and pushed them down her legs, rocking her hips back and forth, inviting. McCullough sat up, reached out, and pulled the woman toward him. Mike took sideways steps and got a fuller view of McCullough pressing his face into her panties. He looked away when McCullough started to push the panties down, but he looked back a moment later, unable to resist the shadow of hair between Alice's legs, unable to break his eyes from her as she bent over and unbuttoned McCullough's slacks.

By the time McCullough pressed Alice onto the mattress again, pushing himself inside of her, Mike could feel the sweat coursing over the skin he had left in the attic. Through long minutes he stood, watching. Alice climaxed, and McCullough climaxed, and Mike left.

Mike and Jake saw other things, too.

Stan Johnson was overweight and had a dark bushy beard. For religious reasons, he refused the Budweiser his friends consumed in bulk, but he jumped at every opportunity to watch a game or go on a hunting trip. He lived in Jake's neighborhood.

"It's kind of an experiment," Mike said. "A place where someone can go, away from home and work and family, and just be close to God. We call it the Prayer Room."

"Prayer Room, huh?" Stan looked at the closed door. "Do you have to make an appointment?"

Mike grinned and patted Stan on the shoulder. "Not yet. There hasn't been much demand for it. Mostly I use it, and Jake Warren, and the other people involved in church business. But it's open to everyone."

"Huh." Stan put a hand on the brass doorknob. The door itself was heavy and thick, insulated against noise. "What's inside?"

"You interested?" Mike asked. He saw a shrug forming in Stan's shoulders and cut it off: "Tell you what. Why don't you go on inside for awhile, and I'll go do a couple of things up in my office. You can stay one minute or five or thirty. If you're an hour, I'll come make sure you're not asleep. Okay?"

"Guess so." Stan opened the door and disappeared.

Mike knew what Stan would see at first. The Room's center was the altar, blue fabric draped over fine wood with an adjoining pad for kneeling. A crucifix hung from the eastern wall. The walls themselves were white as bone. A yellow fixture on the ceiling suffused soft light. A newcomer would not detect the symbols Mike and Jake had painted on the walls with blood.

From his distant desk chair, Mike could watch, but he could not see what Stan saw. Stan shoved his hands into his pockets and made a circuit of the Room. He paused at the crucifix. The large man glanced, and glanced again, at the northern wall. His eyes widened. The wall transformed, but Mike couldn't see how.

Stan almost tripped over the altar as whatever he saw pushed him back. He looked left, right. On both sides, the walls were changing. He looked behind him and released a quick, sharp scream. All Mike saw was that the altar had vanished. He had no idea of what had taken its place.

In the center of the room, Stan spun, seeing something, or some things, lurching at him from the walls. His arms extended, and he screamed again, a bellowing blare. From inside the room, Mike could hear him, but he knew that, back in his office, his eardrums would pick up nothing. The Room had left the Church.

Stan calmed. He took steps toward the wall where the crucifix had been and stared at it, into it, as if into a mirror. His arms folded across his chest. Stan sucked in air, and Mike could hear a stifled sob rattling the man's vocal chords. Releasing breath, Stan placed his hands flat against the wall and let his head fall back. The head rocked forward and slammed into the wall, again and again, until a trickle of red began to move upward, drawing a line to the ceiling.

Screams from Stan's lungs blended with other sounds that Mike was starting to sense, rushing water, the rhythmic wheels of a train, a mass of noises and thought. When the walls themselves began to bend, to shift and swirl, to expand, to open out, Mike realized he was falling, and he remembered what Jake had told him. He stepped backward, not in space but in will, and resumed his safe vantage.

Mike knew of only a few ways that an experience in the Prayer Room could end for an uninitiated visitor. Stan's ending was the most common. Stepping back from the wall where he had smashed his head, Stan placed fingers on closed eyelids. Lids parted, and the fingers pushed inward, crushing and digging until sight was removed.

When Mike returned to fetch Stan, he found him kneeling at the altar. The walls were as white as ever, and Stan's eyes seemed to be where they belonged. Mike knew better.

14

Sara shoved the spade into the soil, deepening the hole for her transplanted rose bush. Mike tended the lilies, removing hints of weeds. They knelt side by side in the dirt. Neither of them had spoken for the last half hour. Mike stopped working and looked at his wife. A brown smudge stood out against the fair skin of her cheek, and her floppy green gardening hat kept the top of her face in shadow. He opened his mouth, hoping his tongue would act on its own, and heard the squeaking hinges of the gate.

"Jake!" he called as he stood. "Come on back. Great day, isn't it?" Mike brushed dirt from his hands and glanced at Sara, who hadn't looked up to greet the approaching visitor.

The men shook hands. "April's not the usual month for planting, is it?" Jake asked. "Good morning, Sara."

Sara did not respond.

"We're not planting," Mike said. "Just maintenance."

"Mm," Jake said. "Listen, Mike, I was wondering if I might have a moment. Something we need to discuss. Church business." He grinned at Sara, whose head turned in his direction. Mike couldn't tell whether her shadowed eyes were glaring.

"Sure, Jake. Sara, would you mind giving us a moment?"

"Yes!" She stabbed the spade into the ground so that its handle pointed skyward. "I can't help but notice," she said, "that in the year since you two met, the amount of church business that needs discussing seems to have tripled. Funny, isn't it?" She stood, placed hands on her hips, and looked at the men in turn.

Mike faked a laugh. "Yeah. Look, honey, I didn't mean to be rude. Why don't you keep working here, and Jake and I will go up to my office. That fine with you, Jake?"

"I would never willingly displace a lady," Jake said. He was still grinning.

"Huh," Sara said. "Well, so you know, I can't promise that I haven't planted listening devices in the attic."

Jake laughed. Perplexity creased Mike's forehead. "You're joking," Mike said. "Right?"

She shrugged and smiled.

"The lady wants to know what we talk about," Jake said.

"The *lady*," Sara said, "has to point out that, since her *marriage* is a lie, and her *religion* is a lie, she's due for some truth." She paused and added, "Goddamn it!"

"Sara!" Mike yelled. Jake laughed.

"Sara," Mike repeated, calmer. "There are some things that Jake and I need to discuss alone. And there are some things," his posture straightened, "that you and I shouldn't discuss in front of other people."

She stepped between Mike and Jake, her back to her husband. "Mr. Warren, my husband offers a curious parallel between your relationship with him and mine. I find that amusing, don't you?"

Jake nodded, chuckling.

"Perhaps you might convince him," her head made a demonstrative tilt toward Mike, "that at this point, the secrets of your little club might be safer if I were allowed to join."

The top of Sara's floppy green hat kept Jake's full expression from view, but Mike could see a gleam in the man's eyes. Jake took Sara's right hand and walked in a circle, turning her so that the two of them, side by side, faced Mike once again. "I see why you married her." He lifted her hand and kissed it.

Mike cleared his throat. "Jake, you're not helping."

"On the contrary," he said, "I think I am. Your wife is absolutely correct."

"She is?"

"I am," Sara said.

"Oh."

Without releasing Sara, Jake took another step and filled his free hand with one of Mike's. Mike had held Jake's hand many times for practical purposes, but this embrace felt awkward. "There's room for the three of us on the swing, right?"

"Oh yes," Sara said. "I insisted on one of the larger swings in case I ever decide to get fat."

Hand in hand, the three left the roses and lilies, walked past azaleas, and settled into the swing, hips against hips, thighs against thighs, Jake in the middle. "So Deacon," Mike said, "what's the business for today?"

Sara pumped her legs, causing the swing to sway.

"First of all," Jake said, "I brought you some mail." Jake removed an envelope from the breast pocket of his short-sleeved shirt. It was yellow, and printed above the plastic address window, in large blue italics, was *AN INVITATION FOR YOU!* The return address said "American Values Federation," and the typing in the window said "To our friend Michael Cox."

"There's no postmark," Sara said.

"There's no *stamp*," Mike added.

"The American Values Federation," Sara read. "That's the one that backed by billionaire, you know, what's-his-name, from Atlanta. Elijah Eagleton." She thought for a moment. "And weren't they mixed up in one of the abortion clinic bombings last year?"

"You're right," Mike said. Everyone in Georgia knew Elijah Eagleton's name, but few people knew him. Eagleton provided a focus for endless speculation. "She's right, isn't she?"

"More or less," Jake said. "Why don't you save that for later?"

"I want him to open it now," Sara said.

Jake showed Mike the back of his silver head as he turned toward Sara: "One thing at a time." He faced forward again, shifting attention to Mike. "We also need to talk about Hadderly."

"Who, Glen Hadderly? The policeman?"

Mike leaned forward to get a clear view around Jake and glared: *Listen, woman, but don't interrupt.*

"Yes, Deputy Hadderly," Jake said. "He's been helping us out with some of the church's business."

"Spicy," Sara said. "I had no idea that your business involved the police."

Spicy? "*Sara*," Mike groaned.

"Well," Jake said, "Glen helped us out with a problem once. Now it's quid pro quo, favors for favors."

Mike's mood became sourer. "I thought we handled that."

"There's an election coming up," Jake said.

Mike leaned back and nodded.

"If you mean Hadderly wants to run for sheriff," Sara said, "he hasn't got a chance against Andy Perkins. Unless you plan to rig the election." She thought for a moment. "Wait, go back. What problem did he help with?"

"Mike?" Jake looked at him.

"You've *got* to be kidding," Mike said.

When Jake shrugged, one shoulder rubbed against Mike. The other must have rubbed against Sara.

"Okay, fine." Mike leaned forward. "Sara, do you remember that robbery last year, when Ness Green got shot?"

"Remember?" Sara said. "Alice talks of nothing else."

"Right." Mike's thoughts wandered to the Sleep E-Z. "Well... anyway, Jake and I were... involved." Leaning as far as he could, he studied his companions' expressions. Neither told him to stop. "And do you remember that the kids who did it disappeared?" He waited. Sara's breathing was loud. "We were involved in that, too."

"Involved," Sara echoed.

"Mike?" Jake said.

The garden threatened to spin out around him. A flood of feelings – disbelief, reluctance, terror, excitement, joy, exasperation, relief – separated him from the moment, so he saw it, the three of them sitting together, talking, *moving*. Into uncharted territory, a new dynamic, a new phase. Mike had never expected to share such things with anyone, least of all his wife. The American Values Federation, Hadderly, Sara – his world was getting bigger in ways he didn't understand.

And so, in a moment, would hers.

"Sara," Mike stood, "do you know anything about the miracles of St. Anthony of Padua? About bilocation?" Jake stood, extending his hands. Mike realized that through that gesture, Jake might save their marriage. "Come with us," Mike said to his wife. "It's time for a demonstration."

15

The American Values Federation's letter to Mike provided facts about the organization that were common to dozens of others: they were building an international ministry, they were dedicated to returning America to the foundational virtues of Christianity, and whatever they did, they did in the hope of bringing greater glory to God. The letter bore no signature. The only sign that a human being had ever touched it were six words at the bottom of the first page, handwritten in blue ink: "Jake Warren is a Founding Member!"

The second page was a slip with an empty box beside the words "Yes, I will join the AVF's mission and sow the seeds of God's Truth!" and a line for a signature. Mike checked the box, signed, and gave the slip to Jake, who said he would make sure the right people received it.

In the months that followed, Mike tended the seeds they had already sown.

Matt McCullough sat on his kitchen floor. He rubbed his eyes and searched for his microwave's glowing clock: 2:25 a.m. Shaking his head, he got to his feet and crossed to the steel double sink. Dishes from yesterday's dinner were stacked high in both basins. As he reached to turn the water on, his elbow knocked over a fork that clanged loudly against steel.

He shouted "Shit!" and covered his mouth with his right hand. He shot a guilty glance over his shoulder, toward the stairs that led to the bedrooms where his wife and children slept. A short wait produced no creaking floorboards. He lowered his hand from his mouth and reached again, more slowly, for the knob marked "C." Mike surmised that McCullough was going to splash cold water on his face, to wash away grogginess so he could figure out how he had gotten from his bed to the kitchen. Whatever his intent, McCullough froze with his hand in midair. He had noticed the marks on his fingers.

The moonlight through the windows was insufficient, so he flipped the switch next to the oven. The small stove light flickered on. Stretching out his hand, palm down, he read one letter on each digit, "C-H-E-A-T." On his left hand, in neater writing, he read "F-R-A-U-D." Something seized him, perhaps a memory, and he dashed for the bathroom. He lifted the blond hair from his forehead and saw the almost illegible word "CORRUPTOR." On his bare chest, in giant letters, he saw "FUCK." Trembling, he reached for the elastic rim of his boxer shorts and looked down. He stretched the skin to read the word scrawled along his penis, this time lowercase, "remove."

Nausea discolored the veterinarian's face, and Mike sharpened his gaze. He sensed disconnection between McCullough's exterior – the shaking hands, the widened eyes, the doubled posture – and McCullough's interior. Mike remembered what Jake had said about Dr. Fincher's prescriptions for reading thoughts. The challenge would be to separate the observer from the observed. Were the thoughts appearing in Mike's head his own speculations, guesses of what he would think in McCullough's position, or the actual workings of another man's mind?

"Remove" was imperative. Someone demanded vengeance against his penis for the qualities inscribed elsewhere. "FRAUD" looked familiar – like "remove," it could have been his own handwriting. "CHEAT" and "CORRUPTOR" were messier, less distinct. The messiness could have been the result of writing on himself. He was right-handed, after all, so the letters on his left hand would have been easiest to write.

In the mirror, both "FUCK" and "CORRUPTOR" moved from left to right. The letters were etched on his skin backward, designed for reflection. Was he sending himself a message? Or was someone else? Should he call a psychiatrist, or the police? How could someone else take him from his bed and touch his hands, his chest, his *dick* without waking him? Was it still sleepwalking if he had the presence of mind to mark his skin without waking himself up? Had someone broken in and drugged him? Had someone—

At that, he ran from the bathroom and toward the stairs. His feet pounded on the steps, forgetting the need for quiet. Mike felt satisfaction; at the precise moment when the thoughts in his own head had led to the possibility that someone had broken into the house, McCullough had bolted to check on his wife and children. Fincher's mind-reading technique was working.

Moonlight in the master bedroom showed Linda asleep on her side of the bed. Fran was sleeping, too, but when McCullough stepped into Brian's room, the boy that Jake called "adversary" sat up and said, "Dad?"

McCullough whispered, "Sorry, Bri. Thought I heard a noise. Go back to sleep." He hoped the obscene letters wouldn't be visible from his son's bed.

The evidence pointed toward him having done this to himself, but what could any of it mean? "CHEAT," "FRAUD," and even "remove" made a kind of sense. He felt guilty for not telling Linda about Alice. Maybe the guilt was deeper than he knew. Castration seemed like an awfully severe punishment for something he didn't consider to be a heinous crime.

The word "FUCK" was peculiar. It wasn't a label along the lines of "CHEAT" and "FRAUD," but it didn't seem like an order, either. McCullough remembered something – a Van Halen album called *For Unlawful Carnal Knowledge*. It came from a false etymology, an idea that "F.U.C.K." was a label put on rapists and adulterers back in the dark ages. Did his superego somehow buy into the fake philology?

Mike didn't think the "etymology" was false at all, but he wasn't in a position to argue.

McCullough's first instinct was to talk to Linda, who was an expert on abnormal psychology, but that would mean a confession he wasn't ready to make. He couldn't talk to anyone else, either, without raising suspicion. So what could he do? He returned to the downstairs bathroom, opened a fresh bar of soap, and scrubbed. As the words gradually faded into skin that turned from white to pink to red, he considered that, if he were going insane, he might have to do this again. And again. In the back of his mind lurked repeating words, something familiar that he couldn't place: *let me let me let me let me.*

Stan Johnson's life didn't change much after his time in the Prayer Room. He threw the football around with his boys on weekends, worked on weekdays, and looked forward to the next hunting trip. It wasn't unusual for him to browse at Rod's Sporting Goods, but he didn't know why he was looking at a handgun. For hunting, nothing could beat his trusty Winchester Wildcat bolt-action .22, especially since he had gotten that new scope for Christmas. Why on Earth would somebody take a subcompact Glock 39 on a hunting trip?

"That one," Stan said.

"What do you mean, 'that one?'" Rod asked. "The Glock's great for law enforcement, not bad for home security. But you're a hunter, aren't you?"

"Yes," Stan said. "But I need this gun." His eyes couldn't part from it. They glazed with desire.

"I hope you don't mind my asking, but why? Is Judy worried about the house? I thought you told me she had a fit when your brother bought you that scope, said she wasn't going to have them in her house anymore."

"That's true." Stan thought maybe he would give up and leave, but instead he said, "but I need this gun." The black, stubby little handle with a fine-textured grip, the elegant barrel – beauty! "There's a waiting period, right?"

"Yeah," Rod said. "I already know you'll pass the background check. But I really would like to know why you think you need a Glock."

"Well, you know. Bears."

"Bears?" Rod laughed. "You don't need a concealed weapon to go after a bear! What you need is one of these." He pulled a shotgun from the wall. "This one's Mossberg, top of the line, real power, easy reload, good weight. Have a feel."

Stan wanted to reach out and touch the shotgun, but he looked at the Glock's cold, metallic sheen and said, "No. I need the Glock."

"All right then." Rod put the shotgun away. "You're the customer, and that means you're the boss."

Two weeks later, Stan found a rusty metal box at a garage sale that Jake told him about. He knew it was wrong because the lock didn't work, but he decided to keep the Glock in the box anyway because it looked like a perfect fit. He thought about building a high shelf so that somebody would at least need a ladder to reach it, but he never got around to doing it.

Cathy Sutton said it was strange for a sixteen-year-old boy to have a spend-the-night party, but since Chad had been doing better at school, she didn't want to rock the boat. She limited the invitations to six. Jake and Mike chose attendees with care, selecting the boys most prone to gossip.

Chad had lost his ears and tongue in the Prayer Room, so Mike could easily get Chad to listen about the opportunity at Stan Johnson's house and tell all his party's invitees. The hard part was getting Chad to have the party at all. Jake or Mike would plant the suggestion, but a day or two later, it would dissipate, and Chad would agree with his mother: a sleepover with a bunch of boys was totally gay. Mike and Jake had to access Chad's mind again and again. Even with the magnifying power of the Room, subjugating another person's will required reinforcement. Jake warned that, eventually, Chad would build up resistance. Eventually, they would have to discard him.

The party went as planned. After Cathy was asleep, Chad asked his guests, "Wanna go look at a gun?" He led the party to the Johnsons' nearby neighborhood, forced his massive body through Stan's garage window, and retrieved the Glock. They went to a nearby patch of trees, set up their beer cans on a fallen branch, and started shooting. The noise of the shots and the whooping of the boys woke half the neighborhood, including Stan. On intuition, Stan climbed out of bed, went downstairs, and checked the rusty box. He saw the gun in its usual place.

Sara and Mike watched Stan together. "How do you make him see it – the gun, I mean?"

"That's not me," Mike answered. "That's Jake, back in the Room. I still can't do half the things he can."

"And why is that?" she asked.

It was a good question, just like another question that had plagued him since he and Jake had introduced Sara to the art of bilocation: why was she willing to join them? Mike and Jake had their mission; no matter how far they moved from Christ's ways, they were dedicated to serving God. Sara had abandoned her Christian faith long ago, but she embraced Fincher with zeal. Why? What could she possibly have to gain?

"I worry about Sara," Mike confessed. "I don't know if we can trust her."

"We can," Jake said. "Believe me. She'll be more valuable to us than any of the others, because we didn't have to use the Room, or anything else, to bring her to our side."

"Why does that make her so valuable?"

"She's more valuable," Jake said, "because the will she has now is more durable than any we could give her. The most valuable people are those who truly believe in our cause."

"And why does she believe?"

"Simple," Jake said. "Because she has nothing else."

16

Mike sat at his desk, and Jake and Sara sat in the two high-backed chairs. "Even if the aftermath wouldn't involve suspicions that would undermine our entire project," Jake said, "The Room just isn't powerful enough to change the outcome of an election. Not yet."

"And what exactly is our 'project?'" Sara asked.

Jake laughed. "You know, in all this time, I don't think your husband ever asked that question."

Mike's back stiffened. "Because I know the answer. We're turning Kenning into a better place. We're bringing the people back to God."

The thought leapt from Sara's mind: *As if Jake Warren could think so small.*

"Kenning is only the beginning, of course," Mike added. "That's why you brought me that letter from the AVF. Eventually, we'll take our ministry further."

"Right," Jake grinned.

Yes, dear, absolutely right. The mockery in Sara's thoughts was palpable.

"But now," Mike said, "we need to solve the problem of making Glen Hadderly sheriff."

Every idea they floated produced a chain of logic that led to defeat. Jake, Mike, and Sara adjourned no closer to a solution. Sara left the office first, and Mike lingered. "You know, Jake, the answer is obvious."

"Yes it is." Jake's toothy grin did not waver.

"The Church has always acknowledged that innocents must be sacrificed in war."

"Yes it has."

Exasperation made controlling his volume difficult. "Then why didn't you just say that!"

"Because," Jake said, "we need Sara to make the suggestion."

So they waited, and Mike observed. The three developed a ritual for Thursday nights: Jake came for dinner, and they discussed church functions, Mike's sermons, and politics. Reading Sara's mind became a way for Mike to hone his skills. He could pluck thoughts from the surface of her consciousness, the passing whims and unuttered responses, without getting a reaction. When he reached deeper, her hand went to her neck, and Mike knew she was feeling the tight skin and stiff hairs that he had felt so many times when Jake was watching. He started to count the seemingly random number of stretches, scratches, and rubs that his and his wife's necks received on Thursday evenings. The numbers were always high.

On a Sunday before the early service, Mike conducted an experiment. He and Jake sat in his office. Mike focused his eyes on Jake's glib expression, and his mind began an inward chant that led him out of his own brain, into the air, and toward Jake's skull. The silver hairs seemed to part before him, and then the skin and bone. Mike's wandering projection slipped between folds of grey tissue.

Mike found an image. A boar grazed on the side of a hill. Its brown hair reflected the blazing sun; it was majestic, perfect, and content with its meal. Mike was thinking that boars weren't known for eating grass when he moved closer and realized that in the grass, with its belly sliced and entrails strewn, a lion lay on its side. The boar looked up at him, its long tusks gleaming red, and charged.

The grassland of thought swirled into suffocation as tusks slid between Mike's ribs, and, in a dark blur, Mike's office reappeared. Jake stood over him, looked down through thin-rimmed glasses, and said, "That was stupid."

For the following Thursday, Mike suggested a more formal dinner in the dining room. Sara responded with excitement, eager to try her hand at filet mignon. Mike said he had a different meal in mind: he had found a delicious-sounding recipe for oven-baked Southern pork loin.

As the men sat at the formal, fully-stocked table, Sara emerged from the kitchen with a bottle and two wine glasses.

"Where did that come from?" Mike asked.

"Oh I didn't tell you," Sara said, "but I picked this up when I went shopping. I know Mike doesn't drink. Jake, is pinot noir okay with you?"

"That would be lovely," Jake said.

Mike thought he detected something along the lines of "Nah nah-nah nah-nah-nah" circling through Sara's head. They started eating. Jake and Sara sipped and savored while Mike sawed at pork. Sara speared a broccoli floret, crunched into it, and said, "Oh my."

Mike dropped his knife. "What is it?"

"I forgot the salt!"

Unaided, the salt shaker slid from its place beside the centerpiece to an empty patch of tablecloth near Sara's left hand. "Oh!" she shouted.

Jake grinned.

Sara looked at him and thought, *Amazing*.

Mike picked up his knife and resumed sawing. The rest of the main course was quiet. As Sara brought out the mousse, she said, "You know, the more I think about this election situation, the more I think it would all just be easier if Andy Perkins were out of the picture. Can you boys do something about that?"

17

Andy worked late, introducing the new deputy to the computerized databases. Winston caught onto the computer stuff about twice as fast as Andy had, but then again, he was half Andy's age. Andy was in pretty good shape, though, more than fit enough to do another stint as sheriff. In the fifteen years since cancer had taken his wife May, fighting off the unsavory side effects of Kenning's expansion had been his chief concern. He had his poodle Randolph, and he had his job. "Good night, Deputy Beecher," he said as he opened one of the glass doors.

"Good night, Sheriff!"

Andy's house was two miles from the station, so unless rain was in the forecast, he walked to and from work on a kind of patrol. As he set out beneath the night's patchwork of clouds and stars, a light breeze put a chill in the autumn air and knocked leaves across asphalt. Their shuffling sound underscored Kenning's prevailing silence. With the cool air and changing leaves, he couldn't help feeling wistful.

He reached around with his left hand and scratched the back of his neck. The breeze was making his hairs stand on end, and the skin felt tight. An anxious feeling traveled from his neck to his fingers, to his elbow, to his shoulder. His right hand settled on the handle of his gun. It was ridiculous to get spooked walking a route he'd walked ten thousand times on a night like ten thousand others. Besides, everybody knew that Sheriff Perkins was not a man to be trifled with. He was fast on the draw and a black belt to boot. Even at sixty-six years old, he could break up a bar fight by himself.

His shoe scuffed against the sidewalk when he stopped. "Hey!" he called.

The night answered with silence, the dark windows of closed shops, the rustling of leaves. The rustling seemed more animated than it had before. There weren't a lot of trees on Main Street, so maybe that spot up ahead was something other than a leaf. It was moving against the wind, in a line that seemed too straight. It was a squirrel, maybe, or a rat, darting from the gutter to some hideaway behind a shop's wooden steps.

Andy kept walking. He whistled a few random notes to take his mind off that scurrying sound, which had to be coming from behind the steps up ahead where he'd seen that little animal, even though it sounded like it was behind him now.

Pushing air through his lips produced a rasp instead of a note, and Andy turned to look behind him. By a streetlight, he saw not one but two moving bodies, almost definitely rats, spreading out in a V. They disappeared into the shadows, and it was stupid to think they were following him.

He thought about Dave Holcomb out at the dump, who said he'd gotten the idea of using his rifle to pick off rats in his spare time from a Stephen King novel. Dave must have mentioned Stephen King to sound tough, but Andy knew the guy sat in his little hut in the middle of all that trash reading nothing but romance novels all day. To each his own. Shooting at rats did seem like a pretty good idea right about now, but he'd be violating the town's noise ordinance if he opened fire in the middle of Main Street, and then what would he do, give himself a citation? The upcoming election was more of a formality, really, but still, a thing like that could give somebody ideas. There were a few guys on the force who might have liked Andy's job.

A rat ran out in front of him and scuttled over his boot, almost tripping him. Andy jumped sideways, trying to squash it, but it was too quick, ducking between the grates of a storm drain by the curb. He wondered what was going on, whether somebody had left food out somewhere that was drawing all the vermin from a ten-mile radius. Scratching noises made him look behind him again, and he saw three or four of them running, crowding one another, heading in his direction. As if responding to his gaze, they dispersed into shadows. He thought of that movie *Willard* he'd taken May to see at the drive-in. He'd read somewhere that they'd had to cover the actors in peanut butter to make the rats swarm like that. Otherwise, rats might attack a baby, but they wouldn't go after a full-grown man.

Andy's steps grew faster, and he wondered, even though it was ridiculous, whether it would take longer to go back to the station or just head home. He could abandon Main Street, duck down an alley, and trim five minutes from the walk. Of course, the lights on

Main Street let him keep an eye on the rats, but then again, seeing them was the problem. It's not like they were really after him, stalking him, gaining numbers as they wove in and out of shadows, tracking him – ridiculous.

He turned into an alley, approached a dumpster. Getting closer, he heard noises, something pounding on a steel drum, claws scratching on a sheet of metal, rats making their way out of the receptacle. Starlight let him see only a few feet in front of him, so he couldn't be sure there were rats running around the edges of the dumpster, but he gave the giant receptacle a wide berth, almost pressing himself against the brick wall opposite. When he emerged on the other side of the alley, with a view of trees and grass and a block of homes, he took a deep breath, feeling relieved, feeling silly.

The sensation on the back of his neck was constant now, but he kept one hand on his gun and the other free, dangling by his side, clenching and unclenching, assuring him that he, the sheriff, a grown man, was not scared of the dark, not scared of rats, and not scared of rats in the dark. His boots left imprints on grass as he made his way into a cluster of trees. Home was a straight shot from here, a few minutes more, tops.

Straw and fallen leaves covered the ground between trees. Every footfall crunched, and the turf seemed slippery. A step landed on a long, rotten branch, and as one end of it went down beneath Andy's weight, the other end launched into the air with an explosive sound like an animal leaping. The gun came out of its holster, steady in Andy's hand, aiming. Enough light made it through half-naked treetops to show him the dead wood sinking as he lifted his foot from the branch. He re-holstered the revolver, cursing himself, hoping to God that the feeling of being watched didn't mean some kids were out there following him and playing tricks. No, that was stupid, too. Nobody was out there. He was just an old man with an overactive imagination.

All the same, he was willing to take the shortest route out of this patch of trees. It'd cost him a few extra seconds of walking, but he wanted the full starlight back, wanted a larger radius of sight around him. The leaves and bark were full of sounds, shifting, crunching, writhing with life, and why wouldn't there be rats running around the roots of the trees? He sensed them everywhere. That the noises seemed to be concentrated behind him didn't matter. He was clearing the trees now, and in a moment, he would be home.

A streetlight shone in a cul-de-sac up ahead, and he moved toward it. He could stop there, look around him, get his head together, figure out whether he needed to go in for a psych evaluation. The urge to get home faster by abandoning all reason and sprinting couldn't bode well for his state of mind. He could lean against the lamppost, take a deep breath, and see for himself that nothing was following him.

He reached the streetlight. He leaned; he breathed. Figuring that the sound of his own voice might break the spell of nighttime silence and rustling leaves, he said, "Get it together, Andy," loud enough to test his vocal chords, quiet enough to be insensible to the sleepers in nearby houses.

The streetlight cast a cone of yellow down at the asphalt. Into the circle of light, a rat scurried and stopped. It looked at him, stood on its rear legs, and screeched. Another rat joined it, and another. When a wave of them broke into the light, Andy started to run.

He wouldn't start screaming, shooting, banging on doors and yelling for help. There was a pretty decent chance he was hallucinating all of this, in need of serious medical attention, and he didn't need to bother his neighbors with that. He'd just run at top speed, thanking God for the treadmill he used in his basement, and get home, and lock his front door, and hold his gun, and watch, and wait until everything seemed all right, and then he'd go to sleep and call a doctor in the morning.

The sounds of his boot heels on the street were loud, but not as loud as the squeaking wave that followed him. He didn't need to turn to get an image of the herd of small black and brown bodies, racing each other, toppling over each other, encroaching, tracing an impossibly precise path behind him. While one part of his mind struggled to convince him that he was insane, the other part, the dominant part, assured him that he was running for his life, that if he tripped on that curb, or slipped on the grass, and fell face-first into the dirt, they would be on top of him before he could stand, and if the weight of the creatures didn't hold him down, the piercing of their teeth would.

His house was in sight. He would have to slow down to shove a hand into his pocket and pull out his keys, but he didn't, couldn't, because they were right behind him. Boots banged on his driveway and found purchase in grass as he skipped the paved walkway to the front door and took a straight line, leaping over the three front steps, crashing into the door, not looking behind him as a hand finally pushed into his pocket. He heard his own voice saying "Come on, come on!" when the keys jangled into freedom, and he imagined dropping them, leaning over to pick them up, and dying. He didn't drop them; he found the right key. It was in the lock and turning when he felt the claws tugging on his pants leg, the rats starting to scale him.

He shook one leg, then another, unable to keep from seeing the diminutive army that had taken over his porch and surrounded him. When the clinging bodies broke loose from his pants and flew back into the multitudes, he withdrew the key and turned the knob at once. He lurched through the doorway and slammed the heavy door behind him. The door bounced back from a body it had crushed. He slammed again, crushed another, slammed again, another. Screeching rats piled at the door. His full body weight forced the door back into its frame, grinding dead rats into pulp. He turned the bolt and stepped back, looking left and right at the few animals that had made it inside. They held their positions, as if waiting for reinforcement.

Stomping on anything in range, he began a circuit of the house, hunting for the windows he had left open so the house would absorb the clean autumn air. A quick rodent was already breaching the windowsill nearest the front door when the slamming window decapitated it. Panes shook, and Andy considered that he had to be careful. If the glass broke, the window would be useless as a defense.

Slam, lock, slam, lock – he secured the house, staying ahead of the bulk of the army that his boots would be powerless to overcome. His heart pounded in his chest, and blood throbbed in his head. It was unbelievable, it was madness, but it was happening, and real or imaginary, the force gathering against his house could kill him. He had no choice. He had to call for help.

Randolph was barking somewhere upstairs, confirming that the attack against their house was not a figment of Andy's imagination. He wanted to run to him, to pick him up and keep him safe from the rats, but the phone was closer, and the phone was crucial. He ran for the kitchen, for the phone mounted next to the refrigerator, and remembered the pet door that led out to the carport.

The bright kitchen light revealed dozens squeezing through the rubber-covered opening. They formed a puddle and then a pool of rodent bodies on the floor. A pain shot through Andy's left arm, and he stumbled back. Once their mass was greater than a human's, the rats surged in his direction. Andy turned to run again, to head for the stairs, to barricade himself and his dog in the bedroom, and without thinking, he stopped, his right hand clutching his chest.

He collapsed face-first in the hall. Barking drowned in squeaking as the feet marched along his body. He felt a distinct bite, and then another, and then another, and then the pain of iron-sharp teeth cutting through cloth and skin became amorphous. He started to crawl, but the rats circled around him, cutting him off. One ran on top of his hand and bit down, ripping flesh. Straining against the pain in his chest, he raised his hands to his face, trying to protect his eyes.

"Keep watching," Jake said. "Follow his thoughts down into death. You'll find the experience... illuminating."

Mike did as he was told.

"You remember the Pied Piper of Hamelin. There is a kernel of truth in every story. First he came for the rats, and then he came for the children. You see, power only comes to you in increments. First, you control the armies of the earth. Then you control the armies of men. If you really want your own power to be like mine, then you will have to work for it. You will have to sacrifice."

Andy let out a scream, and the agony turned into words: "WHO ARE YOU?!!!"

"He can hear you?" Mike asked.

Jake nodded. "And you. I'm letting him see us, standing in front of him, watching him die." Jake's projection knelt in front of the dying man, whose arms were almost too weak to keep the hands over his eyes. "Sheriff Hadderly will conclude that you died from the heart attack. The rats were just a gory sequel. It's better this way, don't you think?"

Andy neither agreed nor disagreed. He was too weak; too much muscle was gone. He let the army have his eyes, and it was over.

18

Chirping birds and bright sunlight: morning, Saturday. The sheet and blanket felt heavy against her bare skin. Summoning willpower, she flipped onto her side and looked at the clock. 8:19. Now that teenagerism had him in its grasp, Brian slept until noon whenever possible, but Fran would be awake. Fran was old enough to help herself to a bowl of cereal, but she wouldn't. She'd sit in front of the TV by herself, hungry and lonely. Still reluctant but more motivated, Linda McCullough sat up and stretched into the day.

Her bare breasts, which still had faint tan lines, caught the glare of the November morning. She wasn't self-conscious about them; her mind didn't explain why she had chosen to sleep in the nude. Any onlooker could have devoured her with his eyes, the shape of her torso, the curves of her thighs as she swung them around the bedside. But she had no reason to suspect any onlookers.

On the other side of the bed, Matt looked comatose. She had felt him getting up in the middle of the night, but she had been asleep whenever he'd returned. He must have had another bad night. She wouldn't wake him. Standing, she spotted her bathrobe hanging from the hook on the bathroom door. As Linda reached for the pink terrycloth with her right hand, her left stretched to scratch the back of her neck. The itch traveled down her shoulder, and her fingernails followed it.

Something felt funny, so she stopped and brought her left hand toward her face. The tips of two fingers were red. Her first thought was blood. She didn't feel any pain, so her mind went to the bed next, hoping she hadn't scratched an insect bite and stained the sheets. She turned and looked: bright red smudges where she had slept. But the red was *too* red to be blood. It was pinkish, artificial. She raised her fingers to her nose, sniffed, and rubbed the messy fingertips against clean ones. A new hypothesis: lipstick. How had she gotten lipstick on her back?

She rushed to the bathroom, stood before the mirror, and twisted, trying to see her back. On the visible section of skin, blurred but legible, she saw writing. She yanked her handheld mirror out from under miscellaneous lotions and grooming supplies. The clatter might have awoken Matt, but at this point she didn't care. Twisting and angling with the two mirrors let her make out the message. The lipstick-writing was shaky, and the diction was that of a thirteen-year-old carving on a tree, "MATT + ALICE 4EVR." Bewildered, frightened, and a little bit amused, she tried to settle on a reaction. Anger took hold, and she raced for Matt's side of the bed. She shook him, insisting but not shouting, "Matt, Matt!"

The heavy body moaned and shifted, but his eyes didn't open.

"Wake up goddamn it and look at this!" Now her voice was louder, and she worried about summoning the kids. Her thoughts flashed back to her bathrobe, revealing that she had at least some sense of decency.

Her husband's eyes flickered open, and his head rose inches from the pillow. Squinting, he said, "What?" He sat up further, shook his head, and said, "What time is it? Good morning."

Linda did an about-face. Her buttocks hovered at the level of Matt's gaze. "What the hell is this?!" she demanded.

"My wife's beautiful behind." He kissed it.

Annoyed, she looked over her shoulder. "Look higher."

Matt's squint became more intent, struggling to discern shapes in the sunlight. When the message became clear, he leapt to his feet, grabbed his wife's shoulders, reread, and said "What the fuck!"

Linda shook off his hands, turned, and said, "That was my question. Who the hell is Alice?"

Matt's legs folded, seating him on the edge of the bed. His eyes were wide and stunned. His mind was a maze, a million thoughts, too many to sift. "Alice," he said. "Alice."

"Yes, Alice!" Her mind was racing, too, but entwined thoughts, about not wanting to involve the kids and about being too righteously indignant to care, broke through.

"Alice. Alice Granger."

"So she's a real person." Linda's chest rose and fell with quickening breath. "She has a last name."

"She works at the drug store. Where the shooting. Was."

Linda sat beside her husband. "I remember. The photo developer. The one who freaked out and almost kept you from saving that man's life."

"Yes, no, I mean, it wasn't like that. She was just... scared."

Linda stared ahead, toward one of the windows with the Venetian blinds that were powerless against the morning glow. "You're sleeping with her."

Matt nodded.

She stood again, spun on the carpet, and slapped his face as hard as she could. "And you decided to fucking tell me by writing on my fucking back with *lipstick*!!!!"

"What? No!" He stood to face his wife, one hand cradling his smacked cheek.

Her hands reached behind her, pressing, pulling, smearing. She put red-coated fingers in front of her husband's face. "Then who did this, huh?" Frustrated, her stained fists fell to her sides, and she marched toward the bathroom. She yanked a washcloth from the towel rack, shoved it in the sink, and began to soak it with warm water and soap.

Matt stayed close. "I," he said. "I, um, I don't remember."

Linda focused on the work she was doing in the sink but glanced in the mirror at Matt, who was standing behind her. Anger receded into fear and bewilderment. Concern etched lines around the corners of her mouth. "If you say you don't remember, then you think it might have been you." Her hands abandoned the soapy washcloth, letting it stopper the sink as she turned off the water.

Matt took a step backward, as if pushed, and stumbled into the vanity chair. His face fell into his hands. "Something... something like this happened before."

He told her about waking in the middle of the night and finding the writing on his fingers, chest, forehead, and penis. He told her that he didn't love Alice, but he did love her, and the affair with Alice was just a form of comfort, more for Alice than for him. And Linda believed him! The stupid bitch sat there listening, crying, nodding, saying how worried she was about their marriage, how she was even more worried about what his "somnambulist" activities could mean about his state of mind. She knew their sex life wasn't what it once was – God knew she had thought more than once about going to bed with another man – but she believed, if they started being honest with each other, they could work through their problems.

Mike was bored after an hour of such drivel, but he felt like he had to keep watching, even though he was pretty sure that the conclusion he wanted wasn't going to come. When the bedroom door opened without a knock, and the little girl wandered in, asking if Mommy and Daddy were coming to breakfast, she walked all the way up to her weeping, naked parents, and accepted the group embrace they offered. It was obscene.

Later, after listening to the tale, Jake said, "Well, I must admit that I didn't see that coming. I thought she'd try to have him committed." He chuckled.

"So what do we do?" Mike asked.

"Your call." Jake took off his golfer's hat and spun it on his finger, watching the plaid whirls. "It's your project. We've got to keep the pressure on, though."

"Why?" Sara asked. "What's so important about the McCulloughs?"

Jake shrugged. "I just have a feeling that they'll be important for us, the boy especially."

For the first time, Mike seriously considered that Jake might be able to see the future.

"That's flattering," Jake said. "Do you want my advice?"

Mike hesitated, and Sara said, "Yes."

"Word needs to get out about those two. Mike isn't the only person in Kenning who might find the McCulloughs' godlessness obscene."

19

Mike and Sara sat on their swing, and Jake stood nearby, surveying the remnants of the flowerbed. "Have you finished all your planting?"

"I think so," Sara said. "We've been... distracted."

Jake nodded. "And what do you find most distracting?" He laced his hands behind his back and faced them, becoming the top point of an isosceles.

Sara put her arm around Mike, who didn't withdraw. "I don't know," she said. "I keep thinking it might not be all that bad."

Jake removed his hat and started twirling. "Oh? And what is 'it?'"

Sara looked at Mike first, then Jake. "An open marriage, you know, the McCulloughs' solution to the little problem we gave them." Her lips stretched skyward.

Jake twirled. Mike coughed. He didn't want to speak. He wanted Jake's reaction first. "It may be venial, but it's still a sin," Jake said.

Mike nodded. "And I wouldn't call it so venial. It's an affront to the very idea of marriage, which is a sacrament."

Sara sighed and removed her arm. "I suppose."

A long silence followed. Mike was about to stand when he heard the squeaking of hinges, the opening of the gate. "Someone's here."

Turning away, Jake stepped toward the fence and called out, "Sheriff!"

Mike and Sara stood. Their legs pushed against the swing, which rebounded and crashed against the backs of their knees. They looked at each other, sharing a silent "ow," and joined Jake at the end of the path lined with withered azaleas.

"Thought I might find you here," Glen said. He wore sunglasses and a shiny new badge.

Moving to the front, Mike said, "What can I do for you, Sheriff Hadderly?"

Glen cocked his head toward Jake. "I meant him."

Jake shifted the twirling hat from his right hand to his left without stopping the motion. Offering a handshake, he said, "Good to see you again, Sheriff. How you liking your new post?"

The look on Glen's face combined disgust and malice. He ignored the offered hand. "Be better if I didn't have so much paper work. There are a lot of unanswered questions. Especially about Andy. That's Sheriff Perkins that was." He nodded, indicating Sara as the intended recipient of exposition.

"Such a tragic loss," Sara said. "I'm just glad the town has someone like you to fill his place." She grinned, eyelashes fluttering.

"Indeed," Mike said. "You do our congregation and our whole town proud."

Glen spat in the half-dead grass. "Cut the bullshit, Reverend. Perhaps the missus would care to give us a moment alone?"

"The missus," Jake said, "has grown accustomed to our company."

"That's all right, Deacon," Sara said. "I'll just go back and wait on the swing." She'd be able to hear every word from that distance. Mike focused his thoughts on silent congratulation, and a look over her shoulder as she walked away suggested she might have received the message.

"Now then," Mike said. "You've taken a tone that suggests we're not friends anymore. Why is that?"

"Of course we're friends," said Jake. "Right, Sherriff?"

"Like I said, there are a lot of questions." Glen hooked his thumbs into his gun belt. "You know, we couldn't help that some of the, uh, details got out, but we managed to keep the nastier facts out of the papers."

"That was friendly." Jake's left hand continued the playful twirling.

Mike felt more severe. "It was nice of you to spare your former boss's memory from ugly sensationalism."

Glen paced. Mike and Jake followed him with swiveling heads, back and forth. "The paper said that neighbors found the body partially eaten by rodents. The truth is, the body was practically stripped."

"How horrible," Mike said. "How long had he been there?"

Glen paused, lowered his sunglasses, and brought his face within inches of Mike's. 'That's the real question. For that many rats to come by, it had to be days and days." Mike nodded. Jake's twirling continued, but his grin began to fade. "But the thing is, one of my deputies saw him less than twenty-four hours before he was found."

"*Your* deputies," Jake said.

Sneering, Glen moved his face in close range of Jake. "Yes, Mr. Warren, *my* deputies."

Jake's face fell into unfamiliar seriousness. "So do you have an explanation?"

Stepping closer to Jake but looking at Mike, Glen answered, "State forensics people said there were enough droppings at the scene for hundreds, maybe a thousand rats or more."

"You're standing very close to me," Jake said.

"I am." Glen took the sunglasses all the way off and dropped them. A cord let them hang around his neck. His face pressed toward Jake's, and then it pressed toward Mike's. "And you know what I'm thinking?"

"No," Mike said. "What are you thinking?"

"I'm thinking it's almost too strange to be real. And then I'm thinking about other things that are too strange to be real, and then I'm thinking about your little vigilante Bible squad."

"I'm thinking," Jake said, "that your thinking is curiously timed. Why didn't any of this come up *before* the election?"

A quick push made Jake stumble back, but he didn't fall, and the hat didn't stop twirling. "I wanted your help, but I didn't want Andy dead."

"Awfully convenient for you to decide that now," Jake said.

"Deacon," Mike said, "there's no reason to fuel the sheriff's suspicions." He tried to step between the other two men, but Glen moved to block. "Surely there's some way to talk this through." From the corner of his eye, Mike saw Sara stand from the swing. Her expression mirrored his feelings.

Glen and Jake stood two feet apart from one another, gazes locked. Jake raised his left hand, still twirling his hat, into the buffering space. He reopened his toothy grin and said, "I think you're in our debt, Sheriff, don't you?"

Glen slapped the hat off of Jake's finger. "Don't you act like you own *me*!"

Instead of disappearing, the grin got bigger, and Jake's eyes spread wide enough to show white expanses around dark irises. "I *do* own you." Jake looked maniacal. A breeze shook bare branches, and Mike felt a chill. He froze. Jake looked at him, looked at Glen, and said, "Now pick up my hat."

As Glen's left boot stomped on the hat and started grinding it in the dirt, his right arm shot outward, aiming for a shove against Jake's chest that would be harder than the last. The hand halted, hovered, palm inches away from its target. The gruff look of authority that Glen had been wearing held for a moment, his face a mask, and then his eyebrows stitched together, and his lips wrinkled, rippled, thinned, contorted, parted, and released a scream. He stumbled back, his left hand reaching for the right one but stopping inches away, repelled. The right hand remained as it had been, with wrist bent so that fingers were perpendicular to the arm, poised to shove. The scream continued, a howl of pain, and Mike watched as the fingers bent backward and cracked, first near the tip, then at the joint, then at the knuckle. The angle between hand and arm collapsed backward as the skin around shattered bone began to split and bleed.

Jake stepped forward, and Glen stumbled back. Alternating steps, advance and retreat, moved the locked pair toward Mike's house. Sara left the swing and rushed to Mike's side. They held each other and watched.

Without touching him, Jake slammed the sheriff into white wood siding. Glen didn't seem to notice the impact. His hand rolled backward up his arm, which snapped with each unnatural turn. The sound from his throat tapered to a gurgle, and tears spilled down his cheeks. Pressing so hard against the boards that his shirt ripped, Glen started to rise. His body slid upward along the wall until Mike could see the bottoms of his boots.

"Jake, the neighbors!" Sara shouted.

Glen fell, smacked against the ground, and curled into a fetal ball, centered on his ruined arm. Jake knelt beside him and said, "I own you."

The large policeman bawled.

"Repeat it," Jake said. "I own you."

"You own me."

"Good, we understand our relationship." He crossed to where his cap lay and retrieved it. "Another one ruined." He threw it down. "Perhaps I'll give them up."

Mike thought he should speak, but he had nothing to say. Sara looked into the distance, checking to see if neighbors were peering over the hedges to investigate the noise.

Jake returned to the reduced man, whose body quivered in the dirt. "When the pain subsides you'll think more about things that are too strange to be real. And you'll think about the power to make those things happen. Won't you?"

The quivering ball stayed silent.

"You'll think about that power, and you'll think that I have it, and you'll think that you want it. Isn't that right?"

Silence.

"Answer me!"

"Yes!"

"Good," Jake said. "You'll have it."

Mike cleared his throat. "Me too."

"What?"

Sara looked at him, a smile dawning. "Me too," Mike repeated. "It's time for me to have more. Tell me what I have to do. Tell me more about sacrifice."

20

On a cold Sunday in February, Fran McCullough stepped into the sanctuary of First Church, wearing a blue dress, black shoes, and high white socks. Mike saw her as soon as she crossed the threshold. She had gathered her shoulder-length hair into a ponytail, tied with a yellow ribbon. The hair was dark brown, a contrast with her absent brother's. Mike and Sara stood in their customary places up front, mingling as the congregation settled into pews. He was careful not to stare; he couldn't seem to take too much of an interest in an unknown child making her first visit to church.

Chad Sutton gave his mother a nudge and pointed to the solitary girl. Impressed by her son's concern, Cathy invited Fran to join her family in a pew near the front. Fran recognized Chad, but she sat by him anyway. Mike extended his hearing to catch what Grant Sutton whispered to his wife: "Isn't that *that couple's* daughter?"

Cathy whispered, "Yes, and now hush!" Mike looked at Jake, who sat near one of the side exits, and nodded.

The crowd was large, and the singing was joyful. Mike's sermon began with a joke about how the new year was already approaching middle age, and he mentioned that the new century, and the new millennium, were old news. He asked the congregation to think about all the things "new" could mean, and he told them that being saved was called being born again because being new, and child-like, is holy, for Jesus tells us to become as little children lest we be denied the kingdom of heaven.

Mike settled his eyes on Fran. "And after telling us to become as children, Jesus says, 'Wherefore if thy hand or thy foot offend thee, cut them off. And if thine eye offend thee, pluck it out.' For redemption, we might have to sacrifice the things closest to us, even parts of ourselves." Mike explained that leading oneself, and others, into suffering, and even into death, is the act that saves oneself, and one's loved ones, from an eternity of suffering in Hell.

"The righteous child," *like you, Franny*, "the Christian born and reborn," *like you*, "is the child who leads through love into sacrifice."

Fran stood and shouted, "Amen!"

21

As Fran waited for sleep, something Reverend Cox had said last Sunday came back to her: when you invite godlessness into your home, it's like letting demons through the front door. Demons. Her parents didn't believe in that sort of thing, and neither did Brian, but when the lights were out, it was hard not to think about what demons could look like. Were they red with pointed tails and pitchforks like in the cartoons? Or were they something worse?

The midsummer twilight became dimmer, and a gust of wind shook the house. Thunderstorms were in the forecast. Daddy said that was good because they needed rain. Brian said she was too old to be scared of lightning. So it would be good if there was rain and thunder and lightning and darkness and no way to see the closet and no way to know what a demon would look like if one was standing at the foot of the bed. Had she checked under the bed tonight? Brian used to do it for her, but he stopped because he said she needed to stop being afraid. She had nothing to be afraid of. If anything bad ever came, he would be there to protect her.

It was dark now. Mommy had gone out with a friend, so she wasn't home. Fran couldn't hear the TV, so Daddy was probably reading. Brian always had his door closed these days, and he wore his headphones when he played PlayStation. That was why it was so quiet. They hadn't really left her all alone.

Thunder rattled the house. When it stopped, she thought she heard a creak. The closet door would creak if it opened. Daddy had said he would use some WD-40 to make it stop, but Fran had said no, it was okay, not telling him that she liked the creak because it was like an alarm. So was that the closet door? Had the thunder shaken it open? It was so quiet except for the thunder. Fran decided to hum, picking up the tune for "I've Got the Joy In My Heart." Where? Down in my heart!

It was a catchy tune. It tended to stay in Mike's head for days.

Rain started beating on the window. Fran wanted a flash of lightning so she could see the closet door. If it was open, she'd get up and close it. If it was closed, everything was okay. A flash – she couldn't be sure, but she thought it was open.

Fran scooted to the edge of the bed and looked over. Through the darkness, she could make out the off-white carpet below. She couldn't see into the black beyond the dangling edge of her bedspread. It was silly, of course, to be afraid to put her feet on the ground next to that blackness, from which something could reach, grab, and pull. Mommy said all kids are afraid of monsters under the bed. She said it was almost funny how everybody could be afraid of the same thing, even when that thing wasn't real. Under the bed would be uncomfortable, she said, for any monster of size. And a little monster – who'd be worried about that?

The closet had plenty of room for a monster of size.

Her feet settled onto the carpet, and she took quick steps away from the black beneath the bed. Closer, she could see that the closet door was open. She *knew* she had closed it all the way, but the doorknob stuck sometimes, so maybe the thunder really had shaken it loose. Brian wouldn't think much of her if he knew she was standing in the dark, too scared to go close the closet door. And if she went over to the closet, well, she could just turn on the closet light, which would let her confirm that no monsters of size were lurking inside, and if she left the closet light on, she'd have less to worry about. When Daddy went to bed, he'd come in and turn the light off because he always did, but if she was asleep by then, that would be okay. So she'd just go turn on the closet light, and things would be fine.

She walked on tiptoe, not wanting the floorboards to creak and let Daddy or anyone know she was up. The open closet door was between her and the closet itself, so when she got closer, she couldn't see inside at all. If she wanted to turn on the light, she'd have to go around the door, and then she'd be standing in front of whatever was there.

She was brave! She would do it!

Mike considered the virtues of cowardice.

The door creaked as she opened it further. She stayed on tiptoe, until she faced the dark inside the closet, which, as far as she could see, was vacant. She couldn't see all the way into the back, though. She couldn't see if something was hiding between the hanging dresses. She reached up for the string connected to the ceiling bulb.

New light revealed exactly what she expected: nothing. Feeling at once brave and silly for going to all this trouble, she turned around to go back to bed. On the carpet, on the side of the bed where she had gotten out, she saw a hand, or a claw, attached to a wrist that vanished back into the black.

She took a step back into the closet, reached up, and turned out the light. Her eyes were playing tricks on her. There was nothing there. When she turned on the light again, she would see that nothing was there.

She turned on the light. A second claw had joined the first, and they had come further out of the black. She saw arms now, and they were pulling at the carpet, dragging a head, round, bald, misshapen, behind them. When the shoulders appeared, Fran ran into the hall.

Brian's door was closed, so she banged on it. No answer, so she tried the knob. Locked. She looked back toward her own door – nothing yet. Was she imagining it? She'd get Daddy.

The first few stairs were behind her when she stopped, looked back, returned to the top, and flipped the light switch. The stairway and the hall were bright. Between her and her bedroom door, she saw nothing, no demon, no clawed thing with a misshapen head. She'd get Daddy anyway.

She paced herself on the stairs, not wanting to seem panicked, not wanting to look as silly as she was. She expected to find Daddy in the living room, sitting in his chair with a book in his lap. No one. She looked in the dining room, and she walked by the bathroom, which was open and empty. Her heartbeat was hard but she still wouldn't run or scream, because she could look in the kitchen, and there he'd be.

He was. He sat at the small table. The oven light was the only one on in the room. "Daddy?" she said.

He didn't respond. He was looking at a piece of paper on the table. In his hand, he held a slender steak knife.

"Daddy?" Fran got closer, close enough to touch his shoulder, trying for his attention.

Daddy stuck the tip of the knife into his forearm, and when he pulled it out, blood pooled. He used it like ink to write on the piece of paper. Fran stood frozen, watching as the knife sketched out the lines and curves of each letter, "S-I-N-N-E-R." Through it all, he never looked at her.

"Marvelous!" Jake cried. "Mike, you've really outdone yourself."

Fran didn't hear Jake's voice. She screamed "Daddy!" and hugged herself, backing away from the deranged man.

Lightning flashed, and Fran looked behind her. There stood the creature from beneath the bed, clawed hands loose at its sides, with its distorted, bare skull, covered in bluish flesh, and it was hunched, naked, and looking at her, lips peeled back from sharp teeth, taking one step, and another, toward her.

Fran screamed and ran for the front door. She had to jump to undo the chain, and as she turned the lock on the knob, she said, "Dear God, please don't let the deadbolt be locked!"

Jake answered her prayer, throwing the bolt. Mike applauded.

Awe halted her for a moment, but when the Bed-Thing appeared at the edge of her vision, she threw open the door and ran down the driveway, down the street, into the rain. In seconds, her pajamas were soaked, but she didn't stop until she turned a corner. She looked behind her.

The figure was small in the distance, seeming to walk, but as she faced it, it met her searching eyes and doubled its speed. She turned to run again and heard a smashing sound in a tree up ahead. The tree was near a streetlight, which let her see, high above, clinging to a branch, the Bed-Thing, gazing down at her. She turned to run in the other direction, back toward her house, and she heard the cracking of wood, a sound like a giant bird leaping from a perch into flight.

She sensed the Bed-Thing soaring over her head, and she saw it land in front of her, knees bent, feet arched like talons, claws ready. Fran screamed, took a backward step, slipped, and fell on the street.

Near her head, rubber screeched against asphalt. A long car, its headlights piercing through the rain, stopped, and a door opened. "Get in!" a voice cried. She recognized it. It was Reverend Cox! Beside him, driving, she recognized another man from church. He had silver hair and glasses and always smiled. Reverend Cox reached out for her, and when she took his hand, he pulled her into the car and slammed the door in a single, smooth gesture.

As they sped away, she turned to look at the monstrous form receding in the distance. "A demon!" she yelled to her saviors.

"I know," the Reverend said, "I know. I'll take you where it's safe. In the church. There's a room in the basement where you'll be safe."

22

Sara left the basement before the first shot fired. Mike and Jake stayed, watching what Jake referred to as a false start, "the catalyst of the long beginning."

The Room had taken Fran's eyes and ears, so controlling her required little concentration. Mike could issue commands while dipping in and out of Fran's thoughts. Even at ten, Fran lacked firm conceptions of death and murder. The significance of her action did not register when the bullet pierced her mother's breast or when her mother, after stumbling back, fell forward. She started to understand when she observed her mother's pain, the sight of her struggling to turn over and the sound of her labored breathing. The girl's compromised senses triggered a cascade of thoughts that washed Mike out of her mind.

Fran stood still, the Glock clenched in her fingers. Mike asked Jake why he couldn't follow her thoughts anymore, and Jake told him not to worry because, even if her mind was closed to him, her behavior was open. Her body belonged to them, tied to their wills by a thousand invisible puppet strings.

Matt McCullough arrived. To save time, Jake had Fran call for him. McCullough stopped near the bottom of the stairs, catching sight of his dead wife. Jake ordered Fran to shoot, but her finger did not squeeze the trigger. A white light appeared behind Fran's father. McCullough didn't see it, but Fran's eyeless face turned toward it, and she saw her mother, clad in the white robes of an angel. The angel told Fran to release her daddy. Seeing that his daughter gazed behind him, not at him, McCullough turned around. She shot him in the back.

Afterward, as they waited upstairs in Fran's bedroom, Mike asked Jake why the girl had to die, too. Weren't the deaths of the parents enough? Might the impact of Fran's survival be even worse for her brother, who would have to take care of her?

Jake said Fran had to die. If she lived, the town would have the luxury of a perpetrator, an empty girl whose obvious insanity would make the tragedy more comprehensible in human terms. Fran's death would make her a victim, turning the cause of the tragedy into an abstraction. Abstraction could motivate the multitudes; humanity would not.

Mike heard hurried footfalls on the stairs. When Brian appeared in the doorway, Mike and Jake turned to look at him, but Fran didn't register his presence. Brian walked toward the girl. The boy stood in front of his sister, hypnotized by the gun and the blood. Jake told her to shoot herself. She was about to comply when Mike told her to halt.

Taking inspiration from what Jake had conjured downstairs, Mike summoned images, the parents, glowing white, behind each shoulder of the shellshocked brother. They called to Fran, welcoming her into heaven.

As far as Mike knew, Brian never told anyone that his sister smiled before she shot herself.

23

Power comes from sacrifice. To be reborn, you have to die.

Mike had helped Sara and Jake dig up the lilies. Now, the bulbs waited, exposed, sitting in a line at the garden's edge. If the delay between the uprooting and the replanting was too long, some of the lilies would die. "Quit complaining," Jake had said. "This is a day of sacrifices." He had grinned, showing teeth.

Sara and Jake shoveled dirt into the deep hole. They moved in rhythm, driving their blades in and heaving the soil back into its place of origin. The clattering of the dirt as it landed was like rain beating at a window. The sounds of the shovels reminded Mike of the creaky springs of an old mattress, a slow bouncing beneath some perfunctory performance.

"Are you comfortable, Mike?" Jake asked. "I don't suppose you're unhappy to miss this sort of work."

The comment didn't deserve a response.

"I keep thinking," Sara said, "that someone is going to come by. That someone is going to trace the... incident... back to us."

"Nah," Jake said. "There's nothing to connect us to it, and even if there were, Sheriff Hadderly would take care of it. All the concerned citizens have their hands full anyway. This town is not equipped for an event of this magnitude. There'll be state police, maybe FBI, psychiatric professionals. And then there'll be reporters. It'll take a few days for them to conclude that Brian isn't responsible. Meanwhile, we'll have to make sure Kenning's more old-fashioned denizens don't form a lynch mob."

Sara shook her head. She shoveled faster.

The brown box in the hole wasn't a regular coffin. It was something they had fashioned themselves, following the prescriptions in one of Dr. Fincher's unpublished papers. Preparation of the wood had involved the same emphasis on body fluids that pervaded *The Alchemy of Will*. Blood and sweat, the stuff of sacrifice, had graced every board. Mike wondered if the scent of biological excrescence would attract insects and worms.

Even the tiniest creatures wouldn't be able to penetrate the container's interior, but they could surround it, forming a little bubble of life around the box of death.

Was it death? Or was it something else, a temporary redefinition of the soul's relationship with the body as it shifted from one life to another? Since he wasn't distracted by the labor of moving dirt, Mike had room to wax philosophical.

The rainstorm-sounds of dirt got softer. The diminishment racked Mike's nerves. Mike tried to concentrate on watching Jake and Sara, but focus was becoming more difficult.

"You went through this yourself?" Sara asked.

"I did," Jake said. "A long time ago." Speaking did not disrupt his rhythm or grin.

Sara paused, set the shovel aside, and wiped sweat from her brow. "How long ago?"

"Why Mrs. Cox," Jake said. "If I didn't know better, I'd think you were trying to pinpoint a gentleman's age."

"You don't know better. That's exactly what I'm trying to do." She leaned on her shovel's handle, making it a cane.

Jake laughed and halted. "I missed some of the best years of the Jazz Age. I didn't come back until October of 1929."

Sara took a deep breath. "So, assuming you were an adult—"

"I was."

"That would make you at least, what, 100?"

Jake resumed his work. Mike felt glad. During the moments when the only sounds were their voices, he became more aware of his body's surroundings. No light. The sensations of the walls around him, bracing his sides, lining his back, and hovering at his nose, would eventually subsume everything. For now, though, he was aware of the wood's scent, not the blood-smell or sweat-smell but the smell of cut lumber. The air brushing past his lips had a taste, too, a mingling of lumber with the dry, acidic flavor of hot air from inside a sealed car on a summer day. Darkness, touch, smell, and taste were all constants; only the noise was changing, the shoveling, the clattering, the voices. When those stopped, his world would become static, and he would be alone, and trapped.

It wouldn't take long. In a few hours, at most, he would lose the ability to bilocate, and he'd have a single reality, the stark enclosure of the box.

Buried alive.

It was the most heinous form of death that poets had ever conjured. Compared to Mike's fate, the suffering of that little girl was nothing. A bullet through the eye was instantaneous. And she had hardly known what was going on. Between her youth and the effects of the Room, the girl was practically under anesthesia. Mike would feel everything.

It might not work. Jake had said it might not. And if it didn't, he would simply die. Here. In a box. In a puddle of his own piss and shit. Unable to bend his knees, stretch his arms, or scream with the hope of anyone hearing him.

He groaned. The sound reverberated, making his skin tingle. He tried to focus on what was happening above him.

"No, no, not *that* old," Jake was saying. "You make it sound like I've been around for centuries. I was in college when Allen... well, died, I guess you'd call it."

Sara looked down at the hole they were filling. "Huh. I never thought dying was such a grey area."

"Really? You're a preacher's wife, aren't you?" The grin.

Dumping another shovelful of dirt onto her husband's coffin, Sara said, "Yes, but we're not a typical church couple."

"You'd be surprised," Jake said.

Jake was so smug. And to think he'd be alone with Sara for years, forever if Fincher's prescriptions didn't work. Mike wasn't concerned about Jake stealing his wife. Jake was – not exactly asexual – but beyond sex. Jake was beyond everything. And he and his beyond-ness would take care of Mike's wife, lounge in Mike's living room, run Mike's church, and lay roots deeper and deeper into Mike's town. And Mike would be here. In the box. With the wood scent and stale taste and the boards pushing—

A cramp seized his arm, and Mike bent his elbow to ease it. The move scraped his knuckles against wood. He lost all sense of the world above, lost everything but the box. The pain in his arm was sharp, and Mike realized that his other muscles might soon follow the arm's example, sending him desperate messages of the need to stretch, to twist, to shift, to step, to spread out and wriggle and writhe and reach and roll and RUN. He would need to curl, to straighten, to give the muscles the full range of their capability or they would rebel, screaming, squeezing his nerves into cobwebs of agony until, releasing, they began to atrophy, leaving him a skeleton bandaged in threads of useless tissue, leaving him, alive or dead, a frozen pile of cells held in place by the memory of hurt.

He had to stop thinking like this. He had to focus on the moment, to keep his mind together so he could sustain his ability to leave the box for as long as possible. There would be enough space to move his arm, to relieve the cramp, if he slid the arm up along the box's side and then slipped it between his chest and the lid. He made the move and shook his arm until the cramp subsided. Better! His hand came to rest on his belly, which swelled with breath until hand-skin touched wood. His jaw dropped in an involuntary gasp.

He shook off the temptation to surrender to sobs. He would reach out with his mind, project himself to the ground above. He heard before he saw, Sara, speaking of him. "Do you know if he's still listening? Still watching us?"

Jake looked around. His eyes didn't land on the exact spot where Mike settled his projection, but it studied the general area. "He's fading, but he's still with us. He'll come and go for awhile."

"Can you communicate with him?"

"Probably, as long as he maintains the serenity to articulate and process thought. Which might not be very long." Jake was teasing him. Mike wanted to snatch the shovel from his hands and whack him on the head, but he couldn't. He didn't have that kind of power, not yet. That's why he was doing this, taking this risk. When, if, he came back, Jake wouldn't be so far *beyond* anymore.

"And I'll be able to communicate with him?" Sara's concern seemed genuine.

"Not at first. For awhile, he'll just observe. And then, when he gets stronger, he'll develop the ability to interact. You'll be like a dutiful wife visiting her husband's grave, talking to his tombstone, and then one day, he'll talk back."

"That would be sweet," Sara said, "if it wasn't so morbid."

Jake nodded.

Sara looked at the ground. "We should stop now. The bulbs need to go back in with about six inches of dirt on top of them."

Jake stopped and tossed the shovel aside. "Yes, I remember. Mike's instructions were very clear. But the bulbs can wait a little, can't they?"

Sara shrugged. "I guess."

No!

"What do you say we take a break," Jake said. "I'm exhausted."

"Sure," Sara said. "Can I get you something to drink?"

"What have you got?"

"There's a nice chardonnay in the fridge," Sara said.

No!

"Sounds lovely!"

No, no, no, NO! Mike's projection stood on the path, trying to block his wife's progress to the kitchen. She passed through him, and he dissolved. He was in the box and nowhere else. "NO!" he cried aloud.

The reverberations registered along every inch of exposed skin. "NO!" he shouted again. He freed his fists and banged against the lid. The first hits were frustration. The solid wood did not yield. The next hits confirmed the findings of the first: he was powerless against the wood. The hits that followed had no purpose. In their tiny space, arms and legs thrashed against wood bindings. The certainty that he was going to suffer and die, having nothing to show for his sacrifice, bled into inarticulate panic, and his whole body erupted in seizure, trying to expand, to burst the boundaries of the box.

Above, there was a sound: the clinking of glasses. And then Mike heard nothing beyond his own screams.

24

Fear of death became longing to die, and longing to die became desperation for life. Desperation gave way to new faith. Without thinking and without ceasing, Mike chanted the words Jake had drilled into memory. His lips continued to shape syllables even after thirst rendered his throat incapable of noise. He was not aware of the moment when the wood walls around him disintegrated into infinite dark.

Time became passageless, and Mike saw a circle. At first the circle was continuous, black and geometric against a white background, but as light around the circle became finer, the space outside and within the circle shaded to blue. The circle itself lost continuity, resolving into separate points, each of which had shape and depth – and hair. He was looking at the tops of people's heads, flanked by shoulders, which hunched over laps, which supported open books. The books were Bibles. The blueness surrounding the circle of Christians was carpet.

A woman's voice: "And what does Paul mean when he writes, 'the letter kills, but the spirit gives life?'"

Mike recognized the speaker: Jeanne Harper. Short brownish hair made her thin face look long, and lines around her eyes suggested age, compassion, and wisdom. Eight people comprised her circle, a Bible study. Mike recognized Kyle Amory and the elder of the two Grayson girls. Struggling to put names to faces, Mike became aware of something closer to him than the circle below: a chandelier. His vantage was from the ceiling of a very nice room.

Memories rushed back, screaming, banging against wood, praying for death, praying for life, simply praying. Something had happened; he had gotten out. He was projecting himself again, and he had ended up here.

"It means we shouldn't get so carried away with what the Bible says that we forget what it all means," answered a woman. Angela. Angela something-or-other. She had long stringy blonde hair and lips that seemed to sneer as she spoke.

"I think so, too," Jeanne said. "I think it's about what it means to be a true Christian ministry, something some of you have worried about since Reverend Simmons took over at First Church. We go to church to hear the word of God, but more importantly, we go to feel the spirit. Why do you think the spirit and the word come into conflict?"

Jeanne directed the question at the entire circle, signaling for contemplation, but Angela, scooting to the edge of her chair, seized attention: "They come into conflict when pig-headed assholes like Michael Cox and Blake Simmons get so carried away with preaching traditional morality that they can't see the harm they're causing! I mean, what's it going to take, another little girl with a gun to get people to do something about what's going on in this town?"

The circle reacted to Angela's profane outburst with gasps and bowed heads. "Hush, woman," one of the men said. "Show some respect."

"Respect?" Angela stood up. "How is it respectful to stay quiet? It's been over a year since the McCullough Tragedy. We need to do something!" She looked around at the circle, which remained quiet. "What's *wrong* with you people?"

"Now Angela," Jeanne said without a hint of irritation, "I know how you feel. I admire your passion. But I don't entirely agree. When I go to First Church on Sundays, I still feel the spirit of God. It comes from all of you. It comes from the believers, not the preachers."

Angela huffed. "Okay, but if the preachers are trying to kill the spirit with their letters, isn't it time to do something?"

Mike willed himself away from the ceiling. He wanted to study the faces more closely and learn whether others had come to see him as a "pig-headed asshole" during his absence. The ceiling receded, and his projection started to take shape – an image of himself, as he had been, before. Creating such an image had once required intense concentration. Now, he felt at ease. He felt control.

He stood behind Jeanne, facing Angela. His hands hovered around Jeanne's neck, and he decided to let a finger brush against her skin. Her spine straightened, thrusting shoulders through his hands. He felt his projection waver, but he maintained his position.

Jeanne stood, and Mike stepped back. The leader stepped into the circle's center and offered distraught Angela a hand. "What would you have us do?"

Angela looked at the other six people before accepting Jeanne's calming grip. "We could start our own church," she said, her voice softer.

"Maybe." Jeanne didn't release Angela's hand as she addressed the whole group. "But I'm not convinced we can't keep reaching people and feeling the spirit as we are, here, in our own way, and at First Church, with a thousand other good people."

Angela returned to her seat. She smiled, making her curled lips seem sincere. Mike stepped closer, examining the woman's face. In contrast to Jeanne's, Angela's long hair made her face look round, and her fair skin made her blue eyes bright. The eyes had something in them, something that Mike couldn't place. The lips stretched out further, pulling away from teeth, showing sparkling white. Mike recognized the force behind the eyes.

Hello, Mike! Jake's voice called from within the woman's head. *Wonderful to see you again!*

25

"Your lilies are doing better than ever," Sara said. The drink in her hand looked like a Coke, but Mike knew about the rum. It was 10:17a.m. "Is it irritating that they've been better off without you?"

She sat on the swing. The sky was whitish-grey, threatening storm. "I wonder if you're listening today. I like it when you answer." She took a deep breath. "Then again, sometimes I like it when you don't." She drank. "Maybe you're here, and maybe you're hovering in some teenage girl's shower. It's fun to speculate." She sighed. "Yep." She drank.

The gate creaked, announcing the arrival that Mike had anticipated. As the first drops of rain spattered the grass, Glen Hadderly walked toward Sara.

"Morning, Sheriff," Sara said. "Jake's not here."

"I know," Glen said. "Just saw him over on Main Street."

Sara lifted her feet into the air, ankles together, making the swing sway. Raindrops splotched her calves. "So Sheriff, how can I help you?"

Glen put his hands on his hips, and then he rested his chin on a fist. He was trying to draw attention to his gloves.

"Are those driving gloves?" Sara asked. "It's a little warm for anything else."

"Necessary," Glen said. He moved forward, stilled the swing, and sat in the gap at Sara's side. His hands spread out on his lap, fingers stretching the gloves' black leather. Sara didn't notice the points at the fingertips that Glen was trying to accentuate. She scooted closer to the swing's armrest. When the added distance became noticeable, Glen inched until their sides touched. "You like them?"

"No." Sara stood. "They're tacky." She took three steps away from the swing and spun to look at him, sloshing her drink. Rain fell faster. "What do you want?"

Glen tugged at the fingers of the glove on his right hand as he stood. The glove was off by the time he had closed to whisper range: "I wanted you to see what your buddy Jake's been doing to me." He waved sharp, clawed fingers in front of Sara's nose. "You like?"

Sara turned her head away. "I prefer the gloves." The look of repulsion on her face didn't mask her fear. Mike watched with interest.

"You know," Glen said, "these new fingers of mine haven't touched anyone yet. I've hardly touched anyone at all since Jake rebuilt my arm."

Sandals squelched in mud as Sara stepped away along the azalea-lined path. Water made her blouse cling to her breasts. She didn't seem uncomfortable with the wet clothes: she focused on Glen, on getting away without ceding control. "So what are you here for? To get me alone with your brand-new hands? To avenge what happened to your arm?"

Glen bowed his head and flashed an aw-shucks grin. "No ma'am. That was a long time ago. Things have gotten better for me since."

He glanced at the ground, and for the first time, Sara noticed his bare feet. Like his fingers, the toes ended in sharp points. High arches linked them to the heels. Bones and tendons stood out under thin flesh. Mike had warned Jake about giving too much to Glen too soon, but Jake had told him not to worry.

"Things," Sara said. "Better things. Right. Well, I hope you'll excuse me, but standing in the rain seems kind of pointless."

He put a hand on her shoulder, and she dropped her drink. He gazed at her chest, where nipples coaxed by rainwater stood out beneath clinging fabric. "How long has it been? Three years since Mike, er, left? Must get lonely."

Sara brushed away his hand. "You must be the stupidest man alive, if you think you can come here and... do this. It can be a lot worse than your arm. Trust me. Mike can do worse. Jake can do worse."

Both of his hands took shoulders. "Mike's not here," Glen said. "And Jake's not here." He pressed himself against her. "I'm not going to give you a bad time." He whispered in her ear, "I just want to make sure you know Mike and Jake aren't the only boys in the club anymore."

"Mike!" Sara called. "Are you watching any of this?"

Glen laughed. Sara wriggled her shoulders away from his hands, but sharp fingers pressed against her back before she could turn toward the house. Her flattened hands slid from Glen's stomach to his chest, distracting him, and, summoning will, she shoved with a force beyond muscle.

The sheriff's backside slammed into mud. Sara stood over him in triumph, preparing a speech, when he leapt to his feet with a single, quick movement. Before she could react, his hands were on her again, clawed fingers piercing her blouse while they pulled her in. Her second will-assisted shove was ineffective: he had her.

"Isn't that one of the perks of your little Bible squad? Mike gets you, Jake gets you—"

"Jake never!"

He ignored her. "Jake gets you, I get you. Right? I don't mind that there's a pecking order, as long as I get to do some pecking." As he congratulated himself on the pun with a snicker, Sara smiled. "There you go!" he said. "I knew you'd come around." Sara licked the rainwater from her lips, tilted her head forward, and gave him a soft kiss. When she pulled away, her gaze went to the space above one of Glen's shoulders. He noticed the shift in her attention, released her, and turned.

A punch connected with Glen's jaw, and the blow's force pushed him toward Sara, who stepped aside to avoid being knocked down. Struggling for balance, Glen planted a foot on the glass Sara had dropped. The glass broke, and the foot rested on shards while Glen searched for his attacker. Except for the rain, the garden was still and silent. He turned to Sara, who backed toward the house.

The second strike landed on Glen's stomach, making him double over and cough. He searched the area in front of him, the area around Sara and the porch and the house, and saw no one. He called out, "I wasn't doing anything, Jake! *She* kissed *me!*"

Another blow struck Glen's chest, and he stumbled away from its invisible source, clawed hands ripping at air. "You stop! Just stop! I only wanted to talk to her, to find out—"

Another to the stomach, and before he could lean in, a slam to the nose, which burst with blood. Rain washed the red from Glen's face in rivulets. Gasping, panting, Glen yelled, "Sara, tell him to stop!"

Sara halted her own retreat and shrugged.

Glen blubbered, "Jake, really, I—"

A rap to an ear, a poke in the ribs. Glen knew the invisible force was playing with him now, knocking him back but not knocking him down, making his glass-pierced heel slide and stomp until he felt a full-body collision and whipped around to see what he'd hit.

His eyes took in a creature of mud: clumps of dark brown and deep orange distorted the outlines of legs, torso, and arms. The head was a dark ball of earth, without eyes or any other facial features, until a slit opened, becoming a mouth that took in dirt along with a greedy gulp of air. Glen stood transfixed while rain chiseled at the mud-man's shape, revealing nose and sockets. The sockets split, white with eyes. Behind the figure, Glen saw a hole in the ground that hadn't been there before. The figure had come from there, with impossible speed and silence. Glen recognized Mike, and he dropped to his knees.

26

Feeling that three years in a small box justified his impatience, Mike asked Jake to be a little more persuasive when he infiltrated Jeanne's Bible studies. Jake's answer was a flat "no," accompanied by an assurance that the timing would ultimately be for the best. When Jeanne announced that her New Church's first service would be Easter Sunday, Mike understood.

During the weeks leading up to the event, Mike tested whether he could match the skill Jake had shown when he sent the rats after Andy Perkins. Limited experiments with rodents showed him that he could influence them with general feelings – fatigue, hunger, aggression – far more easily than with directions for chasing or attacking a specific person. Mike received deeper vexation from the rats' tendency to fall into comas after extended periods of control. Like the visitors to the Prayer Room, they could suffer only a limited amount of use. Once they were spent, Mike killed his test subjects, bagged them, and threw them away.

"I've got an idea," Mike said, "but I need your help."

Jake was lying on the brown sofa in Mike's office. His hands were laced together on his chest, and his eyes, freed from the glasses he'd set on the table near the miniature Noah's ark, were closed. "No you don't," Jake said. "I'm taking a nap."

"I'm thinking – what if, as a trial run, I sent out commands to every animal in town? It seems like a decent way to see if I'm ready for Sunday."

Jake's eyes didn't open, but his lips did, showing teeth. "One hundred rabid puppies, racing through the streets of Kenning." He snickered.

"They don't have to be *rabid*," Mike said. "Though I suppose strong emotion would provide a more accurate test."

Jake sighed. "Good. Do it. You don't need my help."

Mike crossed the room and tapped Jake's shoulder. Jake didn't respond. Mike grabbed Jake's glasses from the table and poked him with them. Jake seemed unfazed. Mike shoved the glasses onto his own face and was about to nudge Jake a third time when focusing through the lenses led to revelation: "These are fake! You don't need glasses at all, do you?"

Jake maintained his repose. "And so you learn another of my secrets. Bravo. Now let me rest."

"What for?" Mike sat on the arm of the sofa closest to Jake's head. "If you're like me, you don't really need much sleep anymore."

"Ah, but I'm not like you," Jake said. "You have a long life ahead of you. Me, I'll be dead by Friday. Dying is... exhausting. Besides, I've been running around making that homosexual reporter catch visions of little Franny McCullough. I made him pleasantly hysterical. And I've been stirring up other sorts of trouble, too, all at your command."

"So you won't help me."

"You have all you need."

Mike slid off the sofa's edge and paced. "And what do I have?"

Jake's hands unclasped, and his right arm pointed toward the opposite side of the office, toward the door with the shiny brass knob that led down to the Room.

Mike recalled a lesson. "You said First Church is a battery. And the Room is an antenna, channeling information, receiving, sending."

"Ain't metaphors grand?" Jake broadened the grin, showing teeth, square incisors and long canines.

"So how do I boost the signal?"

Jake sat up. "Look, Mike, you didn't spend three years underground to come up and be my fawning apprentice for the rest of your life. Be a man. Take charge. Kenning is your town, not mine. You figure it out. I've got bigger fish to fry."

Returning to his desk, Mike shook his head. "Metaphors. Fish. You know, that reminds me – Sara is cooking a salmon Wednesday night. You free for dinner?"

27

The door to the Room stood open, and Jeanne Harper lay on the blue altar. Her naked body looked limp, but she seemed awake, her eyelids fluttering, her breasts rising and falling with rapid breath. Jake bent over her, examining her skin through his fake glasses. He wore a surgical mask.

"She has a younger woman's skin, don't you think?" The latex-covered fingers of Jake's left hand gestured for Mike to come closer. Jake's right hand held a scalpel. "Don't worry," Jake said. He raised the scalpel in the air. "It's not for you." He set a hand on Jeanne's stomach; her body didn't register the intrusion. "It's not for her, either. It's for him."

Jake's head jerked backward, indicating the second altar. A naked man lay pinioned on top of it, arms and legs strapped to spikes driven into dense yellow wood. Mike heard wheezing, like an asthmatic trying to scream.

"One last sacrifice before Sunday's broadcast?" Mike took a tentative step through the doorway and crossed to Jeanne's altar. The Room was twice as large as it had been when he'd last entered. It fluctuated, growing and shrinking to meet their demands. In the early years, Mike had assumed that Jake controlled it. Now he thought otherwise.

Jake tapped the flesh above Jeanne's navel. "Have a look at this exquisite skin. Here's a woman who never wrecked her body with pregnancy, never wore a bikini to go sunbathing, and never went on a yo-yo diet." Jake sighed with appreciation. "She's in fine condition. Her coming here was great luck."

Mike nodded. "Luck" meant something different when Jake was involved. "And the man?"

"Glen brought him over. His name's Holcomb. He works at the dump, and he was making noise about bags of dead animals. Almost like volunteering, wasn't it? Here, hold this, please." Jake placed the scalpel, handle-first, into one of Jeanne's hands. Fingers closed around it. Nothing else moved.

Jake clapped his latex-covered hands. "Now then! Back to your earlier question. Do we need one more sacrifice before Sunday? The answer is yes, we do, but not Jeanne. She's got more work to do."

"So first Holcomb," Mike said, "and then you."

"Bravo! So what we do is, we turn Mr. Holcomb here into a cipher for the whole town. We take his senses as a prefiguration of Sunday's main event. Capiche?"

Mike nodded. He braced himself for the work ahead.

"Actually, I was thinking Jeanne could do the honors. What do you say, Jeanne, care to perform a surgery?"

Jeanne sat up, the scalpel in her hand. Her eyes were still blinking, and her breathing was still fast. Jake took her empty hand into his own and led her to the yellow altar. Holcomb's head thrashed. Below the neck he was paralyzed.

Jake chanted a succession of soft, unintelligible phrases before saying, "Let's start with the nose." Holcomb's wheezing became louder. Mike wondered what Jake had used to stifle the man's screams.

Jeanne walked to the altar, leaned in, and sliced at Holcomb's nose. Mike studied her face as Holcomb's blood started to flow. "Is she going to remember any of this?"

"No," Jake said. He uttered more soft, unintelligible words. "At least, probably not. Hard to say, in the long term." The muffled chant continued. "Now, Jeanne, why don't you cut off his ears? Quick swipes should do away with the external cartilage, and quick jabs should do for the inside. Not too deep! We don't want to damage the brain."

Her expression blank, Jeanne complied. The movement of the man's head made the scalpel less accurate. It abated when Jeanne punctured the eardrums.

"What are we going to do with her," Mike asked, "after?"

"I don't know," Jake said. "We should dump them somewhere. Maybe in the cemetery. Somewhere they'll be found."

Mike nodded.

Jake chanted, becoming louder, more rhythmic, uttering words Mike recognized but could not parse. At the next break, Jake said, "So Jeanne, what do you think – eyes or tongue? We don't want him dying before it's finished, so we'll have to do both pretty quickly."

Jeanne stared at him, blank eyes behind fluttering lashes.

"I'm afraid they don't do too well with choice, not when the Room has them. She'll be back to her old self tomorrow. Mostly. For now, I guess she's all brawn and no brain. Why don't you pry open the mouth and take the tongue?"

Jake's staccato chanting continued. Beneath the streaks of red, Holcomb's face contorted in terror. Weak struggling resumed when Jeanne grabbed at his chin, but he wasn't strong enough to resist her as she removed his tongue. While Jeanne dug out the eyes, Holcomb choked on his own blood. His breathing did not stop completely until after Jeanne had finished.

"Almost done then. Jeanne, please clean off the blade. Use the man's clothes. I don't want any of his blood on that scalpel. Be thorough." Jeanne complied, and Jake snapped the latex gloves as he pulled them off. He took a deep breath, and Mike realized what would come next.

"Are you scared?" Mike asked.

Jake looked at him and pulled off the surgical mask, revealing an expression unlike any Mike had seen. The lips pinched together, covering teeth, and the corners twisted upward. "I'm touched, Mike, truly touched that you would ask. I've been waiting for this for almost a century. Studying, preparing. I'm terrified." Palms up, he held his arms in front of Jeanne. Mike searched for signs of trembling, but the light was too dim. "Now Jeanne, I want you to cut my wrists. No silly teenage slits – I want broad, deep, vertical gashes. Do it."

She drove the blade into Jake's flesh, cutting swaths through veins. When the scalpel emerged, it was clean. Blood did not flow from the openings; it welled up in bubbles and remained, defying the rules of liquid and gravity. The bubbles grew, and Jake's head lolled. "Oh my... it flows fast. I already removed... my shoes... Jeanne, would you... make cuts... in my ankles, please?"

She knelt to comply. Mike could see pain on Jake's face as she gashed around his tendons, but he did not flinch. Clenching his teeth, Jake said, "Thank you. Now be a good girl and faint." Jeanne collapsed.

Mike watched as Jake's blood gathered impossibly around his extremities. "Now what?" Mike asked. "What can I do?"

"Make Sunday... spectacular," Jake said. "Enjoy the music." His voice was soft, breathy. "Burn... the ones who won't... respond... except... the ones... we chose." He grinned in his usual form. "The others... you... Reverend Cox... *Pastor* Cox...." He laughed. "*Herd.*"

Jake's body crumpled onto the floor of the Prayer Room. The blood around his wrists and ankles held its shape for a moment and then broke, spilling upward. Four lines of crimson streamed toward the ceiling, creating splotches that spread out until they touched, joining in a solid pool. Mike tilted his head back as far as he could, letting his jaw gape at the miracle amassing above him. When the last drops of blood flowed up from Jake's body, Mike smiled. "Well, friend, you had to go and leave me with all the heavy lifting, didn't you?" He looked at the three bodies he would have to move. Jeanne would have to be cleaned and dressed, too. "I guess I'll manage." He walked to the doorway, turned back, and addressed Jake's corpse: "See you soon."

Transfiguration

1

The cooking hand connected to an arm. Flame engulfed everything beyond the elbow. Digits extended from a charred mass, curling upward, as if the person had died trying to hold on to something. Brian blinked. The music had been hypnotic, but he had escaped. He couldn't let the burning hand transfix him, transfix them, make them prey to the booming baritone that had said "sister."

Feel the force of the faith of your brothers and your... sister! Yes! We will all *submit to the power of the Lord, to His Divine Might, to his Supreme Will!*

Michael Cox was addressing Brian and Ronald directly, and when he said "sister," he meant Fran. Fran, who hadn't looked like Fran when she was sitting on the edge of the bed, holding the gun. Like Stef, who hadn't looked like Stef when she was circling around him, swinging the handsaw. Michael Cox knew who they were, and he knew more.

"Mel," Brian said.

"What?" Ronald whispered. "She's here?"

"No. We have to find her."

Ronald raised a hand to halt him. "Wait. I know that woman."

Brian didn't know which woman Ronald meant. Michael Cox had moved toward them, but many men and women remained in a circle around the fire. "Oh God," Brian said.

He heard a baritone laugh.

"Shh!" Ronald hissed. "What?"

"That's Tatum Grayson. Mel's mom."

"And that other woman — her name is Kelly Pratt. She's the doctor who came down from the CDC to look into the killer Chihuahua phenomenon."

Brian recognized others. He saw Ted Early, the veterinarian — he'd been at Jeanne's church, not at Michael Cox's, but now he was one of the circle. He saw Jim Bledsoe, the high school principal, whose land they were on. Rod Mason, who had sold the gun that Fran had used. Stan Johnson, who had bought it. Alice Granger.

Brian stood tall, leaving his and Ronald's safe huddle behind the tree. "Get down," Ronald whispered.

"Doesn't matter," Brian said. "He knows we're here."

Michael Cox's baritone laugh repeated. "True. Will you join us?"

Members of the circle left their positions and joined the Reverend, forming a line between the fire and the trees. All heads turned toward Brian and Ronald's position. Ronald stood and said, "I guess that settles that, doesn't it?" He waved at the line with his good arm. "Hi there, crazy magic religious people! Hell of a night for a bonfire, eh?" The line did not move. Ronald turned to Brian. "What are the chances of us getting away, you think?"

"Don't know," Brian said. "Maybe we should stay. See what happens."

"I see two options if we stay. Option one, tend the fire. Option two, fuel the fire. You told me to calm down. Notice how well I am following your advice. Calmly, I suggest we run."

Brian looked at their injured shoulders. "We won't make it."

"You never know," Ronald said.

"Brothers and sisters," said Michael Cox, "will you please show these two gentlemen the way?"

Members of the lines stepped forward in unison. Brian felt a tug on his good arm, took the cue, and was running alongside Ronald once again, dodging trees that became harder and harder to see as the firelight grew more distant. Sounds of twigs cracking and straw shifting as feet pounded earth pushed them on until they broke through to the street. Winded, exhausted, Brian halted and turned. On the farther side of the street, Ronald waited.

Their pursuers emerged from the trees one at a time and stopped at the edge of the road. With greater distance between them than before, they reformed their line, minus leader, and looked out at Brian and Ronald.

Ronald crossed to Brian's side. "They're not chasing us."

"No," Brian said.

"You told me this road – the way blocked by the singers – leads north, out of town, right?"

"Right."

"Okay," Ronald said, "and if we follow it south?"

"Back to Main Street," Brian said. "Back into Kenning. Where they want us."

2

The stiff fabric of her blue Easter dress felt like cardboard around her torso. She'd wanted to look good for Ms. Harper. For Jeanne. She'd wanted to be a symbol, showing that New Church was just as important as all the others. She wished she'd been more practical. The dress's folds rustled and constrained her legs as she walked. Being a symbol wouldn't help Jeanne now, and it wouldn't save Stef.

Melanie's shoes clattered on asphalt as she approached her house's driveway. The empty street made finding anyone seem unlikely, but she had to look anyway, to search for clues about what had happened to Stef. The bells that signaled the Easter service's end meant that First Church's congregation was dispersing to go – somewhere. She had to figure out where.

Before opening her front door, Melanie scanned the fronts of her neighbors' houses. Most of the families went to First Church, but some of them – like the Crandalls – attended the smaller churches. The Crandalls' house looked as abandoned as all the others. Melanie remembered the urge to sing she had fought off while Brian was trying his truck's ignition, and she remembered Stef acting like somebody else was controlling her as she attacked Brian with the saw. Whatever was happening wasn't limited to the people in First Church. It could affect the whole town. Except her, and Brian, and Ronald, and Winston, who had all managed to fight it. How?

The front door wasn't locked, so she opened it and went in. If Dad was home, she'd have to run. After last night, there'd be no talking to him, no reasoning. "Hello?" she called. The sound echoed in the foyer, and she regretted it. Her shoes clomped as she stepped toward the kitchen. The kitchen sink held two frying pans and three plates. Mom had cooked breakfast before they'd gone off to church. Mel and Brian had had Crunch Berries.

Clomp, clomp, clomp, clomp. Her shoes weren't any more practical than her dress. The heels weren't high, but they were clunky. The kitchen's noisy tiles led to the noisy hardwood in the hall, which brought her to the living room. The living room was carpeted, at least, but it was as devoid of clues as the kitchen.

The ceiling creaked. That meant the *floor* was creaking upstairs, like it did when someone walked. If someone, or something, was moving around upstairs, then she, or he, or it would have heard Melanie by now. *Creak, creak.* The sounds moved across the ceiling. Footsteps. If Melanie started walking, her shoes would make noise, and whoever was there would know exactly where to find her. She needed a plan: stay or go, front door or back door? She didn't know.

The footsteps halted, and Melanie realized the room above her was her own bedroom. Stef wouldn't be up there – she had too much big-sister fear to invade the sacred space when Mel wasn't home. Dad almost never went in, as if being around a teenage girl's things might contaminate him.

The steps left the bedroom, moved toward the stairs, and Melanie had to make a decision. She couldn't stand still. Struck by her own stupidity, she slipped off her shoes and tiptoed across the hardwood floor toward the kitchen, toward the back door, which was farthest from the stairs. Picking up speed, she realized that if the deadbolt on the back door were locked, she wouldn't be able to open it without the key, and her key only worked on the front door, so she stopped by the sink and opened the drawer where they kept the spare, which was gone.

Her heartbeat quickened, and she heard a step on the stairs. Whatever was coming moved slowly, toying with her, waiting to pinpoint her position. She had to stay quiet, but she also had to move. They kept more keys in a drawer in Dad's study, in one of the drawers that Dad didn't lock. The study was toward the front of the house. In view of the stairs.

Move! She had to move! But the floor might creak, and her only ways out were close to the stairs, where someone was taking steps down, tentative, slow, patient, step, step, certainly far enough to see into the study, far enough to see her if she went looking for the key to the back door, but she could go around the other way, toward the front door, which was also in view of the stairs, and at least then she might be able to run, impractical dress and naked feet, not fast, but maybe...

"Melanie? Is that you?"

"Mom!" The word rushed out with relief. She moved toward the stairs as fast as her clothes would allow and found her mother waiting. "Thank God it's you!"

Mom ran down the stairs and hugged her close. Looking down at her mother's back, she saw the familiar pattern of the white dress with spring flowers, the same one she had worn to the Easter service the year before. Mom had been to church, and somehow, she had gotten home.

Pulling out of the embrace, Melanie realized she was crying. "Mom, how did you get here? Are you okay?"

"Oh baby," Mom said, hugging her again. "I was so worried." Mom stroked her hair, and it felt good. The arm around her tightened, and Melanie wanted to let her whole body go limp, fall into her mother's grasp, but she was too big for that now. She cried louder, and Mom must have been crying, too, except...

She wasn't. Mom wasn't crying at all. And the stroking of her hair – it seemed measured, and the hand doing it seemed flat and cold. "Mom?"

The hand grabbed her hair and pulled back her head. Her mother's face remained warm and caring as the arm around Mel's back released her, came into view, and smothered her with a damp rag.

Nothing.

Light, coming into focus. Brown colors. Melanie had been in her house, been with her mother, and lost consciousness. Had Mom drugged her?

Melanie heard humming, a tune she recognized, "Jesus be Jesus in Me." The voice was a woman's, but it wasn't her mother's. She tried to move her arms, but she couldn't. They were bound behind her back. She tried to move her legs, but they were bound, too, and she bent forward to bring them into her blurry field of vision. Something silvery covered her calves. Tape. Silver duct tape started at her shoeless feet and circled, tightly, over her ankles, up her calves, and disappeared beneath the folds of her dress.

Her legs could move, but only when she lifted them together. She did, and they slammed back down, hard, against a wooden floor. Eyes perceived more: dark wooden support beams, bolstering rafters. She was in an attic, but it wasn't like the attic in her house because the whole floor was solid, and there was a rug nearby. Trying to get a better look around, she leaned forward and felt a tug at her throat. A twist of her head revealed a noose that secured her to one of the beams.

The humming came from behind her, so she turned, rotating carefully to keep the rope from tightening or burning her skin, until she saw the back of a woman sitting at a desk. The woman wore an Easter dress, pale yellow, pretty, of a fine soft fabric. She was writing in a book.

The woman turned, and Melanie recognized her. "Hello," said Mrs. Cox. "How are you feeling?" When Melanie didn't respond, the woman sighed. "I'll be keeping you for awhile. Apparently, it's necessary." She lifted her eyebrows, and her gaze bent downward. "You can scream if you want, but I'll be terribly annoyed."

3

Intended for *American Sane*:

If I am ever fortunate enough to transfer this writing to the pages of your favorite electronic publication, I'll have to wonder, will you care? You bookmarked *American Sane* because it is a reliable source of social insight, cutting criticism enabled by incisive wit. Horror movies, tales of the supernatural – these things are for *those* people, the ones who waste their lives sitting in front of television screens avoiding intellectual confrontation with the matters of *real* importance with which you, Educated Readers, enrich your lives as you sit daily in front of your computer screens and type in my address.

So I will, therefore, skip over the less savory elements from recent experience dealing with psychic preachers and mystic mind control in order to share with you some details that should be more to your liking.

Conspiracy! It's the stuff of great postmodern fiction. Secret sects and the scheming rich who may or may not be working within governments to hide radical truths and rewrite history – such noble spirits spur our intellects to question the very natures of power and reality. Yet these illuminati are human, more or less, which means one thing: they have to get around somehow. And what sorts of cars do they drive? Any aficionado of conspiracies will tell you: unmarked black vans.

Experts insist that the vans be unmarked because clever conspirators naturally eschew nametags. But why black? Is it the color's power to blend, its fashionable ability to match with anything and thus disappear from notice? Or is it the traditional association of black and white with evil and good, which serves, in some contexts, to perpetuate the injustices of racist hierarchy?

These questions, I argue, are moot, because unmarked black vans have nothing in terrorizing potential next to their dastardly counterparts, the *white* vans.

Marked white vans are for plumbers, exterminators, and handymen. Their drivers infiltrate our existences, and, if we're lucky, they maintain our infrastructures. Unmarked white vans are contemporary hearses. Today's cadaver carriers don't advertise their corpse-y contents like the classic death carts, whose distinct distortions of station-wagon chic once broadcasted death's ubiquity. What greater conspiracy can there be, Observant Readers, than death, sneaking around in white vans, coming to get us and drive us, anonymous, into a hidden realm of abjection?

I spent the greater part of yesterday evening, after the events that would not interest you, in the company of the charismatic young subject of my forthcoming, as-yet-untitled book. Young Brian McCullough felt terribly concerned about his even younger girlfriend, Melanie Grayson, who had gone missing earlier in the day. We checked the girl's house and found nothing. When we emerged from the front door of her house – which, for legal purposes, I must assure you was both unlocked and open when we arrived – we saw an unmarked white van parked on the street.

Knowing from unreported experience that the street and, indeed, the entire town were deserted, we remarked on this vehicle's anomalous presence. Earlier in the day, all of Kenning's vehicles had been rendered inoperable, so we found ourselves in a state of perplexity as we confronted the recently-arrived whiteness. The nearby streetlight gave the van an unsettling glow, but it was insufficient to reveal anyone behind the windshield. We went to the driver-side door and knocked. No answer. We tried the handle, but the door was locked. Fatigued from an excess of mystery, we decided to leave the white van behind.

We were at the mouth of young Miss Grayson's cul-de-sac when we heard the white van's engine crank to life. We walked on, silently daring the thing to run us down. Instead, the white van matched our pace, crawling at our heels for as long as our feet touched asphalt. When Brian led us off the road, into the shortcut back to his house, the van drove away.

Now I sit, on the Monday morning after Easter Sunday, typing this update. I occupy a comfortable chair by a window. The view from the window is picturesque: manicured lawns, evenly-spaced houses, abandoned tricycles. Every half hour or so, a white van drives by. The vans differ in size and shape. I count at least three distinct vehicles. Their purpose?

Their purpose?

4

Jeanne looked down and saw her fingers splayed flat on a piece of paper, which lay atop a dark wooden desk. The paper, a flier, bore big blue and yellow letters that read "Join us at First Church this Easter Sunday for a Revival of Tradition, Fellowship, and Spirit! New members are welcome – don't miss it!"

"Huh?" The word left her lips without volition. She felt lost, displaced – and yet she knew where she was and why she had come.

"Are you all right, Ms. Harper?" asked the man sitting across from her. He was Deacon Warren, with thick silver hair, thin-rimmed glasses, and a big toothy smile. On the desk between them spread a meal: salmon, green beans, bread, something that looked like wine but was, without a doubt, grape juice. "You seem upset about something. Is it this flier?"

"What?" She looked around the room. She sat in a high-backed leather chair. A comfortable-looking brown sofa stretched along a nearby wall. In the far corners were two doors. The one on the left held her attention, and she shivered as her eyes broke away.

"Ms. Harper, I suppose I can guess why you came here today. You're upset about our revival happening at the same time as your grand opening at New Church. Is that right, Ms. Harper? May I call you Jeanne?"

"I don't care what you call me."

"Fine then, Jeanne. Well Jeanne, I really do wish you the best. But you can't expect us not to go ahead with our Easter plans. You know this is one of the two biggest holidays for every church in town, and despite all the bunnies and chocolate eggs, I feel that Easter is the one day of the year that most people devote wholly—"

"Stop." Jeanne looked at Jake Warren's face, at the lines around his eyes. "Easter. Easter already happened. You were there. I—"

"Well, Jeanne, I acknowledge that Easter happens every year, but in light of the week's strange events, I think—"

"You," she said. "You're dead."

He laughed. "Am I really?"

Jeanne stood up, and the backs of her legs bumped against the chair. It was solid, real. The paper under her fingers had the soft texture of paper, and the air in the room tasted like cool office air. The food in front of her smelled good, and she was hungry, just like she had been Thursday, but that was days ago, and so much had happened.

"Jeanne," Jake Warren said, "you look pale. Maybe you should sit back down? Is there somebody at home I can call for you?"

Somebody at home he could call. He knew darned well she lived alone. He had been at her house, had pushed her on the stairs – after he had died. But that was preposterous. The look on his face, very much alive, told her so. The feelings in her eyes and ears, on her tongue and skin, told her so. "This is a trick," Jeanne said. "Or a trap."

Jake Warren circled around the desk, approaching her. "Really, Jeanne, how could I trick or trap you when I didn't even know you were coming?"

"How did I get here?"

"You walked, I presume. Or maybe you drove. I honestly can't recount your day for you, at least not before the moment when you knocked on Mike's door."

"Mike," Jeanne said. "Reverend Cox. Did he do this? Is he here?" She looked around the room, desk, chairs, sofa, doors. The door on the left, with the shiny knob. She knew what was behind it, didn't she? She'd been there, hadn't she? She couldn't remember.

Jake Warren stood at her side, so she moved quickly, jumping toward the door on the left. Her hand was on the knob before she sensed him behind her. The knob turned, and the door started to open.

"You don't want to do that," Jake Warren said.

"I don't want to? Or you don't want me to?" She looked over her shoulder and saw his face, half-sneer, half-grin. "'The Lord is my helper, and I will not fear what man shall do unto me.'" She opened the door.

Around a corner, she saw stairs, leading down. Deacon Warren stood behind her, but he did not reach to stop her. She extended a foot toward the first step. "Where does it go?" The question came without anticipation of answer, but she turned to gauge Jake Warren's reaction. He was gone.

She took the first step, and the next, and the next. The stairwell opened out into a large room with thin, cheap, bluish-grey carpet. Stacks of boxes lined the walls. Rows of music stands and two wardrobe racks of choir and baptismal robes were arranged on the far side of the room. It was a simple basement. She had found First Church's storage room.

To her right, she saw another door. The door was plainer than the one leading from Reverend Cox's office to the stairs, a simple blue-grey rectangle with a simple brass knob. It looked heavy. Jeanne stared at it, and her vision began to blur.

Something edged into her periphery: furniture, a bench, and it must have been there before, but she hadn't noticed it. It was to the right of the door, as if intended for visitors waiting for people to emerge from within. A woman occupied one side of the bench, leaving a polite majority of the space for a new arrival. Her head hung down, concealing her face, but Jeanne could see short hair the same brown as hers. The woman's dress and bearing seemed familiar. Intimate.

Even before the bench's occupant lifted her head, Jeanne knew what she would see. Gazing across the room, her eyes met her own. The woman stood from the bench, unfurling Jeanne's height and build, color and features. She took a step toward herself, and she didn't know which one of them was moving until she realized that each of them was stepping toward the other. They stood inches apart, noses almost touching. One of them tilted her head to one side, and the other tilted to the opposite. Jeanne pushed closer, until their lips touched. Faces twisted, mouths moist with saliva, kissing, and Jeanne's heart raced. Losing track of which woman she was, she felt her bodies colluding, adhering, intermingling, until four lips and four eyes became two and two, and the kiss ended, and she was staring down at thin cheap carpet, moisture at the corners of her mouth, alone.

She looked up, and there she was again. Another Jeanne stood three feet away. When the new Jeanne stepped forward, Jeanne felt herself stay still. The woman with her skin and eyes and mouth and hair crossed the space between them, lifted her arm, and struck Jeanne's face with the hard-knuckled back of her right hand. Jeanne fell.

Mud spattered her dress when her knees hit grey wet earth. Terror seized her, and when she looked up, she saw a tombstone. Her hat had come off when she'd fallen, and her hair was long and wet, so light in color that in direct sunshine it would seem blonde. She was nine years old, kneeling in the rain at Hart's Cemetery, and on her way to her mother's interment.

5

Brian said "Good morning." He didn't mean it.

"Morning," Ronald said. "I couldn't find any coffee filters in your kitchen. Therefore, it is simply morning."

Brian grunted. "You ready?"

"Are *you*?"

Brian half-shrugged. The look on his bruised face was sullen. The black t-shirt hanging over the waist of his faded blue jeans had an aura of deliberate frump. Even though yesterday's sling was absent, he didn't look well. "Let's go," Brian said.

Ronald smoothed the front of his white-and-blue striped oxford shirt and crossed to his crestfallen companion. "We'll find her, you know." He turned away. "We'll find both of them." Brian's concern for longtime girlfriend Melanie was understandable. His own feelings for weeklong boyfriend Winston were not.

"Sure," Brian said. "Let's go."

Ronald studied Brian's expression. "What are you thinking?" He recalled the scent of cooking flesh. "Do you think they...."

Brian shook his head. "I," he said, and speaking stopped. His face looked disconnected from the possibility of utterance. For the first time, the young man before him seemed like the boy Ronald had read about, the traumatized kid who had spent an entire year without speaking.

They stood near the front door, but neither of them moved to exit. Ronald thought about the pages he had written for eventual upload to *American Sane*. Were they funny? He wanted to be funny. In a week populated by deranged dogs and burning bodies, humor seemed as necessary as it was inappropriate.

A loud honk snapped Ronald from his reverie. He stepped toward the nearest window and pulled back a curtain: across the street, a green Volkswagen pulled into a driveway, and a suited man walked toward the passenger-side door. A woman emerged from the house behind him, ran in slippered feet to his side, and offered him a briefcase. The man turned, kissed her cheek, took the briefcase, and got into the car. The car backed out of the driveway and drove away.

"What the *fuck*," Ronald said.

"What?" The question was more animated than anything that had left Brian's lips so far.

Ronald made room at the window and pointed at a pane. "Your neighbors... are... *home.* If I read the hackneyed scene correctly, a man just rushed out to catch his carpool to work, and his devoted wife ran after him with a briefcase full of important papers that he had accidentally left on the breakfast table, undoubtedly beneath his copy of today's *Wall Street Journal.*"

"You saw all that?"

Ronald smiled and was about to say "naturally" when another noise derailed him: the whir and grind of a smaller engine. The window revealed nothing, so he opened the front door, stepped outside, and took in a panorama. On Brian's side of the street, three houses down, a riding lawnmower refreshed a lawn's manicure. Further down, another car pulled out of a driveway. It was almost eight o'clock. Monday morning. People were going to work.

Preparing to remark on the inexplicable normalcy of their surroundings, Ronald felt Brian brush by him. Brian walked past his truck, and when he reached the street, he took the same direction as the last two cars Ronald had seen. Toward town. Without a word, Ronald followed, taking in the surroundings that spring sunlight revealed. People stood by windows, completing quotidian arrangements, in garages, packing cars for work, and in yards, performing regular chores. The only out-of-place details were children playing, reclaiming the tricycles and toys that had earlier seemed ominously abandoned. If this morning were a normal Monday, full of normal people doing normal things, the children would be in their normal schools filled with their normal loathing for teachers and tasks. Apparently, the day after mass delusion and murder was, for children, a holiday.

Brian was getting too far ahead, so Ronald ran to catch up. With Ronald panting beside him, Brian reduced his pace. Ronald said thanks, and Brian said nothing. They continued their journey over asphalt through a reanimated suburbanesque wonderland until Brian stepped over the curb. Ronald knew where they were going. The trail through yards would lead them to Melanie's neighborhood.

"Wait a minute." Ronald didn't expect a response, but he had to try. "Goddamn it, stop!"

Brian halted at the order and turned. "What?"

"What," Ronald said. "Pithy. Don't you think we should talk about what's going on? I mean, what's going on? Someone might have hit the reset button on the town, but Kenning's sudden sanity doesn't mean everything is hunky dory."

"People are home," Brian said. "Mel might be home."

His logic was inarguable. Brian led on, and Ronald followed. As they reentered the Graysons' cul-de-sac, Ronald said, "So you're just going to knock?"

Brian stopped and looked at him.

"I seem to recall a certain someone saying he punched a certain someone else's father in the face. Twice. So again I ask, you're just going to knock?"

Brian looked at his left shoulder, freed from its sling but not free of its injury. "I don't care."

Again, his logic was inarguable. Ronald followed him to the door and stood back as Brian knocked. The door opened, and a heavy man appeared. His face was round, and the top of his head was bald, but between and beneath jowls and wrinkles sat a thin nose and high cheek bones that were unmistakably Grayson. "You," said Mr. Grayson. He meant Brian, who didn't respond. Mr. Grayson held a cell phone in his hand, which was down by his belt. A voice was saying something through it, but Mr. Grayson seemed oblivious as he locked stares with Brian. "Where are they!" the father demanded. On one side of his face, his jaw line was purple, and another bruise on his forehead reminded Ronald of Gorbachev.

"I," Brian said.

"Where are my daughters! And where's Tatum!" Mr. Grayson's exclamations didn't sound like questions, but the blend of worry and fear in his damaged face wanted answers.

"I," Brian said.

Ronald stepped up. "We were going to ask you that. We've been looking for Melanie since last night." Last night, when we saw your wife singing at a bonfire full of human remains.

"You're looking." Mr. Grayson didn't sound convinced, but he lifted the phone to his ear and said, "Hold on, Deputy." To Ronald, he said, "Who are you?"

Ronald offered a handshake. "Ronald Glassner, journalist, author, trav—"

"And you're with him?" Ignoring the offered hand, Mr. Grayson tilted his head toward Brian and winced as the move compressed his jaw.

"In a manner of speaking," Ronald replied.

"Huh." Mr. Grayson walked back into his house but left the door open behind him. He spoke into the phone, asking how long he would have to wait and how many forms he would have to fill out before the police would do something about his missing family. During a pause, he turned toward Ronald and Brian, who stood speechless on the front step, and motioned for them to enter. They approached Mr. Grayson's position in the hall.

"Hold on," Mr. Grayson said. He lowered the phone and looked at Brian. "When's the last time you saw Melanie?"

Brian didn't answer, so Ronald said, "Yesterday afternoon. What about you?"

"Ask *him*," Mr. Grayson said, indicating Brian. He lifted the phone and said "Go." A voice on the other end chattered.

"Stef," Brian said. "When did you last see Stef?"

"Hold on," Mr. Grayson said. Phone down, eyebrows stitched, he answered, "Yesterday. Morning. Church. Night. I don't rem—it must have been last night. I got up this morning, and everyone was gone." He brought the phone to his ear. "I don't care how many calls you've had today, Deputy! I want answers NOW!"

Ronald made out the voice from the phone saying "Now hold on there, sir," and without a thought, his fingers ripped the device from Mr. Grayson's strong hand and held it to his face.

"Winston!"

"Mr. Grayson, this is business, so I'd prefer if you'd call me Deputy Beecher—"

"Winston, my God, it's Ronald!"

"Who?"

"Ronald! Remember? Injured shoulder, hot sex, the city dump, hot sex, crazy singing, your whole ridiculous life for the last week?"

"Ronald? It's the damnedest – Ronald! My God! What's going on? I—"

The line went dead. Before Ronald could verify that the call had ended, an arm pushed him toward a wall, and a hand snatched the phone away. Mr. Grayson pocketed his phone and said, "This is ridiculous. I'm going down there. I can't just stand here when my wife and daughters are – get out of my way!"

The last command was for Brian, who stepped aside, leaving the hall clear for Mr. Grayson's march to the front door. Bewildered, Ronald followed, and he felt Brian close behind him. Mr. Grayson made his way across the lawn toward the station wagon in his driveway before he stopped, glanced at the sky, and lifted his hand. He looked at his watch and said, "Oh no! I'm late for work!"

Ronald and Brian froze, standing on the grass, and let their eyes follow Mr. Grayson's jiggling hurry back into his house. A moment later, the man emerged with his briefcase, locked the front door, and ran to his car. Ronald didn't notice the white van at the mouth of the cul-de-sac until Mr. Grayson drove by it.

6

"Please," Melanie whimpered, "I'm so tired." Her chin nudged the rope. "I can't even lay down or this thing will strangle me." She bowed her head as low as she could. "Please."

Mrs. Cox put down her pen and swiveled her chair toward Melanie. "I suppose the ness isn't noocessary." She chuckled. "Noose isn't necessary. I'm tired, too. I feel like a college kid, staying up all night to finish a paper right before the due date." She sighed and stood. "But you haven't gone to college yet, have you?"

"No ma'am." Melanie sniffled.

"That's too bad." Mrs. Cox's heels clicked on floorboards as she stepped off the rug and approached. "Here's the situation. I've been in these clothes for twenty-four hours. I know, I know, you could say the same thing, and duct tape is undoubtedly uncomfortable, but things are how they are, and I, at least, am in a position to shower and change. To do that, I need to trust you'll stay put."

"I will!" Melanie promised.

"With that noose around your neck, I can be pretty certain. But if I leave you alone, and you faint, and choke to death – well, that might suit our purposes, and it might not. So if I'm going to leave you unattended, it might actually be safer to take off the rope. If I can trust you."

"I promise! I promise!"

Mrs. Cox stood tall and looked down at her. "There's no reason why you shouldn't live through this. Mike and Jake keep talking about sacrifices, and sometimes, sacrifices are necessary, but still, I don't think you need to be sacrificed. But if you try to get away... do you get my meaning?"

Melanie nodded, feeling the coarse fibers against her throat.

"Okay then." Mrs. Cox disappeared behind Melanie's back, and for a moment, the loop around her neck tightened. There was a grunting noise – Mrs. Cox reaching toward the rafters – another tug on the rope, and a sudden decrease of pressure. Melanie's bound hands yearned to slip the circle up over her head, but she had to wait for Mrs. Cox to do it for her. Released, Melanie fell limp on the floor.

"Poor girl," said Mrs. Cox. "Get some rest." The woman left the attic.

Sitting up, Melanie flexed every muscle in her arms, stretching the tape around her wrists. A lifetime ago, when she'd woken in an upright position and found her arms and legs immobilized, she'd thought that getting loose would be impossible. Now her skin was raw, maybe bleeding, and it hurt like hell, but with one more tug, one last squeeze...

Her left hand slipped through the tape, and she was free. Arms snapped forward, and her shoulders, strained from being held in a single position for so long, shuddered with bolts of pain. Pipes groaned. Mrs. Cox was in the shower, but she wouldn't be there forever. Peeling tape from her thighs hurt, but since most of the strands clung to stockings instead of skin, she was able to push down nylon and free the rest of her body with ease.

Using a beam for support, she got to her bare feet and scanned the small room. The only way in or out of the attic was by a pull-down folding stairway. Its hinges squealed every time Mrs. Cox raised or lowered it, which she had done when she'd needed restroom visits. Melanie hadn't had the privilege. Mrs. Cox had complained about the smell of the urine that had ruined Melanie's dress, and small triumph had tinged Melanie's humiliation. She wanted that woman to be uncomfortable. She wanted her to be far worse.

Melanie prayed that the shower was loud and distant enough to conceal the screech of the folding staircase. Hinges screamed, but Melanie forced the stairs downward until gravity took over, unfolding sections with clamorous snaps. The incline was steep: if she didn't go down backward, she'd fall on her face. She'd have to go down blind to what waited behind her back.

She turned and lowered herself onto the top step. The wood felt strange against her bare foot, slippery but raw enough to splinter. When she lowered her other foot, entrusting the stairs with her body weight, the entire structure wobbled, and she thrust her arms out along the attic floor to keep her balance. With fingers clawing at wood flooring, she stepped down. She tried to look over her shoulder, but the movement made the stairway tremble, threatening to shake Melanie off. Mrs. Cox, or Reverend Cox, or someone or something worse, could have been watching at the foot of the stairs, looking up her polluted dress. She had to take another step, stretching her confining dress to keep her balance, and another, curling her feet so they would have purchase on narrow wood, and another and another, even if she landed in the angry arms of her captors.

Near the bottom, a foot slipped, a knee banged, and she tumbled the rest of the way onto hallway carpet. The force of the fall jostled the stairs, which lifted off the ground and smacked back down again. The smacking sound echoed, and Melanie knew the shower had stopped. Forcing her way through disorientation, she pulled herself up and started for the stairs that led down to the main floor and an exit.

"Melanie Grayson!" Mrs. Cox's voice shouted, but Melanie didn't look back. She ran down the stairs, not thinking about slipping or falling, just concentrating on the front door, which came quickly into view and then reach. The knob yielded to her grip and the door swung wide, admitting the white glare of day. Dazzled, Melanie kept going, trusting her feet to find the steps that led down from the door, ignoring the heat of the stones in the front path, and as her vision came into focus, she screamed as loud as she could, "SOMEBODY HELP ME!!!!"

Nobody was in view, just massive empty yards and majestic mailboxes of brick and stone. She'd been to this neighborhood before, seen the big houses of Kenning's wealthiest denizens, but she didn't know exactly where she was. Nearby, one or two streets over, maybe, she'd find Jeanne's house, but she couldn't be sure that anyone would be there to help her, and if Mrs. Cox was close behind, chasing, she might not even get that far. Without a destination, Mel tried to run, and she made it to the edge of the driveway before tires screeched and a vehicle blocked her path.

The driver-side door of the white van swung open, and the figure that emerged brought first relief and then terror. Mom shut the door and smiled at her. "Melanie! What are you doing out? Is he here?"

Before Melanie could speculate about who "he" might be, she felt a tap on her shoulder. Her head turned, neck aching, and showed her Mrs. Cox, arms akimbo and expression vexed. "So much for trust," the woman said. She wore only a towel.

Melanie turned back to her mother, who stood by the van. "Mom?" she said, breathless. "Why are you helping them?"

Mom circled around the front of the van and brushed a lock of Melanie's hair away from her cheek. The tight blue jeans and low-cut pink blouse that her mother wore looked like nothing Melanie had ever seen on a woman that age, let alone her own mother. Nathan Grayson disliked modern fashions and griped about skirts that didn't hang down to the ankle. Tatum Grayson complied with his wishes in silence.

"You know why," her mother said.

The tears that sprung from Melanie's eyes irritated her. The ducts should have gone dry hours ago. "I don't," she said.

Mom stepped back. "You know what he's like. And divorce is a sin. They'll help me. And you won't get hurt if you do what they say!" Her tone conveyed a desperation to be believed and, perhaps, to believe.

"And Stef?" Melanie asked.

Her mother's expression grew darker. She turned and walked back toward the door of the white van.

From behind Melanie, Mrs. Cox said, "Some things can't be helped. Like I said, sometimes, sacrifices are necessary."

"No." Melanie choked on a sob. "You didn't...."

With the van's door reopened, Mom spoke into the vehicle rather than toward them. Melanie heard her anyway: "I'm going to do the route one more time," she said. "Tell Alice we'll switch off in an hour." The van's white door slammed shut, and Melanie's mother drove away.

Melanie swallowed, forcing down the lump in her throat. "There's nowhere to escape to," Mrs. Cox said from behind her. "Come back to the attic and wait with me."

Melanie thought of an escape; she had one person left. He'd have to come for her, though, because she couldn't run away on her own. Even if she managed the speed to flee, she wouldn't be able to see or feel anything but Stef. Mel had failed her sister, and now, she'd go back inside and let Mrs. Cox bind her however she pleased. She was beyond pain and humiliation. She was certainly beyond fighting.

"Good," said Mrs. Cox. "Then maybe we can do without the tape."

7

The single-story police station looked the same as it always did, but the surrounding trees seemed different. Brian wasn't accustomed to thinking about who, or what, could be waiting within trees' protective darkness. For years he had associated basements with blood. Now he would associate groves of trees with burning flesh.

A white van was parked in front of the station. This van was older and smaller than the last one they'd seen, and its rear bumper was missing. Like all the rest, its windows were impenetrably dark. "Hold on," Ronald said. He raised his binoculars to his face and pivoted on the asphalt, searching the area around the building. "Do you think it's clear?"

Brian didn't think anything.

"I see movement through the glass in the front door," Ronald said. "People are in there. But we knew that, didn't we?"

Brian nodded.

"Nobody is waving guns," Ronald said, "and there aren't snarling dogs as far as I can see, so maybe we should just, I don't know, walk through the front door? Wait." Ronald raised the binoculars again, but Brian didn't need magnification to follow what was happening. A deputy, someone younger than Winston whose name Brian didn't know, emerged from the glass front door and crossed the parking lot toward the small cluster of squad cars. He got into one of them, pulled out of the lot, and started down the street. The car's lightbar spun with blue and red, but its siren stayed silent. Brian half-expected the white van to follow the police car, but it did not move. "He put his lights on like he's answering a call," Ronald observed, "but he's driving slow. Where do you think he's going?"

Brian shook his head.

"Hmmm." Ronald scanned the police station with the binoculars. Minutes passed before he concluded, "I just don't know."

"What?" Brian asked.

Ronald looked at him, eyelashes fluttering. "How kind of you to spare a word." After the sentence dropped from his mouth, Ronald seemed sorry. "Anyways, you asked a question. What I don't know is—"

Ronald's jaw fell open, and Brian didn't look to see what startled him until the lights caught his own eye. A police car – the *same* police car – was coming back toward the station from a different direction. It returned to the parking lot, retook its original space, and released its peppy deputy, who walked back into the station.

"He must have driven around the block," Ronald said. "He can't have gone farther." A moment later, an older officer, Ben Pritchard, came through the glass door. He crossed the lot, opened a different police car, and drove off in the same manner, lights flashing, siren silent. Ronald looked at his watch. Brian gestured for Ronald to hand over the binoculars. He did. Sunlight and distance made seeing distinct objects through the front door impossible, so Brian scanned the perimeter of the building. He found nothing more interesting than faded paint. He was lowering the binoculars when a flash of red blinded his right eye.

"Four minutes," Ronald said as Ben Pritchard parked the squad car. "He drove around for four minutes. Kenning's police force is truly dedicated! Wait, I have an idea." Brian was pretty sure he knew what it was, but he was content to let Ronald spell it out. "What if they're coming out in rotation?" Ronald asked. "I mean, there can't be that many of them. What if Winston's turn is next? We just have to wait."

Brian wanted a closer view of the action. He crossed the field of grass and dirt that separated them from the station, stood at the edge of the parking lot, and raised the binoculars. A minute later, Brian sensed Ronald approaching from behind. "I guess waiting isn't your strong suit," Ronald said.

Through the glass door Brian could make out the counter in the station's reception area. The countertop featured three telephones, each with a person standing over it. Phone attendants included Ben Pritchard, the anonymous younger man, and Winston. Brian pushed the binoculars in Ronald's direction. "What?" Ronald asked. Brian pointed at the door, and Ronald observed as directed. "You think..." and he stopped himself. He gave back the binoculars and used his good arm to wrangle the cell phone from his pocket. "Yes! I have service!"

Ronald dialed, and Brian could tell from the impatient bobbing of Ronald's head that the deputies didn't answer on the first ring. Brian returned to lens-assisted spying and focused on Winston just as he was lifting the receiver. "Yes, hello," he heard Ronald say. "May I speak to Deputy Beecher please? Uh-huh. Yes hi Deputy Beecher. You can help me today by sending an officer over to my house. Uh-huh. Yes. The problem is that, oh, I don't know, a gang of Nazis has kidnapped my mother's dog and – yes, Nazis – uh-huh – and yes, I'd like someone to come over and look into it."

At the counter, the officers weren't leaning over to one another to share a laugh. Winston didn't look confused or amused, only diligent as he scribbled notes on a pad by his phone. "I understand that you're very busy today," Ronald said. "Uh-huh. I know you're receiving a lot of calls, sir, but you see, these are *Nazis*. Uh-huh. So you'll send someone? Really. Great. Fantastic. Thank you so much. Bye now."

Brian lowered the binoculars.

"You know," Ronald said, "I didn't even give him an address." He pondered. "Wait a sec." He dialed on the cell phone again and held it to his ear. "Nope, didn't work. I guess Michael Cox's magic barriers only allow local calls."

A moment later, Winston emerged from the front door, and Ronald started toward him, aiming to head him off before he reached the cluster of police cars. Brian stayed close. When they drew near, Winston acknowledged them with a friendly wave.

"Winston!" Ronald shouted.

"That's Deputy Beecher," Winston said. "And I'm on business right now, but if you need help, one of the officers inside will assist you."

Ronald thrust himself directly in front of the much larger man and stood with feet spread, a barrier. "Winston," Ronald repeated, "I'm Ronald, and you know me, intimately, and I insist that you acknowledge me."

"Yes, Ronald, it's nice to see you, but I'm on business right now. If you need help, one of the officers inside will assist you."

Ronald slapped him, and Winston shouted "Ow!" Ronald slapped him again. "Ow!"

"Next time I'll punch you," Ronald said. "Tell me you know who I am."

"Jeez, Ronald, of course I know who you – wait a minute. Why are you hitting me? What the...." Brian wasn't standing close, but he could see the flood of memory rushing into Winston's eyes. "Holy shit!" the officer said.

8

Jeanne sat on a step by Town Hall, observing the center stage of Kenning's Springtime Celebration. She was a thirteen-year-old girl watching a major town event, but she was also a fifty-five-year-old woman. A moment ago, she'd been even younger, a helpless girl bewildered by the towering attendees at her mother's interment. Before that, she'd faced off with replicas of herself in the storage area of First Church. She wanted to focus on her sense of *now*, on being an adolescent girl on a warm day in the 1970s, even though she knew she was lost somewhere in the twenty-first century.

Daddy was going to give a speech. Daddy liked giving speeches. He always had a solution to the problems on people's minds. Daddy believed that God guided him and had chosen him to be mayor of Kenning. From what Jeanne had seen, Daddy was right. The town's agricultural economy was climbing out of a rut as new businesses were moving into the surrounding areas. Daddy had the vision to anticipate the long-term effects of the population shifts of the 1950s and '60s and was turning that vision into opportunities for economic and real estate development. Economic and real estate development? Jeanne was thirteen – she didn't think about things like the economy and real estate!

Today Jeanne would give a speech, too. She'd inherited her father's penchant for public speaking; even as a child, she'd known how to address a crowd. Her job was to announce the schoolhouse renovations for which her father's office had organized the funding. It was a big deal; the town was going to love her father for it. Jeanne would make her announcement, and she'd be greeted with wild applause.

Daddy strolled onto the stage in his light blue suit, white shirt, and red suspenders. He waved at the people on their picnic blankets, and the applause began. From her perch on the Town Hall's steps, Jeanne monitored the audience. Daddy made rallying claims about what the great people of Kenning would accomplish this year. He reminded them that they should be grateful because not everyone was as blessed as they were, with the beauty and comforts of their town and nation. He alluded to the persistent threat of Communism, and he held up Kenning's prosperity as evidence of the favor God showed to the American way of life. The crowd responded with ecstatic approval. Their reaction clashed with Jeanne's future-memory. Had the people been so enthusiastic before? *Before*?

Her turn to speak came. She stood on the step, smoothed the front of her dress, and lowered a foot onto the next level of concrete. The wooden stage overlapped the stairs, so there were only a few more steps between her and the platform. The height of her shoe's heel caught her eye: Daddy had told her she could wear grown-up woman shoes because she was doing a grown-up woman thing. He'd been proud of her, and she'd been proud of his pride. What if her ankle twisted, and she slammed face-first onto the wood behind him? That would be horrible, a disaster, a—

Who was that man?

Jeanne's heel-clad foot froze in midair as her eyes took in the tall, thin, silver-haired man on the lawn near the stage. Her eyes were playing tricks on her, like they had at the interment. The man in the black hat in the back row of mourners had looked familiar, but she had dismissed the idea because she'd known better. This man had the same sort of look, but the suit was white, and so was the hat on the blanket beside him. He sat alone, a contrast to the audience members around him, who clumped in family units. He was alone, and Daddy's speech absorbed his attention.

He couldn't be here! Jake Warren hadn't been at her mother's interment, and he hadn't been at the Springtime Celebration during the speech that made her think that she, like her father, could devote her life to public service. It was a hallucination, an illusion, a trick.

The heel of her shoe made contact with the stone step, and she lowered the next foot. Her eyes stayed with the silver-haired auditor. Daddy was almost to the point in his speech where he'd turn around and introduce her, and she had to be ready and smiling at his side. Another step down, and another, and she was safely on the stage, level wood between her and the podium, and that man, the man who couldn't be Jake Warren forty-two years ago because *he looked exactly the same*, was still there, watching her father, but now, his attention seemed to divide, because he was looking at Daddy and looking at Jeanne, too.

What if it was him? What if Jake Warren had been in Kenning far longer than anyone had supposed? Maybe he had always been here, planning for the day when Kenning would succumb to his demonic powers, to the duplicity of song that carried more than melody.

Singing. She had stood in the pulpit of her own church, railing against perversions of Christ's message, and the doors to her new sanctuary had flown open, scattering an army of Jake Warrens. Was that army here now? Her girl-eyes looked out at the grassy hills around Town Hall, searching. Daddy said her name; people clapped. The man near the front, the only man of Jake Warren's likeness Jeanne could find, clapped, too.

On that Easter Sunday in the future, Jeanne had stayed near the front of the church and greeted members of her new congregation as they approached to tell her how wonderful her sermon had been. She was flattered, awed, and humbled. Every ounce of her strength had gone toward not screaming about the circle of demon images surrounding her, so she had never expected the sermon to be a success, but the people's reactions told her that God had blessed her.

"Daddy!" she said, and her father looked down at her, distress and disapproval stitching his eyebrows. She wanted to tell him about the bad man on the blanket, the man who stared with piercing eyes, who not only should not have been there but simply should not have been, but she couldn't. She had to smile and tell her audience about how the school's renovation would help to guarantee Kenning's children a brighter future – the future when singing voices swarmed through the open front doors of her sanctuary and seized both her and her congregation. Everyone joined in the hymn, and why not? It was Easter, after all, but the singing seemed sinister, and it was drawing her people away from her, luring them from the safety of New Church.

"Ladies and gentlemen," she heard herself saying. They were the words she had rehearsed. She could give the speech her father needed her to give, even if, at this moment, her mind was far more intent on the silver-haired man who should not have been and on a day, forty-two years in the future, that was somehow tied to this moment in a way she never could have anticipated.

"Ladies and gentlemen, we all know that Kenning isn't a very big town. But that doesn't mean we don't have a big future." The cute sound of her voice won good-natured chuckles and spontaneous applause. "And kids like me, we might not be very big yet, but we've got big minds with big potential, so we're going to need room to grow."

"I'm happy," she said, and she swallowed, looking at the silver-haired man, "that my Daddy, I mean my father the mayor," laughter, "has given me the privilege of telling you today that we're finally going to get the room we need. Classroom, that is." More laughs, less sincere. "Starting in the first week of summer, construction on the new classroom building will begin!"

Applause became a standing ovation. When the silver-haired man stood, the last doubt about his identity vanished. He was Jake Warren, just as the dozen men who had surrounded her had all been Jake Warrens that day, that Easter, when the singing had carried away her congregation and taken her with them, through the open doors of her sanctuary, into blinding bright daylight, and then, with a footstep, into the past.

Into the Prayer Room.

But what was a "Prayer Room?" And how did she know about it?

"Now, ladies and gentlemen, please join me in prayer!" Her voice said the words, but they were wrong – she hadn't led a prayer that day. The people standing on the lawn bowed their heads, and she wanted to scream at them, this didn't happen! But it was happening. "Repeat after me," she said. She couldn't control her own mouth. Strange words moved through her but did not come from her.

The words sounded in her own voice and in the voice of her father behind her. They sounded from Jake Warren and from the rest of the audience behind him. Their rhythm was like a Latin mass, pure vowels and careful enunciation, but Jeanne had studied Latin and Greek, and she knew the sounds of Hebrew well enough to know that this language was nothing Biblical. But the words seemed old, and they had power. Their power came less from their obscure meaning than from the unison they created from the cacophony of the town, a single pitch, a single tempo. Through the power of the words, the town changed.

Clouds wove together, vanquishing the sun. The people, even Jake Warren, sank to their hands and knees. Their necks twisted, and their bodies writhed. Some of them started to bay at the dark sky even before their clothing split into tatters, revealing transmogrified skin. Jake Warren's face divided, sprouting tusks. Between the long curves of sharp bone, nostrils widened and flared, and at the sides of his head, ears lengthened and flopped. Jake Warren became a boar, others became wolves, and others became cattle. Behind her, her father transformed into a sheep. Only her own body remained human as everyone around her melted and reformed into beasts. In the distance, on a hilltop, she saw a lion.

The next word was in her voice but nothing akin to hers: "*Feed!*"

The townspeople, transformed, began to tear one another apart. Blood splashed on grass as teeth tore out throats and claws rent limbs. She wanted to cry out, to stop the frenzy her voice had started, but she was impotent. A flash of light burst overhead, not lightning, but pure illumination, endless, white, and total.

Jeanne was on a highway, surrounded by broken glass.

9

"I could use a cup of coffee," Ronald said. He, Brian, and Winston were walking down Main Street. The Starbuck's lay ahead, but Ronald knew they wouldn't, shouldn't, couldn't stop. If they stopped, they could get sucked into a Charybdis of coffee, spinning forever in a cycle of refills, not knowing that they, like Winston and the other deputies, had been co-opted by the unnatural normalcy that held the town in an invisible, all-enveloping fist.

"I could use a shot of whiskey," Winston said. Brian and Ronald hadn't informed the officer of their destination, but Winston was pliable, still bewildered by his recent experiences as a Kenning zombie.

As they walked, Ronald described his and Brian's flame-lit encounter with Michael Cox, and Winston's expression went from bewildered to forlorn. "Don't worry," Ronald concluded. "We've got a plan. We're on our way to the good Reverend's house now."

Winston's foot skidded to a halt. "*That's* where we're going? Do you really think that's a good idea?"

Ronald and Brian stopped, looked at each other, and looked at Winston. "Well," Ronald said, "we don't have any better ideas. And if anyone knows where to find Mel and Stef and Jeanne, it's Michael Cox, right?"

Winston stared at a drainage grate a few feet away. "You said you saw him burning human bodies last night, and you really think that's a good idea?"

"Yes," Brian said. He directed his answer toward Winston's holster.

Winston nodded toward his gun and repeated, "You really think that's a good idea?"

Brian led them down side streets and into Kenning's richest neighborhood. "That's it." He pointed at the white two-story with a stone path and steps that led to a doorway flanked by grand pilasters.

"I had no idea the ministry was so lucrative," Ronald said.

Reluctantly, Winston lifted the brass knocker and let it clap against Cox's door. Brian's quiet face looked stern and ready. Ronald refused to think beyond the knocker, lest the rationality of Winston's reluctance impede them. The knocker clapped again. A third time. A fourth. As Winston turned to go, Brian reached by him and pressed the button for the doorbell.

A woman's voice, marked by the strain of shouting and muffled by distance, came down from the second floor: "Just a minute!" Winston set a hand on his gun handle. A grinding metallic sound preceded a loud thump. "COMING!" the woman shouted, this time closer. A bolt slid, and the front door opened a sliver. The woman who peered at them wore clothes suited for yard work, but she looked clean, her makeup and hair careful. Her eye settled on Winston. "What can I do for you, Deputy...?"

"Beecher, ma'am. I need to ask you a few questions."

She opened the door further, but she blocked the gap with her body. "And who are these gentlemen with you?" she asked.

"That's Ronald Glassner, and that's Brian McCullough."

The woman stepped through the doorway and extended a gracious hand. "I'm Sara Cox," she said. Winston and Ronald shook the hand in turn. The hand paused in front of Brian. "I recognize you. You've grown up quite strong." Her smile and tone of voice oozed charm, almost enough to cover the sinister quality of "grown up," which told Ronald she had been observing Brian's maturation with interest.

Brian refused the handshake.

Mrs. Cox lowered her hand without a glimmer of offense. "Two civilians and a policeman. Your visit seems as unusual as it was unexpected." Another sinister waver in her voice told Ronald that "unexpected" was a lie. They were not only expected, but she had been waiting for them. Was he being paranoid?

"Well, ma'am," Winston said. His hand hadn't moved away from his gun. "These two are helping me on a case. A sort of missing person."

Mrs. Cox shifted her head and hair to one side. "How can a person be 'sort of' missing?"

"Well, technically, it hasn't been long enough yet, and nobody's filed a report, but these guys are worried, and I thought I'd—"

"So you're going door to door, then?" Mrs. Cox punctuated her question with wary glances at all three of them.

"No, ma'am," Winston said. Why didn't Winston say yes? Why was Ronald so completely uncomfortable and so completely sure that this woman would do them tremendous harm?

"So you've come to my house with questions about this sort-of-missing person for a specific reason, then," Mrs. Cox said. "Is that right?"

Brian mumbled something. Ronald turned to him and whispered, "What?" The whispering was silly. Everyone heard Ronald's question and awaited the answer.

"She hasn't even asked us who's missing," Brian said. "She already knows."

Mrs. Cox's rosy cheeks sank, and her eyelashes fluttered. The words she spoke, "Do I?," carried enough insincerity to turn her face's expression of concern into a mask of mockery.

"Step away from the door, ma'am," Winston said. Mrs. Cox stepped back into her doorway, filling the gap once again. She paused, assessing them, and took another step back, creating an opening too small for them to use without pushing her. Ronald waited for Winston to respond. Winston looked at Brian, his face mixing anxiety with an exhortation to patience.

Mrs. Cox took another step back. The opening was big enough now, but it would be tight. "You want to come in, I take it?"

Trap! Trap! Trap! No single syllable had ever held so much truth for Ronald before, but he didn't utter it. Brian and Winston's behavior told him they knew as well as he that all was not right, that Mrs. Cox was playing with them.

"Move," Brian said, and he forced his way inside. He stood at the base of the stairway and shouted, "MELANIE!!"

"You're not looking for Melanie *Grayson*, are you?"

Mrs. Cox's last rhetorical taunt proved too much for Winston. His gun came out of its holster. He marched through the doorway and hollered, "MELANIE, ARE YOU IN HERE?!" Checking corners before taking new steps, Winston began a tour of the house, staying in sight while checking out the antique-filled dining room.

Brian set a foot on the bottom stair, turned around, grabbed Mrs. Cox, and shoved her against the banister. His fist twisted the fabric of her t-shirt as he spat, "Where is she? I swear to God, if you hurt her—"

A muffled cry cut him off. It came from above. Winston rushed from the dining room. Brian let go of Mrs. Cox and leapt upward, taking two steps at a time. Winston stayed close behind, gun ready. Ronald hesitated: face to face with Mrs. Cox, he wanted to say something profound, but he found no words.

"You're the homosexual reporter, aren't you?" she asked.

Nothing he could have said would have been quite as disarming as Mrs. Cox's question. Defeated, he ran to catch up with Brian and Winston, who had traced the noise to a hatch in the ceiling. Winston pulled a string, bringing down a board attached to a folding wooden staircase. Brian climbed the rickety steps, metal hinges grinding under his weight. Winston holstered his gun and followed. Ronald looked back. Mrs. Cox had come to the second floor landing. She picked up the ancient one-eyed cat that was nuzzling against her leg, and together, they observed.

Ronald reached the attic in time to see Brian peeling the duct tape away from Melanie's lips. "Oh God, Mel, oh God, Mel," he said. Stunned, kneeling on the floor in a ruined Easter dress, the girl didn't resist Brian's hands as they pressed against her cheeks and pulled her face to his. The quick kisses that traced her mouth might have hurt against the tape-worn skin, but Melanie didn't protest. She fell into him, revealing more binding around her wrists. Winston walked around to release her arms, and Ronald scanned the room, looking for the mechanism that would trigger at any moment and unleash their doom.

He noticed the hand-woven rug and the elegant cherry wood desk. On the desk, a book with gold-embossed letters on the front announced "Diary." Ronald remembered a conversation with Brian – was that only two days ago? – about the manuscript he'd expected to find in Dave Holcomb's wooden shack.

Melanie got to her feet. She, Brian, Winston, and Ronald stood together in the Coxes' attic and were, for a moment, speechless. Brian said, "What did they do to you?" The girl opened her mouth and uttered nothing but a dry rasp. As if the sound were a summary of torture, Brian hugged her close and said, "Oh God, Mel, oh God."

She cleared her throat. "No," she said. "Not me. Tied me. Tied me up. Kept me. But Stef...."

Ronald's heart fell to his stomach. He didn't know Melanie's twelve-year-old sister, but he could share the sorrow in Melanie's last two words.

"What about Stef?" Brian demanded. "What did they do?"

"What's this?" Winston picked up the diary and pulled on its cover, which seemed locked.

"That's my diary," Mrs. Cox said. Ronald hadn't heard the grinding of hinges as she'd ascended the rickety stairs, but she was there, standing by the hatch. She'd left the cat behind. "And it's private. Deputy Beecher, I insist that you return it to me and leave my home at once." She spoke with the same tone as before, taunting and insincere. She wanted them to take the book. She had left it there just for them. The book was the trap.

"Winston," Ronald said, but what could he say?

Brian's head lowered onto Melanie's shoulder, tightening their tearful embrace. When his face rose, it was red and water-lined. He spoke through clenched teeth: "What did you do to them, you BITCH!" He stormed toward Mrs. Cox, and Ronald and Winston jumped out of the way. Ronald turned in time to see Brian's fist slam into Mrs. Cox's face. The woman's arms flew up, shocked and desperate for balance, and she tipped over, falling through the hatchway. Ronald heard a loud crack that could only have been the wooden stairs breaking under the force of her fall. He and Winston rushed to Brian's side, and all three looked over the edge. The wood was splintered. Mrs. Cox lay motionless below.

"Oh Jesus." Winston looked at Brian. "You killed her."

"It's not the first person we've killed this week." Brian's level tone sent a chill across Ronald's skin.

"It was an accident." Melanie's voice sounded stronger. She joined them at the edge of the hatchway. "Brian was protecting me. She kidnapped me. She – only it wasn't her who did it, it was—" Ronald expected that a sob would follow Melanie's self-interruption, but silence prevailed.

"It's okay," Ronald said, unconvinced. "Don't worry about it... now. Now, we need to get out of here. We've got to get down there somehow. The stairs are broken." He thought of using Mrs. Cox's body as a cushion, but he kept the idea to himself.

"It's not that far," Winston said, "and I'm the tallest." He looked at them. "And I'm the only one without a hurt shoulder who's not wearing a dress. I'll lower myself down, and then I'll help the rest of you." Winston tucked the diary into the back of his pants and began.

Ronald watched the operation with unease. On the floor, within reach of Winston's dangling feet as he lowered himself, Mrs. Cox's body lay still. Her neat hair had gone wild; her makeup remained composed. She wasn't moving, but at this angle, at this distance, and in this light, Ronald couldn't be sure she wasn't breathing. Not that she could do much harm – could she? If she was anything like her husband—

Winston said "Oof" as his fingers released the attic floor and his feet smashed onto broken boards. The barrel-chested man's arms shot out to steady himself. Ronald imagined a cartoon of Winston toppling and flattening Mrs. Cox's corpse, but Winston regained his balance, feet planted firmly at a slight distance from the body's left arm. She was close enough to grab him. She wouldn't, couldn't, and even if her arms would move, what could she do?

"Mel's next," Brian said, and Ronald nodded. Brian and Ronald cooperated awkwardly, grabbing at arms and legs as they guided the girl to the ground. At the bottom, Melanie seemed dazed. When she snapped to attention, she kicked Mrs. Cox's body. It didn't react, but it moved away from them, sliding as if the carpet were a smooth surface. Ronald blinked and shook his head. He wasn't sure. Mrs. Cox's body might not have been touching the ground at all.

"Ronald's turn," Winston said. As the other men lowered him, bodies pressing close, Ronald wondered whether "erotic" had an opposite. He stepped out of the way, and Brian asked Winston to do the same: despite his own shoulder injury, he wanted to get down on his own. When he dropped the distance between dangling feet and messy floor, he stumbled, and he landed butt-first on the rubble of the wooden staircase.

Ronald said "Ouch," but Brian made no noise. He looked at Mrs. Cox's body. His face trembled with something that might have been remorse, but the motion was brief.

"We'll go back to Brian's," Winston said. "We'll read this book. We'll figure out what's going on, and then we'll put a stop to it."

The foursome started home in a shoulder-to-shoulder line, Winston by Ronald, Ronald by Melanie, and Melanie by Brian. They were quiet; they'd have time to talk soon. Ronald hesitated, but he broke away to have one last look behind them, at the Coxes' beautiful white house. Bright green faux shutters bordered its tall second-floor windows. The sun was setting, so the movement of shadows made shapes indistinct and doubtful. Was that a silhouette in one of the windows? Was Mrs. Cox waving goodbye?

10

Melanie reported that strange civility marked her final hours with Mrs. Cox. After her escape attempt, they ate biscuits and jam and slipped into banal conversation. Mrs. Cox told her Faith Healer, the band helmed by Bobby Sutton, would perform at First Church that night. It would be the first event of many: First Church would celebrate Christ's Resurrection every day until next Sunday, which, if Melanie cared to know, the Pope had designated Divine Mercy Sunday. Thinking about Stef and how excited Stef had been about Bobby Sutton's stupid band, Melanie told Mrs. Cox that she didn't give a damn about the Pope. Mrs. Cox said she didn't care for the Pope either; she found the date's Catholic significance "curious and quaint."

"Cunt," Ronald said. Winston nodded.

Melanie smiled, and the sensation was strange on her raw lips. She didn't know if she should be smiling when Stef was probably dead. She didn't know if she should be smiling when her mother, whose betrayal was far worse than anything her father had ever done, was still out there, driving one of the white vans that Ronald said were all over town.

"Tape," Brian said. She looked at him, not sure what he meant. He hadn't said anything since they'd left the Coxes' house.

"I think he means," Winston said, "that you were still taped up when we found you. How'd you eat biscuits"

Brian could have said that himself. "She put that on when you knocked on the door," Melanie said. "She apologized and said she had to do it. She was in a hurry, but she seemed... calm."

"She wanted us to find you," Ronald said. "The question is, why? Why did they take you in the first place?"

All four of them looked down at the coffee table, where Mrs. Cox's diary sat unopened. Melanie had told them how Mrs. Cox had written almost non-stop the entire time that she was there. Whatever the book was, Mrs. Cox had been anxious to finish it.

"She wants us to read it," Ronald said.

Winston leaned over from the sofa, grabbed the book, and put it in his lap. "Now just hold on. I'm not convinced. Ronald, you're saying that they kidnapped Melanie but wanted us to come get her. And Sara Cox bothered to lock up this book," for emphasis, he pulled on the thick front and back covers, which were fastened by a metal clasp, "and told us to leave it alone, all because she really wanted us to read it. That it?"

Ronald raised an eyebrow and frowned. "It all sounds kind of far-fetched when you put it *that* way."

"And don't forget," Winston said, "that she died trying to protect this book."

"I told you I don't think she's dead," Ronald said.

"Right, because you think you saw her floating." Winston patted him on the knee. They sat together on the sofa. Brian sat in his rocking chair. Melanie sat separately, in a chair they had taken from the kitchen. "Most women I know," Winston continued, "don't float."

"Most sheriffs I know don't have claws and fly around in garbage dumps, but your pal Hadderly did. Back me up, Brian."

Brian's chin rose from his chest. He looked at Ronald, then at Winston, and nodded. Melanie didn't know if he was thinking about Stef or his own sister. Maybe both. Whatever it was, it was making him different, less like the Brian she knew and more like the Brian she knew about.

"On the walk home," Ronald said, "I saw a poster on a phone pole. Faith Healer starts playing at nine o'clock. That's in a few minutes. If we want to see what's really going on at First Church, maybe we should go."

"Events for the Young Evangelists aren't usually that late on a school night." Melanie hadn't realized that she'd missed school.

"Nobody went to school today," Ronald said. "I saw too many kids out playing. I'd be willing to bet that there's no school tomorrow, either. Whatever the church's plan might be, education does not seem to be part of it."

"Ronald, you're changing the subject." Winston brandished Mrs. Cox's book.

"I'm not changing the subject!" He stood up. "Okay, I am changing the subject." He pointed at the diary. "Look, I'm only half-kidding when I say that I'm afraid that breaking the lock on that thing is going to fill this room with deadly poison, unleash a legion of demons, or both. I feel like somehow, we've been doing everything they want us to do. It's like they're using their mind control mojo on the whole town, but it's really *us* they're controlling. Think about it. Why are we the only ones immune to what's going on?"

"I wasn't immune," Winston said.

"You are now," Ronald said. "Now, together, we're able to think for ourselves and act for ourselves in a way that nobody else can. I mean, Nathan Grayson seemed like a fucking juggernaut until he went all Stepford on our asses." He cleared his throat. "Sorry, Mel. I mean no disrespect to your father."

"No problem." She tried another smile.

"So we've got this special immunity, and we're able to waltz in and save Melanie from the evil magician's tower without getting so much as a scratch – all due respect to your bruised backside, Brian," who did not respond, "and you're not just a little bit suspicious?"

Winston rose from the sofa and stood inches in front of Ronald. "Maybe you could stop condescending for just a minute and tell us all, please, WHAT THE HECK IT IS THAT YOU SUSPECT!"

Melanie had never heard Winston raise his voice in anger. She didn't like it. She didn't like any of this. None of it made sense. Winston wasn't acting like himself. Brian was losing himself. She'd been tricked, tied up, chased, and bruised. She was sick of everything and everybody being so out of control.

Ronald sat back down, becoming a dwarf in Winston's shadow. "I'm sorry." He put his face in his hands. "I'm sorry, I'm sorry. Christ fuck! I barely slept. Melanie didn't sleep. Winston – well, you probably slept, but you can't say for sure. Mr. Cold Silence over there probably won't *choose* to say."

"I didn't sleep," Brian said.

"Thank you." Ronald took a deep breath and surveyed his audience. He was a young man, but Melanie thought he looked old. "I don't know what I suspect. I don't know what's going on. I know all of this is fucking crazy. I suspect... I suspect there's a big picture that we're not seeing, a big plan, and we're a part of it. I don't know how I drove into town a week ago and wound up being a part of some huge fucking conspiracy, but that's what happened. I suspect everything we do is part of somebody's master plan. Michael Cox's, Jake Warren's, somebody's. I suspect we're doing everything they want us to do, and I suspect that if we keep doing that, they'll get exactly what they want. And I'm pretty fucking sure that we don't want that to happen. Okay?" He sighed and leaned back into the sofa cushions.

Winston sat next to him. "Okay." He dropped the diary back on the coffee table. "So what do we do?"

"Some of my clothes are in Brian's room." Melanie felt herself speaking and knew the words were hers, but she didn't understand what was making her thoughts so clear. "I'm going to change. I'm going to take a quick shower. Ronald, there's stuff for making coffee in the cabinet by the refrigerator. It's on the top shelf. Winston, get it down for him." She was giving orders, and the men were listening, their faces showing comprehension and assent. "Make a pot of coffee. Drink it, because we're not going to sleep for awhile longer."

She took a deep breath, closed her eyes, and let the clarity keep coming. "We'll make it to First Church before the concert is over. We'll see what's happening. We'll see if we can figure out something about this big plan that Ronald keeps talking about. We have to, because Ronald's right. Mrs. Cox knew you were coming." She remembered her mother asking if *he* were here. The *he* she'd meant was Brian. "My mother knew you would come. Everybody thinks they know what's going to happen. Except us. So here's what's going to happen."

The men — all of them older than she was, all of them stronger than she was — waited for her to tell them what to do. "We'll learn what we can at First Church, and we'll come back here, and we'll make a plan. We'll decide if we want to look at that book. I think we will. Ronald, I don't think it'll poison us, because if they wanted us dead—"

"We'd be extra crispy," Ronald said.

Melanie nodded. "But it could trick us. So if, after we learn what we learn, we decide to look at it, we'll be careful. Okay, Ronald?"

"Okay."

"Okay, Winston?"

"Okay."

She looked at Brian. He smiled at her. "Okay," she said. "After all that, we'll make a plan for tomorrow. And then we'll try to sleep. Okay?"

11

Melanie tapped Ronald on the shoulder. "Let me look." Ronald handed her the binoculars and studied her. The ruined Easter dress had made her look like a sad, defenseless orphan. In tight blue jeans and an old t-shirt that complimented her chest, she looked not only more mature but also happier. Her dark hair's neat ponytail made her seem worthy of the authority she had wielded since they'd retrieved her.

Nevertheless, Ronald doubted she'd detect anything new. They were creeping along the outskirts of a sprawling rock concert. First Church and the revival tent were stuffed beyond capacity. Around the building, in Hart's Cemetery, and in a hilly field across the street, additional attendees sat on blankets. Tiki torches and moonlight provided a hint of their numbers: according to Winston, virtually everyone from Kenning and the surrounding areas had shown up to hear a teenager shout "SAVIOR, SAVE ME!" over inexpert power chords. Speakers with gargantuan woofers fed sound to the populace in all locations. Not only had the entire town turned out for the concert, but First Church had *planned* for such attendance.

From the top of an unoccupied hill in a corner of the cemetery, Ronald's binoculars afforded a good view of the church's sanctuary. Through a large clear window, Ronald, Winston, Melanie, and Brian could see people standing among pews. "Hey – I know that guy." Melanie handed Brian the binoculars. "Who is he? Front row, red shirt."

Brian looked, and Ronald waited to see if Brian would report his findings verbally or through obscure nods and gestures. "Chad Sutton." Brian gave the binoculars back to Melanie.

"Bobby's big brother?" she asked. "Why does he look so... bored?"

"May I have a look?" Winston asked. He received the binoculars and searched. "He's not bored. He's scared."

Ronald took the binoculars and searched for the red shirt. Teenagers were the primary occupants of the front pews. In contrast to the grown-ups and younger children further back, many of whom looked dressed for a Sunday sermon, the kids wore tight pants and t-shirts and belly-revealing halter tops. As he pondered an entry on *American Sane* entitled "Sluts for Jesus," Ronald located the red shirt. Chad Sutton looked twenty-something and large, maybe larger than Winston, and he had a ridiculous moustache. He lacked the dropped-jaw glee of his writhing companions. Instead of swaying to the beat, he switched from foot to foot arrhythmically. Quick glances from shoulder to shoulder suggested obsession with his surroundings, a man fearful of attack. "You're right," Ronald said. "He's terrified." Singer Bobby announced that the encore would be a repeat of their smash hit "Kool-Aid Crusade," so Ronald added, "The question isn't why is he scared – the question is, why isn't everyone else?"

"Yeah," Winston said. "Chad is the only person in there who seems to know that something isn't right. That makes him like us. Smart thinking."

Ronald had intended his question as a joke.

"We should talk to him," Melanie said.

"How? If he's scared, he won't talk in front of the others. And I don't think we'll be able to get him alone." Winston took the binoculars and resumed gazing.

Ronald turned to Melanie. "The concert is about to end. Maybe we can approach him in the exit-bound throng?"

"*We* can't," Melanie said. "But I can."

"No," Brian said.

"Why you?" Winston asked.

"Because he'll recognize me. He might trust me. Do you really think he'll trust a cop and a reporter?"

"She's got a point," Ronald said.

Winston shook his head. "If we know anything, it's that First Church is dangerous. She should stay with us."

"If they wanted to hurt Melanie, they already would have," Ronald said.

"No," Brian said.

Melanie turned to him. Ronald recognized the look on the girl's face, feminine self-assertion that a straight man dare not deny. "I have been through so much *shit*. Just because you—" Thunderous applause drowned the rest of her sentence. Lights inside the sanctuary and the tent got brighter. Flashlights came on in the cemetery and the field. Concertgoers began their exodus. As the church's exits burst open, Melanie grabbed Brian, kissed him on the cheek, and mouthed the words "See you soon." She headed for the exit nearest Chad's pew.

Ronald took the binoculars and followed her progress. She mingled with the crowd, fighting against its current.

"Do you see her?" Winston asked.

"Yes!" She broke between a hand-holding couple and dodged a thicket of tweens. As she pressed into the masses, she became less distinct. "No."

Winston turned. "Brian, why don't you – Brian!"

Assuming Winston was trying to jolt Brian from his secret netherworld of silent thought, Ronald resumed his attempt to relocate Melanie. He found her by the door she had selected; she was luring her target into conversation. Ronald lowered the binoculars. The masses were closer now, and their chatter necessitated shouting, "HEY GUYS, SHE GOT HIM!"

"BRIAN!!!!" Winston screamed. "RONALD, HE'S GONE!"

Damn it! Why couldn't that kid just—

"I'M GOING AFTER HIM!" Winston said.

"NO!" Ronald grabbed Winston's arm and pulled him closer. "Brian's going to do what Brian's going to do. He'd want us to look after Melanie. We wait." They crouched and spied. Melanie and Chad looked over their shoulders with conspiratorial frequency as they conversed. They reached some sort of agreement, and Melanie led Chad back to the hill in the cemetery. Ronald and Winston rose to greet Melanie and her new charge.

"Chad, this is Winston. He works in the sheriff's office. And this is Ronald. He's new in town. They're both like us." As he shook hands with the moustached man, Ronald admired the aura of comfort that Melanie had summoned for Chad's benefit.

"How did you?" Chad's muscles tensed, a cat poised to sprint.

Ronald struggled to interpret. "How did we what?"

"How did you get free?"

"Where's Brian?" Melanie asked.

"He, uh...." Winston squirmed. "He went on ahead."

Melanie scowled.

"Free. Yes, you see," Ronald said, "that's an interesting question. Isn't it, Winston?"

"Yes," Winston said. Ronald elbowed him. "I mean yes, it is. Ronald and Melanie's friend Brian did it. For me. They did, I mean, set me free from, you know. I was driving in circles around the police station. They slapped me."

Winston sounded like a jabbering idiot, but Chad seemed to comprehend. "Nobody did it for me," he said. "I broke free myself. They had control over me for years."

"*YEARS?*" The volume of Ronald and Winston's simultaneous exclamation alerted them to the thinning of the crowd. If they wanted to remain undetected, or if they wanted Chad to believe that their meeting was clandestine, they would have to be quieter. "*Years?*" they whispered.

"Yeah. They only got Bobby a little while ago, but I remember, ever since... Brian? Do you mean Brian McCullough?"

"Yes," Melanie said. "Did you see where he went?"

Chad looked over both shoulders and narrowed his eyes to slits. "I can't be with you people." He readied to bolt.

"Hey," Winston said. The word had two long, comforting syllables. The officer placed a hand on the young man's massive shoulder. "I can only imagine what you've been through. But you can trust us."

"They'll burn me!" Chad clapped his hand over his mouth and lowered it. Softer, he said, "They'll burn me anyway. Is there a way out?"

Ronald wanted to repeat the "years" question, but he understood the situation's delicacy.

Winston's steady hand assuaged Chad's urge to flee. "I've got to get out. I can't keep pretending. They'll know!"

"Tell us how to help you," Winston said.

"You? You're with *him!*" The hand clapped over the mouth again. Seconds later, it fell limp at his side.

"Him?" Melanie asked. "You mean Brian?"

Ronald looked around and saw no one; he listened and heard no one. The townspeople in their vicinity had all left for their cars and homes. Where had Brian gone?

"For a long time, it was just like these blank spaces where I couldn't remember. But then it started coming back, and the first ones, the early ones, were about him, starting with the time he beat me up on the playground." Ronald surveyed Chad's size and felt dubious. "It was like, these voices, talking to me, and I did what they said. I didn't have to. I *wanted* to. Can't say why. And one day, I would hear the voices, and I didn't want to as much, but I did it anyway. And then Bobby, a few weeks ago, started coming back from Young Evangelists all strange, and I knew!"

Chad made limited sense, but Winston nodded with complete

understanding. "You said they'd burn you," coaxed the deputy. "What makes you think that?"

"They got her!" Chad said. Ronald expected a mouth-clap, but Chad's hands remained at his sides.

"Got who?" Winston asked.

"Angela. I thought she was crazy, kept talking about a demon possessing her. But then I'm crazy, too, right, so we met sometimes, and talked about it. I saw her yesterday, when there was the singing, and it had a sound like the voices have, and I knew everybody could hear it, and she knew too, because she yelled for everyone not to listen, not to sing, but then they grabbed her! I knew I had to play along. They made me carry her! I watched as they held her against the tree!" He closed his eyes. His entire face was shaking, and at intervals, his arms twitched.

In a soft, fatherly voice, Winston said, "It's not your fault. What did they do to Angela?"

Ronald looked at Melanie. She met his eyes with the same confusion and desperation that he felt. Chad's information was crucial, but they could barely follow it, and the question wasn't *if* the young man would run away, but *when*. Ronald held his tongue, waiting for the calming authoritative presence that Winston had used to befriend Brian years before to pry the facts free.

"Go on," Winston said. "It's okay."

"They used a broken branch. To smash her – her head. They broke open her skull and made me carry her to the fire!"

Shattering all precepts of manly friendship, Winston wrapped his arm around Chad and gave him a sideways hug. "It's okay," Winston said. "It's not your fault."

Ronald caught on. "Yeah, it's okay," he said. "Nobody could help it. It's the voices' fault, not yours." Winston looked at him. The moonlight suggested that the officer was displeased, but Ronald couldn't be sure. "Come on, Chad, this is very important. Whose voices are they, and how did they get to you?"

Chad pushed Winston away. "You! You're with him! They – they'll know! FUCK YOU! YOU'RE FUCKING BURNT AND YOU DON'T EVEN KNOW IT!"

With that, Chad fled.

"Damn it, Ronald!" Winston ran after him, into the night. Melanie followed.

"What'd I do?" Ronald said. Then he ran as fast as his injured arm would allow.

12

Jeanne knew this memory better than any in her head. It replayed through hundreds of quaking reveries spread across dozens of years. They were setting up for a party. Charlie had the full keg in his backseat and the half keg in the passenger seat, so they took separate cars. Jeanne didn't drink, but she didn't mind that Charlie did. Charlie had a rebellious streak summed up in his white t-shirt and tight leather jacket. He was cute and cool, but under his anti-everything veneer, he harbored spirituality more sincere than any she had ever encountered. After graduation, they were getting married.

When the cops arrived, the fat truck driver would say that two motorcycles in a race almost collided in front of him, and he braked and swerved, and the truck jackknifed, and the rest was a deafening blur of smashing metal. Jeanne didn't see the motorcycles, but she did see the truck's cab and trailer fold together and form a barrier across three lanes. Rubber screamed against road; cars spun. A brown pick-up crashed into the trailer, and a blue four-door hit the pick-up. Jeanne braked, pulled right, zoomed into the breakdown lane, scraped against a concrete wall, and stopped, unharmed.

A medical examiner would later explain that the impact killed him instantly, but when she got out of her car and ran into a field of broken glass and twisted metal, she could only think he was hurt, alive but hurt and needing her help. Smoke surrounded her, but she saw no fire. She searched through ruins, detecting the wounded and dead but comprehending nothing but her need for Charlie and Charlie's need for her. She gazed at the jackknifed truck and thought Charlie had gotten away until she recognized the green heap in the corner of her vision, half as long as it should have been – Charlie's Ford. Endless nights of prayer would not erase the image from her mind, his crushed head and mangled torso, bound in the leather jacket, hanging through the driver-side window, almost disconnected at the waist. Slowed, she walked away from her fiancé's body and, with conversational volume, said "help."

People stirred near one of the vehicles at the back of the line. Good. They'd been spared. Later, she would wonder why she hadn't tried to do more, why she hadn't, like the people running toward her, started to pull the injured survivors from the wreckage or offered her help with tourniquets and resuscitation. Instead, she drifted toward the front of the mass of death, toward the cab of the jackknifed truck. She would walk around to the driver's side and see the fat man in the seat shaking his head as if to clear his vision, as if to banish the effects of the concussion, broken arm, and fractured ribs that would add up to "getting off easy." Other than Charlie, there were five dead and eleven wounded, one of them paralyzed for life.

Feeling her body move forward, she prepared herself for her meeting with the driver, his slurred babble and fast tears. He would insist on climbing out of the cab, and she would help him. She wished she could go back to her car and, like so many others, drive across the highway's grassy median and into the traffic crawling away in the opposite direction. She had lived through this scene enough times. She didn't need to walk through it again now, but her young legs kept moving one in front of the other, dazed but steady, bringing her body around for the encounter with the man whose quick stomp on a pedal had broken her life.

Before she arrived, the driver-side door swung open. It wasn't supposed to do that. The legs that emerged from the doorway were not wearing plus-sized jeans. The slacks were brown, creased, and professional, terminating at well-made loafers that clapped onto asphalt with confidence. The man wearing them was tall and thin. Jeanne identified him before her eyes swept over the long facial features and silver hair.

"Are you hurt?" the deacon asked. "Is anyone hurt?"

He knew! He had to know. He was invading her mind, marching through her memories, and he had to have the same doubled perspective as she, reflecting on outcomes before they arrived. He knew Charlie was dead. They were here so he could see it, see her, and savor her trauma. "You *devil*," she seethed.

He ignored her, stepping away from the truck and the wreckage it had caused. "I'll go," he said. "I'll go for help." The question about being hurt and the insistence on going for help — they were the same as before. Jake Warren was speaking the truck driver's lines but revising his actions, exploring new territory in the dimming twilight. Jeanne followed him over the empty highway, not knowing what she would do but not wanting the aberration to escape. She imagined having a scythe and cutting him down, adding his blood to the splatters on the street, but unarmed she could only wade in his wake and wait for his next revision of her history, unless—

Her body turned around and started walking. She passed the truck, and instead of weaving a route back through the smoking debris, she ran through the unoccupied breakdown lane, back to her own car. She got in and twisted the key. The engine turned over on the third try. Shoving the car into gear, she slammed on the gas, dragging metal along the concrete wall until she pulled free and darted past the wrecks. In seconds she was clear, and the road lay open before her. Jake Warren walked in the center lane. She couldn't imagine where he thought he was going. Her foot forced the accelerator to the floor.

Jake Warren's body slammed onto her hood with a satisfying thud and flew up onto the windshield, creating a dent in the glass like a convex spider web. His body rolled upward, disappeared, and reappeared in her rear-view mirror as it hit the ground and rebounded. Her foot moved from the accelerator to the brake, and when she stopped, she initiated a three-point turn. She'd run over him again. She wasn't killing a man – she was fighting for possession of her mind.

Before she got the car pointed back toward the wreckage, she glimpsed herself in the mirror. She wasn't the twenty-two year-old girl she had been when Charlie died. She was the older woman that Jake Warren's ghost had thrown on the stairs, and she was something else. Her short hair had new streaks of grey. She was grizzled, a warrior, and the battle had begun.

As her foot returned to the accelerator, she noted without interest that the scenery had changed. The jackknifed truck and smashed cars were gone. The road in front of her looked the same as the road behind her, an unlimited, empty expanse of highway with only one other occupant, the well-dressed man who was standing up and about to be run down.

This time the collision sent the body rolling under the car, which wobbled as tires crunched bone. Terrible glee surged behind Jeanne's eyes, and she told herself again that she was not killing a man but fighting an illusion, battling for her soul and her God.

Jerking the wheel before she came to a stop, she spun her car around for a third attack.

She expected to see a spectacle like the one before: a crumpled body impossibly rising from asphalt and shifting its misplaced parts back into the semblance of upright humanity. Instead, Jake Warren was already standing, legs in a firm V-stance, shoulders square. She couldn't see his face or hair because the twilight had faded into dark. Behind him a row of headlights, five pairs, glared at her. The demon-man was a silhouette in a flood of white, illuminated by a fleet at his back. She didn't need vision to see the toothy grin that defied her to charge.

She had nothing to lose. Her headlights came on, the accelerator hit floor, and she careened forward. Jake Warren leapt at her approach, and she heard his feet land on the roof of her car. Ahead, the ten headlights became more distinct, and Jeanne saw the vehicles, the deacon's Lincoln in the center and two vans at either side. They held their ground as she sped toward them.

Her scalp must have split as her head smashed through glass, but she didn't feel pain. She felt cool night air as she flew through her windshield and into the sky, over the blue Lincoln, between the white vans, soaring high until ground arced upward and bounced her back into the air. She landed as Jake Warren had, a ball of twisted limbs, but she was conscious, able, and *strong*. With clicks and cracks, her legs rediscovered their shapes, and she felt herself rise to her feet. The movements happened consciously – she was choosing to rise – but the choice itself lacked the immediacy of the present and instead seemed to well from a past as distant as Charlie's death. Even though she was living new events, she moved through them with the same momentum of inevitability that had guided her toward the cab, the cab of the truck where Jake Warren had launched his new invasion of her history.

She took a V-stance and squared her shoulders. The Lincoln and the vans bathed her in the same light as before. She had smashed into them from the other direction and flown onto the street behind them, but their undamaged fronts now faced her. Jake Warren didn't stand in the headlights as he had before; his outline hung over the wheel of the center car. It was his turn to charge.

Following his example, she held her ground as the five vehicles raced toward her. Trusting the inevitability that governed her body, she felt her knees bend and her legs thrust. She landed on the roof of the car in triumph, but her balance failed, and a second later she tumbled onto the road. As she struggled to regain her stance, she heard the vehicles screech to a halt. When she looked at them, she saw their backs, fifty yards away.

One van's rear doors were open, and a figure climbed out. The figure was too short and lithe to be Jake Warren's. Jeanne approached, wary but confident. As the distance between her and the van diminished, the twin senses of inevitability and historicity faded. She was moving out of memory and into a new present. The image of the figure climbing out of the van became sharper. Jeanne was looking at a girl, and the girl was not alone.

"Hello, Melanie," Jeanne said. "Welcome to the Prayer Room." The words left her lips, but they were not her own.

13

Mel, Ronald, and Winston would have noticed by now that he was gone. Once they noticed, they'd be able to guess what he was doing. They should have known what he'd think. Too much was going on for them to turn down useful information, and a diary by Mel's captor could be crucial, even if Mrs. Cox wanted them to find it. Brian had to know. He used a flathead screwdriver to chisel the lock from the book's faux-leather cover, opening the diary one hammered stab at a time. He pulled back the cover and read: *A Memoir of the Long Beginning.*

What kind of person gives her diary a title?

"I am to create a record. Jake told me to focus on <u>what</u> we accomplished, not <u>how</u>. People greater than myself – those on a level near his friend Allen, I suppose – record the hows. The whys, Jake said, will vary. For Mike, it still has to do with faith. Jake keeps his motivations to himself, but I have my theories. My own why is even more inscrutable than Jake's. I wish I believed as Mike does. That would be easier. I suppose I do believe that all the sacrifices we have made in the last seven years will eventually bring about some form of good. My husband and I have at least that in common.

"So then, to <u>what</u>. What was the beginning of the beginning? We've known Jake for seven years, but maybe it started earlier. While Jake was scouring the southeast, and Mike and I were deciding to stay married because it was God's will, the pieces were already finding their positions on the board. I think Jake studied Kenning long before he made his arrival known. Even though he took months and months to identify his aim, he always knew his targets. The McCulloughs brought him here."

Brian set the diary, still open to the first page, on the coffee table. He was not surprised to see his family's name. The revelation felt like confirmation. Vindication. Intuition had brought him back to his house, alone, to read the book that scared the others. He picked up the diary and turned the page.

14

The run seemed too short for Melanie to feel as awful as she did, but when Chad tripped on his own feet and crashed onto asphalt, she felt glad – she couldn't have gone much farther. Slowing to a walk, she approached and offered him a hand. He took it, and while she helped him stand, he asked, "Why... are you... chasing?" He was breathless, more exhausted than she. She hadn't slept well in days. Chad had been involved for *years*.

"I." Melanie's head felt light. Her knees bent, and her backside hit the street. "Uh," she said. Chad sat next to her.

Winston arrived next, followed by Ronald. Winston acknowledged them with a nod, leaned over, and sucked at air. When Ronald drew within ten yards, he shouted "THANK GOD!" and dropped to the ground with a faint "Ow."

"Help you," Mel said. "Want to help you." She thought for a moment as her heart settled into a reasonable rhythm. "We want to help you, and we want you to help us."

"Ronald!" Winston called. "You okay over there?"

Ronald's torso slumped over splayed legs, signing a definitive *no*. "Coming. Be right... there." He leaned back and merged with the road.

"Okay." Winston stood erect. "You two all right?"

Melanie nodded, and Chad looked like he was trying to stand. "Got to get out," Chad said. "Burnt. All of you. Burnt."

"Yeah, you mentioned that," Winston said. "What are we supposed to do about it?"

"Get away."

"How?"

Chad looked at Winston with an accusation of stupidity: "Get away *from me*."

"Be right there!" Ronald called from his supine position.

"Chad," Melanie said, "we'll get away from you, or we'll help you get out of town, whatever you want, but first, you have to help us. Why are we burnt? What do you mean?"

Chad shook his head. "If they can't control you anymore, you're dead. I'm dead. You're dead. Sorry."

"We won't let them get to you," Winston said, his hand on his gun. "You're not alone anymore. You're with friends."

Chad let a soft laugh escape as his chin dropped to his chest. "Doesn't matter."

"When did he turn all glum and grim?" The voice was Ronald's – Melanie hadn't seen him moving, but he'd gotten up, spanned the distance, and taken a place leaning on Winston, who shifted his legs to support the smaller man's weight.

"Chad," Melanie said, "what about the Young Evangelists? How are they involved?"

"They've been using them all week, making fliers, getting ready," Chad said. "My brother... isn't my brother anymore."

"My sister," Melanie said. "Do you know Stefanie? Have you seen her?"

"Sure. But not since before."

"Were any of the Young Evangelists... in the fire?" Melanie asked.

Chad shook his head. "I don't know. Didn't see any."

Melanie felt her chest expand, as if the vice around it had loosened a fraction of an inch. "Then maybe she's alive."

"We'll find her," Winston said. "We will."

"Who are *they*?" Ronald asked. "Chad, you keep talking about *they*."

"Reverend Cox," he said. "And the deacon. And people in the church. Ever since... he built that place. That Room."

"What place, Chad? What room?" Winston leaned in close, disturbing Ronald's balance.

Chad resumed his efforts to stand. "The Prayer Room. Took me in it. Made me... hear things. My ears were bleeding, and I – I was just a kid." His lolling face struggled against tears; the exertion helped him to his feet.

Melanie stood with him, ignoring the ache that filled her. "The renovations, right? When they redid First Church. That's when they built the room you're talking about?"

Chad nodded. "Not last time, when they made the sanctuary bigger. The first time. When they redid the basement. The Room is in the basement." He shuffled down the road, toward the town line.

"Wait," Winston said. "Let us help you. We're better off together."

"And we've hit a spot of luck, too." Ronald pointed in the direction where Chad was shuffling. "If we go a little further that way, we'll end up at my motel. At the Jeep. We've been assuming that someone would keep us from leaving. Now that the cars are working again, let's test that assumption."

"We can't," Melanie said. "Brian. And Stef. And Jeanne. We can't leave them."

"We won't," Winston said. "But Ronald's right. Let's get Chad to safety. And then we can get help, and come back for Brian and Stef and everybody else."

In a haze of exhaustion, they made their way to the Sleep E-Z. Ronald's Jeep and Brian's truck were where they'd left them. A few other cars were in spaces close to the main office, and light shone through several windows' closed curtains. "You see that sign?" Winston said, pointing. Melanie squinted and made out a rectangle. "That's the town limit. We're close."

Melanie heard a jingle from Ronald's direction. "The keys," he said. He led them toward the Jeep. Melanie and Chad took the small backseat, Winston took the passenger side, and Ronald took the wheel. Melanie kept a hand on the door handle, nervous, and when the noise began, the hand jerked. The door swung open, amplifying the booming beep, a blaring car horn.

"Aw hell," Winston said.

"What is it what is it what IS IT?" Chad bounced on the narrow seat, making Melanie's attempt to reclose the door more difficult.

"The ignition will work, and the car will start," Ronald said with imperative calm. As Melanie pulled her door closed, she heard the Jeep's engine cough, struggling to turn over. She looked over her shoulder, toward the noise, beep, beep, BEEP, and she saw the white van on the road by the entrance to the Sleep E-Z's parking lot.

The blaring was a clear warning: the van would not let them leave. Everyone in the car felt the sound's significance, but no one said anything. She held her breath and waited for the Jeep's engine, which struggled, struggled, sounded close, but didn't turn.

"You'll flood it," Winston said. "Take it easy!"

"Start, goddamn you!" Ronald slammed his head on the wheel as he cursed, his good arm never releasing the key in the ignition. The engine kicked and revved, running and ready. "Ha-ha! Hitting things *always* works."

Melanie looked at the white van. She saw the shape of the driver, thin, probably male, but she couldn't tell who it was. "He won't let us go."

Chad mumbled; Melanie heard "burn" and "dead." The engine revved, and Ronald shifted into reverse. He watched the van in the rearview mirror as he pulled the Jeep from its spot.

"I've never been in a car chase," Winston said.

The Jeep backed up until its taillights hit the van and lurched as Ronald yanked it into neutral. Melanie hunted for a seatbelt and couldn't find one. She saw Ronald's hand get ready to switch the automatic transmission into drive. "One," he said.

"Don't count," Winston urged.

Ronald looked at him. "Two."

"Dead dead dead DEAD!" Chad yelled.

BEEEEEEEEEEEEEEEEEEEEEEEEEEEEEEEEEEP!

"Three!" He slammed into gear and pressed on the accelerator. Melanie's hand searched for something to steady her as the vehicle zoomed forward. She found Chad's thigh; her grip quieted him and steadied her. The Jeep tore through the parking lot, jumped a curb that made Winston hit his head on the roof, ran over grass, and ended up on the street between the van and the rectangular sign for the town limit. Melanie kept her attention on the road ahead of them and on the signpost, which got closer and closer. In seconds they'd be free. The beeping got quieter. Her head snapped around and glimpsed the van, which wasn't chasing them.

Brakes squealed, and the Jeep spun out. Winston rammed into the passenger door, and Melanie landed in Chad's lap. Ronald held on to the wheel, and he kept driving, now in a different direction.

"Ronald, what are you doing!" Winston yelled.

"Ooooooooooh shiiiiiiiiiii—" Ronald wasn't in control of his actions as he sped back toward the van, which had stopped beeping. Melanie braced herself for impact, squinting, not willing to shut her eyes completely, so she was able to see as they drove not into but past the van, past the Sleep E-Z, and back toward town.

"Stop, stop, stop!" Chad chanted.

Brakes squealed again, and the Jeep halted. Ronald switched off the ignition. "What the fuck," he said.

"You turned around, that's what," Winston said. "You turned around and stopped."

"I didn't mean to. Honest!"

"It's okay," Winston said. "For a second, as we crossed the line, I wanted you to go back. It's what you told us about. An invisible wall or something." He took a deep breath. "Now we know for sure. We can't leave."

Melanie was trying to figure out something to say when Chad pushed her off of him, opened his door, and got out. "Chad, wait!"

"What's he doing?" Ronald said. Melanie watched Chad walk toward the rear of the Jeep, toward the van and the town line. The van started to move, making a U-turn. Headlights engulfed them.

Chad hesitated, standing by the Jeep. "BOBBY!" he yelled.

Melanie understood. "Oh God," she said. "It's his brother. His brother's driving the van."

Winston got out of the Jeep. "Chad, stay where you are!"

Chad ran toward his brother, the van, and the town line. Winston ran after him. Melanie got out of the Jeep, and Ronald followed her lead. Chad and Winston were too far ahead for them to catch up, and the white van was already moving, driving toward them, playing chicken. Winston slammed into Chad, keeping his feet while pushing Chad to the ground and out of the van's path, and he drew his gun. Melanie heard the pistol go off at the moment she saw the impact. The van lifted Winston from his feet, swerved with Winston rolling on the hood, barreled over Chad, corrected to stay on the road, and sped in their direction.

"Ronald!" Melanie cried. The van headed for the Jeep, ready to plow them down. Ronald froze, staring at Winston, whose empty hand locked on a windshield wiper to keep him from falling. Melanie grabbed Ronald's good arm and used her full body weight to pull him away from the van's path. The wiper blade snapped off just before metal and flesh crunched in a deafening collision. The Jeep moved with the van's momentum, teetering, but both vehicles stopped before the Jeep overturned.

Ronald was on his feet. "Winston!" He ran, half-limping, toward the conjoined vehicles.

Melanie watched through blurred vision. Ronald was almost to the smoking masses of metal, to the figure pinched between them, before Melanie thought to go forward, and she thought of the question that Ronald was already trying to answer: was there any chance that Winston had survived?

As she moved toward the crash, the pinched figure became more visible within the smoke. An arm hung free from the wreckage. Its hand still held the gun. Melanie could see the arm's shoulder, but the torso was buried in the crash. Winston's head was completely hidden by the metal that had crushed it from both sides.

She looked at Ronald, who looked from the body, to the Jeep, to the van, to the body. They were both stunned, processing. Melanie thought of Chad, crushed beneath tires, and she heard the sound, a short, accidental beep.

Bobby sat up behind the van's steering wheel. Its windshield was intact. Winston's bullet hadn't hit. Melanie's muscles clenched for fight or flight, and she heard a shot, another, and another. Holes appeared in the van's windshield, and Bobby's face lost its shape.

Melanie turned and saw Ronald's good arm sinking to his side, the hand still holding the gun he had pried from Winston's dead fingers. She turned again and saw Bobby, shot, dead, murdered at the wheel of the van.

Melanie was going to turn, to offer whatever comfort she could pull through the smoke and confusion, but staring at Bobby's body, she froze. She saw beyond the body, into the van, to the rear doors. They were open; the crash might have thrown them open. But through them, she could see a road, and it was not the same road where they were standing. "Ronald," she whispered.

She heard the gun clatter on the ground, but she didn't hear a reply.

"Ronald!" She walked to the van's passenger door. The front of the van was crumpled, but the door was unaffected. It opened.

"Wha... Melanie? Melanie, Winston, no. Stay – help. Melanie?" Ronald sounded strong through tears.

A wave of reality hit her, and she felt she should go away from the van, join Ronald in grief, and look for help. But there wouldn't *be* any help. They couldn't leave, and they couldn't stay, and something was wrong with the van, something they needed to understand. She backed away from the passenger door and walked to the van's rear doors, which were shut. Returning to the front, she looked through the van again and saw open rear doors and a street she didn't recognize, a place not here, not in Kenning, not anywhere she had ever been.

She turned. Ronald knelt by Winston's arm, looking at the mesh of metal that hid the rest of him. Melanie approached and put a hand on his good shoulder. "I didn't really know him," Ronald said. "Not really. But I thought," he looked up at her, his face shining in the streetlight, "I thought I might." Quieter, he repeated, "I thought I might."

Melanie felt sobs collecting in her throat, and she swallowed them. "Ronald," she said, her voice cracking, "my father beat me up, my mother kidnapped me, and my sister might be dead. Ronald." She felt a tear on her cheek that contradicted the tone she was trying to raise. "Ronald, we have to keep going."

Ronald looked at her, took a deep breath, picked up the gun, and rose from his knees. "Fine." He glanced at the crash and closed his eyes. "Where to?"

She opened the van's door. They climbed inside, passed the dead teenage boy, and crawled over the seat, into the van's rear. The street on the other side was colder than the place they were leaving. Someone was coming toward them. Melanie recognized her, and as she climbed out of the van's back, into an unknown place, she heard Jeanne say, "Hello, Melanie. Welcome to the Prayer Room."

15

Ronald studied Winston's handgun and remembered the sensation of firing it. He had known Winston for a week, which meant their relationship ranked among the longest in Ronald's life, but he hadn't known him. He hadn't known him, but he hadn't hesitated to shoot and keep shooting until the kid driving the van was dead. Bobby Sutton was dead, and Ronald thought *good*, and Winston Beecher was dead, and Ronald didn't know how to think. He nestled the gun in the back of his pants.

Jeanne and Melanie embraced. The hug was one-sided, Melanie all cling and desperation, Jeanne reciprocating perfunctorily. Jeanne pulled away, and Melanie said, "Where are we?"

Jeanne looked at them. Ronald stepped toward her, away from the van. "We...." the woman said, and Ronald detected a struggle between her brain and her lips. "I think I just told you. We're in something called the Prayer Room. I don't know how I know."

"Chad said the Prayer Room was a place in the basement of First Church," Melanie said.

"We're not in the church," Jeanne said.

"Yes we are," a voice said from a different location. Ronald turned to find the voice's source, which was close, female, and familiar. About-face, the van had vanished, and in its place an empty road stretched out and terminated in blackness. Ronald turned further, taking in more highway bounded by darkness, until his eyes landed on Jeanne. A second Jeanne. She wore the same clothes and hairstyle. Under the streetlight, Ronald noticed new streaks of silver. A quick glance revealed streaks in the other Jeanne's hair, too.

Melanie and the first Jeanne faced the newcomer, and together with Ronald, they formed a circle. Ronald noticed that the highway around them lacked the echoes of distant cars and the buzzing of near streetlights. The only sound was the wind, blowing around them as if it were the essence of the blackness that framed the road. They were four people – or perhaps three – standing on a road that was not a road, in a place that was not a place.

"I don't know," the first Jeanne said, "how you got here," she looked at Melanie and Ronald, "but I've been reliving memories. This road, it is, or at least it used to be, where Charlie, my fiancé, died more than twenty years ago, and—"

"Think about it," the second Jeanne said. "Where did this all begin?"

The first Jeanne paused to reflect. Ronald looked at Melanie and read his own confusion on her face. Jeanne didn't seem at all surprised by the conversation she was having with herself. Tempted to point out that their situation had transitioned from strangeness to full-on surreality, Ronald stayed quiet. He looked at the highway's black boundary and stepped toward it. The horizon did not recede as he approached; black got closer. He stepped toward the edge, which was a jagged boundary, as if someone had broken the highway off from the land around it and thrown it into a vacuum. They stood on an island, floating in black ether that was the Prayer Room, Jeanne's memory, or somewhere else.

"It began," the first Jeanne said, "when I was in Reverend Cox's office, talking to Jake Warren about First Church's fliers."

The second Jeanne shook her head. "No. You arrived here on Easter. After your sermon. There was the singing."

"We heard it," Melanie said. "Did it... take you?"

The first Jeanne looked at Melanie without comprehension, and the second Jeanne nodded. Ronald thought about stepping away from the edge, back into the circle of women, but he needed to be close to the blackness. Was he considering a jump? It would be melodramatic, but it had appeal.

"I walked through the open doors of New Church," the first Jeanne said.

Staying by the edge, Ronald turned to watch the exchange.

"The doors that we opened," the second Jeanne said, "with the force of our will."

"'We,'" Ronald said. The three women turned toward him. "You said 'we.' Are you both Jeanne?"

The two Jeannes looked at each other. "I," said the first Jeanne, who then looked at her counterpart, "we, we started singing like everyone else. And we started walking. We walked to First Church."

"We found Reverend Cox. He congratulated us on our sermon."

"We followed him down the stairs, to the Prayer Room."

"He called it an antenna, and he said there were satellites."

"The white vans, and the Lincoln. They extend the reach—"

"Of the Room. We are all in the Room."

Melanie looked back and forth between the two Jeannes. "You mean we're all in First Church now? When we got in the van, we ended up in First Church?"

"Yes."

"No."

"Yes and no," the second Jeanne conceded. "The Prayer Room is a place of thought, constituted by the will."

The first Jeanne put her hands on the sides of her head, clutching her hair. "I don't know these things!" She looked at the second Jeanne. "Who are you? Who, who—"

The sounds of the wind in the blackness became louder, blotting out speech. It rippled Ronald's clothes and stirred his hair; he shifted his stance to keep balance. When it quieted, Melanie's was the first voice he heard: "Is he still there?"

Taking slow, solid, deliberate steps, Ronald left the edge and joined the circle. "Who?"

"Reverend Cox," the first Jeanne answered. "He led us into the Room."

The second Jeanne nodded. "And he's still there now."

"Here," Melanie finished. "He's *here*."

16

Sara Cox's handwriting became more difficult to read with each successive page, but the long, elegant pen-strokes remained comprehensible as they spelled out truth.

"I acted out of trust and from a sense that all my questions would, sooner or later, have answers. I didn't understand why they took Fran to the Room instead of Brian, but Jake assured me that it was right. Brian's will has to be pure. I acquiesced, but I would not watch. I know what happened. They told me before, and they would tell me after. I did not need to see the girl holding the gun. I did not need to see what they wanted the boy to see. I might have been able to stand the deaths of the adulterers, but the girl? Sacrifices are necessary. The deaths of a few are a small price for the salvation of an entire town, an entire country, the entire world. But I could not watch a little girl put a gun to her head and pull the trigger."

Brian saw past the pages. Feeling that the deaths were senseless was bad; realizing that they made perfect sense to someone was worse. He had known, hadn't he? Sitting in his hospital room, night after night, he had searched for explanations for why his family had been annihilated and he had been spared. Now, reading the reflections of this pious woman, wife of Reverend Cox, a man among Kenning's most admired, most influential, who had preached the sermon that had sparked Franny to action, who had presided over the burning of human bodies, such a man, such a woman, so pious and pure in their senses of right and wrong – Brian could comprehend. Brian saw past their truth, into his own purpose.

17

When her double spoke, the words became facts that had always been in Jeanne's mind. Some of the words that came from her own mouth – the welcome to the Prayer Room, the truths about the vans and the Lincoln – appeared without foreknowledge or volition. But like everything belonging to the other woman who wore her face, they were hers and not hers, identical and alien.

"He's *here*," Melanie said.

"So what do we do?" Ronald asked. "How do we help Jeanne – excuse me, ladies – Jeanne*s*, and get the hell out of here?"

"How do we *beat* him?" one of the Jeannes asked.

The other one nodded. "'Lord, even the devils are subject unto us through thy name.'"

"Amen."

"Jeanne?" Ronald stepped closer. "No disrespect, but what on earth does that mean?"

The winds quickened. Michael Cox watched them, listened to them, and feared them. He would try to silence them, but he would fail. "Faith," the Jeannes said. "Faith and the will."

"Faith, huh." Ronald turned toward the darkness at the edge of the road, ran, and jumped.

"RONALD!" Melanie screamed. She followed him and stopped at the edge, leaning over.

The Jeannes walked to the girl and stood on either side of her. "Take my hand," they said. Reluctant, the girl opened her clenched fists and accepted Jeannes' grips. Together, they leapt from the highway and into the black.

18

Her eyes told her she wasn't moving at all. The blackness didn't swirl or rush. The only sense of motion came from the wind that pushed against her body and made her fingers strain to keep their hold on the Jeannes' hands. The wind blew harder, and the black started to change. Melanie saw distant grey, and the grey became light, with greens and yellows and reds dispersing, taking shapes. She recognized a garden before the ground flew at her, slammed her, knocked her hands loose and sent her rolling alone into briars, thorns and dirt and vines, sharp and green with buds of red ready to open, roses, fresh, blooming on a bright spring day. The thorns should have torn her skin and clothes, but they didn't. The impact should have broken her, but she felt whole. Melanie lay in a rose garden unhurt, and when she moved, her hands passed through the briared stalks like a ghost's.

She sat up and saw dogwoods with only a few blossoms left – it was May. Was she back in the real world, weeks after she had left it? Birds sang, and puffs of cloud hung in the air like wispy balls of cotton. "Hey there, Reverend!" called a voice. Melanie turned and saw a white house with a porch at ground level and a balcony above. Michael Cox's house.

A creak brought Melanie's attention to the side of the house where the gate was opening. Jeanne entered the backyard and shut the gate behind her. She wore a man's clothes and a funny white hat. As Jeanne approached the garden, Melanie knew she was neither of the women whose hands she had held a moment before.

"I appreciate the invitation," said white-hat Jeanne. "I had no idea this side of town had such lovely houses."

Michael Cox stood by a double swing. Something lay on one side of the wooden seat – a book with a red cover. "We're blessed to have such a nice place in such a nice town," Cox said.

A tap on Melanie's shoulder triggered a scream, short, high-pitched, and loud. Melanie covered her mouth as she looked over her shoulder to see what had touched her. Crouching in the roses, one of the Jeannes who had jumped with her held a finger to her lips. "*Shhhhhh.*"

White-hat Jeanne stopped a few feet away from Michael Cox. "I've been thinking," she said, "about other things we might do to raise money for the church. Bake sales are fine, but an attendance drive would work better."

White-hat Jeanne spoke as if she hadn't heard Melanie's sharp cry. Michael Cox hadn't registered the noise, either. Calculating, Melanie yelled "HEY!"

White-hat Jeanne and the Reverend didn't react.

"HEY!" returned a tenor's voice. Ronald stood up in a patch of lilies. He crossed to Michael Cox, held up a demonstrative fist, and punched through the Reverend's head.

"I appreciate the thought, Mr. Warren," Cox said, "but I'm afraid I've had to reconsider our... partnership."

Ronald walked through the swing to reach the rose garden where Melanie and a Jeanne stood dumbfounded. "They can't see or hear us. It's like we're not even here." He scratched his chin. "What do you think?"

Another Jeanne emerged from behind a dogwood. "I think you're right," she said.

Three Jeannes?

White-hat Jeanne continued her conversation with Michael Cox. "I see you found my book." She sat on the swing and opened the book. "Looks like you might have read some of it." She closed the book and set it in her lap.

"Mr. Warren, I—"

The two Jeannes who had jumped with Melanie stood together. "Why is he calling us 'Mr. Warren?'" one of them said.

"Because." The other shook her head. "Isn't it obvious?"

"Pardon me, ma'am," Ronald said, "but you've got a fucked up idea of obvious."

"You stopped calling me Jake," said white-hat Jeanne. "Didn't like what you read very much, did you?"

"It's blasphemous!" Cox yelled.

"They don't know each other," Melanie said. She looked at Michael Cox, looked at the white-hat Jeanne, and squinted, envisioning Jake Warren.

"We're in another time," said one of the true – or at least truer – Jeannes. "Before, I was moving around in time, through my own memories."

"But that's not *you*," Ronald said. "You don't remember this, do you?"

White-hat Jeanne set her hat on top of the book. "Come now," she said, "I agree that Dr. Fincher wasn't a traditional Christian, but does that make what he has to say blasphemous? Allen was an anthropologist, so he writes from a more... global... perspective. Don't tell me you're the type of preacher who refuses to read about others' beliefs."

"Allen?" Cox asked. "Do you know this man?"

Ronald, the two familiar Jeannes, and Melanie walked around to the front of the swing, half-surrounding the exchange. "This isn't my memory," said one of the familiar Jeannes.

"It's not mine," Melanie said. Reverend Cox looked younger, like he had when Melanie was a kid. The Jeanne who was talking to him looked the same age as the other Jeannes.

The Jeanne with Michael Cox laughed. "No, Mike. Allen Fincher died almost a century ago, in Massachusetts. He was a Harvard professor. I just happen to have studied a lot of his work."

"And that's precisely my point! What I'm saying – what I mean to say – is that I don't see how a man of the sort you claim to be could study such garbage." Cox took a deep breath, composing a sermon. "And it's not garbage because it's different from what I believe. It's garbage because it attacks the foundation of my belief! You know this book compares the Crucifixion to pagan forms of human sacrifice, as if God had to sacrifice His son to work some kind of hocus-pocus?"

"Well it's definitely not *my* memory," Ronald said. "Look at them. Michael Cox isn't seeing what we're seeing. He thinks he's arguing with Jake Warren."

"Maybe he is," said one of the Jeannes.

Melanie pressed a palm against her forehead. Weirdness was causing a headache.

"Sit down, please," Jake-Jeanne said, "and maybe we can stop shouting." Mike took a seat. "Look, I know that Dr. Fincher can be hard to take. You have to understand the times he was living in. Even half a century after Darwin's drivel, no scholar, no matter how tactful, could challenge the mainstream way of seeing things without being ostracized. So Dr. Fincher decided not to be tactful at all."

Reverend Cox shook his head. "Mr. Warren, are you trying to tell me that there's a tactful way to say that the redemption of mankind was like black magic?"

"Yes," Jake-Jeanne said. "Believe it or not, I am." She gestured toward the book. "That's the point of *Alchemy of Will* – there's a way of understanding the powers of all religion, all mysticism, as manifestations of the one true God Almighty. Allen Fincher was pious in his own way. Martin Luther was accused of blasphemy, too."

Ronald reached for the book, and his hand passed through. He shrugged. "Worth a shot."

"That's it," Melanie said. "That's what all of this is about, isn't it? That book."

"Come on," said one of the familiar Jeannes. "That's not Michael Cox. It's a shadow."

"All of this," said the other familiar Jeanne, "is shadows, conjurations of the Prayer Room. It's using us. It's time for us to start using it."

The conversation between Michael Cox and Jake-Jeanne continued, but Melanie tuned it out. None of the three Jeannes sounded exactly like the Jeanne Melanie knew. If Michael Cox was a shadow, how many of the Jeannes were shadows? All of them?

"Okay," Ronald said. "I can go with this. Sure. Why not. This Prayer Room thingy – how do we make it work?"

The Jeannes walked down an azalea-lined path. "We keep going. We find the source of the shadows."

"Okey-dokey." Ronald looked at Melanie with a wide-eyed, maniacal grin. "Follow the yellow-brick road, right?"

Melanie looked down and saw the brown dirt path with the colorful azalea border. When she looked up, the familiar Jeannes stepped off the path and moved toward the gate where Jake-Jeanne had entered. Ronald followed. Melanie hesitated and then ran to catch up. Rushing through the gate and turning a corner, she expected to see the driveway where she had last met her mother. Instead, the ground terminated in a jagged break, dead-ending as it had on the highway, but at the border, blue, the same as the bright spring sky, stretched out to infinity. Melanie looked back, expecting to see Jake-Jeanne, but no one stood behind her. The backyard was empty.

"Come on," Ronald said. "Nowhere to go but down, right?"

They leapt.

19

When he jumped into the endless blue, Ronald expected another journey of wind and weightlessness, but the hooks of gravity caught him and pulled at his chest and stomach as he reeled toward an unknown destination. The blue changed, separated into distinct patches of light and dark that shifted, swirled, contracted, and expanded. The color around him morphed, *breathed*, and as it changed, noise poured through the living patchwork's seams. At first, it sounded like rushing water, and then, the rhythmic wheels of a train. Next, voices, a babbling crowd indistinguishable until, louder than the rest, a woman's voice exploded:

"THE LORD IS MY HELPER!!!" The voice was Jeanne's, and its message was command. "GOD WILL LEAD ME FORTH, AND DELIVER ME FROM TROUBLE!" With each word, the voice became louder, and it seemed to come from all directions. Jeanne's voice wasn't within the void; somehow it *was* the void, a thread in its fabric. "LORD JESUS CHRIST, DIRECT OUR WAY UNTO YOU!!"

As Jeanne shouted her Biblical commands, the patchwork of blue tightened around him, forming a cone, a funnel, pouring Ronald toward—

Hard wood wrenched his wounded arm as he crashed and rolled, downward and at an angle. Spinning around him were a sloped ceiling, a handrail, dim yellow light, and stairs, one, two, ow, ow, OWWWWWW—

Ronald came to a stop, sat up and, just as the bump on his head began to allow coherent vision, felt another body slam into his back. He turned and saw Melanie splayed on the stairs. She stared at the ceiling with incredulity. "Uh," she said.

Ronald shook his head. "Yes, I agree. Uh." He faced front and saw the stairway's end, a large room with bluish-grey carpet and stacks of boxes along the walls. A Jeanne lay at the bottom of the stairs. Just one. "Jeanne!"

The woman sat up and looked at him. "Are you and Melanie alright?"

Ronald noticed blood on his shirt. More stitches had popped. "No." He looked back at Melanie, who had shifted her body on the steps so she could see Jeanne below. "How about you, Melanie – aren't you not alright?"

"No." Melanie put a hand on her forehead. "I mean yes. I mean, where are we?"

Jeanne looked around the room, and Ronald did likewise. He saw music stands and racks of robes. "We're back in First Church," Jeanne said. "The basement." She took a step toward the edge of Ronald's view. "There." She pointed to the door with the brass knob. "That's the door to the Prayer Room."

Weren't they already *in* the Prayer Room?

20

I regret that the Grayson girl had to die as well.

Brian reread the sentence three times and closed the diary. He had read enough. He paced. His mind told him that he needed a plan, a better plan than what he was considering, but what could be better? Too much thought would impede. Upstairs on his bedroom closet's high shelf, he found his rifle's locked case. He opened the case, took the weapon, and attached the shoulder strap. He filled his pockets with shells. Back in the bedroom, he collected an armful of old t-shirts.

In the garage, he found two canisters for gasoline. Two bigger ones were in the back of his truck along with a pile of rags. Together with the t-shirts, which he stuffed into a large black garbage bag, they would be all he needed. The truck was still parked at the Sleep E-Z motel.

Outside, the sky brightened. Soon, the sun would appear on the horizon's edge. Brian didn't know how long he'd been reading. His mind had wandered, again and again, reseeing, reliving. Mrs. Cox spelled out the story that underpinned his entire existence. For years, they had manipulated and ruined, taking Mom and Dad, taking Fran, torturing him, torturing Mel, and then they had done to Mel what they had done to him. It could not stand.

People were leaving their houses for work, but if they noticed Brian's gun, canisters, and garbage bag as he marched past their driveways, they gave no signal. By the time he crossed through the center of town, the sun was up, and people were on the streets. Mr. Hoberman waved at him, oblivious to his armaments. The Hobermans were members of Michael Cox's congregation. They were no longer friends.

Leaving the densest part of town, Brian noticed people's reactions to him changing. Conversations ceased as he walked by, and people turned to watch. As he approached the Sleep E-Z, a cluster of women spread into a line of staring, expressionless faces. Brian passed them, determined not to be distracted, but when the faces reached the far edge of his periphery, frozen and staring, he stopped and looked back. On the street and the sidewalks behind him, every human being stood still, watching. He resumed his course.

The wreckage and the motel came into view simultaneously. He recognized the larger vehicle as one of the patrolling white vans before the crumpled shape of the smaller vehicle, the Jeep, relayed its significance. Brian dropped the canisters and trash bag and ran, thinking of Mel, wondering who else the Coxes and their followers had taken.

The first visible sign of death sat behind the wheel of the van. The shape of the chest and shoulders suggested an adolescent boy. The remains of the face were too fragmented to reveal identity. The passenger-side door of the van was open. A bulge in the boy's pocket must have been a wallet, so Brian dug for it. Before the billfold flopped open, Brian guessed his identity: Bobby Sutton. Brian knew about Faith Healer and the Young Evangelists. Bobby Sutton was one of *them*. Brian thought of searching the van's rear when the view through the shattered windshield captured his attention.

Where the van's front merged with the ruined Jeep, a portion of a man protruded. Brian climbed out of the van and knelt by the body. He couldn't see a face – the head was smashed within metal – but he saw the arm and the blood-soaked uniform. His lips quivered. He thrust his weight against the Jeep, trying to pry metal from metal. Neither vehicle budged. He picked up the hand. It was cold and familiar. Part of him wanted to see a face to be sure, but that part was small. Who else would they have taken? The body was Winston's. The man who had carried him to safety That Day. If Brian had ever had a brother...

He moved to retrieve the canisters and bag. As he walked, he noticed someone standing in the parking lot of the Sleep E-Z, Phil Rather, the motel's owner. His face bore the same expressionless stare that Brian had seen in town. Brian thought about yelling at him, asking why he just stood there instead of calling someone, everyone, about the tragic wreckage that blocked the street. But there was no point in speaking, no one left to call.

The rifle bounced against his back as Brian made his way past Phil and into the motel parking lot. His truck was as he'd left it. If the Jeep had started, which it mostly likely had, his truck would start, too. He set the rifle on the seat beside him and turned the key. The engine struggled at first, but it turned, and his truck spat exhaust into morning air. He drove on the grass to get around the wreckage and sped through the quarter mile to Hank Winfrey's gas station. As he parked at the pump, he realized he'd have to go in to pay.

A bell rang as Brian pulled open the convenient store's front door. "Morning, Brian," Hank said. His eyes didn't acknowledge the rifle.

Brian nodded. He approached the counter, took out his wallet, and counted cash. He had one twelve-gallon can, one ten-gallon, and two five-gallons. The cans were mostly empty, so he took five twenties from his wallet and set them on the counter. Hank looked at him without comprehension. Clearing his throat, Brian said, "Pump three."

Hank said, "You got it," swept up the twenties, and pushed some buttons by the register. Brian noticed the box of free matchbooks by the register and took a handful. He was almost to the door when Hank said, "Closing early today, you know."

Brian stopped. He looked back at Hank, his face asking *why*.

"The Church went late last night, and it's starting early today. We'll start the praying and the singing in the sanctuary at three." Hank laughed. "Or as many as can fit in the sanctuary. I'd come early if I was you."

Brian nodded.

Hank narrowed his eyes. "You'll be there?"

Brian nodded as he pushed his way out.

21

"This door," Jeanne placed her hand on the brass knob, "leads to the Prayer Room's representation of itself." She didn't know how she knew, but she did. Maybe she had captured the knowledge through prayer, using what Jake Warren called "the alchemy of will." Maybe she had summoned power just as she had in the blue void, shouting Bible verses and imploring God to lead her here, to First Church, where Michael Cox waited.

She spun around when she heard Melanie pound her fist against a wall – a wall that stood where a stairway had been a moment before. "I looked back," Melanie said, "and this... just... appeared."

Ronald crossed to Melanie and smacked his fist into solidity. "Ow." His shirt was bloody. "It's a real wall, or at least it's as real as anything else in here." He gestured toward the door to the Prayer Room. "That's where it wants us to go, right?"

"It might be where *we* want to go," Jeanne said.

"I want to go home," Melanie said. For once, she sounded her age, maybe younger.

"To get out we have to get in." Jeanne found her statement odd, but she didn't question its truth.

Ronald crossed to the door and reached for the knob. Jeanne knew that something, perhaps even God, was leading her to the door, but the thought of the door opening summoned a whirlwind of terror that shook her insides and froze her limbs. She didn't remember passing through the door before, but she knew she had. When it opened, she would recognize what she saw. She didn't want to see, didn't want to go.

The knob rattled in Ronald's hand. 'Well, maybe it doesn't want us to get in-and-out, because it's locked."

"Listen!" Mel said.

"To what?" Ronald asked.

Jeanne held up her hand to silence him and bowed her head, focusing her ears on their surroundings. At first she heard nothing but blood throbbing in her head, but gradually distinct noises, scratches, became audible. They were loudest at the wall that had blocked off the stairway, but they spread elsewhere, in the corner by a rack of robes, behind the boxes, and in the wall that held the door. Scratches, like long fingernails on dry wood, surrounded them. They grew louder. They grew fiercer.

Ronald put a hand on his forehead. "No. Nuh-uh. I am not at all interested in knowing what that is."

Scratch scratch scratch scratch scratch. Some scratches were slow, and others were quick, but all were urgent. Jeanne imagined layers of wall peeling away beneath scampering claws. She held her hand out to Melanie, who took it and pressed near, side by side with her, examining the walls, waiting to see if something would break through.

Ronald backed away from the door. "We're not the only ones trying to get *out* by getting *in*, are we?"

"There are so many of them," Melanie whispered. The noises originated in five, six, maybe seven distinct places, fourteen hands, one hundred and forty scratching fingers, to the north, south, east, and west. The scratching was too loud to be coming from the exterior. They had to be inside the walls, scratching to get out, to get in, to get *them*.

They grew louder. Jeanne felt Melanie tremble, pressed against her side. Ronald's upper body was still, but his legs wobbled, struggled for balance. Jeanne looked at her hands, which were calm, and her feet, which were planted firmly on the ground. The others needed her to lead them. The others needed her to save them, to get them out, to take them through the door and into the Room, but the sounds were getting louder, scratching as if on her eardrums themselves. She imagined forcing fingers into her ears and pushing inward until the scratching stopped. Imagination became desire. *Need.*

Ronald and Melanie pressed palms to their ears. Melanie's left palm pulled back and slapped against her head, and soon both of her hands hammered at her ears, as if to crush them. Ronald rubbed his outer ear with his right hand. His fingers separated, and one of them started to slip in.

A flash of memory: Dave Holcomb's body, stripped of senses. Straining her lungs for a sound that could overpower the scratching, Jeanne yelled "STOP!" She grabbed her companions' arms, yanking Ronald's fingers from his face and halting Melanie's hammering. "No! You can't give in to it."

Scratch, scratch, scratch. The noise was like a million insects parading over her flesh, urging her, begging her to make it cease. She could see her own reactions in her friends' faces. They struggled to obey her, to keep their hands at their sides, to resist the urge to stop hearing forever. Scratch! Scratch! Do it! DO IT!

Jeanne pushed past Ronald and Melanie. Facing the door, she swallowed terror and kicked, once, twice, a third time. "HELP ME!"

Melanie and Ronald ran to her. The door was too narrow to allow three of them to kick, so Ronald stood at Jeanne's side, and Melanie waited behind. They found rhythm, slamming the soles of their shoes into the door. Scratch, kick, scratch, kick—

The door cracked in its frame, and the next kick flung it open. What lay beyond assaulted Jeanne with instant recognition and memory. She screamed.

22

Jeanne was screaming, but Melanie couldn't see the cause. Jeanne and Ronald filled the doorway. Around the edges of their bodies shone light from the Room beyond, dim and yellow.

"Oh God." Ronald was almost inaudible beneath Jeanne's screams. Melanie wanted to push him out of the way, to see what he was seeing, but she couldn't. The screams or the Room or something else entirely froze her in place and left her no other choice but to listen and wait.

"Right on time." The voice was rich baritone: Michael Cox. "Welcome. Come inside." He huffed, a derisive laugh. "Ms. Harper, Jeanne, we get the point. You can stop screaming. Wait. Not you. The other one. The one in the doorway."

Melanie found his words confusing until Jeanne stepped forward and silenced her scream. She revealed a chamber with wavering white walls and two altars, one yellow and one blue. The blue altar was vacant, but the yellow supported a man's body. Jeanne, a different one from the woman who had stepped through the doorway, hovered above the man's bloody face. She was naked and held a scalpel. The movement of the man's head made the scalpel's blade jerk back and forth in the wound it was creating. The naked Jeanne was cutting off the man's ear.

Standing to Melanie's right, another Jeanne watched the operation. She wore a man's clothes and a surgeon's white mask, and she was saying something, chanting, guiding the naked Jeanne's actions in a language that Melanie couldn't understand. The chanting stopped, and surgeon-Jeanne said, "So, Jeanne, what do you think – eyes or tongue? We don't want him dying before it's finished, so we'll have to do both pretty quickly."

Ronald moved inward, leaving Melanie alone at the doorway. He approached surgeon-Jeanne and said, "So you're the Jake Warren in this picture. You're the one running the show."

He grabbed the surgeon's mask and pulled it down, revealing a mouth that looked just like the other Jeannes'.

"Good guess," Michael Cox said, "but wrong." Cox stood to Melanie's left, on the opposite side of the Room from surgeon-Jeanne and Ronald. At center, naked-Jeanne stood by the yellow altar.

"I'm afraid they don't do too well with choice," surgeon-Jeanne said, "not when the Room has them. She'll be back to her old self tomorrow. Mostly. For now, I guess she's all brawn and no brain. Why don't you pry open the mouth and take the tongue?"

Naked-Jeanne opened the man's mouth and cut out his tongue. The Jeanne who had kicked open the door dropped to her knees and buried her face in her hands.

Melanie stepped into the Prayer Room, not ready to engage the scene but not willing to be excluded. The scratching noises followed her.

"What did you do to her?" Ronald moved to the kneeling Jeanne and put a hand on her right shoulder.

"You should ask what she did," Cox said. He indicated naked-Jeanne, who was cleaning off a scalpel while she watched a man choke to death on his own blood.

"But this isn't real," Ronald countered.

Melanie understood. "It is." She moved toward the kneeling Jeanne and put a hand on her left shoulder. "Jeanne did this. They *made* Jeanne do this." Naked-Jeanne and surgeon-Jeanne were playing out a scene from Jeanne's past. Remembering had brought Jeanne to her knees.

Cox circled around the blue altar and stood opposite the kneeling Jeanne. He obscured Melanie's view of naked-Jeanne, who had moved toward surgeon-Jeanne and begun a new operation. "In a way, you're right," Cox said. "We made her do it. But in a way, you're wrong. The Room channels the wills of everyone inside it. It channels the communal will of the entire town. Who knows? It might even channel the Will of God." Cox shrugged, and Melanie heard scratching in the walls. "Jeanne's will remains in the hands that sacrificed Dave Holcomb. Nobody here is innocent."

The scratching got louder, insistent hands, clawing to get in, desperate to get out. Melanie's eyes left the Reverend and moved along the Room's boundaries, white walls, yellowish in the light, rolling like the surface of a pond. When she saw the shape of a hand with fingertips pushing outward beneath the wall's surface, she looked away, back at the Reverend.

Behind him, naked-Jeanne fell to the floor, and a moment later, surgeon-Jeanne collapsed. Melanie kept her eyes on the Reverend as the scratching grew louder and surrounded them. "What you just saw," he said, "happened days ago, when Jeanne paid Jake Warren an unexpected visit. What happens next, happens now, and has been anticipated for years."

"Why?" The question came from the Jeanne who knelt at the blue altar. "How does any of this serve God?"

"Look around you!" Cox raised his arms and praised the walls with open hands. "Could any of this *be* without Him? Can you doubt the evidence of your eyes?" On the walls' rippling surfaces, bright characters and symbols appeared, figures from an unrecognizable alphabet, lines and curves that were almost blinding in their brilliance. Around the symbols' glowing edges, fingers pierced the walls. "The sacrifices become part of the Room itself, part of its strength, its glory, and now—"

The Reverend's cadence broke, and he looked at the ceiling. The kneeling Jeanne looked, and Ronald looked, but Melanie resisted, fixating on the hands that reached out from the walls in worshipful adoration of the man at the Room's center. When the hands began to reach up instead of out, Melanie let her eyes follow. The ceiling wavered like the walls, but its waves were red. "It's his blood," Jeanne said. "It's Jake Warren's blood."

"It's much more than that," Cox said. Desperate and confused, Melanie's eyes moved to the kneeling Jeanne, whose head tilted back so her face pointed upward, toward the ceiling's lake of blood. As the woman's jaw fell open, every muscle in Melanie's body clenched. She knew what would happen before the first drop fell. A trickling line became a steady stream, and then the liquid poured down, a column of rushing red, entering Jeanne through her gaping mouth.

Ronald acted first, thrusting his body toward Jeanne to push her away from the jet of crimson. Before his body made contact, it halted in the air, petrified. Melanie watched Ronald rise from the floor, linger in the air unsupported, and fly to the wall on her right. Michael Cox stared at him, holding out a hand as if it were pressing in place the man who was pinned to a wall half a room away. "Stay," Cox said, and he lowered his hand. Ronald remained on the wall, his feet inches from the floor, his body flat, eyes wild, and lips wriggling to form words of protest that the force holding him would not allow.

The blood continued to flow from the ceiling into Jeanne's mouth. Melanie stepped forward and felt Michael Cox's gaze shift to her. He'd stop her if she moved closer. She could only watch as the red column decreased to a line. The last drops fell into Jeanne, whose body flopped onto the blue altar in front of her as if drained instead of filled.

Michael Cox clapped. Ronald wriggled helpless against the wall. Melanie closed her eyes.

When they opened, her surroundings had changed. White walls were closer, solid and unmarked. The only altar was blue, and it supported the kneeling, unconscious Jeanne. Naked-Jeanne was gone, but surgeon-Jeanne remained on the floor by the back wall, where a crucifix hung in mockery. To Melanie's right, Ronald was pinned just as he had been, and to Melanie's left was Michael Cox. He stared at her.

23

"What's happening?" Melanie asked. "Where are we?"

She faced Reverend Cox. Ronald heard bravery commingled with the girl's bewilderment, and he admired her. Then again, being brave was much easier for people who weren't glued to a wall by the force of an evil preacher's unholy will. Ronald had to maintain perspective.

In a blink, the Room had changed from a monstrous nebulous thing into a simple chamber with bright white walls. Not a trace remained of the hands or the glowing symbols or the waterfall of blood or any of the other midnight-movie special effects. Ronald, however, was stuck in the same predicament. Reverend Cox had him. He was trapped, a prisoner, a damsel in distress with nary a hero on the way. He pushed aside the memory of Winston's limp arm.

Where the hell was Brian, anyway?

"You know where we are," the preacher said.

Actually, we don't, Ronald thought.

Michael Cox smiled. "Okay, maybe you don't."

Mind-reading was *deeply* annoying.

"You get used to it," the Reverend said. He turned to Melanie, who was trying to rouse the unconscious Jeanne at the altar. "Now, little girl, to answer your question. You're in the basement of First Church, a place called the Prayer Room, and you've been there since you got into the back of that van."

"Is it... now?" Melanie's attention turned back to Jeanne. She stroked the woman's hair, which was almost completely white. "What did you do to her!"

In his periphery, Ronald saw movement. The Jeanne with the surgeon's mask was still with them, crumpled by the back wall and starting to stir.

"One question at a time, please." Michael Cox knelt by Melanie. One of his hands stroked her brown hair with the same affection that Melanie was showing Jeanne. Melanie's face withered in disgust. "Yes, it's *now*, the unmitigated present. This is the Room at its simplest state, when it's not working its... well, why not call it magic?"

A magical room, the newest ride at Disney World!

Michael Cox looked at him. "You people pride yourselves on inappropriate humor, don't you?"

We're the masters, bub.

Michael Cox laughed. He curled Melanie's hair around one of his fingers, and Melanie stopped stroking Jeanne, suspended at the man's touch. Michael Cox sniffed demonstratively. "Ah, there it is. You're almost out of time."

Ronald couldn't help obeying the Reverend's example: he sniffed and detected a faint scent. Smoke. Something burning.

"If we can smell it down here," the Reverend said, "it must really be getting going upstairs." Melanie sniffed and then stood tall. She looked at Ronald, and he looked at her. They didn't know what was happening, but they both knew they needed to leave. Now.

"Stay a bit." Michael Cox stood, towering over Melanie. "See it to the end."

By the back wall, the Jeanne with the surgeon's mask propped herself up on hands and knees. She looked around the room, confused by her surroundings. Ronald tried to watch her without focusing on her. If Michael Cox hadn't lied − if she really wasn't Jake Warren in a Jeanne disguise − she might be able to help them, and she might have the element of surprise if Ronald didn't give her away with his eyes or thoughts.

Michael Cox remained oblivious. "The two of you have been so helpful, you'd almost think we had planned for you from the beginning. We didn't, or at least, I didn't."

The smoke smell was stronger, and the Jeanne with the surgeon's mask was getting to her feet. She looked at Ronald, and dragging his eyes along with hers, she looked at Melanie. Ronald tried not to think, not to interpret what he instinctively knew. If he turned his sense of Jeanne's meaning into articulate thought, into a coherent plan, Michael Cox would know.

The Reverend focused on Melanie. He did not detect Ronald's growing hope or the woman moving toward him, quiet steps, ready to lunge. When Michael Cox finally turned, the Jeanne with the surgeon's mask was already tackling him. "Get Mel out of here!"

The glue holding Ronald to the wall vanished, and he fell. Melanie helped him to his feet, and together, they faced the struggling mass of Jeanne Harper and Michael Cox. Ronald understood that Jeanne was using everything she had to buy them the time to get out, to *run*.

Ronald and Melanie fled the Prayer Room, leaving the Jeannes and Michael Cox behind. They ran through the room that stored robes and boxes, and with Melanie leading, they hurried onto the stairs. Halfway up, Ronald saw the smoke above them. The fire was close, and every step up brought it closer.

24

Brian unloaded his cargo in the bushes at the rear of First Church and parked his truck on the far side of Hart's Cemetery. He tied some of the t-shirts and rags together to make the ropes that would serve as fuses. He soaked the rest of the shirts and rags for kindling. Staying low, he surrounded the windows and doors with wet fabric. Nobody who had seen him on his way over had made a move to stop him, but if somebody inside First Church's overcrowded sanctuary caught a glimpse, people would overwhelm him before he could strike the first match.

The singing from the church was loud. Brian heard "Jesus," "God," and "good," and he wanted to laugh. They were such hypocrites.

Bricks composed most of the church's base, but some sections of the walls looked like solid wood. The window frames and the shutters around them were definitely wooden, as were the roof and beams visible at the building's many right angles. The new part of the sanctuary, the add-on that Michael Cox had built to support his growing numbers, was made entirely from wood. Inside, the pews and crosses were wood, and the carpet, wall-hangings, and Bibles would be even better than wood. He wouldn't obliterate First Church, but he'd burn most of it. Enough.

He doused as much as he could with gasoline and stuffed rags into areas he thought might be slow to catch. He left the makeshift fuses where they'd be easy to reach until he had everything set up. The fuses caught one by one, and the flames traveled fast. In minutes, every door and window that people might use to escape was burning, all except one.

From a high hill in the cemetery, Brian could still hear the singing. The single door he had left for escape was narrower than the sanctuary's main door; only one or two people would be able to get through at a time. That would keep the stream of panicking churchgoers from moving too quickly. Leaning on a tombstone,

Brian viewed the door through the scope of his rifle. He wished the tombstone belonged to Mom or Dad or Fran.

25

Melanie held a hand over her mouth as she stumbled into Michael Cox's office. The dark, windowless wood of the walls, the oversized desk with the clutter and bookends, the high-backed leather chairs, and the model of Noah's ark by the sofa had always looked wrong to her, and now the smoke-filled room in front of her looked like death. She didn't see fire yet, but she knew it waited ahead, and she knew that Cox would come for them from behind.

"Come on!" Ronald pushed her further into the office. "Keep moving!"

She stayed still. Going ahead seemed as impossible as going back. "But Jeanne!" was all she could say.

Ronald looked back through the doorway. "She wanted me to get you out of here, and that's what I'm going to do." He took her hand and yanked her toward the exit.

A noise, like scratching in the walls. Melanie froze, listening.

"Come on!" Ronald yanked again before surrendering to a cough.

The scratching became rumbling. Melanie couldn't tell which wall it came from, but it was close and insistent, like before. It couldn't be! They were out of the Room now, back in reality – they had to be! The fire and the man chasing them were already too much to deal with. More reaching hands and blazing symbols would destroy what nerve she had left, reducing her to helplessness. Ronald's grip on her hand slackened. He heard what she heard, and the weakness in his fingers conveyed something of what she felt.

From behind her, laughter, and she turned around, knowing what she would see. Michael Cox sauntered into the room, his proud and mocking face bisected by a diagonal streak of fresh blood. Through smoke she saw his eyes gleaming.

The rumbling in the wall became pounding, fists against wood, syncopating muffled screams. Melanie tried to press her hands to her ears, but Ronald grabbed one arm and pulled. She stumbled against his force; he combined the strength of his good arm with his body weight to drag her. When they reached the exit, he released her arm and mashed his hand against the door, testing it. "Okay, hold your breath and stand back." He threw open the door, and a cloud of smoke overwhelmed them.

"NOT YET!" Cox screamed. Ronald fell backward, and the door cut through the cloud, slamming shut. "I want you to stay with me, an offering made by fire unto the Lord." The preacher chortled as he uttered the Biblical phrase.

Melanie faced the Reverend, and Ronald pressed close at her side. Thick smoke hung above them, and haze filled the room. Seeing was hard. Breathing was harder. Ronald fought a cough. "So we all burn, is that it?"

Cox moved toward them and paused at the side of his desk. Melanie heard the pounding in the wall, and Cox looked over his left shoulder, toward the door opposite the stairs to the Prayer Room. He looked back at them. "Most of us, but not all."

The smoke got thicker, and Melanie felt woozy, but she could still see Michael Cox, his gleaming eyes, standing in what seemed like a bubble of light. The smoke didn't touch him. Somehow he was safe, waiting for them to succumb.

"Get down!" Ronald dropped to his knees. Melanie knew he meant they should stay low to escape suffocation, but when she saw him on his knees, she thought of Jeanne at the altar, kneeling and defeated. Melanie didn't want to kneel, not to *him*. Her head swam; she struggled to suck pure air through pursed lips.

Ronald delivered a quick karate-chop to the back of her knee, and she joined him on the floor. Breathing was easier – he was right – but Cox loomed over them, leaning on the desk and looking down. The preacher knew he had won, and he'd savor watching them die.

The pounding in the wall was louder, but the noises were further apart. Something was behind the door opposite the stairway. Something wanted to get out.

"Nothing to lose," Ronald whispered. "I'll rush him, and you run for the door. Do it, Melanie. Don't let Jeanne's d—don't let what Jeanne did be for nothing." She hesitated, and he screamed "GO!" before he lurched from the floor and crashed into Michael Cox's bubble of breathable air. Melanie crawled for the exit, and Michael Cox brushed Ronald off like a gnat. Ronald crashed into one of the leather chairs, which toppled beneath him. Melanie got to the door, reached for the knob, turned it, and pulled.

The door opened. The hallway was smoky, but she couldn't see fire. She looked back and saw Ronald on his knees and good hand, following her like a three-legged dog. She couldn't leave without him, but the door might close. She thrust her body into the doorway, and as Ronald hobbled toward her, Cox loomed behind him, enjoying the show, waiting to strike. The man's dark hair had wilted in the sweat that poured over the blood on his face, but he remained unfazed by the smoke, impervious, invincible. They could escape only if he let them, and he wouldn't. Ronald crouched next to her now, and they could crawl into the hallway. She faced it and readied herself for a race she knew she would lose.

A sound, a scream, different from the one in the wall, called her attention back. Jeanne, not surgeon-Jeanne or naked-Jeanne but the other Jeanne, whose hair had gone white, tackled Cox on his desk. Like Cox's, Jeanne's form repelled smoke, caused it to recede, a billow in reverse. It traveled around Ronald, past Melanie, and into the hall. Jeanne's body radiated power as it pinned the preacher to his desk. She held the cloth of Cox's shirt in tight fists, lifted his upper body from the desktop, and slammed it back down. The look on her face was unlike any Melanie had seen, triumphant, almost gleeful. Jeanne slammed Cox down again, and a third time, and the Reverend's baritone voice sounded in protest, "Stop, stop, stop!" The man looked desperate and confused, as if, at last, something had happened for which he had not planned. Melanie felt the thought welling inside of her and relished it: *kill him!* She looked at Ronald, who watched from his position in the doorway with the same fascination. Silent, they rooted for their unexpected heroine, and when Jeanne grabbed the heavy-looking bookend, they both knew what she would do with it and longed for her to continue. The weapon was a statuette, a lion, and when it crashed into Michael Cox's blood- and sweat-streaked face, it made a satisfying crunch. Lifting the lion again in both hands, she brought it back down and spattered herself with the Reverend's blood. She smashed again and again until the man's skull collapsed.

"You should have known better, Mike." She grinned, showing teeth. The swagger, the sneer – Melanie realized that the woman before them couldn't be Jeanne. The gloating killer hardly looked human. The woman dropped the lion, climbed off the desk, stood, and faced Ronald and Melanie. "Shouldn't the two of you be going?"

Melanie looked at Ronald, who looked back at her, astounded. She stared up at the Jeanne who was not Jeanne, aghast, and the not-Jeanne grinned down at her. The woman turned and walked back toward the doorway that led downstairs, and Melanie knew. Jake. She didn't understand how, but Jake Warren had killed Michael Cox, and now he, or she, proceeded downstairs in inexplicable triumph.

Melanie heard the pounding noise again. It was softer than before, less menacing. The smell of smoke tickled her nose. Grey-white clouds rushed around her and Ronald, refilling the office. "Melanie," Ronald said, "we have to go."

"Wait." They weren't in the Prayer Room anymore – the noise was not an illusion. Something real, some*one* real, someone weak, someone desperate, was banging on the door, pleading to get in, needing to get out. Melanie dashed across the room, allowing her eyes to linger only a moment on Cox's bleeding body as she maneuvered around the desk. When she tried the door, the pounding got louder, as if the would-be entrant had shifted from knocking with a fist to kicking with a foot, encouraging her efforts. After a few more beats, the pounding stopped, and Melanie listened.

The voice was soft, weak, and feminine: "*Hello?*"

Melanie clenched the doorknob. "Ronald, somebody's trapped!" He ran to her. "We need a key!" Together, they looked to the most probable source: Cox's body.

Ronald coughed. "If he rises from the dead, I quit, okay?" His hands dove into Cox's pants pockets. Melanie felt along the blood- and sweat-soaked fabric of his shirt and found nothing. "Unfair, totally unfair," Ronald said. "We have to flip him over. Back pockets. Help me turn him."

The smoke thickened. Melanie didn't know if she had the strength to help, but she wrapped her hands around the dead man's side, bracing herself for a sick ripple of reviving muscle, and pushed. The body rolled, and the battered head split open as it moved. Ronald looked away, and Melanie lost control: the body slipped from the desk and landed on the floor. Ronald searched the pockets that clung to the Reverend's backside. With an audible grimace, he said "Eureka." He took the key-ring. "What does he do, sit on them?" They tried keys until one fit. The door swung open.

"Mel Mel Mel thank God I was so scared!"

Melanie's heart and eyes swelled with disbelief and wonder. Her sister sat in the closet hugging her knees, ragged and dirty but *alive*. Melanie reached down and accomplished something she hadn't in years: she lifted her sister from the floor, wrapped her in an embrace, kissed her, and told her everything would be okay.

"That depends," Ronald said, "on whether we die from smoke inhalation."

Melanie understood. She lowered Stef, and when Ronald got to his knees, both girls followed his example. "Try breathing through your shirts," he said, "and stay low." They crawled from the office into the hallway. When they turned a corner, Melanie saw an exit engulfed in flame. Ronald yelled for them to go back. Hobbling with only one arm to balance him, he tried to lead, but he was slow. They were all too slow – even along the floor, the smoke was becoming too dense to breathe. Realizing that height no longer made a difference, Melanie stood and motioned for Stefanie and Ronald to do the same. On their feet and half-blinded by smoke, they ran.

Every door and window they found was on fire, and the further they got from Cox's office, the closer the flames seemed. They turned another corner and arrived at the vestibule, the inner doors to the sanctuary on their left, a wall of flame on their right. The sanctuary doors were closed, but they didn't stop the sounds of people screaming. Ronald opened the doors and revealed chaos, a mass of bodies crushed together, pushing and yelling, all trying to go through one narrow door near the front pews. Fire framed every other door and every window. It spread along the wall opposite the viable exit, seeming to herd the townspeople toward a single point of egress. Melanie looked at Ronald and her sister, and all three understood. They had no choice. They had to press into the throng.

26

The first people who fled through the doorway escaped unharmed. Brian watched them through the rifle's scope, but he didn't recognize them, and they moved away before he decided whether to pull the trigger. Ten, fifteen, maybe twenty people ran through the crosshairs, and then one of them prompted reaction. Stan Johnson's fat body and bushy beard filled the scope's circle of vision, and Brian's finger squeezed. The bullet caught Mr. Johnson in the throat, and he fell. The woman behind him tripped on his body, and the next person back tried to leap over them both and fell face-first onto the concrete sidewalk. People swarmed around the three felled forms. The woman on top of Mr. Johnson, Monica, kept trying to get up, but the people rushing around her bumped into her and left her no room to get a foothold. Brian pulled the trigger again, and she lay down.

The people were already screaming when they came through the door, so the gunshots didn't alter their sound. The shots did redirect their flow: instead of running into the cemetery, people sensed the direction of the shooter and scattered to the sides as they came through the door. Brian saw Jim Bledsoe and shot. The bullet hit the man's side, and he didn't fall. Brian shot again, and Bledsoe fell with the others. The person behind Bledsoe didn't generate any reflection or identification, just a gunshot. The pile of bodies grew larger. People coming through the door began to push at the obstacle; bodies rolled, and the pile leveled. Trampling began.

Distracted by the stampede of churchgoers showing no regard for their wounded brethren, Brian had time to realize that two pockets full of bullets wouldn't support many more random shots. The whole congregation was complicit, but he'd have to choose his targets more carefully. After reloading, he waited to pull the trigger until he saw another face he had recognized at the Easter bonfire: Alice Granger. The bullet caught her in the breast, and she fell. Brian didn't think the bullet was close enough to the heart, but the stampede would finish her.

Clambering over corpses, Michael Cox's congregation rushed faster and faster through the bottleneck Brian had constructed for their slaughter. His trigger finger shook, the muscles ready to squeeze, and he marveled at the accuracy of his aim. When they'd gone hunting, Winston had always been the better shot. But Winston was dead. The finger jerked, and another churchgoer fell.

Brian recognized Ted Early and took some satisfaction in killing the man who had bought his father's practice, even though, before Easter, Brian had always liked him. Brian recognized Jon Hoberman and fired. He was about Brian's age, and he might not have done anything to harm anyone – directly. But they didn't have to be direct, did they? Sara Cox's diary made the power of the congregation's indirect participation in their plans very clear.

Where was *he*? Where was Michael Cox? Brian stopped, looked away from his target area, and emptied his pockets. He still had a good number of shells, but he'd have to be careful. He needed to save one in case the Reverend showed himself.

Staring at the bullets risked missing the goal, so he refocused his eye through the scope and shot someone. He tried to keep his aim high so he wouldn't hit any children. Someone Bobby Sutton's age might be blamable – they might all be blamable – but the little kids at least had the excuse of not knowing better.

Hundreds of people got away as Brian tried to measure the justice he administered. The fire might take some of them. It wasn't isolated at the places where he'd set the gas-soaked rags anymore. It was spreading to the roof, which might cave in before everyone got through the bottleneck. The whole building would be a bonfire soon enough. *Have some sacrifices on me, Reverend Cox, and while you're at it, show yourself.* Brian pulled the trigger and someone fell.

He hesitated when he saw Nathan Grayson, but when he thought of what the man had done to Melanie, what he might do again, he shot.

Brian lost track of the number of bodies piled near the door. He was starting to think that Michael Cox wouldn't show himself. With a few bullets left, Brian would have to decide how long to wait. It wouldn't be long before the first escapees would come back with fire trucks and guns of their own. The window of opportunity was closing. He pulled the trigger without looking but trained his eye on the man's fall. He didn't recognize Ronald until the red-haired reporter hit the ground.

Behind Ronald, Brian saw Mel, and he yanked his hand away from the trigger. She had Stef with her. Stef! She was alive! She was alive? The diary had said...

He dropped the rifle and looked around him. Thoughts rushed through his head, about fingerprints, about witnesses, but they would know it was him, and if they knew, Mel would know. Nathan Grayson and Ronald and – what was he doing?

Without the scope he couldn't see features well enough to identify Mel and Stef, but he could tell who they were from their positions and actions. They were trying to drag Ronald away from the dregs of the stampede. They were trying to undo some of what Brian had done.

He ran down to help Ronald. Only Ronald.

27

First Church of Kenning burned to the ground. By the time they arrived, the firefighters from the next town over had to push their way through the crowd of people that could do nothing but watch as the flames worked. The firefighters tried, but in the end, they were little more than onlookers themselves. They didn't see anyone alive in the sanctuary, and to venture further would be suicide. Anyone left in the building would die.

Holding Stef in her arms, Melanie was like everyone else, watching. She, Brian, and Stef had kept Ronald from getting trampled, but they couldn't do anything else for him. Ronald got carried away along with the rest of the people whom the arsonist had shot. Brian disappeared after that, leaving Melanie and Stefanie to fend for themselves.

No one doubted that the shooter and the arsonist were one and the same. How could Kenning be host to more than one mass murderer? All of it had to be the work of one man.

Melanie didn't find out that her father had been shot and killed until the next day. She and Stef were staying at Brian's house. Brian wasn't there. Melanie didn't know where he was, but when she looked over the diary she found in the living room, she guessed why he had left.

As far as she knew, her mother had survived the blaze and the shootings. Tatum Grayson's name didn't show up in the news the next day. The television reported seventeen dead, more than forty injured. Some people said it was a miracle that more weren't killed. If the murderer had waited awhile longer, more people would have been in and around the church, compounding the chaos and the body count. Nevertheless, the town, the county, the state, and the entire nation would mourn the losses. People gave special lamentation for the passing of Michael Cox. His body was burnt beyond recognition, and even the local dentist had difficulty with the preacher's smashed head, but eventually, authorities made the identification. Since the body was in the back of the church, people decided that the Reverend had gone back to make sure nobody got left behind. Michael Cox was a hero.

People from all over America and all over the world came to help Kenning cope. The power that had made Kenning's boundaries impermeable was gone, vanquished, perhaps, with Michael Cox, or dispelled because its purpose was served.

Brian McCullough was the top story three days after the conflagration. The investigators didn't have to look long for evidence that pointed to him as the arsonist. Friday morning, Hank Winfrey was on the news saying that Brian had come to his station to fill up a few gas canisters. Hank didn't think much of it at the time, or even after. Who would have thought that Brian McCullough was capable of such a thing? The whole town had more or less adopted him after the tragedy that befell the McCullough family. He was a familiar sight on every street, a hard worker, a quiet, good-looking young man. Who would have thought?

Some of the news shows said that *everyone* should have thought. Brian McCullough spent time in a mental institution after his parents died. His sister was a murderer – weren't these things genetic? He should have been watched for instability. Somebody should have known. Somebody should have done something.

Kenning's police force was devastated by the disappearance of Glen Hadderly and the death of Winston Beecher, so the state police took over everything, and they weren't taking any chances with the evidence in the McCullough house. Melanie had to leave, so she took Stef to the only place they had – their parents' house.

Melanie spared her sister the sight of what waited in their parents' bathroom. People said Tatum Grayson's suicide was a response to the loss of her husband, but Melanie thought otherwise. No one understood what had happened in Kenning between Easter Sunday and the following Tuesday, but everyone remembered those days, in fragments if not in their entirety. Melanie's mom must have remembered what she did. Part of Melanie couldn't forgive her mom the role she played in Melanie's captivity at the Coxes' house. The death was horrible, and together with all the others, it was unbearable, but part of Melanie thought her mother's death might have been for the best. As for her father's death, she hadn't wanted it, but he had almost killed Brian on the ladder that night. Nathan Grayson was not the good man everyone said he was.

The Tuesday after Easter received many names. "Black Tuesday" was the most common, even though the day's blackness had little to do with the stock market crash that had another claim to that appellation. Some people called it "Christianity's 9/11," for what was the target of Brian McCullough, the maniac child of two self-avowed atheists, if not religion? He was more than a murderer or a spree killer. He was a terrorist, no better than Osama bin Laden and Saddam Hussein.

On Saturday, Melanie was questioned and told not to leave town. Evidence linked her to Brian in ways the authorities didn't like. They asked her about Winston Beecher and Ronald Glassner. They asked about Jeanne Harper. People said that there was some sort of conspiracy against First Church. The state police called in the FBI to help investigate. They didn't believe in any conspiracy, but they had to know for sure so they could put suspicions to rest. Suspicions of conspiracy tend to make people do bad things.

Melanie didn't know what to do. Would they decide she was an accomplice? People were saying that Black Tuesday wasn't an isolated event. The FBI had found bones in the ashes of the Easter bonfire. They were still being identified, but people suspected they belonged to Angela Jenkins and the other people unaccounted for since the massacre. People talked about the murder of Dave Holcomb and the disappearance of the sheriff, who was presumed dead. People even suggested that Brian was responsible for that weird thing with the animals. Everyone knows that psychopaths like to torture animals. It was too much of a coincidence, wasn't it?

Whatever happened, she'd keep Stefanie with her. If she had to run, she'd take her sister. Melanie would be eighteen soon, so maybe she could become the legal guardian. Legal or not, she wouldn't let anyone separate them again.

Stefanie remembered what had happened, but she didn't understand it. She remembered attacking Brian, and she remembered the fight between Dad and Melanie. She said she remembered going to church Sunday morning and all the beautiful singing. After that, she remembered Reverend Cox asking her to come help him with some special work. And then for some reason, he locked her in the closet. People brought food and took her to the bathroom when she needed it, but otherwise, she had to stay in the closet. When she asked why, she said they were waiting for someone and told her not to ask questions. She found that she didn't *want* to ask questions, and she felt like everything was okay until she started smelling smoke.

Melanie didn't consider the possibility that Jeanne could be alive until she appeared on television Sunday morning. Jeanne's hair was silver, as silver as Jake Warren's, and it was longer than it had been, almost long enough for a ponytail. She wore clothes that Melanie didn't recognize, a conservative blue skirt and suit jacket with a snazzy large-rimmed hat. When she talked, her lips curled up from her teeth.

She stood in front of the open doors of New Church. "These doors have been open all week, and they will remain open until all of Kenning understands how welcome they are here. I particularly welcome people who worshipped with Reverend Cox at First Church. I regret that Reverend Cox and I had our differences, but I don't doubt that he was a good man. Some have even called him a martyr, and I don't think they're too far off the mark." When she spoke, Jeanne's accent sounded unnatural, not like her own at all.

She continued, "I want the people of Kenning and anyone else who watches this broadcast to understand that I will *not* let the recent deaths be as meaningless as the ruthless killer wanted them to be. Whether they knew it or not, when the people of faith walked into church that day, they sacrificed their lives to God, and believe me, God *always* has a plan." The sneer became broader, a ghastly grin. "First Church was a force of good in this town, and in a way, it will be forever. Let First Church be the battery that powers a new movement, a movement of the faithful to revitalize our town in the wake of tragedy, and let New Church be an engine to drive us into a future where we realize God's Will!"

Melanie watched the broadcast on her living room sofa wearing her white bathrobe and pink bunny slippers. Stef was in the kitchen, eating a breakfast of Crunch Berries. Melanie wanted to cry. She had lost so many people – her parents, Winston, Brian, and Jeanne – and now here was this person wearing Jeanne's face, a monster whom everyone in town would adore as a saint. No one would believe her if she said that the woman on TV, the woman in the pulpit at New Church, was a man named Jake Warren. Somehow his will, not God's, had done it all, brought all the horror, all the death, into being. The desire to cry gave way to anger. They couldn't get away with it. It was wrong.

She heard a knock on the door. It was soft, but it startled her. Her first thought was to grab Stef from the kitchen, run upstairs, and hide. Maybe it was the police, come to charge her as an accessory to murder, come to take Stef and send her into foster care. If it was them, though, she couldn't, wouldn't get away. Resigned, she opened the front door.

The porch was empty. Sunday morning was bright with a warm blue sky. A breeze swung the branches and stirred up leaves that had lingered in the bushes since last fall. "Hello?" she called. The police wouldn't knock on her door and hide. If they wanted her, they would take her. "Is anybody here?"

No answer. She stepped back inside the house and closed the door behind her. She was about to turn the lock when she heard another tap. Without hesitating, she stepped back and pulled open the door.

Brian, wide-eyed, unshaven, and dirty, jumped through the opening and slammed the door behind him. "Please, if you want me to go, I'll go. Just give me ten minutes before you call the cops. I risked everything to see you."

Tears sprung up instantly, and Melanie covered her mouth to keep from sobbing. When she was sure she had control, she folded her arms across her chest, covering the lapels of her robe and clasping at her shoulders. "You can't be here. They're after you."

"I know." He looked distant. Older.

"I thought I'd never see you again." She sobbed quietly.

He looked at her with his head tilted to one side. He didn't have a full beard, not yet, but the blond stubble was filling in. "I'm so sorry."

"I." She buried her face in her hands. "You don't know what's happened."

"Yes I do. It's all on the news, about… your mom… and about… what I did… your dad… oh, God, Mel, I know it doesn't mean anything, but I'm so, so sorry." He cried, too.

"Stop it." She moved her hands down her cheeks, smearing tears. "How can you be sorry when… when I don't know if I am? About… Dad… and—"

He took a giant step toward her and wrapped her in his arms. "Shhhh. I'm sorry."

She pushed him away but grabbed his t-shirt to stay connected. "Stop it, I said!"

"Mel?" Stef called the kitchen. "Who's at the door?"

"Nothing!" Mel called back. "Just finish your breakfast!"

"How is she?" Brian asked.

"Still in shock, the doctor said. I think I am, too." She sniffled and wiped her nose with her robe's sleeve. "I mean, how do we come out of it? They tell me we have to grieve. But how can I grieve when I can't understand?"

Brian nodded. "I know." He pushed a lock of hair away from her face and let his fingers linger against her cheek. His hands were warm, his touch electric. She pressed up against him and kissed him. His stubble tickled her skin, but she wouldn't pull away. She put her arms around his waist and pushed as close as she could push, never letting her lips break from his, feeling his tongue and his saliva, feeling the length of his body, his solidness, his heat.

When the kiss ended, their faces stayed together. "Stay with me," she whispered. "Stay with us."

"We have to leave. We have to go. We won't have money."

"I don't care," she said. "Take us with you."

"Do you love me?" he asked.

"Yes!"

"Do you trust me?"

In the background, she heard the trumpets signaling the end of the newscast. Local news was ending, and national news would follow. Kenning would still be the top story. Everyone knew Brian's name. She wanted to answer him, but instead, she leaned her head against his chest and told him she loved him.

Epilogue: The Start of War

Ronald reread the text he intended for the first print edition of *American Sane*:

The entire experience has changed me. I am something new. Something *sinister*.

Bear with me, Sane Readers, as I explain my quaint little pun. I resort to this linguistic economy in honor of a fallen friend, and if you don't love it, I don't love you.

Sinister. I am a criminal, a Wanted Man. Who would believe that to be Wanted by men and women across America would be so unpleasant? Trust me, though, it is not the party you might imagine. I have changed my appearance. I have a fake ID, for Dog's sake. I never even had one of those in college because sophisticated older gentlemen always competed to buy me drinks. Frankly, I find being someone other than myself to be frightfully awkward.

"Underground" always sounds so fashionable, but actually to have *gone* underground is tedious. I have been set back by decades. My web server in New York has been confiscated, but even if I still had it, I couldn't write to you online without leaving a trail that the G-Men could trace. Thus, you hold this sinister, illegal little rag, reading every sinister, illegal little word.

Where am I, you might wonder? Let's leave it at this: I am in Your Imagination. Now, as you read, I am infecting you with my criminal thoughts. Exciting, right?

If, as I suspect, you are one of the many people who think that I am as insane as Bugbear-of-the-Decade Brian McCullough, perhaps I can win your affection via sympathy instead of subversion, which brings me to the other half of my pun. I am sinister in the etymological sense. *Sinistral*. Since blond, beautiful Brian shot me (I don't blame him, Sane Reader, as I do not think he intended me harm), I have not regained the use of my right arm. Thus, now that my left arm has finally recovered from repeated mauling by dogs and deacons, I once again type to you one-handed for reasons that are entirely unprovocative. While I suppose I've been a lefty in more than one of the colloquial senses for quite some time, this literal leftiness is not particularly desirable, as it makes typing my wisdom more difficult. I will, therefore, leave off from this punning digression and return to my narrative.

If I am to be completely honest, I am not entirely innocent. While I deny accusations related to teenage God-rocker Robert Sutton, I cannot say that I am altogether surprised that they linked me to the death of Glen Hadderly after they found his body in the garbage dump. They discovered a reddish hair in the burial ground, and I cannot accuse them of faking the evidence of it having once been connected to my scalp. Damn my X chromosome! However, I think that Kenning's body count is somewhere in the forties (if you include the bones found in the basement of the burnt church), and I can honestly tell you that I bear no responsibility in any of the other murders. Other than the Sheriff's, the only murder with which I believed I might rightly be associated turned out to be a non-event.

I was watching television in an electronics store in a town located in Your Imagination, U.S.A., and I saw yet another news report about the heroic work being done by "Kenning's Survivors." This report focused on a woman about whose death my opinion was overruled: Sara Cox, wife of the late and lauded Reverend Michael Cox, his partner in heinousness. The last time I saw her, she was lying in a pile of splintered wood at the bottom of a broken stepladder, looking quite dead. I suspected that she was up to something, but my friends assured me that she had snuffed it. And then I forgot about her until she pranced merrily onto the television screen.

The setting: an airport, on a runway hosting a private jet. I assume the airport was in Atlanta, but I'm not entirely sure. She walked with an entourage of reporters and men in suits with wires dangling from their ears. The men might have been secret service, except the man with whom she was walking is not officially a participant in our government. Mrs. Cox and the unofficial man weren't arm-in-arm because that would have been wrong for a woman so recently widowed in a national tragedy, but they might as well have been because I am sure that he has filled the late Reverend Cox's place.

And who is "he," you might ask? None other than billionaire-recluse-fundamentalist Elijah Eagleton, the new leader of everyone's favorite political organization, the American Values Federation. Mr. Eagleton maintained his usual silence in front of the camera, but Mrs. Cox explained that she had left Kenning to work full time for the AVF. Just like her sainted sister-in-faith Jeanne Harper, Sara Cox has dedicated her life to making meaning from Kenning's losses. Kenning's tragedy really was Christianity's 9/11, and she hopes it will bring together Christians in the same way that 9/11 brought together Americans. Despite recent setbacks, the AVF will mold willing Christians into a united front, and through the force of their goodwill, they will return this glorious country to the Christian virtues upon which it was founded!

Hallelujah, Sane Readers, and Amen.

As he put down the pages, Ronald wondered if he would ever return to the project that had brought him to Kenning in the first place. His target audience had had just about enough of still-at-large Brian McCullough. Maybe it wasn't worth writing about anymore.

Even if Ronald could finish his book about The McCullough Tragedies, he wouldn't be the first to have one on bookstore shelves. Within two months of the event, no fewer than three exposés appeared about Brian McCullough and the horrifying truths of Kenning, Georgia. Two of them ended up on the bestsellers list, and one was a finalist for a Pulitzer. Besides, the American people had hope that their nation was on the brink of recovery. What good would dire forecasts unrelated to economic upheaval do for a people ready for rebirth?

Black Tuesday was not an isolated event. Like another shooting spree in another April more than a decade earlier, it spawned copycats. Churches in Texas and Kentucky burned; a shooter killed twelve in Michigan. The shooter who took out a group of kids in a public park in Utah wrote a blog about atheism that mentioned Brian McCullough more than once. When enucleated corpses began to appear in California and Nebraska looking scarily similar to tabloid pictures of Dave Holcomb, and when a woman in Vermont drowned after removing her own tongue, a small number of fundamentalists tied all the events together with Kenning at their center. Stepping back from the complex tapestry, they connected Kenning to the End of Days.

A greater number of fundamentalists saw all of these gruesome crimes as motivated by hatred of Christianity. That all of the victims were not Christian didn't deter their proclamations. Christians were a persecuted majority, and it was time for the government to protect their rights in the same ways they protected the rights of the gays and the atheists. These grim occurrences were nothing more and nothing less than a cry for help from the very fabric of society. It was time for change, and a new day would soon dawn.

Whenever Ronald tried to write a serious piece about those who would exploit America's ideological divides or about the many things that Brian McCullough had come to symbolize in the American imagination, he would get stuck on more practical concerns. Where was Brian? Where could any of them go now that they knew what they knew and were who they were? Why did Brian have to do what he did? Ronald understood Brian's motive. What he didn't understand was *their* motive. With all the power they had, why couldn't they have staged the shootings? Why did they need to spend years driving a young man to commit mass murder? They turned people into puppets, took away their humanity, and used them however they willed. Why did Brian's humanity remain intact? Why did he have to choose? Jeanne didn't have any choice but to become what she had become, but in the end, her part was smaller than Brian's. The ramifications of Brian's choice were only beginning. Why did someone have to *choose* to start a war?

About the Author

L. Andrew Cooper thinks the smartest people like horror, fantasy, and sci-fi. Early in life, he couldn't handle the scary stuff—he'd sneak and watch horror films and then keep his parents up all night with his nightmares. In the third grade, he finally convinced his parents to let him read grown-up horror novels: he started with Stephen King's *Firestarter*, and by grade five, he was doing book reports on *The Stand*.

When his parents weren't being kept up late by his nightmares, they worried that his fascination with horror fiction would keep him from experiencing more respectable culture. That all changed when he transitioned from his public high school in the suburbs of Atlanta, Georgia to uber-respectable Harvard University, where he studied English Literature. From there, he went on to get a Ph.D. in English from Princeton, turning his longstanding engagement with horror into a dissertation. The dissertation became the basis for his first book, *Gothic Realities* (2010). More recently, his obsession with horror movies turned into a book about one of his favorite directors, *Dario Argento* (2012). He also co-edited the textbook *Monsters* (2012), an attempt to infect others with the idea that scary things are worth people's serious attention.

After living in Georgia, Massachusetts, New Jersey, and California, Andrew now lives in Louisville, Kentucky, where he teaches at the University of Louisville and chairs the board of the Louisville Film Society, the city's premiere movie-buff institution. *Burning the Middle Ground* is his debut novel.

Remnants of Life: Legends of Darkness
by Georgia L. Jones

Samantha Garrett lives and dies a good life in the human world. She awakens a new creature, Samoda, a vampire-like warrior in the army of Nuem. She is forced to realize that she has become a part of a world that humans believe to be only "Legends of Darkness." Samoda finds her new life is entwined with the age old story of greed, love, betrayal, and vengeance. [Urban Fantasy, ages 14+]

THE MAN IN THE BOX
by Andrew Toy

The box was his drug. It lulled him, cared for him and fulfilled his deepest desires... for a cost too high to pay.

Robbie Lake inadvertently climbs inside a cardboard box, which mentally transports him to a dangerous and mysterious island. He finds his identity in a secret world where he is hailed as a savior. The box quickly becomes his escape from reality. [Fantasy Adventure, ages 14+]

www.ingramcontent.com/pod-product-compliance
Lightning Source LLC
Chambersburg PA
CBHW070540260626
47161CB00002B/462